SILENT SCREAMS

C. E. LAWRENCE

PINNACLE BOOKS
KENSINGTON PUBLISHING CORP.
www.kensingtonbooks.com

PINNACLE BOOKS are published by

Kensington Publishing Corp.
119 West 40th Street
New York, NY 10018

All Kensington titles, imprints, and distributed lines are available at special quantity discounts for bulk purchases for sales promotions, premiums, fund-raising, educational, or institutional use. Special book excerpts or customized printings can also be created to fit specific needs. For details, write or phone the office of the Kensington special sales manager: Kensington Publishing Corp., 119 West 40th Street, New York, NY 10018, attn: Special Sales Department; phone 1-800-221-2647.

This book is a work of fiction. Names, characters, businesses, organizations, places, events, and incidents either are the product of the author's imagination or are used fictitiously. Any resemblance to actual persons, living or dead, events, or locales is entirely coincidental.

PINNACLE BOOKS and the Pinnacle logo are Reg. U.S. Pat. & TM Off.

ISBN-13: 978-0-7860-2148-2
ISBN-10: 0-7860-2148-9

First printing: December 2009

10 9 8 7 6 5 4 3 2 1

Printed in the United States of America

For Mom and Charles

ACKNOWLEDGMENTS

Thanks first and foremost to my editor, Michaela Hamilton, whose vision, wisdom and insight proved invaluable throughout the rewrite process. Thanks also to my agent, Paige Wheeler, for her unfailing good cheer and support, and to Dr. Lewis Schlesinger, a fine teacher whose excellent course in criminal psychology at John Jay College for Criminal Justice was essential to my research. Thanks to my colleague Marvin Kaye for his support and friendship, and special thanks to Gregg McCrary, for his invaluable advice and generosity. Special thanks also to Robert Murphy and Rachel Fallon for providing the ideal retreats in which to work—and to Fred and the other fine folks at the Long Eddy Hotel for the delicious sustenance during the long rewrite process. My deepest gratitude to the Byrdcliffe Arts Colony in Woodstock, New York, for the five years I spent in my beloved cabin, Varenka. It is the happiest place I have ever lived. Thanks too to Hawthornden Castle International Writers Retreat for providing a wonderful month in the most idyllic setting I can imagine— and to Martin, Angie, Mary and Doris for putting up with me. Thanks and gratitude to Chris Buggé for bailing me out of a tight spot, to Beth Andrasak for her insight and friendship, and to Susan Schulman for her patience and continued support. Thanks to my mother and Joan Lawrence for their insightful feedback, to Anthony Moore for his companionship and advice, and to NYPD Detectives Joseph Cavitolo and John Sweeney, as well as civilian NYPD liaison John Kelly, for their patience and professional advice. Last but far from least, my deepest gratitude to Amanda George for her guidance and willingness to shepherd me through a very dark forest.

Chapter One

Lee Campbell stood looking at the naked body draped over the altar of the church. The girl's delicate white skin was pale as the cold marble floor beneath his feet, in stark contrast to the vivid red wounds slashed across her torso and the purple bruising around her neck.

"Come on, Marie, talk to me," he whispered. He bent down over her, looking for petechial hemorrhaging in or around the eyes, but could find none. The lack of patterned abrasions meant there had been no ligature. "So he used his hands," he murmured. Some strangulation victims had no sign of injuries at all, so he was grateful for the bruising around her neck—pronounced enough to suggest that this, and not the slash wounds, was the cause of death. He thought about what her last moments were like: eleven pounds of pressure for ten seconds could cause unconsciousness, and thirty pounds of pressure, for four or five minutes, would result in death.

He observed the blue creeping into her lips, the porcelain smoothness of her dead cheeks. *At least he left her face alone.* He had always found it odd that strangulation victims sometimes looked strangely peaceful, with all of life's pain, suffering, and uncertainty behind them now. Lee felt a stab of envy in his stomach, and a warning sounded in his head. He could not allow himself to linger over such thoughts. He closed the door of his mind to the desire to be where this dead girl was now, to be done with the mad dance of life and its many trials.

But, of course, there had been nothing peaceful about her death. His eyes fell on the jagged letters carved into her naked torso: *Our father who art in heaven.* The *O* encircled her left breast like a red halo, the blood droplets symmetrical on her pale flesh. For some reason, he was reminded of a red and white hula hoop his sister had as a child. The writing was uneven and slanted downward—a job done in haste, he concluded, by a killer who was not yet comfortable with this part of his work.

The blood had dried and was caked in little mountainous crusts of crimson on her pale skin. The word "Heaven" was cut into her abdomen, just over the light dusting of dark pubic hair on her pelvis. There was little excess blood around the altar, and no signs of struggle, suggesting that she was killed elsewhere.

"What happened to you?" Lee whispered. "Who did this to you?" Even at a whisper, his voice echoed and fluttered, ghostlike, through the tall stone columns of the chapel's interior. Lee had never been on the Bronx campus of Fordham University before, and he was surprised by the size of the campus chapel. But then, Fordham was a Catholic school—in fact, the college seminary was just across the quad.

Lee studied the dead girl's face, waiting for the eyes to flutter open, and realized with a start that she resembled his sister—the same curly dark hair and white skin. He had often imagined seeing Laura like this, wondering what he would do or say, but her body had never been found. And so that encounter hung in suspended animation, waiting for him in some near or distant future. He looked down at Marie, cold and unmoving upon the altar, not a line creasing her smooth cheeks, her youth a rebuke to the person who had squeezed the life from her body. Lee was relatively new to such intimacy with the dead, and it held a fascination he knew was not entirely healthy.

But Leonard Butts, the Bronx detective assigned to this case, had no such fascination, nor was he of a sentimental turn of mind.

"Okay, Doc," he said, approaching Lee. "You 'bout done there? ME's here, and we'd like to get the vic downtown ASAP."

Butts indicated several men unloading a stretcher from a van outside the chapel. Lee could see the words MEDICAL EXAMINER in large yellow letters emblazoned on the backs of their dark blue jackets as they brought in the stretcher, its wheels clacking on the stone floor. A couple of members of the forensics team glanced up briefly, then went on with their work—dusting, photographing, inspecting. They worked with swift, practiced gestures, moving smoothly through the crime scene, gathering evidence. A thin young Asian woman snapped photographs of Marie from every angle, her face set in a stoic, businesslike expression.

Looking around, Lee felt that he was the only one out of place here—he alone had nothing to contribute, nothing to offer toward the solving of this terrible crime, this trespass against society and decency. He wondered if his friend Chuck Morton, commander of the Bronx Major Case Unit, had made a mistake in calling him out to this crime scene in the predawn hours. After two years as the NYPD's only full-time criminal profiler, Lee still had doubts about whether he was up to the job.

"Well, Doc, whaddya think?" Detective Butts's Bronx accent bit through the solemn atmosphere of the chapel.

Lee glanced up at Detective Butts, who had an unlit cigar dangling from his mouth. He had told the man twice that he had a PhD in psychology, and was not a medical doctor, yet Butts still insisted on calling him Doc. With his beard stubble and unkempt hair, the detective looked like the kind of man you might see lurking around an off-track betting parlor. Lee couldn't blame him for the beard stubble; after all, it was 6 A.M., and he could feel the scratchiness on his own chin. But he suspected that even with a shave and a haircut Butts would still look disreputable.

Instead of the handsome, regular features of a stereotypical Irish cop, the detective had a decidedly uneven face, with flaccid jowls, a bulbous lower lip, small eyes, and a complexion like an unkempt gravel road. There was no discernible change in the thickness where his skull began and his neck ended; his neck rose in an unbroken line up to the top of his head, crosshatched tanned skin fading into gray hair stubble. Lee was reminded of the mesas he had seen in Arizona. To top it off, Butts was short and thick—Elmer Fudd in a trench coat. Lee thought the unlit cigar was a bit much, as though Butts was deliberately trying to look cartoonish.

"Well, whaddya think?" Butts repeated. "Boyfriend did it?"

"No," Lee replied. "I don't think so."

"Strangulation is typical of domestic violence cases, y'know," said Butts, his small eyes narrowing even more in the dim light of the chapel. When Lee didn't respond, he added, "You know what percentage of murder victims know their killer?"

"Eighty percent," Lee replied, bending down over Marie again.

"Yeah," Butts said, sounding surprised that he knew the answer.

Lee straightened up and stretched his cramped back muscles. At just under six foot two, he was half a foot taller than the stubby detective. He ran a hand through his own curly black hair, which was getting shaggy in the back.

Butts frowned and deepened his bite on the cigar. "So who do you think did it?"

Lee stepped aside as the men from the medical examiner's office loaded the body onto the stretcher. All around him, the forensics team members continued with their work; silent and efficient, they were the opposite of this stubby detective with his battered cigar and bad skin.

Lee looked down at his hands, feeling their uselessness. "I don't know," he answered.

Butts made a sound between a grunt and a sigh. "Humph. Okay, Doc—well, when you get some ideas, let me know."

"Oh, I have some ideas," Lee replied. "I just don't know what they add up to yet."

Butts moved the cigar to the other side of his mouth. "Yeah? Well, let's have 'em."

"It's too early yet to draw a lot of conclusions, but I don't think the attacker knew his victim."

"Really?" Butt's voice conveyed his disapproval and disdain.

"This was not a personal crime—this was a ritualistic murder."

Butts cocked his head, letting the cigar dangle from his thick lips. "How do you figure that?"

"Look at the positioning of the body—he wants to shock us. And then there's the carving."

"Well, yeah, I can *see* that," the detective said irritably. "I'm not saying this perp isn't a creep. You should see some of the things I seen these guys do to their girlfriends."

"And leave her in a church?"

Butts sniffed at the body like a bird dog. "She wasn't killed here—she was brought here."

"Exactly my point."

"These days you got a lotta weirdos out there. You never know what they'll do."

"Who ID'd the body?"

"Chapel priest. Same one who discovered her. Said he came in for early prayers and found her here." The detective lowered his voice as though he was afraid someone might overhear. "You know, I had a guy once who killed his mother, then dressed her up for church."

"Someone who kills like this is displacing his rage onto a stranger. This is a ritualistic display of the body—it's impersonal."

Butts plucked the cigar from his mouth and stuffed it into his shirt pocket. "Okay, Doc—you're the one with the degree." He turned to the forensics team. "You boys 'bout done there? I'm gettin' hungry." He turned back to Lee. "Wanna go for some eggs? I know a great little place on Arthur Avenue."

Lee did his best not to be irritated at this homely little detective for his casual attitude toward death. "Thanks—another time, maybe."

The detective didn't appear to take the rejection personally. He shuffled across the smooth floor toward the side exit, scratching his chin. "Okay, Doc, catch you later."

"I'll be out in a minute," Lee called after him. It was only then he noticed the young priest huddled in the corner, his arms wrapped around his body, a mournful expression on his face.

He walked over to the man, who looked even younger close up, with his smooth pink skin and sleek black hair. There was no stubble on his face—he looked almost too young to have any.

"You knew the victim, Father . . . ?" Lee asked.

The priest's eyes were dark and pleading, like a puppy's. "Michael. Father Michael Flaherty."

"You were able to ID the body?"

"As I told him, I knew her because she was one of my—"

"Flock?"

"One of my comparative religion students." His voice was thin and ragged; he looked away, perhaps suppressing tears.

"I see."

"As I told the detective, she wasn't a regular in church. She attends another one, I believe." He sighed and rubbed his eyes. "Ralph is going to be so devastated when he hears about this."

"Ralph?"

"Her boyfriend. Nice kid, a science major." Father Flaherty let his hands fall to his sides, a gesture of surrender. "I, uh . . . I just came in to pray and tidy up the altar." He glanced at the vases of drooping and withered lilies to one side of the altar. A CSI worker was bent over them, dusting for fingerprints.

The priest swallowed hard. "And . . . there she was." He gave Lee a searching look. It was clear he was studying Lee to see how his explanation was being received. The priest was obviously concerned about establishing his own innocence, but that didn't necessarily mean he had anything to hide. Lee knew that even innocent people are often nervous in the presence of the police.

"Okay, thank you, Father Michael," he said, handing him a business card. "Here's my card if you think of anything else."

The priest looked at the card. "The detective already gave me one of his. Aren't you working together?"

"Yes, we are, except that—well, we sometimes work on cases from . . . different angles." He hoped that was enough to satisfy the priest. He had no wish to discuss the tension between criminal profilers and traditional law enforcement.

The priest fished a handkerchief from his pocket and gave it a swipe across his nose. "All right. He already asked me the usual questions—could I think of anyone who would want to hurt her, and all that. I couldn't think of anyone."

Lee wasn't surprised. He was beginning to believe that no one would be able to think of anyone who wanted to hurt this unfortunate girl—except, of course, her killer. He shuddered as the team from the ME's office loaded poor Marie into a shiny black body bag. *Marie.* He forced himself to recite her name, to think of her as a person, not as "the vic," as precinct detectives often referred to their crime victims. It was more painful to keep a sense of her as a person, but it helped to motivate him. Lee held his breath as they zipped up the body bag. He hated the sound of the metal teeth as they caught one another—so cold, so final, a young life reduced to that terrible, sad sound of metal on metal.

He approached one of the techs from the ME's office, the thin young Asian woman who had been taking the photographs earlier. Her skin was as uncreased and pristine as Marie's—he thought she might be Korean, or possibly Chinese. Her shiny black hair was looped back in a ponytail, and her jumpsuit looked two sizes too big for her slender body.

"Can you tell me if the wounds were postmortem or—" Lee began.

She replied quickly, as if wanting to get this over with as soon as possible. "Most likely postmortem. There wasn't much bleeding."

"Most likely? Is there any chance—?"

She shook her head, her black ponytail slicing the air. "It can be difficult to tell, but here you can see where the blood trickle ends. I can't say for sure, but my best guess is that these wounds were postmortem . . . I hope to God," she added in a low voice. Lee thought he saw her shiver inside her oversized jumpsuit.

"And the weapon?"

She frowned. "Hard to say for sure, but nothing fancy—possibly an ordinary knife, the kind you could get anywhere."

"Thank you," he said, turning away.

As he left the chapel, a wicked wind whipped up around Lee's ankles, flipping his coattails skyward, scattering a few wisps of dead leaves up into a spiral swirl, like a miniature tornado. The sharp, dry gust took his breath away. He shivered and shoved his hands into the pockets of his green tweed overcoat. A thin, pale dawn began to bloom in the eastern sky as he gazed down at the southern end of Manhattan, where a smoldering gash in the earth was all that was left of the once-proud towers. It was barely five months ago that the planes dropped from the sky like some mythic beasts, their tongues dripping with fire and destruction . . . and despair. . . .

He forced his mind back to the present.

Hearing footsteps, he turned to see a man standing next to a blue van parked at the back of the church. He was dressed in a workman's jumpsuit and carried a tool case.

"Who's that?" he asked Butts, who had stopped by the side exit to speak to one of the crime scene technicians.

"I dunno," the detective answered, walking over to converse with the man.

"Locksmith," he said, returning to where Lee stood. "Got a call from the college administration that there was a broken lock in the basement. I told him to come back tomorrow."

Lee turned to Father Michael, who had wandered out of the church. The priest looked lost, and had the glazed look of someone in shock. "Were you aware of a broken lock in the basement?"

Father Michael shook his head. "No. But the maintenance staff might have put the call in. You'd have to ask them."

"Right," Butts said, writing it in his notebook. "Do you think there's a connection?" he asked Lee.

"I don't see one, really—I mean, the killer came right in through the unlocked side door, and presumably left the same way."

"I'll check it out anyway," Butts said.

"He took something," Lee murmured to himself, "but what?"

"Whaddya mean, he took somethin'?" Butts asked.

Lee gazed over the wounded landscape of the city, soaking in its stark and terrible beauty. "A souvenir, a memento."

"Jeez. What for?"

Lee turned to face him. "What was the last trip you took?"

Butts pushed back his battered fedora and scratched his head. He reminded Lee of a character out of a 1940s screwball comedy.

"I dunno . . . The Adirondacks, I guess."

"And did you buy anything there?"

"Uh, the wife bought some dish towels."

"Did she need dish towels?"

Butts frowned. "Actually, come to think of it, she's got dozens of 'em. She always buys one when we go somewhere."

"Right. So why buy what you don't need?"

Butts snorted. "Look, Doc, I learned a long time ago that when it comes to women, it's better not to ask certain questions, know what I'm sayin'?"

"But there is an answer to this one."

Butts jabbed the toe of his shoe into the dirt, kicking up the soft black soil.

"She says it reminds her of the trip."

"Exactly. That's why sexual murderers often take something from their victims: to remind them. It's like hunting trophies—they serve no purpose, other than to bring the killer memories of the crime itself. The souvenirs help them relive the whole thing over and over."

Butts tore off a piece of a jagged fingernail with his teeth and spit it out. "Man, this is twisted stuff. Mostly I just handle homicides, you know? Drug deals gone bad, abusive boyfriends, family fights that escalate—run-of-the-mill stuff. This is a whole new kinda weird."

"Yes, it is."

Butts looked at Lee suspiciously. "Doesn't this stuff keep you up at night?"

"Sometimes. But knowing those people are still out there keeps me up even more."

"Don't take this the wrong way, Doc, but you don't seem

like the type. . . . I mean, how did you get into this kind of thing?"

"It's kind of personal."

"Sure, sure," the detective answered, his homely face crinkled in sympathy. "No problem—I get it. Didn't mean to pry."

Lee looked away—he didn't trust his reactions around other people. He wasn't entirely in control of himself yet, not quite recovered from his breakdown.

The two men stood side by side, looking southward, watching the thin gray mist of smoke snaking upward from the ruined earth.

Butts shifted his weight from one foot to the other. "Well, then, I'm gonna move along now. I'll, uh, catch you later. I'll call you when we find the boyfriend."

"Sure. See you later."

He watched as the detective trundled off after the forensic team, his rumpled gray trench coat flapping in the wind.

Lee closed his eyes and let his head fall back. He could hear bagpipes, faraway and sad—their thin, plaintive tones carrying across the East River to where he stood on this melancholy bluff. He often imagined he heard bagpipes in times of stress and sorrow, and he had come to welcome the sound rather than taking it as a sign of deepening mental illness. It comforted him, bringing him back to the hills of his Celtic ancestors, where mountains rose sharp and bare from rushing riverbeds below, a mysterious and stark landscape that ran through his veins as strongly as his own blood.

He gazed up at the sky, where a lone crow scraped its way north, black and solitary against the creeping dawn.

Chapter Two

As it turned out, the boyfriend wasn't difficult to locate. Within an hour Lee was standing outside a grimy interrogation room inside a Bronx precinct house, watching through the one-way mirror as he waited for Butts to question the young man. The interrogation room was small and stuffy, its pale green walls scarred with stains and scuff marks. Lee imagined the scenes that had taken place in this room—the outbursts of rage, poundings by fists or boots or both. Some of the black smudge marks on the walls did appear to come from kicks—they were the right height and size. But others—coffee splotches, the occasional streak of blue ink, even a few ominous red patches, dried to a dark rust color—were more mysterious.

The young man inside the room sat quietly, hands folded on his lap. He was slight of build, with narrow, bony shoulders—a boy who wouldn't stand out in any crowd. Lee took an inventory of his regular but unremarkable features: straight brown hair over a thin, sensitive mouth and sad brown eyes. Under the harsh fluorescent lights his face had an unhealthy gray pallor, the circles under his eyes pronounced. He looked young—even younger than poor Marie—and very, very frightened. *Not in a guilty way*, Lee thought, *just plain scared*. He would bet that this boy had never seen the inside of a police station before, and certainly never as a suspect.

Ever since he could remember, Lee had an unusual ability to "read" people. He used to think that everyone could do this, and it wasn't until after his training in psychology that he had realized how uncommon his gift was. He studied aspects of human behavior in textbooks explaining things he had always known instinctively. He could see into people— into their souls, so to speak.

Now, looking at the scared young man sitting in front of him, Lee was quite certain that the boy was not guilty of his girlfriend's murder.

Detective Butts entered the room with two paper cups of coffee and slid one across the scarred Formica table to the boy.

"Thought maybe you could use one too," he said, sitting down across from him. "Hope you take it regular."

In western New Jersey, where Lee grew up, "regular" meant milk, no sugar, but in New York City, regular coffee always included a liberal amount of sugar.

"Thank you," the boy replied in a small voice, but he didn't touch the coffee. Butts flipped back the plastic lid of his own cup with a well-practiced gesture and slurped it noisily.

"That's better," he said, leaning back in his chair. He appeared to be enjoying himself. "I hate to start the day without it, y'know?"

The young man stared at Butts, his face still frozen in fear. He reminded Lee of a fox he had once seen cornered— the animal had the same expression of wariness and creeping panic. This interrogation was going to be a waste of time; he knew Butts was showing off for him, trying to impress him with interrogative skills. *First soften him up, become his friend, then close in for the kill.* This technique seemed so obvious to Lee that he couldn't imagine any criminal—even the simplest shoplifter—not seeing right through it. This kid was no criminal, though, and he figured that Butts knew this—but procedure was procedure. You had to jump through the right hoops.

"Okay," the detective said, setting his coffee down and glancing at a file on the table, "Mr. . . . Winters. Rough luck, by the way—sorry about what happened to your girlfriend."

"Yeah," Winters responded softly.

"Can I call you Ralph?"

"Okay," the boy answered, his voice still barely above a whisper. Lee had the impulse to intervene, but that was out of the question. This was Butts's investigation, and the last thing he wanted was to alienate the burly detective.

Ralph sat staring at the untouched coffee in front of him, as a thin ribbon of steam spiraled upward through a tiny hole in the lid.

"Okay, Ralph," Butts said, "why don't you tell me anything you can think of that might help?"

Ralph gulped twice, his Adam's apple rising and falling sharply in his thin throat. He appeared to be on the verge of tears.

"Says here you're a chem major," Butts continued, maybe to save Ralph the embarrassment of tears. Whatever his motive was, it apparently worked. The boy leaned forward, and his eyes seemed to focus on Butts for the first time. He reached for the coffee, his hand trembling.

"Yeah. Organic chemistry. I'm studying to be a pathologist." He took a sip of coffee.

"Oh, really?" Butts's tone was friendly, jocular. "You interested in forensics?"

"Uh, I want to specialize in diseases, actually."

"Well, well," Butts replied, smiling. "How 'bout that? You

gotta be real smart to do that kinda stuff, I know that much. Me, I was no good in science. I envy guys like you."

Ralph seemed suspicious of this attempt to butter him up. He sat looking at Butts, his hands wrapped around the paper coffee cup.

"So, Ralph, what can you tell me?" Butts said, his tone indicating it was time to get down to business. "How long have you known Marie?"

"Since last semester. We, uh—we were in the same comparative lit class."

Butts frowned. "But you're a science major."

"It's a required course. I need it to graduate."

Butts cocked his head to one side. "I get it. And Marie was a religion major?"

"Comparative religion, yeah. She wanted to teach eventually."

"I see. So you guys just sorta hit it off?"

Ralph winced. "Yeah. I mean, at first I didn't believe a girl like her would be interested in me. I mean, she's so pretty and lively and everything, and I'm . . . well, a science geek, you know?"

Butts gulped down some more coffee. "Yeah. I know what you mean—never could figure out what the wife sees in me. Women are a mystery."

This admission seemed to put Ralph more at ease, and he sipped at his coffee, though without taking his eyes off the detective.

"Tell you what, Ralph," Butts said. "I'm not gonna keep you here very long, but can you think of anyone who'd want to hurt Marie? Anyone at all?"

"Well, she was really sweet and trusting. I can't think of anyone who didn't like her. I mean, she didn't *try* to be popular or anything, but there was just something about her, you know?"

"Yeah, sure."

Ralph shifted in his chair. "There *was* one thing. . . ."

"Yeah? What's that?"

"Well, I had the feeling she was seeing someone—someone else, I mean. I don't really have any evidence of it. It was more of a feeling, I guess."

"Okay. Any idea who it was?"

Ralph looked down at his hands, which were clasped tightly in his lap. "No. I was meaning to ask her about it, but . . . I guess I didn't want to pry. It's not like we were engaged or anything, you know?"

"Yeah, sure. Will you excuse me for a moment?"

He got up and lumbered out of the room, closing the door behind him. He came over to Lee and slumped his stocky body against the wall.

"That kid's clean as my mother-in-law's kitchen. No way he did it—and I don't think he has any idea who did." Butts pulled a cigar stub from his breast pocket. Placing it between his sturdy teeth, he bit down on it hard.

"Do you ever actually smoke those things?" Lee asked.

"Not anymore. Used to, wife hated the smell, said it got into everything. So I gave it up. This is the closest thing I have now to a vice. . . . I miss it, but I'll tell you, this is a helluva lot cheaper. I used to buy the good ones—you know, the Cubans—when I could get 'em, and they set you back a buck or two."

Butts shifted the cigar to the other side of his mouth. "This other guy he mentioned—that could be a lead. That is, if she really was seeing anyone else."

"Maybe," Lee replied. "I wonder if you'd just let me ask him one thing?"

Butts shrugged. "Go ahead—knock yourself out. Then we should let the poor bastard go home."

"Thanks."

Lee entered the interrogation room and felt the oppressiveness of its windowless silence. The one-way mirror behind which Butts now stood watching only added to the sense of isolation and paranoia the suspects must feel.

Ralph Winters looked up at him apprehensively when he entered the room. Lee tried to dispel his fear with a friendly smile, but the boy's body didn't relax as Lee sat down opposite him.

"Hi, I'm Lee Campbell. I'm helping with this investigation."

Ralph responded with a twitch of his head and wrapped his hands tighter around his coffee cup.

"Look, Ralph," Lee said gently, "we're going to let you go soon. I just want to see if there's *anything* else you can tell us about Marie that might help us catch her killer."

The boy's face reddened, and his eyes welled up with tears. "You—you don't think I did it, then?"

"No, we don't. But we hope you can help us by telling us about Marie—anything you can think of."

Ralph swallowed hard. "Well, like I told the other detective, she was really sweet, and everyone liked her."

"Yes," Lee replied. "I know." *On the last day of her life Fate swooped down upon her, a slap out of nowhere, a sudden shock as she rounded the corner of her life.* It was a line from a poem he had written about his sister, and he shook it out of his head. "Why don't you just tell me what you can about Marie?"

"Well, she was kinda religious—Catholic, you know."

"So she went to church how often?"

"Oh, not more than twice a week. She went Sundays, and then sometimes to Wednesday night mass. But she didn't like people who swore and took the Lord's name in vain, you know? And she had a crucifix over her bed—kind of creepy, if you ask me, but I wasn't raised religious." His lower lip trembled. "Have they called her parents yet?"

"We're taking care of that. They live in Jersey somewhere, I think."

"Yeah—Nutley." He swallowed again and took another sip of coffee.

"Did she have any special friends at church?"

"Not that I can think of. A couple of girlfriends. She didn't really socialize all that much. She did volunteer to feed the homeless at the church once a month."

"Did you go with her?"

"Sometimes."

"You mentioned her girlfriends—are they religious?"

"I don't think so."

"But Marie was?"

"Yeah. She wore a cross around her neck all the time."

"Can you describe it?"

"Uh, yeah . . . it was plain gold—oh, with a tiny little pearl in the center."

"A white pearl?"

"Yeah. She never took it off."

Lee felt his heart quicken. He carried a clear image of Marie as she was in death, and he could swear that when they found her there was no cross around her neck.

"Never?"

"No. She kept it on even in the shower—said it was like keeping Jesus with her all the time. I remember it scratched me one time when we were . . ." His face crumpled, and his thin shoulders sagged under the weight of his grief. "Oh, God, oh, God!" He collapsed sobbing, burying his head in his arms. Lee laid a hand on his shoulder just as Butts reentered the room.

"Come on, kid, we got a car to take you home."

Ralph raised his head and looked up at the detective through tearstained eyes.

"You don't have any more questions?" He sounded disappointed.

"Not right now. We know where to find you if we do." Butts spat out a piece of cigar into the trash can and handed Ralph a business card. "Give me a call if you think of anything else. Especially if you have any ideas about who this other guy might be. Sorry you had to go through this."

"That's okay," said Ralph, clutching the coffee cup as he stood up unsteadily.

"Officer Lambert here will take you home," said Butts, indicating a thin, sallow-faced policeman standing just outside the room.

"Can you make it okay?" asked Lee.

"Yes, thank you—I'll be all right," Ralph replied, and followed Officer Lambert meekly down the hall.

"I know what he took," Lee said as soon as the boy had gone.

"Who took what?"

"The killer. I know what he took as a souvenir."

"Oh yeah? What?"

"The gold cross—the one she never took off."

"But there was no cross on her when we found her."

"Exactly."

Butts rolled his eyes. "Okay. So all's we have to do is find some pervert wearing this girl's cross."

"No, he wouldn't wear it himself. He would either put it away in a drawer or give it to a woman in his life—someone important to him, someone he wants to impress."

Butts shuddered. "Kinda like my cat bringing in a mouse head and dropping it on my pillow."

"That's a good analogy, actually."

"Do creeps like this have girlfriends?"

"Some of them do. I doubt this guy does, though."

"A sister, maybe?"

"Maybe. He's an introvert, though, and my guess is that if he gives his trophy away to anyone, it'll be to his mother."

Butts shivered again. "Oh, man, that's just too weird."

Lee felt his own spine tingle as a thin finger of dread wound its way up his back. "Yes. We're dealing with someone who is profoundly disturbed."

"You can call it what you want, Doc," Butts replied. "I call it creepy."

Chapter Three

An hour later Lee entered his empty, darkened apartment on East Seventh Street, savoring the stillness before turning on the hall light. He removed his coat, hanging it on the Victorian bentwood coatrack, a gift from his mother. She loved all things Victorian: burgundy velvet drapes, satin-lined Chinese scarves with fat laughing cherubs, lace curtains, painted china tea sets, opera capes. Men were unreliable, and would come and go, but the Victorian era had a solid, carved-oak heaviness that she seemed to find comforting.

"Well, it's a theory, anyway," Lee muttered as he walked to the kitchen.

His piano sat in the corner under the window, waiting for him. But right now he wanted a cup of coffee, strong and bitter and hot, with a dollop of milk and a teaspoon of sugar. His insides ached from the strain of digging around among the demons that continued to plague him. There was something in the back of his mind, something he couldn't quite grasp. He had a feeling that it related to Marie's death in some way. As he put the water on to boil, the phone rang.

The sound was jarring, cutting through the stillness of the air like a summons. He picked up the receiver and held his breath.

"Hello?"

"Hello, dear." It was his mother, brisk and cheerful as usual. Her voice was a shield, with a veneer of warmth and optimism, but he could sense the fear and sadness underneath.

"So how are things?" His mother's cheeriness was resolute, implacable—an immovable object.

"Fine, Mom." There was only one answer to this question in the Campbell family. Nothing else was acceptable. *Fine, Mom. Everything's just fine. Laura's murderer is still out there, and there's a college girl in the city morgue with her chest carved up, but everything's fine.*

"Isn't this weather just awful? It's hard to believe there are only six weeks until spring."

Weather—a safe topic. Weather, food, home improvement, gardening—all safe topics for Fiona Campbell.

"I just can hardly wait to get my roses in. I've got three different colors of tea roses this year." She was always planting things: roses, begonias, petunias.

"Oh, good."

"Stan thinks it's too early. He says we'll have another frost, but I don't believe him."

Stan Paloggia was her next-door neighbor who hovered around her like an eager beagle. Actually, he was a lot like beagles Lee had known: short and stocky, with a voracious appetite, thick around the middle. His voice, too, was a kind of a bray, like the hoarse baying of a hound on the hunt. He followed Fiona Campbell around like a one-man posse, being helpful in any way he could, whether it was gardening advice or plumbing repairs. Lee had often wished he could tell the man he was wasting his time—his mother was only attracted to remote, elegant men like his father. Tall, glamorous, and handsome, Duncan Campbell was Stan's opposite in every way—but Stan seemed to enjoy the quest, and panted happily along whenever he could. His mother tolerated his attention, and treated him about as well as she treated anyone.

"Well, if Stan says so, maybe you'd better listen," Lee said, pouring coffee beans into the white Krups grinder.

"I don't know; I just hate waiting," his mother replied.

Lee turned the grinder on and took the phone into the living room as the machine whirred into action, screeching harshly as the beans tumbled over each other.

"How's Kylie?" he asked.

"Oh, she's just fine—growing like a weed, you know. It's hard to believe she's almost seven!"

Lee looked at one of the snapshots of Laura on the door of his refrigerator. It was taken in front of his mother's house, and she was squinting into the sun, her hand raised to push back a few stray strands of long brown hair. He remembered the day well—he had taken the picture shortly before her graduation from college.

But his niece would have no memories of her—she would know her mother only through photographs like this one, or in the stories people told about her. Kylie lived with her father, but she spent Saturdays and Sundays with her grandmother, as he worked the ER shift at the local hospital most weekends. George Callahan was a big, bluff man without an evil thought in his head. Lee always wished Laura had married him, but he wasn't her type. Steady, unexciting, and kind to a fault, George was nothing like the vain, high-strung father Laura had never stopped searching for in the men she dated. Even after Kylie was born, Laura refused to marry George, even though he had begged her.

"You're still planning on spending Saturday with her, aren't you?" His mother sounded wary—lately Lee had been less than reliable.

"Uh, sure."

"Do you want to say hello to her? She's right here."

"Sure."

In the background, Lee could hear his niece talking to his mother's cat, Groucho. He pictured the scene: Fiona in the kitchen, cooking breakfast, her portable phone cradled on her shoulder as she stirred the potatoes, Kylie sitting in the corner kitchen nook with Groucho on her lap, trying to dress him in baby clothes.

There was a pause, and he could hear his mother in the background. "Put the cat down now—no, he doesn't like being held like that."

He smiled. Kylie was just like his sister, ferociously independent and stubborn. At six and a half, she already displayed Laura's ironic wit. There was the sound of the cat hissing in the background, then a sharp "Ow!" and the sound of a chair falling. Moments later, his niece came to the phone.

"Hello, Uncle Lee."

"Hi, Kylie. What were you doing with the kitty just now?"

"Playing." Her voice carried a note of gleeful guilt.

"Really? What sort of game were you playing?"

"Um . . . dress up."

"You were dressing up Groucho?"

"Um . . . yeah."

"Did he enjoy that?"

"Not really. He tried to run away."

"But you stopped him?"

"Yeah—until he bit my hand."

"That must have hurt."

"Uh-huh . . . Grandmom is putting a Band-Aid on it."

Kylie's relationship with Groucho was one of hunter and hunted—and, when she managed to corner him, it was torturer and victim. Her favorite game was dress up, and she clothed the cat in a dazzling array of humiliating outfits. The aging and dyspeptic tabby was far from child friendly, but Fiona Campbell had had him for years and wasn't about to give him up now.

"My Band-Aid has Winnie the Pooh on it," Kylie said.

"Oh, that's nice. Did your grandmom buy them for you?"

"Uh-huh. I picked it out, though."

Lee heard the whistle of the teakettle and went into the kitchen. "That's good. I'll bet it feels better already."

"Yes." There was a pause. Talking to a young child on the phone was a job. You had to constantly initiate topics, keep the conversation moving. As Lee poured hot water over the coffee grounds, he was aware of something in the back of his mind trying to press its way to the front, but he couldn't quite grasp what it was—a thought, an idea, an image of some kind.

"Are you having fun in school?" he said into the phone.

"Um, yes."

"What do you like best?"

"Art class. I drew pictures of Mommy today."

"You did?"

"Yeah. We were apposed to bring a picture in and draw from that, so I brought one of Mommy from the scrapbook." Kylie had trouble with "sp" sounds, and pronounced "supposed" as "apposed." She also said "Francanscisco" for "San Francisco" and "pissghetti" for "spaghetti." Lee found all of these child-hood speech patterns charming, and was sorry the day would come—as he knew it would—when his niece would outgrow them.

A silence hung in the air, and Lee couldn't think of any-thing to say. He knew his mother kept a scrapbook filled with pictures of Laura, but he didn't know Kylie had seen it.

"And then when she comes back I can show it to her."

Lee bit his lip. It was bad enough that his mother had never accepted Laura's death, but it made him furious that she insisted on sharing her unreasonable hopes with her granddaughter.

"Okay, well, I'll see you tomorrow. Can I talk to your grandmom now?"

"Okay. Grandmom!"

His mother came and took the phone.

"Yes, dear?"

Lee wanted to tear into her for what he considered her irresponsible behavior, but he didn't have the energy. All he wanted to do was lie down, pull the blankets over his head and shut out everything.

"Was there something you wanted to tell me?"

"No—I just wanted to say good-bye."

"Fine. Take care of yourself—and remember to eat!" His mother often ended conversations that way. He had lost so much weight during his depression that she became worried.

"Okay, I will. 'Bye."

Lee hung up and lifted the filter from his coffee mug. The liquid inside was hot and strong and black—opaque and impenetrable, like his mother. Again the thought in the back of his mind struggled to make its way forward. He added a drop of milk to his coffee and took it over to the window seat. It was something about Marie, and yet not about her. Something related to her death . . . but what? He stared out at the gray February morning. A thin rain was falling, and he noticed the lights were on in the Ukrainian church across the street. In a flash, he remembered what had been bothering him all morning.

He picked up the phone and dialed the number for the Bronx Major Case Unit.

Chapter Four

The campus is quiet, still as a tomb. The thought came to Samuel as he tiptoed across the quad, toward the dormitory building with the one light burning in the first-floor corner room. The light cast a blurry yellow halo around the window, a protective aura surrounding the room's inhabitants. He shivered as he drew closer. He could hear music playing— something classical, with flutes and violins. A couple of other rooms on the third floor had their lights blazing—late-night studying, he supposed.

He stood beneath the windows and looked up at the occupants of the rooms. Three coeds, as far as he could make out, sat around a low table, talking and laughing. He watched the girls moving through the windows, the outline of their bodies blurred through the white lace curtains, their faces muted and indistinct, as if in a dream. Why didn't they want him? Why couldn't they see his specialness? He could hardly dare to desire them, but as he sat gazing at their soft forms, lit from behind by yellow lamplight, translucent and misty mermaids, the gentle glow of the room, the light breath of breeze on his cheeks induced a trancelike state in which he floated, caught in a sweet web of longing.

Then one of the girls threw back her head, laughing at something (he couldn't make out the words), exposing her throat. He watched as the light fell upon the sudden curve of her neck, so open, so vulnerable. He imagined his hands wrapped around that white neck, pressing, squeezing, tighter and tighter, until the life within seeped into his fingers. He imagined his hands growing stronger as the life force drained away from the girl's body and into his own.

It was a thrilling thought—and it seized him with a force that shook him to his bones. He trembled, he sweated, he burned with a fierce flame from deep within him, from a place he had not known existed until now, a place his mother could not see, could not even imagine. This was his secret, his delicious fantasy. He trembled at the idea of keeping something from his mother—it made him swell with a sense of his own manhood. He turned and walked away from the window, putting his hand on the key ring that hung from his belt to stop the keys from jangling.

For the first time in his life that he could remember, he felt powerful.

Chapter Five

Captain Chuck Morton leaned back in his chair and studied the man sitting on the other side of his desk. He looked thin, even leaner than when Chuck had last seen him two months ago, and definitely thinner than he had been when the two of them shared a suite of rooms at Princeton all those years ago. His friend's angular, handsome face was pale and drawn, and his long body was slumped forward, his elbows braced on the chair's armrests. Chuck knew Lee had been up since well before dawn. Morton leaned forward in his chair and fingered the glass paperweight next to his phone. It was a butterfly spread out beneath a glistening prism, and it gave him the creeps, but it was a gift from his son, so he kept it on his desk. The butterfly's multicolored wings gleamed like tiny rainbows under the fluorescent light.

He sighed and looked at Lee Campbell. Even sitting there studying crime photos, his friend gave the impression of restlessness. It had been a long time since their carefree days at Nassau Hall, days when all that seemed to matter were rugby, girls, and grades—in that order. Now Lee looked anything but carefree—Chuck could see his long fingers twitching as they gripped the photos. Chuck felt sorry for his old friend; this was not the Lee Campbell he had known at Princeton.

Mental. That's what some of the beat cops called him behind his back, but Chuck felt a fierce loyalty to this intense, earnest man with the haunted eyes and nervous hands, a loyalty that extended beyond their days together romping the ivy-drenched quadrangles of Princeton. On the rugby field, Lee was the team captain, with quick hands and an even quicker mind, playing the key position of fly half, while Chuck, with his speed, played wing or outside center. Maybe it was their opposite temperaments that made their friendship possible: Lee was always keyed up, charismatic, intense, while Chuck's own flame burned lower, with a steady blue glow. Lee was a born leader, and he was a born sidekick. The two of them bonded as roommates their freshman year in Blair Hall. Not even women could come between them, though Chuck still wondered occasionally if Susan ever regretted marrying him instead of Lee.

"You know," Chuck said, "maybe I shouldn't have called you in on this. Maybe it was—"

"A mistake?" Lee interrupted. "Cut it out, Chuck—it's obvious that this case needs a profiler."

"No, that's not what I mean. I was just thinking that because of . . ." Chuck paused, not wanting to say the words. He felt like a coward.

"Christ, Chuck, you can't second-guess every case I'm on because it might bring up memories of my sister's disappearance."

Five years ago, Lee Campbell's younger sister Laura had disappeared without a trace from her Greenwich Village apartment, and everything had changed. He had never been the same since then. It was as though a dark chord had been struck in his soul and the reverberations still had not stopped. He'd had a thriving private practice as a psychologist, and

Chuck was surprised when Lee called a few months after his sister's disappearance to say he was attending John Jay College for an advanced degree in forensic psychology. Later he came to realize that the disappearance of Lee's sister had affected his friend in ways he couldn't quantify. Once Lee graduated, Chuck had been instrumental in getting him his present position as the only full-time profiler in the NYPD. Lately, though, he had been wondering if he had made a mistake—emotionally, his friend didn't seem up to it.

Chuck looked out the grimy window of his office, absentmindedly fingering the butterfly paperweight on his desk.

"So no signs of sexual assault, right?" Lee muttered, still studying the photos.

"Right," Chuck said. "The lab report just came in. But how did you—"

"I'm telling you, Chuck, the same guy who did Jane Doe also killed Marie Kelleher last night!"

Chuck looked back at him.

"You really think they're connected?"

"Yes, I do."

Morton shook his head. "I dunno, Lee. Seems like a stretch to me."

Lee ran a hand through his curly black hair, something he did when he was upset. His friend's hair was longer, too, Chuck thought—even shaggy, by his own standards. He wore his own sandy blond hair short—like the bristles of a hairbrush, his wife said. He had left her soft warm body with particular reluctance this morning. When he rose from bed, the house still so dark and quiet, Susan had flung an arm out after him and moaned a little, and he had wanted nothing more than to climb back under the covers next to her and plant kisses everywhere his lips could reach.

The crime photos Lee was studying were from an unsolved murder out in Queens a few weeks ago—*Jane Doe*

Number Five, they called her. She was well groomed and wasn't dressed like a hooker, and it was odd that no one had called yet to report her missing.

Outside his office, Morton could hear the morning shift of cops arriving, as the building that housed the Bronx Major Case Unit stirred with the beginning of a new workday. The aroma of fresh coffee seeped through the closed office door, making Morton's mouth swim with saliva. He looked wistfully at the empty coffee mug on his desk, swallowed, and rubbed his stinging eyes, dry from lack of sleep.

"I just know they're related, Chuck," Lee was saying, his dark eyes intense in the stark fluorescent lighting. "The posing of the bodies—"

"But there was no mutilation on Jane Doe," Chuck protested.

"No, because he didn't feel comfortable enough—she was probably his first kill."

"Okay, okay," Morton answered. "I believe you. Trouble is, I don't know who else will."

Lee stood up and paced the small office. "The same perp that killed this girl in Queens also killed Marie Kelleher. I know he did!" He thrust a photo in front of Chuck's face. The glossy print showed a well-dressed young woman lying on her back, her arms flung out from her body, so that if you stood her up she would be in the same position as a crucifixion victim. But there was no cross anywhere in sight—the body lay in a ditch on the edge of Greenlawn Cemetery in Queens.

"Look at that!" Lee said, his voice tight with emotion. "Look at the positioning of the body! It's exactly the same as Marie Kelleher, except this time he managed to get a little closer to his fantasy."

"And what's that?"

"Leaving the body in a church. There was nothing random about that. And the carving—that's part of the fantasy too."

Chuck leaned back in his chair. "I don't know, Lee. It seems a little thin."

"I'll tell you something else. He won't stop until he's caught."

"So you say we're dealing with a serial offender here?"

"That's right."

Something in his voice made Morton believe him.

"Please, Chuck," Lee said. "Please. I need to study the file on the Queens killing."

Morton and rose from his chair. He felt stiff and old and tired. Seeing his friend like this didn't help.

"Okay, okay," he said. "I had to call in some favors just to get a copy of these photos. Let me run it past the guys upstairs, okay? I don't have to tell you that detectives can get very territorial about their cases."

"All right."

"So," Chuck said after a pause that threatened to swallow them both, "how's the *Frau ohne Schatten*?"

The old Lee Campbell would have smiled at this. But now his friend just raised an eyebrow, his face devoid of mirth. "Oh, some things never change, you know. Brisk as ever."

Lee had come up with the nickname for his mother after seeing the Strauss opera in college. Chuck, who had some German ancestry on his mother's side, found it amusing, having experienced Fiona Campbell's relentless cheerfulness firsthand. They used to joke about how she was really the original *Frau ohne Schatten*—woman without a shadow. But now the shadows had fallen heavily over his friend.

Campbell turned to leave, but he swayed and caught himself by grabbing the door frame.

"You okay?" Chuck asked, reaching a hand out to him.

Lee waved him off. "Fine. Just a little tired, that's all."

Morton didn't believe him, but he kept silent. He recalled Lee's Presbyterian stoicism only too well from their days on the rugby field, and still remembered the day Lee refused to leave a tournament game after breaking his nose on a tackle. Blood spurting from his nose, he insisted on finishing the game; he muttered something about "setting an example." Chuck called it masochism, but he would never say that to his friend.

"Can I speak with the pathologist doing Marie's autopsy?" Lee asked.

"I don't see why not. I'll be in touch," he added.

"Right," said Campbell. He paused at the door to Chuck's office, as if he were about to say something else, but then turned, opened the door, and was gone.

Morton leaned back in his chair and ran a hand over his stiff bristle of blond hair. Then he stood, picked up his mug, and headed out of his office toward the coffee station. The mug—a gift from his daughter—proclaimed him as "World's Greatest Dad," but today he didn't feel like the world's greatest anything.

When he got to the coffee station, he saw that a few beat cops were gathered in the corner, heads lowered, talking quietly, and he heard one of them snicker. Then another one said, "Yeah—real *mental*, I guess." They all laughed—until one of the conspirators saw Chuck and nudged the others with his elbow, at which point they abruptly stopped laughing. Rage gathered in Chuck's chest, constricting his throat and making his forehead burn. He was noted for his even temper most of the time, but when he lost it, he truly lost it.

"What the *hell* are you looking at, Peters?" he bellowed.

Everyone in the station house stopped what they were doing and looked at him. He advanced on the group of subordinates, who shrank from him, averting their eyes as he approached.

"Let me tell you something," he said, his voice lowered to a steely calm. "If you don't get back to work right this minute, some heads are going to roll around here. Do you understand me?" he said, addressing himself to a young sergeant, Jeff Peters.

"Yes, sir," Peters replied, his blunt face sulky. He was short and black-haired and built like a prizewinning Angus.

Chuck felt his face redden. "I didn't hear you, Peters!"

"Yes, sir."

"And you, O'Connell—do you have anything to say to me?"

"No, sir." Danny O'Connell was a tall, skinny redhead who followed any lead that Peters set. Chuck knew this, and knew that the rest of them were just playing along. One of the rules of group dynamics—which functioned in station houses exactly as it did in high school locker rooms—was to make fun of others to deflect the possibility that others might make fun of you. Peters was the ringleader, as usual, and Chuck knew he had a mean streak. He came from an unstable home, had a drunken failure for a father, and was angry at the world. Chuck put his face close to Peters's face, so close that he could smell his wintergreen aftershave.

"Or maybe you wanted to transfer out of Homicide? Because that could be arranged."

"No, sir."

"You sure about that?"

"Yes, sir."

"Then you'd better keep your nose clean. You understand me?"

"Yes, sir."

Chuck took a look around the station to see that he had things under control. He was satisfied with the results. Everyone was looking at him with respect tinged with fear, and that was the way he wanted it. There would be opportunities for joking later, for loosening the reins a bit, but what he needed now was respect. He glanced at Peters one last time and stalked back into his office, being sure to slam the door behind him.

Once inside, he closed the venetian blinds and sank into his chair. Being in command was part theatrics, part intimidation, and part setting an example. He didn't enjoy the theatrics or the intimidation, but he dreaded even more losing control of his men. Once that happened, he knew, you might as well turn in your badge.

He was not a natural leader—he knew that. At Princeton, Lee was always the alpha male, and Chuck had been happy with his role as sidekick. But then a miracle had happened: he had finally attracted the attention of Susan Beaumont, the most glamorous and beautiful woman he had ever known. For a long time she seemed to have fixed her sights on Lee, and then they had broken up and she was pursuing him. Even now it seemed like a dream from which he would awaken someday, but until then, he had resolved to do everything in his power to keep her interested. Being a lowly policeman would not do for the likes of her, so he set his eyes on precinct commander—and he made it, though it was not a natural fit. Chuck Morton was tailor-made to be second-in-command. He was diligent, honest, and intelligent, but not especially imaginative or charismatic. Still, he worked hard—harder than anyone would ever know—to get what he wanted, to please Susan, to make her proud of him.

And now here he was, commander of the Bronx Major Case Unit. It was a demanding job, especially now, after what had happened on the southern tip of Manhattan just a few short months ago. Everyone was jittery, and his men looked to him to set an example. And by God, he would set one if it killed him.

He looked out the window at the soot-covered sill, where a pigeon pecked away at some invisible scraps. He wished there was something he could do to take away his friend's pain, but he knew that the demons dancing in Lee's soul were beyond anyone's reach. But at least he could keep the men from making fun of his friend behind his back. He looked down at his empty coffee mug—he had forgotten to fill it. He sighed and leaned back in his chair. He knew that to go back out there now would spoil the dramatic effect of his stormy exit. The coffee would have to wait.

Lee Campbell stepped out of the police station into the dismal dog days of February, that time of year when all holiday cheer has evaporated, leaving in its place only a lingering shiver of wistfulness. The days were still short, and the cold weather a brusque reminder that spring was still a distant reality.

This year the cheer had been thin in New York, the holiday meetings filled with a sense of loss, of those suddenly gone, ripped brutally from their lives, like a conversation interrupted mid-sentence. There had been much talk in the media about healing, and of a "return to normalcy," but he knew that for many people the words were empty ones. The healing process would never be finished, and "normalcy" would never come. He didn't know about the rest of the country, but New Yorkers now lived in two time zones: before and after.

Lee wrapped his knee-length tweed coat tighter around himself and headed for the subway. Like so many of the nicer things he owned, the Scottish tweed was a present from his mother, brought back from a recent trip to Edinburgh. He caught a glimpse of his reflection in a store window, his haggard face looking mismatched with the elegant coat.

He ducked his head low against the biting wind and hurried onward. At times like this, there was one man he could turn to, who always seemed to know what to say, what to do.

He smiled as he slipped through the turnstile to make a trip he had made a hundred times before, during his student days at John Jay College of Criminal Justice. He needed to see his old mentor: the irascible, brilliant, moody, and thoroughly misanthropic John Paul Nelson.

Chapter Six

Professor John Paul Farragut Nelson was not a happy man.

"Good God, Lee! Can't you give it a rest? You just got out of the hospital, for Chrissakes!"

Nelson savagely stubbed out his half-smoked cigarette in the glass ashtray on his desk and stalked over to the window. His office at John Jay College was spacious but cluttered, with books and research papers stacked on the floor on both sides of his desk.

Lee shifted in his chair and looked down at his shoes. He had expected a lecture, but his old professor was more worked up than he had anticipated. Nelson jammed one freckled hand into his right pants pocket and ran the other one through his wavy auburn hair.

"Do you *really* think you can be of any help in this case?"

"Well—"

"You had a *nervous breakdown*, for God's sake! And you think you can come waltzing back to work a few weeks later as if nothing ever happened?"

Lee stared at the floor. He knew Nelson well enough to

know that when he got like this, arguing with him would only infuriate him more, like waving a red flag in front of a bull. Nelson actually resembled a bull at this moment, with his short, thick body tensed, nostrils dilated, his face as red as Lee had ever seen it—redder even than after an evening of Nelson's legendary bar crawling and untold shots of single-malt scotch.

A tall, skinny student with a punk hairstyle and a silver nose ring wandered past the office and poked his head in the door—but after one look at Nelson's face, quickly withdrew. Lee watched as the kid's spiky, bright orange hair disappeared down the hall. He looked back at Nelson, who was rummaging through his desk—probably looking for cigarettes. He never seemed to be able to remember which drawer he kept them in. Lee had always been a little mystified by the interest the celebrated Professor Nelson took in him, an interest that began the first day he took his seat in Nelson's Criminal Psychology 101, nicknamed "Creeps for Geeks." It was a required course, even for the technicians who investigated crime scenes, the CSIs who were generally thought of as nerds by the other students.

Nelson's teaching style reflected his personality. Imperious, brilliant, and impatient, he had a temper that could sweep up as suddenly as a storm over the waters of Killarney Bay, where he had traced his ancestry back for centuries. It was rumored that his father had been a member of the notorious Westies, a murderous Irish gang in Hell's Kitchen that flourished in the middle of the twentieth century. It was said their ruthlessness and brutality made the Mafia look like choirboys.

In spite of Nelson's reputation for remoteness, his interest in Lee had been immediate and fatherly. Lee thought maybe it was because he was a good ten years older than the average John Jay student, or perhaps it was their similar Celtic heritage. Nelson treated Lee with a kindness he did not display to the other students. In fact, he didn't seem to regard the human race as worthy of the kind of affection he usually reserved for his Irish setter, Rex. Nelson doted on the animal and spoiled him as extravagantly as any Upper East Side lapdog.

Nelson's interest in Lee's career continued after he left John Jay to join the NYPD as its only criminal profiler, an appointment Nelson helped make possible. The bar crawling continued, as did the late-night discussions of German composers, French philosophers, and Celtic poets.

Now, however, Nelson did not appear at all pleased with his prize student.

"I thought you had more sense than that, I really did," he said as he lit the cigarette he had dug out of the recesses of his desk.

Lee couldn't help noticing that Nelson's hands were trembling. Taking a deep drag from the cigarette, Nelson absently twisted the wedding ring on his left hand. His wife had been dead for nearly three months now, but he continued to wear the ring. Lee wondered why. To keep potential mates away? Out of loyalty and devotion to her memory? Nelson rarely discussed Karen, but her picture hung in the living room of his spacious apartment, showing her fresh faced and smiling from the stern of a sailing yacht, her short brown curls blowing in the wind—with no hint of the cancer that was to gnaw stealthily away at her in the years to come.

The wind seemed to leave Nelson's sails. He blew out a puff of smoke and sat down behind his desk, linking his hands behind his neck.

"All right, lad," he said. "What is so compelling about this case that it can't wait?"

Lee was used to Nelson's abrupt mood changes.

"I just have a feeling I can help here, that I—well, there's something about this killer that I can *feel*, that I understand."

Nelson leaned forward and studied the younger man.

"I don't know that that's necessarily a good thing."

"Yes, I know. I realize the danger of—"

"Of compromising your objectivity."

Now it was Lee's turn to be angry.

"This whole notion of objectivity is a fantasy, you know."

Nelson looked startled, but Lee continued.

"There is no such thing! It's a comforting fiction created by people who don't want to get too close to things that go bump in the night."

Nelson took another drag from his cigarette. "If you're suggesting that it's relative, I would agree with you."

"No, what I'm suggesting is that it doesn't exist *at all.* The whole idea is some outdated Age of Reason notion, some classical model that went out with powdered wigs and knee breeches—only we just haven't realized it yet. It's an impossible ideal."

Nelson grunted and stubbed his cigarette out on the floor. "Impossible or not, as a criminal investigator you owe it to your victims—and to yourself—to be as objective as possible. Otherwise your conclusions become clouded by emotion."

Lee felt his shoulders go rigid as he looked at Nelson. "What are you saying?"

Nelson held his gaze. "I think you know."

Lee didn't reply, and the silence between them lay thick as the layers of books and manuscripts stuffed everywhere in the cluttered office. He glanced at the brass busts of Beethoven and Bach on Nelson's desk. Beethoven's face was tragic: the tightly compressed lips and broad nose, the stormy, tortured eyes under a mane of wild hair; the stubborn chin, jutting out defensively against the world, as if bracing himself for what Fate was to throw at him . . . the picture of determination, the triumph of human will in adversity. How different from the bourgeois contentment of Bach, with his big nose and face ringed by a wig of riotous Baroque curls. Nelson had a particular fondness for Beethoven. He had read Lee excerpts from the Heiligenstadt Testament, Beethoven's tragic letter to his brother after learning of his impeding deafness.

Lee laid a hand on the bust of Beethoven, the metal cold and hard under his palm. "You think this is about my sister, don't you?"

Nelson raised his left eyebrow. "This victim is about the same age Laura was when she . . ." he looked away as if embarrassed.

Lee's grip on the bust tightened. "When she died," he said.

Even though Laura's body had never been found, Lee was certain that his sister was dead. He had known it from the very day of her disappearance, so finally and irrevocably that the countless questions and speculations from well-meaning friends, family, and news reporters became intolerable. *"She's dead!"* he wanted to scream at them. *"Isn't it obvious?"* But his mother's denial was like a wall of granite between them.

He needed no such pretense around Nelson, who understood the inside of a criminal's mind better than anyone Lee knew. Looking unblinkingly at hard human truths was what the criminal psychologist did, his raison d'être.

"She *is* dead, you know," Lee said, his voice as steady as he could manage. "And like it or not, to some degree, for me every case is about Laura."

Nelson sighed. "All right. I just think maybe you're getting in too deep too soon."

Lee paced the small room impatiently. "I know I can *see into* this killer, if I can only get a chance! I'm already beginning to see his patterns at work—"

"What patterns? There's only been one body."

He stopped pacing and faced Nelson. "Oh, no, that's where you're wrong. There's another one—I'm sure of it."

"I didn't hear any—" Nelson put his hand to his forehead. "Wait a minute—there was a girl out in Queens a few weeks ago, a Jane Doe. Is that the one you mean?"

"Yes," Lee said. "They called her 'Jane Doe Number Five.' I'm certain the two are linked."

"Same signature?"

"Not exactly, but—"

"Wasn't the girl in Queens found outdoors—not far from Greenlawn Cemetery, if I remember?"

"Yes, but she wasn't far from a church, and I'm convinced that he would have left her there if something hadn't stopped him."

Nelson rubbed his chin, thick with reddish-brown beard stubble.

"I'll be damned. I wonder if there are others."

"I don't think so. The Queens killing was hurried, opportunistic. I wouldn't be surprised if it was completely unplanned. The one yesterday was much more organized, very carefully thought out. And he—" Lee paused and looked at Nelson.

"He what?"

"It hasn't been released to the public, but he carved her up."

Nelson sucked in a large quantity of smoke and flicked cigarette ash into a solid green jade ashtray he had brought back from Turkey.

"Go on," he said quietly.

"The words to the Lord's Prayer—or at least the beginning of it. Post mortem, thank God."

"Jesus."

"That took some time to do."

Nelson rubbed a hand over his face. "God, Lee, I'm still afraid you'll be getting in over your head on this one. Are you taking your medication?"

Lee fished a bottle of pills from his jacket and held them in front of Nelson's nose. Nelson studied the bottle.

"Not much of a dosage. When Karen was sick I was on twice that much."

Lee put the bottle back in his pocket. "This stuff is expensive."

Nelson gave a laugh—a short, mirthless puff of air. "Tell me about it."

Lee looked out the window at the cars and pedestrians on Tenth Avenue, everyone hustling up the avenue—jostling, honking, competing for space in the rush hour traffic, all in a big hurry to get somewhere, to be part of the endless, restless motion that is New York City. He remembered being one of those people, before depression came along, lifted him off his feet, and slammed him facedown into the pavement.

The view from down there was different. It was strange to look up and see people still hurrying along with their lives intact, while for him just getting out of bed was an act of enormous willpower. Now, looking down at them on the street below, he had the same feeling of distance, of being an alien in a world where everyone except him seemed to know where they were going. He envied them, but he also felt that he knew something they could never know. He had seen into the very center of things, into hell itself, and come back alive somehow—damaged, perhaps, but alive.

He felt a hand on his shoulder and turned to see Nelson standing behind him. Was it Lee's imagination, or were his blue eyes moist? It was hard to tell with the light coming from behind him.

"I can see that nothing I say is going to stop you. So let me just say this: be careful, Lee."

"I will."

"Good. Now go out and get that son of a bitch."

Lee looked down at the street again. Somewhere, in the

throng of people, with a face that could blend into any crowd, a pair of footsteps clicked along the sidewalk next to a hundred others, footsteps belonging to a murderer with only one thing on his mind: his next victim. Lee silently vowed to do whatever he could—at whatever cost—to get between that killer and his goal.

Chapter Seven

"You know," Detective Butts remarked, "all this hocus-pocus stuff doesn't solve crimes. Shoe leather does."

"Right," Lee answered. He had heard it all before, and was tired of defending himself to cops. He wasn't an official member of the police force—he had not attended the academy, and carried only an ID card identifying him as a civilian consultant to the NYPD. He was keenly aware of the separation between him and the gun-toting members of the police force. People like him were not necessarily included in the tight, exclusive circle of the Brotherhood of Blue.

It was the next morning, and they were standing in front of an examination room at the medical examiner's office, waiting for the pathologist who had done Marie Kelleher's autopsy. She entered hurriedly, apologizing for her lateness. Gretchen Rilke was a rather glamorous-looking woman, blue-eyed and pink-cheeked, with thick, dyed blond hair and a suggestive lilt of Alpine hills in her accent.

"I was in a conference call that went late," she said, pushing a strand of implausibly yellow hair from her eyes. With one hand she pulled the body from the morgue freezer compartment, the oversized drawer sliding smoothly on its metal rollers. With the other hand she pulled back the sheet covering Marie's body just enough to expose her neck. In spite of the bluish tinge to her pale skin, it was still hard to think of her as dead.

"You see the bruises?" Gretchen asked.

Lee looked at the thick collar of purple discoloration that ringed Marie's neck. It appeared darker now, which could be a result of the harsh fluorescent lighting—but he knew that bruises could deepen or even appear after death. Now, under the bright lights, he could see several separate bands of bruising.

"I see," he said.

"This indicates that he repositioned his fingers, probably several times."

"So he didn't kill her all at once?" Butts asked.

The pathologist shook her head. "No. There's no crushed cartilage, and no serious damage to the larynx."

"So," Lee said, "that means he applies minimum force—enough to make her lose consciousness. And then he waits until she comes to and starts all over again."

"That scenario would be consistent with the physical evidence," Dr. Rilke agreed.

"Shit," Butts muttered. "This is one sick bastard."

"Okay," Lee said, almost to himself. "He's not in a hurry. This means that he's comfortable where he is—that he's not worried about getting caught. He's killing them somewhere other than the church. And no sign of sexual assault?"

"Right," Dr. Rilke answered.

"And no sign of a struggle?"

"Her fingernails aren't even broken, so she didn't have time to fight back. There are no defensive knife wounds, so I'm guessing he took that out after she was already subdued."

Lee gulped in some air, avoiding breathing through his nose. "So the carving was postmortem?"

"That would be consistent with the amount of bleeding—or lack of it," she replied. "On the other hand . . ."

"What?" Lee said, his stomach twisting around itself. He swallowed hard. He hated visiting the morgue.

"Well, he didn't carve that deeply, so it's just possible it was done while she was still alive."

Lee felt his stomach give a heave. He swallowed again and concentrated on taking deep breaths.

"How would he get her to stay still, though?" Butts asked.

"There were no signs of ligature around her wrists or ankles, right?" Lee asked.

"No," Rilke answered. "But she might have been too weak to struggle by that time."

"Any idea what he used?" Butts asked.

"Nothing fancy. An ordinary kitchen paring knife would do the job. Something with a pretty short blade—probably a couple of inches at most."

"Could it have been a scalpel?"

"The wounds are too jagged for that—even in unskilled hands, a scalpel would do a neater job."

"Too bad we can't use handwriting analysis on this," Butts remarked.

"No, I doubt there would be a correlation," Lee agreed, "although there might be something about the way he forms certain letters . . ."

"It's not much of a sample to go on," Dr. Rilke pointed out.

None of them wanted to say what they were all thinking: the last thing they wanted was to have a larger sample, because that would mean having another victim.

"No prints at all?" Lee asked.

"No," said Rilke. "We superglued the body—nothing. He must have worn gloves."

"Supergluing" meant using cyanoacrylate (superglue) to develop latent prints that might not otherwise be visible.

"We gotta get going," Butts said, looking at his watch. "The parents in Jersey are expecting us."

"Okay, thank you," Lee said to Gretchen, who smiled grimly.

"Good luck."

"Thanks," he replied, thinking, *We'll need it.*

Forty minutes later Lee and Butts were seated next to each other on the DeCamp bus to Nutley, New Jersey. As the bus rumbled out of the Lincoln Tunnel and onto the corkscrew stretch of highway leading up the hill past the town of Wee-hawken, Lee turned to look across the river at Manhattan. The mid-morning sun lingered low in the eastern horizon, lurking behind the buildings, its furtive rays refracted by the glass skyscrapers of Midtown. The river appeared perfectly still and opaque under the hazy gray February sky.

Marie Kelleher's parents had already come into the city once to identify their daughter's body, and Chuck Morton, trying to spare them further grief and stress, had dispatched Lee and Butts out to the couple's house in Nutley to inter-view them.

Lee leaned back in his seat and stretched his legs out under the empty seat in front of him. The DeCamp bus was expensive, but it was comfortable and quiet. It wasn't crowded at this hour; they were traveling in the opposite direction of the commuters headed into the city. The few people scattered around the bus were reading, staring out the window, or nap-ping. Talking on cell phones was forbidden, according to the sign behind the driver. Thick block letters warned that pas-sengers who disobeyed could be ejected from the bus.

"Good old-fashioned detective work—*that's* what solves crimes," Butts remarked as he opened the magazine in his lap and leafed through it. "Yep," he murmured, "that's what it's all about: knockin' on doors, gathering evidence."

Lee gazed out the window as the gray granite cliffs of Weehawken whizzed by. He'd heard this line before, many times, not just from beat cops and guys like Butts, but also at John Jay. The culture of law enforcement had little patience for what most cops considered the "touchy-feely" aspect of crime solving. Most cops were not comfortable around profilers, any more than they were comfortable around psychiatrists.

"It's not that I think it doesn't figure into the equation," Butts said, staring down at a print ad promising whiter teeth. The woman in the picture grinned up at them, her parted lips displaying a row of broad, perfectly even teeth that gleamed like ivory dominoes. "But it's really all about evidence in the end, you know? Cold, hard evidence—*that's* what catches criminals."

Lee didn't reply. They *had* no evidence so far: no hair, no fibers, no DNA—nothing. He didn't feel optimistic about getting any, either. This killer would only get better at covering his tracks as time went on.

Detective Butts was leafing through the magazine, his bulbous head bent low over the pages. Lee couldn't help liking the man, in spite of his bluntness—or maybe because of it. He was like a lumbering old bulldog—grumpy, moody, eccentric—and yet Lee had the feeling he was someone you could count on in a crisis.

"What did you find out about that broken lock in the church basement?" he asked.

Butts looked up from the magazine. "The maintenance staff didn't know anything about a broken lock, and no one I talked to in administration remembered making the call. But sure enough, there was one down there when they looked, so someone must have known about it."

"Hmm," Lee said. "That's interesting."

"Coincidence, you think?"

"Maybe, maybe not."

Nutley was not a long ride—about thirty minutes, with the light traffic they encountered traveling westward—and soon they were trudging from the bus stop up the hill to the modest middle-class neighborhood where the Kellehers lived. The house itself was a tidy little white clapboard structure, with green awnings over the windows and a small wooden windmill on the front lawn. *Nothing looks its best this time of year*, Lee thought as they walked up the narrow sidewalk to the front door. The grass in front of the house was brown and windswept, and even the little windmill looked desolate and abandoned in the dull late winter light.

The Kellehers were expecting them, and they were soon seated on opposite ends of the living room sofa, cradling cups of instant coffee in their hands. Their hosts sat opposite them in matching wing chairs. A fake electric log gave off an eerie red light in the hearth behind them.

Mrs. Kelleher had a face like a deflated muffin—as though someone had taken a pin to it. Her flesh puckered softly, gathering under her eyes in doughy little pouches, lying in crinkled pockets around her small, pursed mouth, the flesh sinking into itself in tiny, concave crevices. Lee figured her for no older than sixty, but knew without asking that she was a longtime smoker. The room reeked of cigarettes.

Her husband was as square and hard as she was fleshy. Short and broad of shoulder, he had the rugged build of a miner or a construction worker. Wisps of curly graying hair clung to the top of his big, square Irish head. A road map of spidery red blood vessels sprouted on either side of his straight, high-ridged nose, but his blue eyes were clear. Lee concluded that the broken blood vessels were more likely from excessive sun and exertion than alcohol. Or, if he was a drinker, he was off the bottle now.

"Can you think of any reason that your daughter might have been a target? Anything at all?" Butts asked them. The opening condolences were out of the way, and he was zeroing in on the heart of the matter with his usual forthrightness—or tactlessness.

Brian Kelleher cleared his throat and looked down at his wife. "We're just simple people," he said in a throaty, faintly accented voice. "We've never been associated with bad people—you know, criminal types." A wave of stale tobacco floated from his clothing, the remnants of many cigarettes, and Lee realized that he, too, was a smoker.

"What makes you think we'd know our daughter's killer?" Mrs. Kelleher asked, her eyes wide with anxiety. "We don't know people like that."

Butts was fidgeting with his notebook, and his eyes roamed the room restlessly. "We're not saying you do," he replied. "It's just that sometimes people remember seeing and hearing something that can later be useful in an investigation. Can you think of anything that might stand out as strange or unusual in your daughter's life—especially in the last few weeks or so?"

The Kellehers appeared to consider his question, but to Lee it looked as if they were merely marking time. They frowned as if in concentration, studied their hands, and looked around the room. Finally Mrs. Kelleher spoke.

"I can't think of anything. Can you, dear?" she said to her husband. Mr. Kelleher looked at his wife—clearly, he took his cues from her.

He shook his big square head sadly. "Not really. Marie was a straight-A student, you know," he added, with a glance at his wife.

"Did you ever see her with anyone strange or unusual?" Butts asked. "I mean, anyone who set off alarm bells or anything?"

The couple looked indignant, as if he had called their dead daughter's virtue into question.

"Oh, Lordy, no," Mrs. Kelleher replied. "She was dating that nice boy. He was respectful. We liked him, didn't we, dear?" she said to her husband, who nodded obediently.

"He told us that he thought she might be seeing someone else," Butts said.

"What do you mean?" Mrs. Kelleher demanded. Her soft, round face resembled a recently vacated couch cushion.

"Did you know anything about another boyfriend?" Butts asked.

Mrs. Kelleher's prim face puckered like a prune. "No, of course not! Marie wasn't that kind of girl."

"What kind of girl is that?" Lee asked.

"The kind of girl who would be seeing two men at once, of course," she snapped back. "Marie wouldn't do that."

"Because she was a good girl?" Lee said.

"Because she was a good *Catholic* girl. And, I might add," she said, leaning forward and placing a plump hand on Lee's arm, "we both trust in the good Lord to bring her killer to justice. We know he's watching over us, and that he will help you capture this evil, evil man."

"I guess He was looking the other way when your daughter was murdered," Butts muttered under his breath.

"Excuse me?" Mrs. Kelleher said, her little button eyes bright with suspicion.

Lee felt sour distaste gathering in his mouth. Brian and Francis Kelleher held their faith in front of them like a banner. He recognized the smugness lurking behind her eyes: even devastated as she was by grief, Mrs. Kelleher's voice had the sanctimonious tone of the true believer. These people brandished their beliefs like a weapon. One sweep of the sword of their faith opened a swath between them and the world of nonbelievers—a swift and tidy demarcation.

It set his teeth on edge and angered him beyond reason.

He didn't know why—perhaps he heard echoes of his mother's stalwart stoicism and superiority. It was hubris in the guise of humility, close-mindedness masquerading as wisdom.

He knew he would have to overcome his distaste, and tried to arrange his face in a proper attitude of sympathy and concern.

"You know, my wife and I worked long and hard to raise our girl with solid Christian values," Mr. Kelleher said, as if reciting a well-memorized speech. The words had all the spontaneity of a church litany. All the while, his wife watched him, smiling. Lee felt such a visceral distaste for them that he forced his thoughts once again to the unspeakable tragedy they had just suffered.

"You see, Inspector—" Mrs. Kelleher began.

"It's Detective," Butts corrected.

She was not deterred a bit, though, and continued without a pause.

"You see, Detective, the Lord giveth, and the Lord taketh away. He must have had a reason for wanting our Marie up there with him—because that's where she is now, sitting in heaven beside God the Father. He must have some plan for her, or He wouldn't have taken her away from us like this."

"So your daughter was religious, too?" Lee asked.

Mrs. Kelleher shifted her focus to him. "Oh, goodness me, yes! She never missed church. Marie was the very best child that anyone could hope to have," she added, dabbing at her eye with the corner of a flowered handkerchief, which gave off an oppressively heavy floral scent. Lee tried to place it: Was it mimosa? Patchouli? Lilies of some kind?

Brian Kelleher put a protective hand on his wife's shoulder. Lee had more sympathy for him. It looked as though he was just playing along with his wife's religious passion, and that left to his own devices, he might be a sensible, rational man. Mrs. Kelleher sighed, though Lee had the impression that she was feeling sorry for herself rather than mourning her daughter. Something about this woman rubbed him the wrong way and set off alarm bells in his head.

Another half hour of questioning brought them no closer to useful information about poor·Marie. Her parents merely corroborated everything they already knew about her. She was a good student, quiet but well liked. She honored her parents' faith by attending church regularly—she even worked as a volunteer to feed the homeless in a program her church ran at a local shelter once a month. After refusing another cup of lukewarm instant coffee, Lee and Butts made their escape. Lee felt the Kellehers' eyes on them as they walked down the short walkway to the street. Neither of them said a word until they rounded the corner toward the bus stop; then Butts exploded.

"What *is* it with people?" he bellowed. "Those two were more interested in their reputation than in finding out who killed their daughter." He snorted and pulled a cigar out of his breast pocket. "What the hell," he muttered as he placed it between his teeth. "Sometimes I just don't know about people. I mean, why do we even bother, you know?" He bit off the end of the cigar and spat it out into the waste can. "You ever feel that way, Doc?"

"Yeah," Lee said, "sometimes." He didn't want to suggest or even hint to Butts how deeply he had drunk from the well of despair.

"I dunno," Butts said. "I just don't goddamn know."

Neither do I, Lee thought, but he said nothing.

"They're hiding something," Butts fumed, biting his lower lip. "I swear to God, they know something they're not telling. I just don't know what it is."

Lee looked at the detective, who was chewing furiously on the cigar, working his jaw as if he wanted to pulverize it.

"I don't know," he answered, shaking his head. "It did seem like they were hiding something, but I'm not sure it related to Marie's death. They did seem more interested in preserving their self-image than tracking down their daughter's killer, but I'm not sure it adds up to collusion. Sometimes people react to grief in strange, unpredictable ways."

"Funny, isn't it?" Butts remarked as they walked down the hill toward the bus stop. "I mean, you say this guy is some kinda religious nut, right?"

"Something like that."

"Right. So who does he go after? The kid of a coupla religious freaks. Talk about irony, huh? I mean, if that's not irony, what is?"

Lee mumbled some words of agreement. It *was* ironic—or was it? He was beginning to wonder if Butts was on to something after all. What if the Kellehers *did* know more than they were letting on? And if so, what exactly did they know?

Chapter Eight

Dr. Georgina F. Williams was an African American woman of imposing dignity, with a formal manner and precise way of speaking that bordered on frosty—except for the occasional wayward smile that began at the corners of her eyes and culminated in a wry, upward twisting of the lips, first the right side, then the left.

Lee had learned to anticipate that smile and often did his best to provoke it; his ability to make this stern woman laugh was one of the few things in his favor in the unequal balance of power between them. He remembered when he used to sit where she was, treating patients—when he was the one with the power. Fortunately, though, he was comfortable around strong women, no doubt because of his mother, Fiona Campbell, who, even at seventy-two years of age, was a force of nature.

Dr. Williams crossed her elegant legs at the ankle, pressed her fingertips together, and leaned back in her chair. She wore a rust-colored suit with a full, flowing skirt, and a pendant with an African design around her neck. Her office matched her perfectly: understated, tasteful, refined. Soft track lighting and a potted palm tree in the corner set off the apricot-colored walls, lined with prints of Monet, Klee, and Matisse. Ethiopian sculptures decorated the bookshelf in the far corner of the room, nestled in between the rows of books, mostly psychology texts. There was always a vase of fresh flowers on the table next to her chair. Today it was a bouquet of peach-colored roses.

Dr. Williams regarded Lee with her large, prominent eyes. "So. How are you this week?"

"Not great." It was always a struggle to admit this, to block his mother's voice from his head: *I'm fine, just fine—everything's fine.*

"Are you still having nightmares?"

"Sometimes."

Dr. Williams shifted in her chair. "A lot of people continue to have trouble with the events of September eleventh, you know."

"But not everyone had a nervous breakdown."

"No. But don't you think it's time you started forgiving yourself for it?"

Lee looked at the window behind her, where a fat gray and white pigeon was pecking at something on the windowsill. The bird cocked its head, regarding Lee with its perfectly round, tiny orange eye. Lee made the sound of a pigeon cooing under his breath. The bird on the windowsill took a few stiff steps to the edge of the ledge—then, with a rush of wings, was gone.

The corners of Dr. Williams's eyes crinkled. Lee watched for the smile to spread down her face, but instead she spoke.

"What did you say to it?"

"What?"

"The pigeon. What did you say to it?"

Lee looked away.

"Don't think—just answer."

"But I—"

"Say the first thing that comes into your head."

"Uh, be careful."

"You told it to be careful?"

"That's what popped into my head."

Dr. Williams uncrossed her legs and leaned forward.

"Be careful of what?"

"Everything, I guess."

"So you feel there's danger lurking everywhere?"

Lee looked out at the empty window ledge.

"Yeah, I guess I do."

"What kind of danger?"

"Human danger. Bad people—people who want only to kill, to hurt others."

"Like the terrorists?"

Lee looked down at his shoes. "Yes. Like them, and . . ."

"And the person who took your sister?"

Lee felt hot, stinging tears spring into his eyes, and he brought his hand up to wipe them away. He hated crying in front of this woman, with her long, elegant legs and understanding eyes.

"Do you always have to bring up my sister?" His voice was harsh, tight.

Dr. Williams leaned back and uncrossed her legs.

"Is there something you're not telling me?"

Lee looked out at the empty windowsill.

"I'm on a new case."

He expected Dr. Williams to disapprove; they had discussed the inadvisability of Lee taking on a case just yet. To his surprise, though, her face betrayed no emotional reaction.

"I see," she said. "So perhaps you were thinking about the new case when you made the comment."

"Right," he answered, though he didn't believe it himself. He looked at her for a response, but her face was composed, unreadable. "You're not angry?"

"Should I be?"

"Well, we both agreed that it was probably a bit early for me to be . . . I mean, this just sort of landed in my lap, but I thought you'd be angry."

"Are you disappointed I'm not?"

Lee was caught off guard by the question. "What do you mean? Why would I be disappointed?"

Dr. Williams smiled. "Sometimes when you're expecting a certain reaction and you don't get it, it can be disappointing."

"Are you saying I *wanted* you to be angry?"

"It's not about wanting, exactly. It's about using other people as a counterbalance to your own actions. We've talked about your tendency to not take care of yourself, for example—"

"Yes, I know." Lee suddenly wanted to leave this tasteful room with its muted lighting and faint scent of eucalyptus. It all felt oppressive, confining, and he wanted to flee out the door.

"And how you have managed to delegate the duty to other people from time to time."

"Right." He didn't even try to hide his irritation. He *knew* all of this; as a psychologist himself, he could jump through the same intellectual hoops as Dr. Williams. But when it came to his own unconscious mind, he was continually amazed at his own blind spots—and he resented her knowledge of his inner life. "So what are you saying?"

"Only that it's possible that you count on me to some extent to worry about you, so you don't have to worry about yourself. So you expected me to be upset when I found out that you had taken on a case, and when I didn't appear to be, you may have found that disappointing."

Lee refused to consider what she was saying. He hated his own defensive reaction, but felt helpless to avert it. He was finding it difficult to concentrate.

"And maybe it even made you angry," Dr. Williams continued.

"Now why would that make me angry?"

"Because you felt I let you down—because I refused to fill the role you assigned me to."

Lee rolled his eyes. "Oh, *please*. That's a little farfetched, don't you think?"

Dr. Williams smiled. "What do you think?"

Lee squirmed in his chair and looked at the door.

"Have you noticed that often when we encounter a difficult or painful subject, your first impulse is to leave?"

Lee looked back at her. "No shit, Sherlock."

To his surprise, Dr. Williams laughed. Then she said, "That's not how your mother would react to such vulgarity, is it?"

"No. When I was a kid, the bar of Ivory soap would be in my mouth so fast I wouldn't know what hit me. So what?"

"So maybe you were testing me. I don't have to tell you that often in therapy, as in our relationships, we're 'testing the waters,' trying to evoke a different response from the one we grew up with."

"Right. You don't have to tell me. Classic transference, yadda yadda. So what?"

"So nothing. Either it's useful to you or it isn't. It's not important whether I'm right or not—what matters is whether or not it helps you."

Lee looked down at his hands. *Nothing can help me*, he thought. A silence widened between them, a chasm built of his unwillingness to wade into the murky depths of his mind, to grapple with the monsters lurking there.

"He carves them up," he said abruptly, hoping to shock her, to punish her with his words. He hated her calm, her confident poise, and he wanted to shake her out of it.

"Who does?" she asked.

"The killer. He slashes words into their bodies."

"What kind of words?"

"The Lord's Prayer, for God's sake!"

A thought sprouted in his head, a tiny seed that blossomed as he spoke.

"He's searching too." He spoke slowly, the idea still forming.

"Who is?"

"The killer. For him, it's an eternal search for a better outcome. Only it never happens: The moment passes. Then the rage takes over, and the only thing left for him is to kill. But each time he goes in hoping it won't come to that."

"How do you know this?"

"I don't *know*—I just have a feeling about it."

"An instinct."

"Right—an instinct. There's something about him, his MO, his signature—he's killing as a last resort."

"So you feel you understand him."

"Yes, I do."

"And his rage? Do you understand that?"

Lee looked out the window. The pigeon was back again, strutting and pecking, his bright orange eye impersonal as Nature herself.

"Oh, yes," he said, biting out each word. "I understand his rage."

Chapter Nine

Samuel was drawn back to the campus again, hoping to catch another glance of the misty mermaids behind their translucent lace curtains. It was a Friday night, though, and the mermaids were gone—out having fun, no doubt. *Girls like that are sluts, Samuel! Sluts! They will corrupt you!*

He shook off the harsh echo of his mother's voice in his head and walked toward the dormitory. A couple of lights shone on the second floor, and he could see bookish students seated at desks, heads bent over their studies. As he approached, he saw light in the windows of one room on the first floor. The first-floor room was different—the lighting was dim, with a warm orange glow to it.

It was the glimmer of intimacy.

He crept to the window and crouched down behind some bushes, listening. There were sounds coming from inside the room, unclean sounds that made his heart pound faster, as a sickly excitement filled his veins. His stomach felt like a vast cavern carved out of his flesh. His palms leaked sweat, and all the blood seemed to drain from his head, leaving it light and empty. He closed his eyes tightly and concentrated on breathing so he wouldn't pass out.

"Oh, Roger, oh, oh . . . *Roger.*"

The girl's voice was slurred and heavy with passion, and sliced into his consciousness as he crouched there in the darkness, knees digging into the damp ground, a patch of wetness creeping up his pants leg. He brushed a strand of hair from his eyes and clasped his knees, making himself invisible in the darkness. Ever since he was a child, the darkness had been his friend, hiding him from the intrusive glares of his mother and the inquisitive insolence of his classmates. In the darkness he was safe, at one with the velvety blackness surrounding him.

He had never been afraid of the dark, never cried when the lights were switched off in his bedroom at night. He longed to retreat into the silence and stillness of the night, while others slept around him, listening to the subtle murmurings of the creatures who also felt at home in the dark. He would lie in his bed and pick out the various sounds: the metallic clicking of the crickets, the soft hoot of an owl, all the rustlings of the nocturnal creatures of the woods.

He especially liked walking from the bright sunlight of a Sunday morning into the tall, vaulted interior of the church— he loved the cool stillness of the stone columns. He knew that his mother was gratified by his interest in church, but she had no idea how much he loved the dimness of the chapel, especially on dull grainy days, when the weak light could barely make it through the tall stained-glass windows, and the congregation sat shrouded in a holy gloom. It was moments like that when he felt closest to God, when he could almost imagine His forgiveness for his own dark desires . . .

"Oh, oh, God . . . R-r-r-o-ger!"

The girl's voice tightened and exploded in a wail of pleasure. He put his hands over his ears as he felt his face redden, warmth spreading up from his neck. Hot tears of shame slid down his cheeks, falling from his chin and gathering in the hollow of his collarbone. He felt violated by his proximity to her unholy passion, and knew then what he had to do. He leaned over on the damp ground and cradled his head in his hands, rocking back and forth as the wetness seeped deeper into his skin, his veins, his bones. He moaned softly. There was only one thing to do now, and the awesome responsibility of it humbled him.

The hand of God. He looked at his own hands, so white and delicate that they might almost be the hands of a woman. He knew how could it be done—he'd seen it. Now he was ready to do it himself.

Thy Kingdom come, Thy will be done . . .

He rose from his lonely lookout and retreated into the welcoming darkness. It was time to do God's will.

Chapter Ten

"You know, it's funny," Lee remarked to Butts, "but I have more sympathy for these tortured, driven guys than for your run-of-the-mill murderer—you know, the ones who kill for 'logical' reasons."

They were sitting on the uptown A train as it rattled its way to the Bronx, on their way to interview Christine Riley, Marie Kelleher's roommate at Fordham.

"What exactly do you mean by 'logical'?" Butts asked.

"Oh, you know . . . jealousy, greed, revenge, money, prestige—or killing to get rid of an inconvenient spouse or family member. The usual stuff."

"You feel more sympathy for these psychos? How come?"

"There's something cold blooded about killing . . . for money, for example. But sexual homicides—well, they may be planned, but there's usually a compulsion involved. Especially for the repeat offenders."

"Yeah? So what?" Butts asked as the train pulled into the station and jerked to a stop.

"Once they start it's virtually impossible for them to stop."

"Why do they start in the first place?"

"Usually some stressor occurs in their life, and bingo—they go over the edge."

"So what do you think the stressor was in this guy's life?" Butts asked as they trudged up the subway stairs.

They were greeted at the top of the stairs by a leaden gray sky. A low cloud cover had settled like a slab of granite over the city. February was not the best month to be in New York, and the Bronx was hardly the most glamorous of the five boroughs. As they walked up the Grand Concourse, a chill wind nipped at their backs, scattering dried leaves and loose bits of paper around their feet. Even the buildings looked cold—four- and five-story structures of grim gray granite, with the occasional decorative flourish or wrought-iron railing a welcome relief from the massive, stolid rock walls. The Grand Concourse was one of the widest avenues in the city, with a thick median strip down the center. In the spring it was probably festive, with all the trees in bloom and beds of crocuses lining the strip, but now it was just grim. Still, there was a grandeur and dignity in its winter desolation that made Lee sort of glad he was there.

"I don't know what might have pushed him over the edge, but I'm sure he's been hovering there for quite a while," he answered as they turned onto the block Christine Riley lived on with her family.

The buildings on the side streets were smaller in scale than the ones lining the avenue, and Christine's family occupied the second floor of a cozy little four-story walk-up. Dead clumps of chrysanthemums drooped in flower beds lining the neat little white fence in front.

They rang and were buzzed into the building. The knock on the door of the Rileys' place produced a burst of rapid-fire barking from inside the apartment—high-pitched yapping from what sounded like a small and annoying dog. Sure enough, when Christine's mother opened the door, at her feet was a ratty old white West Highland terrier. Fat and rheumy-eyed, the dog took little leaps up at them, barking in a shrill yelping that cut the air like bursts from automatic weapons.

"Stop it, Fritzy!" the woman commanded. The animal ignored her and continued its barrage of barking. Each bark lifted the tiny dog right off the ground, all four feet rising about an inch from the floor with every yap.

"Mrs. Riley?" said Butts.

"Yes?" She was a striking blonde with an athletic build— a swimmer's body, with broad shoulders and long arms. She was young looking, but her eyes were worn and weary, and her pale, big-boned hands clutched the door frame.

Detective Butts showed her his badge.

"Oh, yes, we've been expecting you," she said. "Please come in." She led them through a cluttered hallway full of religious icons to a spacious living room, also decorated with the same theme of religious kitsch. A heavy, lavishly framed oil painting dominated the east wall—a young, beautiful Mary looking up at Christ on the cross, her tearstained eyes full of saintly love and loss. Fritzy followed after them, barking and bouncing, as if he were made of rubber. It was as if the barking were a kind of unique propulsion system, moving him forward with a little jerk each time he made a sound. Mrs. Riley motioned for them to sit on a flowered couch, sheathed in plastic. It reminded Lee of a huge condom.

Brought up to sneer at such lower-middle-class ideas of home furnishing, Lee had trouble understanding why anyone would choose the discomfort of sitting on plastic just to keep their furniture clean.

"Please sit down," Mrs. Riley said.

He and Butts complied, the plastic making a crinkling sound as they sat.

"I'll tell Christine you're here. Would you like some coffee?"

"No, thanks, Ma'am—we're fine," Butts replied, hands on his knees. He looked uncomfortable, his sturdy body perching on the edge of the sofa, as if he were afraid to lean back, lest he might be swallowed in a sea of plastic.

Mrs. Riley left the room, but Fritzy stayed behind to guard his quarry. The dog's barking had subsided to a few hiccough-like eruptions deep in its throat, disgruntled rumbling sounds that served as a warning that, come what may, Fritzy was on the job. He sat lopsidedly a few feet away, leaning on one pink haunch, his bright little eyes shining out from under overhanging terrier brows, fixed on his prisoners.

"I don't get how they can see through all that fur," Butts whispered, "but the wife tells me that they do. That's a lousy excuse for a dog," he added, shaking his head.

As if he had heard the insult, Fritzy looked in the direction of the kitchen, then jumped up and followed his mistress out of the room.

Lee and Butts looked around the living room. Everything was flowered—the couch, the rug, the curtains, even the wallpaper. The excess of floral patterns made Lee's head ache.

"Geez," Butts said, "this place is nice, huh? My wife would love this."

Lee had an uncomfortable image of the Butts household, and wondered if it included plastic on the furniture. His musings were interrupted by the arrival of Mrs. Riley and her daughter Christine. The girl's resemblance to her mother was striking: the same pale eyes, so light they appeared colorless, the same husky, athletic build, all shoulders and right angles. Christine had more color in her face than her mother— her cheeks were ruddier, her lips fuller.

She walked over to the chair opposite them and sat down. Fritzy trotted officiously after her, settling himself down at her feet.

Mrs. Riley stood behind her, as if unsure of her role in this matter.

"Do you want me to leave you alone with her?" she asked.

"No, you can stay if you want," Butts said, taking out his little notebook. Lee noticed that he rarely wrote in it, but he seemed to like holding it.

Mrs. Riley perched on the arm of her daughter's chair and put a hand on her shoulder, in a gesture of maternal protectiveness.

"So," Butts said to the girl, "I'm Detective Butts, and this is Lee Campbell."

"Is he a detective too?"

"No, but we're both cops," Butts replied with a little cough. "He's a criminal profiler."

Her eyes widened, and Lee could see the pale blue irises.

"Like on TV?"

"Yeah, like on TV," Butts sighed before Lee could say anything. "Just like on TV," he repeated, his jaw tight. He leaned back against the plastic couch cover, which made a little sucking sound. Fritzy looked up, cocked his head, and licked his lips.

"So you were Marie's roommate?" Butts asked Christine.

"Yeah," she replied. "We lived in Wykopf East. It's an all-girls dorm," she added, with a glance at her mother.

"Okay," Butts answered. "Were there any weird guys hanging around, anyone who caught your attention?"

Christine frowned. Her strong-looking hands played with a strand of her lank blond hair, twisting and curling it around her fingers. "Uh, not really. I can't think of anyone. I mean, her boyfriend is a little weird, but he's a sweetheart. You don't think he would—" She broke off and looked up at her mother.

"Mr. Winters is not a suspect at this time," Butts replied.

"Oh, good. Because if you thought he—I mean, that would just really be awful. Not that it isn't awful already," she added.

"Like I said," Butts repeated, "he isn't a suspect at this time."

"Is there anything you can think of, anything out of the ordinary, that you think might help us with our investigation?" Lee asked. "Anything that struck you as odd or un-usual?"

Christine frowned and looked at her hands. "I wish I could be more helpful, but I can't think of anything."

"It's okay," Lee said gently. "If you think of anything, you can always call us."

"How would you describe Marie Kelleher?" Butts asked.

"Oh, she was really sweet—quiet, studied hard, just a real good girl . . . " Her voice trailed off.

"A good *Catholic* girl," her mother interjected.

"I see you're Catholic too, Mrs. Riley," Butts said.

"The one true religion," she replied sharply.

"Is that why your daughter and Ms. Kelleher were room-mates? They shared the same religious beliefs?"

Mrs. Riley picked at an invisible piece of lint on her im-maculate carpet. "That's one of the reasons. They had other common interests."

"She was the kind of girl who would talk to anyone, you know?" Christine said. "She wasn't snobby or anything. She was . . . well, she was very kind, okay? She'd help anyone in need. Why does it always seem like those people are the ones who die young, who are killed by crazy people? Why is that?"

"Maybe it's because those deaths strike us harder, as more cruel or unjust somehow," Lee answered.

Fritzy wagged his tail and licked Christine's exposed ankle.

"Oh, Fritzy," she said, bursting into tears. "You always seem to know what I'm feeling." She picked up the dog, pressed him to her chest, and sobbed into his fur. Butts looked at Mrs. Riley and cleared his throat.

"That's—uh, that's enough for today. Thanks for your time."

He struggled up from the sofa, fumbling with his note-book. "We'll be in touch if there's anything further we need. Don't hesitate to call if you think of something," he said, handing her his card.

"I'm sorry, Detective," Mrs. Riley said as she walked them to the door. "It's been a really hard time for us."

"No need to apologize," Butts assured her. "I'm sorry if we caused your daughter any more distress."

"You were just doing your job."

Butts coughed and looked down at his feet. "Yeah, well, not everyone understands that. I wish everyone was more like you—sure would make my job a lot easier."

"Forgive me," Lee said, "but is there a Mr. Riley?"

Mrs. Riley's mouth tightened. "There was. Not anymore."

She didn't offer any further explanation, so they thanked her and left the house, heading back toward the subway. When they were some distance from the building, they heard footsteps and turned to see Christine running after them. She wasn't wearing a coat, and her cheeks were flushed from cold and exertion.

"Please," she said, catching up with them. "Please—I just can't go any longer without telling someone!"

"What?" Lee said. "What is it you need to tell?"

"They don't want me to tell, but I have to—I just can't keep quiet anymore!"

"Who doesn't want you to tell?"

"My mom—and Marie's parents. They know about it—or at least I think they do."

"What is it they know?" said Butts.

"It's—it's Father Michael."

"What about him?"

"He . . . he was having an affair with Marie."

"How do you know that?"

"Because he was having sex with me too."

And with that, she burst into tears.

Chapter Eleven

"So you just didn't bother to mention that one little detail, huh?" Detective Butts said, putting his face close to the priest's. "That you were having sex with a girl who just happens to end up dead *in your church*?"

Father Michael Flaherty sat, hands folded on his lap, staring at the floor. Butts paced around him, his stocky body vibrating with rage.

It was less than two hours since Christine's revelation about the priest's sexual involvement with her and Marie. Lee and Butts were in an interrogation room in the Bronx Major Case precinct house while Chuck Morton watched through the one-way mirror from the hallway outside.

"How many others were there?" Butts continued. "Huh? Pretty good pickings, undergraduate coeds, I guess. You must have had a field day with all those nice Catholic girls. Is it true what the song says, Father? *Are* Catholic girls more fun?"

The priest stared at his hands. "I'd like a lawyer, please," he said.

"Oh, don't worry—there's one on the way," Butts said with disgust, and plopped down in the chair next to Lee.

Chuck opened the door and motioned to both of them to come outside.

"Okay, that's it—no more questions until he's lawyered up," he said once they were out in the hall. "I don't want to risk losing him, so we go by the book. We don't have anything on him, so unless he confesses, we'll have to let him walk."

"Can we put a tail on him, have him watched?" Butts asked.

"Sure, but I don't know how much good that'll do. He hasn't committed any crime—having sex with these girls was unethical, but it wasn't illegal. They were both over eighteen. I did call the administration at Fordham, and they're going to deal with him on the ethics charges." He turned to Lee. "What do you think? Does he fit your profile so far?"

Lee looked at the priest, who sat staring at the empty space in front of him, hands still in his lap. "My instinct tells me no, but he is the right age and race. And the religious angle fits—almost. But something's not right . . . I don't think the killer is going to be someone in a religious profession. This is more the work of an outsider, someone who *longs* for religious absolution, but doesn't quite believe he's worthy of it."

"So if the priest isn't the Slasher, we're back to square one," Butts said.

Butts had nicknamed the killer the Slasher. Lee didn't like the word much, but he and Butts were just beginning to get comfortable with each other, and he didn't want to rock that boat, so he went along with it.

"We've got a search warrant for his rooms, so if the missing necklace is there, we'll find it," Chuck said.

"I don't think you'll find the necklace," Lee answered and

turned to Butts. "Remember the boyfriend thought Marie was seeing someone? It must have been Father Michael he was talking about."

"Son of a bitch. Taking advantage of those girls. And you know what really gets me? The families knew about it, and they didn't say anything."

"Well, there are different levels of knowing, and we can't say exactly what they knew—maybe they just suspected," Lee pointed out.

"But why cover up a thing like that?"

"Because they were 'good Catholics,'" Chuck said.

Butts scratched his head. "I don't follow."

"How could they allow themselves to believe their daughter's priest is capable of that?" Lee said. "It throws their whole belief system into chaos."

"Oh, man," said Butts. "That really burns me."

"It's bad, I agree," Lee replied. "But what the killer is doing is worse—much worse."

Chapter Twelve

Lee sat off to the side in the drafty lecture hall at John Jay College, watching his old mentor in action. It was after 3 P.M., but the heat wasn't on in the cavernous room, and the students sat bundled in their down jackets, rubbing their hands and blowing on them. In spite of the chill, though, attendance was good. Nelson's lectures always drew a crowd. This was a new course, something a bit daring for the typical John Jay curriculum: The Psychology and Philosophy of the Serial Offender.

Up on the stage, Nelson paced in front of the podium, hands jammed into his pants pockets. He lectured without notes, and the machine-gun delivery of his lectures had often been parodied by his students. When Lee was a senior at John Jay, the class sketch show included a satire of Nelson, played by a student in a red fright wig, chain-smoking several cigarettes at once and barking out his lectures so fast that they were unintelligible. To his credit, Nelson laughed himself silly over it. He later said it was the most flattering portrayal he had ever seen of himself.

"I want to continue today with a quote from the renowned

FBI profiler John Douglas," Nelson said, stopping his pacing to pull down a large projection screen at the front of the room. "In his book, *Mindhunter,* he writes, 'To understand the artist, look at his work.'"

Nelson perched on the edge of his desk and rubbed the back of his neck. "Now, what exactly does this mean?"

He looked out over the sea of eager faces. "It's been said that there is a fine line between genius and madness. If you carry that idea far enough, you might even surmise that beneath every genius lurks a potential madman. And certainly in cases like van Gogh or Lord Byron, you had both. Trying to separate a genius from his 'madness' is like trying to pull dye out of a fabric after it has set. It's a chicken-and-egg question. Who's to say which feeds which? Would van Gogh have painted sunflowers or the garden at Arles if he didn't suffer from bipolar disorder? My guess is probably not. He may have painted—he may even have painted well—but he would not have been van Gogh."

He paused to adjust the slide projector on the desk next to him. The students sat, captured by his intellect and charisma. Lee remembered that when he was a student, there were girls who had crushes on Nelson, following him around between classes, soaking in the heat of his forceful personality.

"So that takes us back to John Douglas," Nelson said, rising from his perch on the desk and picking up a remote control for the slide projector. "'To understand the artist, look at his work.' And if you view a serial offender the same way you would look at an artist, then we can begin to understand what Mr. Douglas is saying. After all, the root for both is the same: obsession. It's only the form and content that differs, the degree of sublimation, of social acceptability."

"Now this," he said, clicking his remote control so that a picture of the garden at Arles appeared on the screen, "is socially acceptable. But this"—another click and it was replaced by a photograph of a young woman with dark red strangulation marks around her neck—"is not."

There were murmurs from his audience. Nelson's lips twitched, and one side of his mouth curved upward in a smile. He liked shocking his students. Without this dark side, Lee thought, Nelson would not be Nelson.

A girl in the third row raised her hand. She was a thin blonde, with a pale, waifish face.

"Are you implying that there's no difference between a serial predator and a great artist?" Her voice quavered, though Lee couldn't tell if it was from nerves or anger.

"Not at all," Nelson replied. "I merely suggest that what drives them springs from the same source. The form of expression couldn't be more different."

The girl's pale face reddened, and her voice shook even more. "So it's just a question of *form*?"

"But form *is* content, on some very profound level. Consider the irreducibility of a poem, for example. It's like the artificial separation between mind and body, something eastern medicine has recognized for centuries. Is a migraine headache a product of too much red wine, a genetic predisposition, or a fight with one's husband? Who's to say? The doctor says it's the result of an expanded blood vessel in the forehead, the allergist claims it's an aversion to tannins and nitrate, the reiki healer claims it's an imbalance of the energies—and maybe they're all right."

He settled himself on the front of the desk again, his arms crossed.

"As to the difference between an artist and a criminal, I would maintain that van Gogh, who was actually psychotic, was lucky to have found an expression for his spirit, for his demons, that was socially acceptable. Or take Beethoven, for example, who was a famously eccentric and tortured soul. They were better adapters than your average criminal. On the other hand, there are people who are both criminals and talented creative artists—like the playwright Jean Genet, for example."

A boy in the second row raised his hand. "You said they spring from the same source—what's the source?"

"Libido—the life force. Passion. Without passion, there is no creativity—or destruction. Passion in Greek means 'to suffer,' as in the passion of Christ. But in our culture it has come to mean the force that drives sex, not creativity. I might remind you," he continued, "that Adolf Hitler was an aspiring artist before he became a dictator.

"In fact, it's been argued that had the art critics of Vienna been kinder to young Adolf, World War II might have been avoided. It was partly his frustration as an artist that turned him toward politics. As R. D. Laing points out, it is necessary for a person to feel they have made a difference—that they are being 'received' by others. So the ignored artist becomes the politician, and he ensures that he is listened to. Both his art and his political speeches were his attempts to impose his will—his *self*—upon the world. Like all cult leaders, he preys on his followers' fears and dreams—"

A dark-haired girl in the front row raised her hand. "The Nazis were a cult?"

Nelson cocked his head to one side. "Of course they were a cult—a very successful one, for a while. All cults eventually self-destruct, of course. But that's another topic."

Nelson stood up from his perch on the front of the desk and pulled himself up to his full height of five foot six inches. "The ignored artist, or son, or lover, can also become a serial offender." He clicked the remote in his hand and the slide of the young woman was replaced by a close-up of a smiling Ted Bundy.

"Most of you recognize this man. Handsome, intelligent, and charming, he was the sort of man your mother might wish you would marry." Lee wasn't sure, but he thought Nelson glanced at the blond girl when he said this. "But he was the very icon of the creature society fears most—the monster in its midst. And some deeply antisocial personalities, like Bundy, learn to imitate social behavior very, very well— you might even say they are masquerading as human beings."

Nelson put down the remote and stood facing his audience.

"But he *was* a human being, and our job is to understand him, not merely judge him. It is a profoundly more difficult and disturbing task, of course, but it is the one we have chosen."

A thin boy in the back raised his hand. "Would you say that Ted Bundy was evil?"

"That's just a label—irrelevant, for our purposes. Leave it to the professional philosophers and theologians. The profiler and psychologist have no need to answer that question."

The boy sat up in his seat. Lee couldn't see his face, but he was slight and blond, and had a thin, raspy voice. "So do you believe there is such a thing as evil in the world?"

Nelson ran a hand through his wavy auburn hair. "The most profound questions are the very ones we should never assume to answer conclusively. Learning to live in a state of uncertainty is one of the most difficult tasks we have as human beings, but one of the most important. As soon as we feel we have all the answers, something inside us begins to die. But that's for another lecture," he added, glancing at his watch. "Any more questions?"

The thin blond boy raised his hand again.

"Freud said that if the id is left unchecked, it can run wild."

Nelson flipped off the power switch to the slide projector. "The word for what we call the 'id,' by the way, in its original

German, is 'das Es'—the It. A much bolder statement, I think, than the flaccid Latin word. Compare 'ego' with the *Ich*, the *I*. And Germans, as you may or may not know, capitalize all of their pronouns."

The blond girl raised her hand. "Their nouns, actually."

Nelson smiled. "Thank you for that correction, Ms. Davenport. Okay, everyone, see you all next week."

Lee smiled too—he wasn't sure if she was one of Nelson's admirers or not. As she gathered up her books and placed them in her knapsack, he thought she was sending lingering glances in Nelson's direction, though, and she was the last to leave the lecture hall. When the room was empty Nelson sauntered up the steps to where Lee sat in the back row.

"Well, well, just like old times. Drop in for a refresher course?"

Lee smiled. "Something like that."

"How about a drink? I'm buying. I need to wash the taste of undergraduate minds from my mouth."

"Sure, why not? As long as you're buying."

The bar at Armstrong's was one of Nelson's favorite watering holes on Tenth Avenue. The menu was capricious and varied—and, more importantly to Nelson, the draft pints of Bass were reliable and cheap. Armstrong's was one of Hell's Kitchen's best-kept secrets, known to locals but not to tourists, or to the bridge-and-tunnel crowd that swept down Ninth Avenue during rush hour.

"That was quite a far-ranging lecture," Lee remarked as the bartender set a pair of dripping amber pints in front of them.

"Mostly these days I just try to keep myself amused," Nelson replied, drinking deeply from the sweating glass. He wiped his upper lip and plunked the glass down on the bar. "Now *that* is what A. E. Housman was talking about when he said, 'Malt does more than Milton can to justify God's ways to man.'"

"Still, we need our Milton as well as our malt."

Nelson dipped a hand into the bowl of fresh popcorn sitting on the bar. "True. It's funny, but I still remember reading *Paradise Lost* in school and thinking how interesting Satan was—and how boring Christ was."

"Satan is more human," Lee agreed. "He's *conflicted*, whereas Christ has everything figured out. Who can identify with that?"

"Or maybe we just like our villains," Nelson replied with a smile. He lit a cigarette and blew the smoke in the other direction. It smelled sharp and aromatic, like herbs.

"Clove cigarettes," he replied in answer to Lee's look. "Some of my students smoke them. Supposedly they're better for you."

"I don't think Christ's virtue is what makes him so opaque," Lee remarked. "It's his *certainty*. But even virtuous people are full of doubts and uncertainty. That's what we relate to about Satan: he's in pain, his soul is in torment. Christ is just so damn serene! Who can identify with that?"

"Not me, my lad, not me," Nelson answered with a wave to the bartender. "Another for me, my good man. You'll have to catch up," he added, seeing Lee's half-full glass.

Lee was concerned over the pace of his friend's drinking. Nelson evidently picked up on this, because he laid a hand on Lee's arm.

"Don't worry, lad, I don't have any more lectures today. I've never yet turned up to class under the influence, and I don't plan to start now. So how's your case coming?"

"We've got a suspect, but I don't think he's the man."

Lee told Nelson about Father Michael and his relationship with the dead girl. Nelson listened intently, his eyes narrowed.

"He clammed up as soon as his lawyer arrived?"

"Yeah. His lawyer kept saying it was the girl's word against his, and that we had no crime to charge him with."

Nelson sighed. "He's right, of course. You may be right that this priest isn't the killer, but you should keep an eye on him."

"We are."

"Good. Now, how about one more round?"

"No, thanks," Lee replied, feeling uncomfortable. "I can't drink quite as much as I used to."

"Keep such admissions to yourself, or they'll have you thrown out of this place!" Nelson said loudly enough that the bartender could hear.

He clearly did not want to discuss his drinking, and the force of his personality was like a wall between them. Lee was partly relieved. He had no desire to turn the tables on their tenuous father-son relationship. He was pretty certain his friend's drinking had accelerated since his wife's death, but the thought of confronting Nelson about it was daunting. He vowed to keep an eye on his friend, but babysitting Nelson's drinking would have to take a backseat to finding the man who was stalking and strangling young women.

He looked at the happy, relaxed faces all around him: the young Latino couple in the corner, the pair of students at the other end of the bar, the young mother with her son at the video game machine. He felt an irrational sense of responsibility to protect them all from a killer who—Lee was certain—would not stop until he was caught.

Chapter Thirteen

Lee's visit to Nelson's lecture and to Armstrong's had done little to dispel the unsettling feeling he had had ever since morning. He couldn't shake the twisting sensation in his stomach. As he was heading for the kitchen to make tea, the phone rang. He picked up the portable receiver and continued into the kitchen.

"Hello?"

"Lee, it's Chuck."

"Hi. What's up?" He pulled a blue enameled canister of tea from the top shelf and put the kettle on. *Nothing a good cup of tea can't fix*, his mother liked to say. *Yeah, right, Mom.*

"It's about our Jane Doe."

Chuck Morton had never been good at disguising his feelings. Lee decided to try to spare him the difficult task of breaking the news.

"No one believes me, right?" he said, plucking a tea bag from the canister. It was Lifeboat Tea, a good strong blend he discovered at Cardullo's on his last trip to Boston.

"*I* believe you, but the brass isn't buying your theory

about Jane Doe Number Five. The detectives in Queens are determined to hold on to the file—they say it's their case."

"She's this guy's work, too—I *know* it!"

There was an uncomfortable pause. Lee looked out the window at the people lined up waiting to get into McSorley's. He never went in there at night—afternoons were the best time, when the sun flooded in through the dusty windows, dancing across the sawdust-strewn floors and gleaming off the row of antique brass beer taps.

"You know how some of them feel about profilers," Chuck said. "They're not buying the idea that we've got a serial offender on our hands." His voice was apologetic.

"Well, they'll find out sooner or later they're wrong— when another girl dies."

Down on the street, a couple was having an argument. The girl leaned against the building, arms crossed, while her boyfriend ranted and paced in front of her, throwing his arms around. Lee couldn't hear what he was saying, but judging from the sulky expression on the girl's face, it wasn't welcome. The boyfriend was bulky and blond, built like a bull terrier; she was lanky and dark-haired, with one of those Irish faces—sharp dark eyes and a pert, upturned nose. Her expression was defiant; she looked like she could handle him.

"You don't think it's the priest, do you?" Chuck said.

"No—and even if I did, you have to let him go unless you're going to charge him with something."

"Oh, hell, Lee, I wish there was something I could do."

The kettle screamed its shrill crescendo, and Lee pulled it from the gas flame.

"Look, it's not your fault," he said. "I hope I'm wrong—I really do."

"Well, maybe we've got enough to go on with this one up in the Bronx."

"We'll see," he said, pouring the steaming water into a

blue and white tin mug. "A killer's progression tells us important things about him. The second killing was already more organized than the first." He didn't say what else he was thinking: *And more violent.*

"We've been interviewing anyone who works at the church, but so far no one's given us anything. If it isn't the priest, do you think this guy could be a member of the congregation?"

"I don't think so. If we had enough manpower, though, it might be worth tracking down people to interview."

He added milk and sugar to his tea and checked back in on the couple in the street. The girl was still leaning against the wall, smoking a cigarette. There was no sign of the boyfriend.

"For the time being we're trying to rule out some local sex offenders," Chuck said. "Butts and I are interviewing some possible suspects this afternoon—want to sit in?"

"Sure. What time?"

"In about an hour."

"I'll be there."

The interrogation room was tiny and stuffy. Chuck had brought in a man named Jerry Walker. Walker was on the maintenance staff at Fordham, and had a record of two arrests and one conviction—both for sexual offenses against young girls. As they waited for Detective Butts to arrive, Lee leafed through Walker's file. He had been convicted eight years ago of statutory rape, and had served five years of his ten-year sentence, with time off for good behavior. He was paroled three years ago. So far he appeared to have kept his nose clean, though with these guys you never knew. How on earth he'd managed to get a job doing maintenance at a college, Lee couldn't imagine.

The door was flung open, and Butts entered, sweating and out of breath.

"Sorry," he said, sounding more irritated than apologetic. "Damn fire on the A train." He loosened his tie and took a drink of water from the cooler in the corner.

Walker smiled and leaned back in his chair as though he was enjoying himself. He was a cocky, macho type Lee was familiar with. He always wondered if these guys were for real—their behavior was full of clichés layered on top of clichés.

But Jerry Walker did not include self-awareness in his arsenal of personality quirks. He sat across from them at the interrogation table, legs spread wide, the insolent set of his shoulders expressing his disdain for the whole process. A pack of Camels was tucked into the sleeve of his T-shirt—*another cliché*, Lee thought. He was dressed like a biker from the fifties: white T-shirt, blue jeans, heavy black boots, slicked-back hair.

His pumped-up arms were crossed, the tattoos on his biceps bulging—a curvy mermaid on the left arm, "I Love Jenny" in Gothic lettering on the right. Lee wondered who Jenny was, and if she knew that she had been memorialized in ink on the muscular flesh of Jerry Walker's right arm.

Detective Butts finished his water and paced behind Walker, rubbing his stubby hands together, while Chuck sat on the corner of the table across from him. Lee recognized the technique. *Invade his territory, crowd him, make him feel cornered, creating feelings of insecurity.* But judging by the smirk on Walker's face, it wasn't working.

"So you guys actually think I might be the killer?" Walker said, his mouth curled into a contemptuous smile.

"You tell us," Chuck answered, his voice failing to conceal his dislike of Walker. "We've been asked by the mayor to interview a few sex offenders living in the area. And that would include you."

"Hey, that stuff's all behind me," Walker protested. "I got a new life now, a steady job, a girlfriend—the works. I'm even seeing a therapist," he added, "not that it's any of your business."

"You're right," Chuck replied, "it's not my business. What I'm interested in is where you were on February eleventh."

Walked smiled broadly, revealing a gold tooth. "No sweat. On the eleventh I was out of town. Went to see my dear old mom—I'm a very devoted son. I can show you the plane tickets to prove it."

Chuck held his gaze. "Plane tickets can be forged."

"Call my mother and ask her."

Butts left his pacing and came around behind Walker. "Oh, that's a good idea," he said. "I'm sure she wouldn't be interested in covering for her only son—I know she wouldn't think of lying to the police."

Lee touched Chuck's elbow.

"What?" Chuck said.

Lee leaned in to whisper into his ear. "It's not him. This isn't our guy."

"Okay," Chuck whispered back, "but I still have to go through with this."

"Your friend is right, you know," Walker said. "I'm not your guy."

Chuck's fair face reddened. "You know what? I'll decide that for myself."

Walked shrugged and leaned back in his chair. "Suit yourself," he said, cleaning his fingernails with a book of matches. The picture on the matchbook cover was of a tall, curvaceous feline wearing black lingerie. The logo read PUSSYCAT LOUNGE.

"You know," he said, "I don't go for Catholic girls. Too uptight."

Chuck leaned into Walker's face. "This may be just a game to you, you son of a bitch, but it's not to us, and if you make one more crack like that, I swear—"

"Hey, easy, there," Walker said, holding up his callused

hands. "I didn't mean anything by it, man. Just trying to let you know I'm not your guy."

"Jesus," Chuck muttered. "What is it with you guys that you can laugh about something like this? What was left out when they put you together, huh?"

"I'm not any happier than you are about this guy," Walker snarled. "Hell, I'm no killer. It would never occur to me to hurt a woman—ask my girlfriend. I'm a pussycat."

"Like the dancers at the Pussycat Lounge?" Butts said, indicating the matches on the table.

"Hey, hey—my girlfriend works there, okay?"

"Figures," Butts muttered.

"She's a *waitress*, okay?" Walker said, going for a cigarette.

"No smoking in here," Chuck snapped. He tried to snatch the cigarette from Walker's mouth, but Walker was faster, and put it back in the pack.

"Hands off, man—these things are *expensive*! Jeez, what do you guys do around here for fun?"

"Beat the crap out of guys like you," Butts shot back.

"No shit. And you don't get busted for police brutality?" Walker asked with mock innocence.

"Why don't we find out?" Butts replied.

"That's enough!" Chuck snapped at the detective.

Walker smiled, and Lee was taken aback by the cruelty in that smile. "You know, every minute you spend with me is time you're not spending catching this guy. Why, he could be out there right now, selecting his next victim, some good little Catholic girl. Nice piece of virgin ass. He could be putting his hands—"

Lee's vision seemed to contract, and he felt as if the air in the room was pressing in on him. "That's *enough*!" he bellowed, springing to his feet. He lunged at Walker and managed to wrap his hands around Walker's throat.

But Walker was bigger than he was, and very quick. He

broke Lee's grip and landed a series of punches with such speed that no one in the room could move fast enough to stop him. The first blow connected with Lee's stomach, knocking the air out of him, and then Walker aimed for his face, an uppercut to the chin followed by a roundhouse that caught Lee in the upper cheekbone, right at the bridge of his nose.

He staggered backward, feeling the blood rushing from his nose, blinded by the force of the blow. He hit the floor hard, dazed and shaken.

Chuck seized Walker by the shoulders, at the same moment calling for backup. Butts was right behind him, pinning Walker's hands down as two uniformed officers rushed into the room, guns drawn.

"Handcuff this guy," Chuck said, and one of the officers quickly slipped a pair of cuffs around Walker's wrists. "Now get him out of here!"

As the officers escorted Walker out of the room, he called out over his shoulder to Chuck.

"Hey, why don't you get your friend some lithium to calm him down?"

"Shut up!" Butts shot back.

"You'll be hearing from my lawyer!" Walker said as they dragged him away.

"Whatever," Chuck muttered. He looked at Lee, who stood leaning against the wall, breathing heavily, blood trickling from his nose.

"You're hurt."

"I'm fine."

Chuck had heard that answer before.

"I'll call a doctor."

"No!" Lee tried to calm his breathing and realized he was trembling—not with fear, but with rage.

"I think we've had enough today."

"I'm sorry."

"Okay, but you can't let that happen again."

"Right. I won't."

Chuck sighed. "So what about Walker? Could he—"

"No. The Slasher isn't a child molester. His rage is directed against women—and God. And I think he could be a virgin."

"How do you figure that?"

"I know it's a stretch, but I think the knife is a phallic substitute. There's been no sign of actual penetration. Which means he would probably come across as emotionally immature."

Chuck snorted. "When's the last time you met an emotionally mature criminal?"

"No, I mean seriously emotionally challenged. Like if you met him, you'd really notice it. Shy, withdrawn, odd—not your cocky sleazeball type like Walker. Sort of childlike."

"The priest is pretty childlike."

"Yeah, I guess he is," Lee admitted.

"And he would be totally unthreatening to women."

Even Lee had to admit that Father Michael Flaherty was beginning to look better as a suspect. But there was one thing they could all agree on: time was running out, and if they didn't close in soon, another woman would die.

Chapter Fourteen

It was dark when Lee walked up the steps to his apartment on the third floor. As soon as he put his keys down on the table next to the front door, the phone rang. He reached it in two steps and picked it up.

"Hello?"

"Heya, Boss Man, it's me."

There was no mistaking that voice, high and squeaky, with a pronounced Bronx accent. It was Eddie Pepitone—hustler, Vietnam vet, professional gambler, sometime con man—and quite possibly the one person to whom Lee owed his life.

"Hi, Eddie. What's up?"

"What's up? What's *up*?" Eddie's tone was mock irritation. "You tell me, Boss Man—you're the one with the dead girl on your hands."

"How did you—?"

"News travels fast in my circle, my friend. I keep my ear close to the ground, know what I mean?"

"I mean, how did you know I was—?"

"On the case? Oh, I just figured—kinda put two and two

together, you know? Seemed like it was up your alley and all."

"Okay, but—"

Eddie cut him off. "Look, I got a little time right now. What do you say we meet at McHale's in about half an hour?"

"Well, I—"

"Come on, you got nothin' better to do right now. Am I right?"

Lee had to admit Eddie was right. Seeing Eddie would distract him from his disappointment at not having the Jane Doe file to work with.

"Okay, half an hour."

"Right, see you then—and I'm buying."

There was a click, and the phone went dead. It sounded as though Eddie was calling from a pay phone. Lee hoped he wasn't out on the street again. Since he gave up gambling, it had become difficult for Eddie to make a living. Eddie was the most unlikely friend he could imagine, but not a day went by that he didn't thank his lucky stars that during his stay in the psych ward of St. Vincent's Hospital, Eddie Pepitone had been his roommate.

It was a short subway ride to McHale's, one of the throwbacks to the old days of Hell's Kitchen before it was renamed Clinton, and expensive sushi restaurants began to replace the old Irish bars, with their steam tables, cheap beer, and all the free pickles you could eat. McHale's wasn't as grungy as the late, lamented Shandon Star, but it wasn't a tourist trap either. You could get a pork chop with all the side dishes you could want for about twelve dollars. The bathrooms smelled of mildew, and some of the red leatherette booths were torn and clumsily mended with duct tape, but Lee loved the place. Unpretentious and welcoming, it was comfortable as an old shoe. Snuggled on the northeast corner of Eighth Avenue and Forty-sixth Street, at the edge of the theatre district, McHale's brought in a steady crowd of locals that included actors both famous and unknown, playwrights, directors, and other assorted theater types.

McHale's was also Eddie Pepitone's favorite watering hole.

Lee arrived first and chose a booth in the bar, near the front door. He knew Eddie sometimes liked to smoke, and while he didn't like the smell, he wanted to accommodate his friend. McHale's was dark and quiet, and the lamps were already lit. The lights of the cars on Eighth Avenue shone diffusely through the grime on the windows, casting a sullen shadow across the back wall of the bar.

Lee had hardly been there a minute when the front door swung open and Eddie entered.

He looked like a bad hangover. His dirty blond hair—or what was left of it—was rumpled, there was a two-day growth on his chin, and his fingernails looked like they needed sandblasting. Yet somehow he exuded optimism. He had the bright, restless eyes of a con man, and his slovenly appearance was deceiving—Eddie was one of the most perceptive people Lee had ever met. He didn't know what Eddie did for money now that he had given up gambling, and he wasn't sure he wanted to know. But he would always remember what Eddie's presence had meant in that hospital room a few months ago. They would sit up all night and talk and talk, as they poured cup after cup of black coffee down their throats, until the graveyard shift at the nurses' station gave way to the morning shift and the gray dawn crept across the faded yellow hospital walls.

Eddie Pepitone settled himself into the booth and put his elbows on the table. "So, how ya been, Boss Man?"

For some reason, during those dark days last fall, Eddie had taken to calling Lee "Boss Man." Lee had never asked him the reason for this—during that time, just getting through a day was an accomplishment. Eddie seemed to like the nickname, and Lee didn't mind.

Eddie leaned forward. His breath reeked of cheap cigarettes and gingivitis.

"What's on your mind? Is this case getting to you?

"How did you know I was on a case?"

"Come on, now, Boss—I read the papers," Eddie said, flipping a grin at the waitress as she went by. She was neither young nor pretty, but that didn't matter to Eddie—he was an equal opportunity lech. He once said about himself, "Hell, I'd flirt with anyone with a uterus, and if I'm drunk enough, I don't even draw the line there."

To Lee's surprise, the waitress returned the smile. Eddie was neither young nor handsome, but women responded to him. He was like a big, happy leprechaun, or the dopey, eternally cheerful uncle who turns up at family occasions with a whoopee cushion. He might not exemplify class, but Lee thought you had to be a pretty sour person not to like him.

"I don't think I'm mentioned in any of the articles," Lee said.

Eddie rolled his eyes. "What, you think I believe only what I read in the paper? If you're not in on the killing of that girl in the Bronx, I'll eat my hat."

Lee raised his hands in surrender. "I don't know, Eddie. Sometimes I think you should be the professional, not me."

Eddie frowned. "What do you mean? I *am* a pro!" He turned to flag down the waitress, who was passing with a tray of drinks. "Hiya, darlin'—can we get something here?"

She glanced at him and nodded ever so slightly as she passed.

Lee leaned forward in his seat. "You know what I mean."

"Yeah, yeah. I'm a professional at what I do, but let me tell you, I wouldn't wanna do what you do, Boss—not for a bundle of change."

As the waitress walked back toward the bar, Eddie's hand casually brushed against her thigh. When she turned to look at him, her eyes narrowed, but Eddie just grinned, showing yellowed, crooked teeth.

"Sorry, sweetheart, but my friend's tongue is about to fall out of his mouth. He's a mean drunk, but he's even meaner sober."

The waitress smiled wearily. "What can I get you?"

Lee sensed the resignation in her voice and in the slump of her shoulders. It was late in her shift, he imagined, and her feet must be hurting. Her mascara was smudged, her sprayed hair was beginning to droop, and her makeup could no longer cover the circles under her eyes.

"I'll take a draft Sam Adams," Lee said.

"Make it two," Eddie responded. "And do you have some chips or something you could bring over?"

"There's nachos or chips with salsa."

"Great. We'll take one of each. Thanks," he said, giving her arm a squeeze. To Lee's surprise, she looked at him warmly, as if grateful for the contact. A lot of men would get into trouble if they tried what Eddie did, but somehow he always seemed to get away with it. Looking at Eddie's round, smiling face, Lee had an uncomfortable thought. *The killer will appear unthreatening to his victims until it is too late.*

When the waitress arrived with their drinks and chips, Eddie pressed a bill into her hand.

"Thanks, sweetheart—keep the change." Lee couldn't see how much it was, but he had seen Eddie tip twenty dollars on a thirty-dollar bar tab.

The waitress looked at the bill in her hand.

"Th—thanks," she said, frowning.

"Don't worry—I'm not hitting on you," Eddie said, popping a chip into his mouth. "Not that you're not very attractive," he added.

"Uh, okay. Thanks." She raised one eyebrow and walked away, shaking her head.

"A habit left over from my Vegas days," Eddie told Lee when she had gone. "You take care of the waitstaff there, they take care of you—y'know?"

"So I've heard. How's that going, by the way?"

Eddie fished a small round wooden token from his jacket pocket and held it between his thumb and forefinger.

"Six months this week. Clean . . . and poor." He laughed and shoved the token back into his pocket.

"What are you doing for money these days?"

"Oh, this and that. Mostly that." Eddie grinned. "You know, I was one of a rare breed—a gambler who actually made money. I was good, you know—damn good."

"I'm sure you were."

Eddie fingered the cardboard coaster on the table, turning it over between his fingers as if it were a blackjack card. "Those days are behind me. Too bad—I miss it. Any addict who tells you he doesn't miss his addiction is a liar."

"I'll remember that."

"You know, it's kind of too bad we ended up in St. Vincent's."

"Why?"

"Oh, it's just that it would have been cool to be in Bellevue, like the crazy people in the old days, y'know? I mean, we still talk about people ending up in Bellevue, but nobody talks about being crazy enough to end up in St. Vincent's, right?"

Lee smiled for the first time in days. Eddie had that effect on him.

He took a long drink from his pint, the amber liquid cold and bitter on his tongue. It was a familiar and comforting taste, a ritual that took him back through all the years of bars and patio parties, back to his college days, to dorm parties and rugby games, late-night pool halls, back to his sister's first drink in a bar with him there playing the role of protective older brother . . . but in the end, of course, he had failed to protect her.

" . . . so then she asks if she should bring her twin sister in on the deal, and I'm like—hey, are you listening to me?"

Eddie leaned forward and waved his hand in front of Lee's face.

Just then the door to the bar swung open, and two of the most singular-looking men Lee had ever seen entered the room.

The taller of the two, an African American with coffee-colored skin, had an elaborate swirl of colorful tattoos on his powerful arms, only partially hidden by the sleeves of his blue flannel shirt, rolled up to the middle of his bulging biceps. His shoulders looked as though they had been stuffed into his denim jacket, and his shiny bald head rose directly from his collarbone, without the intervention of a neck. Everything about him suggested enormous physical strength. His face was dominated by thick, sensual lips, set between wide cheekbones, and his deep-set eyes looked yellow in the dim light. Lee estimated his height to be about six foot seven inches.

His companion was at least a foot shorter. Also powerful of build, his body was like a study in Cubism—all right angles and edges, not so much muscular as square. His palms were broad, with stubby pink fingers thick as sausages. Even his head, with its flattop crew cut, resembled a cube, with a sturdy chin that was as wide as his forehead. His rock scrabble nose twisted in oblique angles, suggesting it had been broken more than once. But his most striking feature was his hair. White-blond, pale as summer wheat, it perfectly matched his eyebrows, set over blue eyes. A tiny gold hoop glinted from his left ear, but unlike his companion, he sported no visible tattoos. He was dressed all in black, creating a dramatic contrast to his pale complexion.

"Hey there, fellows!" Eddie sang out in his high, squeaky

voice. "Come join us!" The pair came over to their table and slid into the booth, one on each side. Lee was surprised the taller one could fit at all, his legs were so long. Lee was just over six feet, but sitting next to this guy, he felt like a toy poodle squeezed next to a St. Bernard.

"I'd like you to meet my pals," Eddie said as he signaled the waitress for another round. "This here is Diesel," he continued, indicating the giant sitting next to Lee, "and his buddy is Rhino. That's what we call him. His real name's Rhinehardt, John Rhinehardt, but he likes his nickname, don't you, Rhino?"

John Rhinehardt, a.k.a. Rhino, pursed his lips and gave a small nod of assent. With his stocky build, crooked nose, and small eyes, he did bring to mind an albino rhinoceros.

"Pleased to meet you," said Lee.

Rhino responded with another lip pursing.

"And his buddy is Diesel," Eddie went on, "named on account of—come to think of it, no one knows how you got your nickname."

"I used to drive the eighteen-wheelers," Diesel responded in an elegant baritone. "And I like to drink quite a bit."

"I don't even remember your real name," Eddie admitted.

"No one uses it anymore," Diesel answered. "I prefer Diesel."

"Right," Eddie agreed as the waitress approached their table.

"What'll you have?" she said, standing over them, pen in hand.

"We'll have another round of the same, thanks, sweetheart," Eddie replied. "And add my buddies' drinks to my check."

She turned to Diesel. If she thought he was odd looking, her face didn't betray it. Lee figured that working in a bar a block from Times Square, she had pretty much seen it all.

"What'll it be?" Her voice was ragged with fatigue.

"Two pints of Guinness, please," Diesel said. As she turned to go, he added, "And a Diet Coke for my friend."

The waitress did a double take that consisted of one raised eyebrow; then she turned and headed for the bar.

"What's the idea of ordering a Diet Coke?" Eddie demanded.

In response, Rhino patted what appeared to be a rock-hard stomach.

"He's always calorie counting," Diesel said with a disgusted snort. "Oh, well, looks like I'll have to do the drinking for both of us."

"Bet you'll never guess what these guys do for a living?" Eddie chirped.

Break kneecaps? Lee wanted to answer, but he said nothing.

"Tell 'em, boys." Eddie leaned back in the red leatherette booth, enjoying himself hugely.

"We are currently working as hospital orderlies," said Diesel. Evidently he was the talkative one.

"Oh," said Lee, not sure what he was supposed to make of that information.

"But you didn't tell him the best part!" Eddie said. He leaned across the table toward Lee, and Lee could smell his tobacco-stained teeth. "These boys work at *Bellevue*!" He pronounced the word as though he were announcing the discovery of the Holy Grail. "So I figure they can get the lowdown on all sorts of nutcases—maybe your guy, for instance."

"Wait a minute," Lee interrupted. "That would be illegal *and* unethical, violating doctor-patient privilege."

"But these guys ain't docs," Eddie protested.

"This guy is probably flying under the radar," Lee said. "Not in treatment, probably not in the system at all. Even if he is, the chances of him coming through Bellevue—"

"Are roughly one in one hundred and forty-six thousand, if he lives in Manhattan," Diesel said solemnly. When Lee stared at him, he leaned back and folded his powerful hands in front of him. "I enjoy statistics. It's kind of a hobby."

"Diesel's a college graduate," Eddie said proudly. "Somewhere in Michigan—?"

"Michigan State," Diesel replied. "Magna cum laude."

Lee guessed that Eddie knew both of them through Gamblers Anonymous, but he wasn't about to ask. Eddie was very casual about the whole notion of his anonymity, and would tell anyone that he was attending meetings—whether they asked or not—but Lee didn't want to compromise the privacy of Eddie's friends.

"Look, isn't there something we can do to help?" Eddie asked.

Lee looked around the bar, with its comfortable low lighting, the softly glowing yellow lamps casting shadows on the walls. The bar was filling up with theatergoers, all in a festive mood. It seemed odd, sitting here with Eddie and his two powerful-looking friends, that somewhere out there, a predator was ruthlessly stalking and carving up young women.

"I don't know," he said. "Maybe I'll think of something."

Eddie winked. "These guys get around—know what I mean?"

Lee looked at the two companions. Rhino's deep-set blue eyes were azure in the dim light, and his pale skin was a sharp contrast to Diesel's richly hued coffee-colored skin. No doubt about it: singly, they were unusual looking. As a pair, they were striking.

"They used to be homeless," Eddie continued, snapping a chip between his tobacco-stained fingers before popping it into his mouth. "Addicts, both of 'em. Hard to believe now, huh?"

Lee looked at the pair. With their well-muscled bodies and clear eyes, they looked like anything but addicts.

"Methamphetamines," said Diesel. "My drug of choice, when I could get it. And Rhino was addicted to heroin."

Rhino sipped at his soda and looked away.

"So not only do they have connections in the hospital nursing field," Eddie said, "but they also know most of the guys who run the shelters around town—and most of the clients."

"I don't see how that can help us," Lee replied.

Diesel leaned forward. "There is an underclass of people in this city who go places other people don't, who see what other people miss. There are eyes and ears out there that the police have yet to fully appreciate."

"Sort of like the Baker Street Irregulars in the Sherlock Holmes stories—right, Boss?" Eddie said.

Diesel took a sip of beer and wiped his mouth delicately. "We have access to those ears and eyes—what goes on in the dark of night when most people are looking the other way."

"Methamphetamines and heroin, huh?" Lee said. "Those must have been hard ones to kick. Those are both really addictive."

"You can accomplish anything," Diesel said, "if you have the willpower and determination."

Looking at the pair sitting across from him, Lee didn't doubt that he was right. Then, against his own will, the words popped into his head: *Thy kingdom come, Thy will be done.* But he imagined that if the Slasher's will prevailed, it would not be either as in earth or as in heaven, but as in hell.

Chapter Fifteen

Her breasts were small and round, the skin smooth and white as the inside of a clamshell. The nipples were marbled mother-of-pearl—like faded pink summer roses. He thought he would faint at the sight of them. His head grew light, and a tingling came to his forehead, even as his eyes drank in the sight of them greedily. He felt like a starving man who had been watching a feast through a window all his life, and now that he was here, the table of delicacies spread out before him, his stomach rebelled at the sight of such abundance. Her body was achingly beautiful—and still it was not his to touch, to caress, to possess. Her mouth, marred by lipstick, was a red slash in the middle of the perfect white skin of her face.

He watched her through the crack in the white lace curtains, as her body rose and fell with passion. He felt his own body swell in response. She was his neighbor's daughter, and the space between their bedroom windows was so narrow that he felt as if he could reach out and touch her.

Samuel! Sam-u-el! You will burn in hell if you don't stop that right now!

If only he could make it stop, the sound of his mother's voice, harsh as a crow's, cawing at him, bleating, berating him, until he felt his ears would bleed.

Stop that right now, Samuel! The hand of God Himself will come down and strike you dead, and you'll go straight to hell forever!

He turned his head to avoid the arrows of her eyes, his face hot with shame. Even with his face turned toward the wall, he could feel the heat of her anger on the back of his head. He closed his eyes and waited for her rage to pass, to burn itself out. . . .

Afterward it wasn't so bad, though—when she calmed down they would pray together, sometimes for hours at a time.

Pray with me, Samuel. Let God wash clean your spirit.

She would burn incense, and they would kneel together, the Bible spread out on the bed in front of them—though she had it memorized anyway. They would kneel in front of their little makeshift altar, with the figure of the bleeding Christ hanging over the head of the bed, the air thick with the smell of incense. Sometimes she would pray from Genesis, other times from Revelations or Ecclesiastes. After a while he had memorized the passages too, and he would kneel beside his mother until his knees ached. . . . But still he was proud to be sharing her passion for God, proud that he could endure the discomfort and pain—a cleansing pain, to relieve him of the stain of his sinful ways—as long as she could, until his toes were pins and needles and he could no longer feel his legs.

He welcomed the numbness, the release from the shameful feelings of lust. He was grateful to his mother for saving him, and if it was difficult and painful, that was proof to him that he was on the right road. After all, as his mother had told him over and over, nothing worth having is gotten easily.

She had brought him to God, and now he would bring these girls too, offering them as proof of his devotion, his faith, his earnestness. He would save them from their own lustful urges—and from his own.

That Sunday, after the second girl, he sat in the cold, darkened confessional, perched on the hard, narrow bench, until the little door slid open and he could hear Father Neill's thick breathing, smell the spearmint mouthwash, and just beneath it the hint of Scotch whiskey.

"Father, forgive me, for I have sinned."

The priest stifled a belch. Samuel heard the rustling of his robes as he shifted on his bench, heard his smoker's cough.

"It has been two weeks since my last confession."

"Yes, my son?"

"I have had unclean thoughts."

"How many times?"

Samuel paused. It was important to be accurate.

"Three times."

"Say twelve Hail Marys."

It never occurred to him to mention the girls whose lives he had taken. That was not sin, because he was acting as the agent of God. He fingered the paper in his jacket pocket, snuggled next to the sharpened blade of his knife. The instructions on it were clear—and tonight he would do the work of his Master.

He left the church slowly, savoring the solemnity and grandness of the house of the Lord. He was at home here—everything was so much simpler, and he knew what was expected of him.

Chapter Sixteen

Lee sat on the hard bench in the back of the courtroom, watching the trial in progress. He had been wandering around downtown, and when he found himself standing on the steps of the criminal court building, he decided to go inside. It was Friday afternoon, and he felt at loose ends, with the weekend looming ahead. Lately he wasn't dealing well with long stretches of unstructured time. He found courtrooms to be comforting places—they reminded him that sometimes criminals really *were* brought to trial and convicted.

The judge looked down on the proceedings with a weary expression. He had a long, jowly face topped by a brace of bushy black eyebrows so thick that it appeared a pair of caterpillars had attached themselves to his forehead.

This particular trial was a murder case, and the defendant—the victim's husband—sat flanked by his attorneys. He sat quietly, hands folded in his lap, a slight, balding, unremarkable-looking man. Lee knew that a defendant's behavior in court had little bearing on guilt or innocence. The most vicious killers could be brilliant actors once the public eye was on them.

The prosecutor, a slim, dapper Asian man with slicked-down thinning hair, stood and buttoned his jacket.

"We call Dr. Katherine Azarian to the stand, Your Honor."

The judge nodded and pulled at his extravagant right eyebrow.

A small, compact woman rose from the gallery and walked to the witness box. Something about the quiet, contained way she moved caught Lee's eye. She was dressed in a dark green business suit with a fitted jacket, nothing flashy—but on her somehow it looked glamorous. Her hair was dark and wavy, cut close to her head, emphasizing the curve of her cheekbones and firm, pointed chin.

". . . the truth and nothing but the truth, so help you God?" The bailiff, a fat, red-faced man, finished his recitation in a monotone.

"I do," Dr. Azarian replied in a clear, firm voice, removing her hand from the Bible held by the bailiff and turning toward the witness box. Lee watched as she sat, her eyes on the prosecutor, waiting for his first question. Her manner was self-assured and yet entirely lacking in arrogance. He found it hard not to look at her.

The prosecutor approached her, smiling. "Would you please state your profession, Dr. Azarian?"

"I'm a forensic anthropologist." A tiny dimple danced on the end of her chin when she spoke.

"And what exactly does a forensic anthropologist do?

"I aid in the identification of victims' bodies and the causes of death through examination of their skeletons."

"So you're a bone specialist?"

"Yes."

The prosecutor plucked a photograph from the exhibit table and held it aloft.

"Exhibit A, Your Honor. If I may, I'd like to show it to the witness and then to the jury."

The judge nodded, his eyes heavy under the weight of his

prodigious eyebrows. The prosecutor presented the photo to Dr. Azarian.

"Do you recognize this?"

"Yes. It's a photograph of the victim's skull."

The prosecutor passed the photo on to the jurors, whose reactions were varied. Some stared at it with fascination, others with detachment, and a few were visibly upset by it. The prosecutor retrieved the photo from the jury foreman and turned to his witness.

"Did you also have an opportunity to study the skull itself?"

"I did."

"And what conclusion did you reach as to cause of death?"

"Blunt force trauma to the head."

"And could the damage you observed have been caused by a fall?"

"No. The wounds are inconsistent with a fall. For one thing, they occur on both sides of the skull. For another, the shape and size of the indentations indicate the victim was struck by a heavy object—most probably a horseshoe."

"Like this one?"

There was a murmur from the courtroom as the prosecutor lifted a large horseshoe from the exhibit table.

"Yes. The curve of the indentations in the skull, as well as the peculiar mark made by the knob here"—she pointed to the raised edge at the crest of the U-shaped curve—"are unique."

"You might even say unmistakable?"

"Yes."

"Objection!" The defense counsel yelped, leaping to his feet. "Leading the witness!"

"Very well, Mr. Passiano—your objection is sustained," the judge replied, but his voice implied what everyone in the courtroom knew: the damage had been done. Kathy Azarian was not just a good witness, she was the prosecution's star witness, and Lee knew that anyone putting money on the defendant now was making a fool's bet. He smiled to himself and slipped out the back door of the courtroom.

When he reached the corridor, his cell phone rang. He found a quiet corner by the restrooms before answering it. He hated talking on his phone in public, and thought people who did were "coarse," as his mother would say.

"Campbell here."

"Lee?" It was Chuck Morton, and he sounded nervous.

"Yes. Chuck? What's happened?"

"Now, Lee, don't get excited, please—"

"What? What is it?"

"Now, don't call your mother until we know more—"

"It's about Laura, isn't it? What's happened?" Lee heard his own voice rising in pitch and volume, and felt himself starting to hyperventilate.

"Lee, please calm down. It may be nothing at all."

Spots danced in front of his eyes. He forced himself to take a deep breath before he spoke again. "What have you found?"

"A couple of kids came across some bones in Inwood Park."

Inwood Park was an unlikely place for a body drop, especially if Laura was abducted near her apartment in Greenwich Village, he thought.

"What makes you think it's her?"

"The medical examiner's office thinks it may be about the right age and, uh, gender, but we—uh, they—want to do a reverse DNA analysis."

Lee forced himself to breathe again, doing his best to sound professional.

"No clothing or other identifying—"

Chuck interrupted him. "No, nothing. But if we can get DNA samples from you and your mother—"

"Yeah, I know how it works. I'll be right there."

"Wait—I'm not in my office. I'm at the ME's office."

"Okay. Be right there."

He turned off his phone and shoved it into his pocket, but his hand was trembling and sweaty, and the phone slid from his hand, clattering to the floor. It skidded across the smooth tiled floor and came to rest at the feet of Dr. Katherine Azarian.

"You dropped your phone," she said, picking it up.

"Uh, thanks," Lee mumbled, taking it from her.

"No problem," she said, and continued on toward the ladies' room. She carried a cream-colored lamb's wool overcoat in one hand and a leather briefcase in the other.

"Uh—wait!" he cried.

"Excuse me?" She turned back to face him, her expression wary.

"Please—please just wait a second. I'm with the NYPD—" Lee fumbled for his ID, trying desperately to keep her from leaving.

"I knew that," she said. "You don't have to show me your ID." She smiled, revealing teeth that were unreasonably white. They gleamed like polished porcelain, and Lee found himself staring at them, unable to look away.

"How did you—"

"Oh, please," she said. "I've been around them long enough to be able to spot one at a hundred paces."

"Oh, okay," Lee said. "I just saw you testify in court, and—"

"Oh? Are you on that case?"

"No, no. I just had some time to kill—but that's not important. I want to ask you something." In this light, her eyes were the color of roasted almonds, and rimmed with thick, dark lashes. "Would you—would you possibly be willing to help identify a body?"

She cocked her head to one side and shifted her backpack to the other shoulder. "Well, that's what I do. Do you mean right now?"

"Are you finished testifying?"

"Yes."

"Then right now—unless you have other plans."

She laughed. "They can wait. You seem very anxious to have your answer. Where is this body?"

"At the medical examiner's office."

"Okay—I have some time to kill, too, actually," she said, putting on her coat and gloves. Her hands were small and fine, delicate as the hands of a child, with perfectly manicured pink fingernails. He couldn't imagine those hands in a laboratory, handling the gruesome remains of murder victims. "When did this body turn up?" she said, buttoning her coat.

"I just found out about it."

"One of your cases?"

"Sort of. It—it may be my sister."

She stopped midway through putting on her second glove. "Oh my God. What happened to her?"

"That's what I'm trying to find out. She disappeared five years ago."

"I'm so sorry to hear it. I hope I can be of some help."

"Thanks."

"Okay, let's go," she said.

"What about—?" Lee said, glancing toward the bathroom.

"It can wait."

As they left the courtroom a brisk wind was blowing from the west, and Lee pulled his coat tighter around his neck. He looked at Katherine Azarian, who had flung a hand skyward in hopes of snagging one of the yellow cabs barreling up Center Street. Even flagging a cab, she looked confident, authoritative.

She glanced at her watch. "This is a lousy time to try for a cab. I think we should take the bus. It's not far."

"Okay."

"There's a stop for the M15 right around the corner at Chatham Square."

He followed her, bent forward against the wind, past the Tombs, with their stark vertical stone walls, the long grim columns rising like the Death Star from the streets below. They hurried past the statue of Lin Zexu, the Fujian hero who defied the British, standing tall on his pedestal in the center of the square. He looked cold, draped in his gray granite robes, gazing northeast toward the rising sun, his stone face shielded by a broad-brimmed hat. Across from the statue stood the Republic National Bank, with its flashy red-tipped pagoda, marking the entrance to the heart of China-town. Another time, he might have thought it charming, but right now, to Lee, the color red only evoked one thing: blood.

Chapter Seventeen

The medical examiner's office was housed in a stolid, bland structure typical of the 1960s genre of institutional buildings. Dull and functional, its rectangular glass windows were bordered by metal rims set in a featureless brick façade.

Just down the block from the Victorian opulence of Bellevue Hospital, with its dark red brick, heavy, ornate balustrades, and carved gargoyles hanging from ivy-covered eaves, the ME's building was like the prim Lutheran cousin who came to visit for the weekend and ended up staying.

They entered the lobby, with its scuffed yellow plastic chairs and cheap carpeting. Within these bland walls were the laboratories and autopsy rooms filled with corpses of people who had been drowned, poisoned, shot, stabbed, beaten, and hacked to death.

The desk attendant wasn't sure which direction to send them, so they headed for the main autopsy room. Standing in front of a glass window so clean it was invisible, they looked around for a medical examiner or lab technician, but the room was empty of all living beings, quiet as a tomb. The only occupants were half a dozen bodies on steel gurneys, in various stages of decay. Even the pressed white sheets covering them couldn't hide the ravages of death on the human body—here a livid arm protruded, there a brown stain seeped through the pristine covering.

Lee looked away. At least Laura, when they found her, would be nothing more than clean white bones, none of this messy and gruesome horror. He looked at Kathy, but her face was grim and unreadable. Maybe she didn't like seeing corpses any more than he did.

Chuck Morton came walking down the long hallway with his cell phone to his ear. He waved at Lee and said into the phone, "Look, I've got to go. I'll call you later." He put the phone in his breast pocket and approached them with a rueful expression. "Missing soccer again. Afraid I'm not much of a dad lately." Seeing Kathy, he held out his hand. "Chuck Morton, Captain, Bronx Major Case Unit."

She shook his hand. "Katherine Azarian, forensic pathologist. I'm just here to give my opinion, for what it's worth."

"Oh, yes, I've heard of you. You're out of Philadelphia, aren't you?"

"Yes. I'm here testifying in the Lorenzo case."

"Right, right—the skeleton that turned up in Queens." He turned to Lee, his face apologetic.

"I'm sorry to call you here like this. It could be there's no connection, but I just thought—"

"It's all right," Lee answered. "I'm glad you called. Where is . . ." *She? It?* He couldn't bring himself to say either word, so his sentence trailed off into thin air.

"Elaine's just bringing the . . . uh, remains . . . from the main morgue." Chuck also seemed to have trouble finding the right words.

Lee swallowed, his Adam's apple tight and dry in his throat.

A short blond woman with a tight pixie face came down

the hall wheeling a metal gurney. Under the white sheet was the clear outline of a skeleton. Lee forced himself to concentrate on his breathing as the woman wheeled the gurney into the autopsy room. The three of them followed her, and Lee wasn't prepared for the smell as the door opened. In spite of the strong odor of disinfectant, as well as formaldehyde and various other laboratory chemicals, the stench lingered underneath, clinging to his nostrils with a noxious insistence, causing a deep, instinctive repulsion.

It was the smell of death.

"This is Elaine Margolies," Chuck said, introducing the blond woman. "She's chief assistant medical examiner."

Elaine Margolies was all business. "A couple of boys came across this in some caves in the woods in Inwood Park, called it in. Cops took photos of the scene and then brought it in."

"I've seen the photos, and they're not very revealing," Chuck Morton commented.

Kathy Azarian wasn't listening. "May I have a look?" she asked Elaine.

Lee held his breath as Margolies lifted the sheet, revealing a nearly complete human skeleton, clean except for a few bits of dirt and leaves still clinging to it.

"Well, it's definitely female," she concluded after a brief glance.

"And in remarkably good condition, considering," Elaine Margolies agreed. "Not much evidence of any molestation by animals."

"Well, that makes sense—there isn't much in Inwood Park other than squirrels," Morton remarked, glancing at Lee to see how he was taking it.

Lee looked down at the bones. If this really was his sister, he could handle it, seeing her this way—better this way than one of the bloated, oozing corpses on the other gurneys.

But Kathy Azarian shook her head. "This isn't your sister."

Morton frowned. "How can you tell?"

"Development of the pelvic bone. This girl was no more than fifteen when she died. In more mature individuals," she continued, "there is considerably more development of the pelvic bone. Not only that," she said to Lee, "you told me that your sister had given birth?"

"Yes," Lee said. "She has—had—a daughter." He remembered now talking incessantly on the bus all the way up First Avenue, rattling on as if filling up the air between them would make the ride go faster. He could barely remember what he had said, but he knew he had mentioned Kylie at least once, and the fact that she was living with her father.

"This is not the body of a woman in her twenties," Kathy said, "much less one who has given birth. Absolutely not."

Chuck Morton rubbed a hand over his short buff of blond hair. Lee thought he looked relieved.

"Well," he said. "You're sure, huh?"

"Positive," she replied.

The tension drained from the room like water from a sieve. Lee knew at that moment that he wasn't that different from his mother after all: as long as no body surfaced, in the back of his head there was still a tiny seed of hope, ready to burst into bloom.

He looked at Chuck Morton. To his surprise, his old friend was sweating.

Chuck's cell phone rang—a jaunty Latin melody that was a jarring contrast to the solemn surroundings.

"Hello?" He listened and then said, "Okay, thanks for telling me."

He hung up, his face grim.

"I'm afraid there's some bad news."

"What is it?" said Lee.

"Father Michael Flaherty is dead. Hanged himself."

"Oh, God."

"There's a suicide note. He apologizes for his sexual behavior."

"But that's it? No mention of—?"

"No."

Neither of them said what they were both thinking: they were back to square one. And Lee had another uncomfortable thought: what if the bones on the table in front of him belonged to an even earlier victim of the Slasher?

Chapter Eighteen

The woods lay silent all around him, the tree branches hanging low over the winding stream, their leaves a lush canopy of gold and green, hiding him, protecting him from the inquisitive, prying eyes of people who might judge him.

He stood looking at the running brook, at the soft clear water burbling over the stones in its path. He was like the water, gliding over the rocks and pebbles in his path, smoothing them over time until they became rounded, the rough edges now as curved as the white limbs of the women he had rescued.

They had to be saved from the path they were choosing before it was too late. He was the only one who could save them—except the Master, of course. They both understood the importance of purity, and he had kept himself pure: unblemished, clean and clear as the water running so swiftly over the stones lining the brook. It was a heavy burden to bear—at times almost intolerable—but the importance of his work drove him onward.

He lay down upon the stones and let the purifying water flow over him. It was icy cold, but he didn't mind. It helped to quench the fire raging in his soul. He closed his eyes and let the pictures float through his mind like the running water over his skin. Whenever he closed his eyes, the images of their faces were there, in his mind's eye, one face melting into another, their features weaving in an endless tapestry of memory and desire. . . .

He had conquered desire, overcome his own lust for these women by an act of willpower, to follow a purer impulse. The Master understood the importance of saving a soul, by stopping the sinner before she could sin again.

And what if they had desired him, these women with their soft white skin and doelike eyes, eyes that widened and filled with terror as he bent over them, applying his hands to their necks, bearing down with just enough force to cut off their breath, then watching, waiting, as the last breath left their body, watching for that moment when the soul made its escape, set free from the prison of the body, to fly—fly up and away through the ether and into the waiting arms of the Lord. And then the ritual of cutting the Lord's words into their dead flesh, consecrating them even as they lay before him, their bodies still warm . . .

A smile moved across his face just as a tiny silver water snake slid by, brushing its shiny skin against his trouser leg. He was unaware of the snake, but perhaps he felt its presence, because he shivered as he thought of all the work he had yet ahead of him.

He thought about the girls, alluring and fresh. . . . He catalogued their charms one by one: the soft shimmer of their hair, their gentle eyes and pliant bodies, the tender fullness of their young breasts.

He rose from where he lay, brushing stray twigs from his clothes, and shook himself as a dog might, flinging water in all directions. The droplets spun and twirled in the sunlight filtering through the trees, catching the light and turning into a thousand tiny prisms. Once again he was struck by the pristine beauty of the woods—the one place he could go without the defiling presence of human beings. He took a deep breath and walked back in the direction he had come from. The comforting jangling of the keys hanging from his belt made him smile, and his hand closed around the freshly sharpened knife tucked away in his pocket.

There was work to be done.

Chapter Nineteen

Lee woke up the next morning in a clammy sweat, anxiety squeezing his stomach like an evil fist.

Mornings were the worst. With the demands of the day looming, the terror could drain him of will, crippling him and leaving him paralyzed. Sometimes he knew the reason for his anxiety, and sometimes he didn't. It was much worse when he didn't. Then it would grip him hour after hour, pressing like a vise upon his consciousness, until even the simplest action, like brushing his teeth, required an enormous act of will.

Today he knew the reason for his anxiety: it was Kathy Azarian. Meeting her had upset his carefully calibrated world. He feared that whatever control he had managed over his emotions would be thrown to the wind. More than anything, he wanted never to return to the months following his sister's disappearance.

That was when it had started—when the darkness had descended around him, a blackness that he had never known before. Since then, he had come to know the many faces of depression. Most often, it would hit him first thing in the morning, upon waking, a cold, hard hand around his heart and a burning, as though his soul were on fire. Familiar objects become foreign, food lost its ability to comfort, landscapes he once found charming looked utterly blank. There was no seeing beyond the thick fog of pain.

Now, lying in bed, he felt the familiar restlessness coupled with frozen immobility. He lay curled up in his bed for a while, stomach churning, his mind circling around itself like a lion pacing in a cage. He looked over at the digital alarm clock next to his bed. The red numbers read 10:32, the dots between them flashing like warning signal lights.

At one point after Laura's death, he had developed a fear of his answering machine. He dreaded getting up in the morning and seeing the blinking red light indicating he had messages. It was like the glaring red eye of a great, devouring beast waiting to swallow him whole. He was terrified of other people's needs and demands on him, afraid he would fail them—or worse, that he would be engulfed by them.

He was also certain that each message would be the police calling to say they had found his sister's body. In spite of his certainty that she was dead, he dreaded receiving that call.

He pulled himself out of bed, dragged himself to the bathroom, bathed, and shaved in a haze, hardly aware of what he was doing, as though he were sleepwalking. He forced himself to look at the answering machine. To his relief, there were no messages.

Hands trembling, he picked up the phone and called his therapist. After leaving a message, he felt what little will he had draining away with each passing minute. He went to the kitchen, opened the refrigerator, and tried to imagine desiring food. No coffee, not today—when he was this jittery, caffeine was the last thing he needed. He stared at a bowl of bananas on the table, but they looked uninviting. He sat down at the piano but couldn't focus on the notes in front of him.

Finally, the phone rang. He picked it up on the second ring.

"Hello?"

"Hello, Lee, it's Georgina Williams." Her voice was cool and yet intimate, with just the right amount of professional detachment.

He got right to the point. "Do you have any openings or cancellations today?"

"Actually, I have one in an hour, if you can get here that quickly."

"Great. I'll see you in an hour."

He put the phone down and forced his breath all the way down into his belly, making himself exhale slowly. Then he went to the kitchen, snagged a banana from the bowl, and forced himself to eat it.

An hour later he was seated in the familiar office, with its comforting collection of objects, books, and paintings. A vase of carnations sat on the table next to Dr. Williams, casting off an aroma of nutmeg.

"Okay, you're anxious today," Dr. Williams was saying in her smooth, cultivated voice. "But are you anything else?"

"Sad, maybe."

"Anything else?"

Lee looked at her. "Like what?"

"Like . . . angry, perhaps?"

His stomach burned—boiled with—yes, rage.

"Okay," he said, "so I'm angry. What do I do about it?"

"Well, allowing yourself to acknowledge it is a start. Then you might tell me all the things you're angry about."

Lee felt his jaw tighten.

"Okay," he said stiffly. "I'm angry at my mother for not recognizing the truth: that Laura is gone, that she's never coming back. She just can't accept that Laura is dead."

"So you're angry at your mother for holding on to hope."

"Yes. There's a time to let it go, to see reality for what it is."

"What if reality is too painful?"

"Reality is often too painful. That's not a good excuse. You still have to face it."

"So you wish your mother had your courage?"

"Yeah, I guess I do. Because then I could—I could grieve with her. It's something we could go through together, instead of living in these parallel realities."

Dr. Williams nodded, sympathy stamped across her high-cheekboned face. "Yes, it's hard when people we care about continue to disappoint us."

"There's something else." *How to say it?* "I've met someone."

Dr. Williams folded her elegant hands in her lap and leaned back in her chair. "Well, that sounds like a good thing."

"It *sounds* great—but it feels scary."

"Why don't we talk about why it feels scary?"

"Well, it's a chance to have something I want, but it's also a chance to fail, to lose what I want."

"So as long as you don't want anything you're safe?"

Lee considered the question. "Yeah, pretty much. That's no way to live, though. The thing is, I'm not sure I'm ready for something like this. I mean, the timing—I feel caught off guard."

"Wouldn't it be great if opportunity only knocked when we asked it to?"

"Do I sense a little sarcasm?"

"No, not at all. Just irony. I don't think it's unreasonable for you to feel that way at all, but life often throws you a curve just when—"

"When you were hoping for a fastball."

Dr. Williams laughed, a low, bell-like sound that emanated from deep in her throat. Lee was reminded of a didgeridoo, the Australian musical instrument that produced amazing waves of overtones when played correctly.

"What does she look like?"

"She's, uh . . . kind of short, with curly dark hair."

"Like your sister."

"Oh, come *on*—does everything have to be about Laura?"

"No. I'm just pointing it out. It's interesting that you became so immediately defensive about it."

"All right, all *right*!"

"You know, it isn't unusual for someone to try to construct a surrogate family when their family of origin is inadequate—or, in this case, torn away from you."

"Okay, okay," Lee said impatiently. "And John Nelson is my substitute father figure, who doesn't abandon me, but chooses me from among all the others."

"Why does that make you so angry?"

"That's what I'm here to find out, isn't it?"

"Okay." Dr. Williams rarely took bait, even when it was dangled in front of her. It was one of the things Lee liked about her—she had that kind of confidence as a therapist.

There was a pause, and then Lee said, "You know, my mother doesn't really approve of what I do for a living."

"You think not?"

"It's too messy, too involved with things she'd rather not think about."

"The dark side of human nature?"

"She was all right with my being a psychologist, but this 'profiling thing,' as she calls it, takes me to places she doesn't want to admit even exist."

"So you think she finds it threatening?"

"I'm sure of it."

"And you? Do you find it threatening?"

"Yes. Yes, I do."

"This woman you've met—do you think she finds it threatening?"

"Well, that's the thing: she seems fascinated by it. I don't know how I feel about that. Part of me is glad, and part of me wonders . . ."

"What's wrong with her?"

He thought about it. "Yeah, maybe."

"So you think you should marry a girl just like dear old Mom?"

"Well, now, which is it, Dr. Williams—my mother or my sister? Make up your mind."

They both laughed, but Lee had a sticky feeling of discomfort. It was one thing to read about these things in a textbook, or even to go through it with a patient, but it was another thing to experience it yourself.

Lee left Dr. Williams's office feeling a weight had been lifted from his shoulders. It was such a relief to be able to say "I'm afraid." In his family, those were forbidden words. No one was ever afraid—not strong, worthy people, at any rate. Fear was for the rest of humanity, those inferior beings who had not the good fortune to be born Campbells. As Lee turned the corner onto University Place, past the University Coffee Shop, the smell of grilled beef assailed his nostrils, and he was suddenly ravenous.

His cell phone beeped inside his jacket, indicating that he had a message. He dug it out of his pocket and looked at the screen. NEW TEXT MESSAGE. He scrolled over to the message and read it. It was a single sentence.

What about the red dress?

He stood in the middle of the sidewalk, stunned. No one knew about the red dress, the one his sister was last seen wearing before she disappeared. That detail had never been released to the public—only the police knew about the red dress.

Except that now someone else knew too.

Chapter Twenty

Later that afternoon Lee sat in the overstuffed brown leather armchair by the window, his feet propped up on the window-sill, a cup of strong coffee on the round rosewood table by his side. He opened the yellow file folder on his lap. The red tab marking said simply *Kelleher, Marie*, followed by the case number. This young girl, who once had a life ahead of her, was now reduced to a manila folder, a few horrific photos, and a case number. A good girl, a practicing Catholic, pious and churchgoing, without an enemy in the world. His sister hadn't had an enemy either, and yet someday someone would be sitting with a file like this one on his lap, and the tab would read *Campbell, Laura* . . . if her body was ever found.

What about the red dress?

Lee rubbed his forehead. There was no way to trace who might have left the text message—you could buy a disposable cell phone at any bodega in New York, use it for one call, and throw it in the East River. Lee debated whether to call Chuck and tell him about the message.

He forced his mind back to the file in front of him and

looked at the forensic data, or lack of it: no semen, no prints, and—other than the victim's—no blood. He studied the crime scene photographs, and was struck by the orderliness of the scene. Nothing out of place, the vase of flowers exactly where the priest said he had last seen them, the pulpit right where it belonged—very little had been touched, except for the awful presence of Marie's body on the altar. The lack of defensive wounds meant she was probably blindsided—a blitzkrieg attack. The killer didn't necessarily know her well, but she didn't feel threatened by him—until it was too late.

The phone rang, jarring him out of his reverie. He picked it up on the second ring.

"Hello?"

"Heya, Boss."

"Hi, Eddie."

"I think I got something for you."

"Really? What?"

"I can't talk right now, but it might be good. Diesel and Rhino have been snooping around, you know."

"Okay, listen—give me your number and I'll call you."

"No can do, Boss. I'll have to call you back."

"Okay."

"When would be a good time?"

Just then Lee heard the beep of call waiting.

"Look, I have to go. Call me tomorrow, okay?"

"Right. Will do."

Lee pressed the receiver and answered the other line.

"Hello?"

"Lee, it's Chuck." Something in his voice made Lee's stomach clench. Before he spoke again, Lee already knew what was coming next. "There's been another one—same MO. It's him, Lee."

"Where?"

"Brooklyn. The victim's name is Annie O'Donnell. They found her in a church in the Heights."

"Damn. Are you there now?"

"On my way. It's in Park Slope—Two-two-five Sixth Avenue."

"Okay, I'm leaving now. I'll meet you there."

Lee took a gulp from the cooling cup of coffee, threw on his coat, and grabbed his house keys, shoving them in his pocket.

He stepped out into the dimming February twilight and looked at the lights in the windows of the apartments lining Seventh Street. The apartment opposite his had cream-colored French lace curtains, and the soft yellow glow of lamplight inside was inviting. But behind even the most inviting glow of lamplight there could live a killer, plotting his next act of rage against society. Lee jogged a half block to the west to look for a cab at the intersection where the Bowery bifurcated into Third Avenue to the east and Fourth Avenue to the west.

As he stepped out from the curb to hail a cab, he heard the sound of a car backfiring. It wasn't an unusual sound to hear on Third Avenue, but an instant later something whizzed by his head, embedding itself with a tinny thud in the lamppost behind him. He turned to look at the lamppost, but just then a cab pulled up in front of him. He looked around Third Avenue, but there was no sign of the shooter. No one on the street seemed to notice that anything unusual had happened. He searched the crowd, but no one was running away—even the sound of the gun firing had been swallowed up by the blare of car horns and traffic noise.

He glanced at the lamppost. Whatever the object was, it had cut deeply into the metal. He took a step toward it, but the cabbie honked his horn impatiently.

"Hey mister—do you wanna go somewhere or not?"

Lee looked down Third Avenue. A light rain had begun to fall, and this was the only free cab in sight.

"Yeah, thanks," he said, climbing in and closing the door.

There was no doubt in his mind that the dent in the lamp-post was made by a bullet. What he wasn't sure of was whether or not he was the intended victim.

The pursuer becomes the pursued, he thought grimly as the cab rattled up Third Avenue.

Chapter Twenty-one

Saint Francis Xavier was a graceful granite and limestone structure smiling down over the low buildings of Park Slope like a kindly uncle. The stone looked as though it had recently been cleaned; even in the feeble February sun, Lee had to squint against the glare. The elegant vaulted ceiling loomed above him as he walked past tall stained-glass windows of unusual beauty. The light cascaded onto the stone floor, magnified as it sliced through cut-glass figures of saints and apostles, sinners and deities, in their flowing vermillion and sapphire robes. In happier times, he would have stopped to study them, but he continued walking, his footsteps clicking rhythmically on the polished floor.

The heavy marble altar was magnificent, its splendor only serving to heighten the gloom he felt as he approached it. The CSI team was already there, moving about the church with their usual efficiency, dusting for prints, scanning the pews for any stray scrap of evidence. He approached the little group around the pulpit. Chuck Morton was there, still wearing his overcoat, which was cream colored and looked pricey. Chuck's wife, Susan, had a knack for buying clothes that weren't expensive but looked like they were.

When Chuck heard Lee approach, he looked up.

"Thanks for coming out on such short notice."

Lee looked at the body draped over the altar.

The victim in this attack was eerily similar to the one at Fordham—young, with dark curly hair and a decidedly Irish look about her. This time, however, the crime scene showed evidence of a frenzied attack. Several hymnals had been ripped from their racks in the front choir loft surrounding the altar and lay scattered about, their pages ripped and spattered with blood. A large blue and white flower vase lay a few feet from the victim's body, broken in two, its contents strewn over the thick carpet covering the floor of the altar. Yellow roses— ironic, Lee thought, since they were the symbol for friendship.

But what he couldn't take his eyes off were the words carved into her chest.

Hallowed be thy name.

The cuts were deeper than last time, the slashes cruder— the *e* in *Hallowed* bisecting her right nipple so deeply that it had almost come off. There was more blood, too—*a lot more blood*. He thought about what the pathologist at the morgue had said about postmortem injuries—and these injuries did not appear to be postmortem. He turned away, sickened.

Hallowed be thy name.

The phrase circled his brain rhythmically, mockingly. *Hal-low-ed be thy na . . .*

"Jesus," Lee muttered. He had another horrifying thought. The Slasher was only two lines into the prayer—not even a quarter of the way through it.

"It's him—it's the same guy," Chuck sighed, coming up to stand next to him. "You were right about one thing: he isn't going to stop."

"And there was less than a week between these two killings,"

Lee pointed out. "The last time he waited a month, but this time—well, he's either more driven, more confident, or both. What do you have on the victim so far?"

Chuck looked down at the girl. "Poor kid. Name's Annie O'Donnell." He indicated a nearby detective interviewing a middle-aged Hispanic man in a drab green uniform, who appeared to be distraught. "Even the janitor recognized her—said she attended this church. Apparently she's fairly quiet, but he says he has an eye for pretty girls." Chuck glanced over at the man. "He's not . . . is he?" he asked.

"Too old, wrong race. The Slasher is younger, and probably white. Interracial sex crimes aren't unknown, but they're rare, and this guy seems to be a preferential killer."

"Meaning—?"

"He targets a specific kind of victim."

"Yeah, okay," Chuck said, with a glance at the technicians quietly dusting for prints, gathering and bagging evidence. "The CSI team is doing what it can, but I wouldn't expect much."

"No," Lee agreed. "If he covered his tracks last time, he will this time too. He knows what he's doing. On the other hand, this time there is evidence of a struggle, so it's always possible—"

"Lee," said Chuck, "do you think that John Nelson would consider . . . "

"What?"

"Well, you guys are pretty close, right? So I thought maybe you could ask him if he would—if he would like to consult?"

"Yeah, sure."

"I mean, no offense, but we could really use all the help we can get, right?"

"Sure," Lee said. "When it comes to criminal psychology, he's the guy. There isn't anyone better outside of Quantico."

The detective who had been talking to the janitor had finished with him, and walked over to where Lee and Chuck stood. He carried a small notebook, an essential tool for any detective, and was dressed in the usual "uniform": a tan raincoat over a somber suit, black shoes, dark socks. Lee wondered why the man was dressed this way on a Saturday afternoon. It seemed a little out of the ordinary on a weekend, but maybe he was already on duty when the call came in.

Chuck made the introductions. "Detective Florette, this is Lee Campbell. Lee, this is Detective Clyde Florette, Brooklyn SVU." SVU was short for Special Victims Unit, which dealt exclusively with sex crimes.

"How do you do?" Clyde Florette reached for Lee's hand. His grip was firm and assertive without being aggressive. He was the physical opposite of Detective Butts: a tall black man, slim and elegant, with slicked-back graying hair. His features were too aquiline to be conventionally handsome, with thin lips and a long nose, but with his neatly trimmed graying beard and luminous eyes, Lee guessed that women went for him, especially the ones who liked the professorial type. His voice was low and cultured, with a hint of an island lilt—from Haiti, perhaps, or Barbados.

"Captain Morton tells me that you're working on a multiple, and that this is his second victim," Florette said. "Multiple" was police shorthand for "multiple homicides," and like a lot of cop jargon, it fell stiffly on Lee's ears. It seemed to him the lingo itself was an attempt to distance cops from the things they encountered in the line of duty.

"That's right," Lee answered, "except that it's his third victim."

Detective Florette raised an eyebrow and looked at Morton.

"We haven't yet determined that," Chuck said, an edge of irritation in his voice.

"Well, whether this is his second or third," Florette went on, "he somehow managed to get in and out of here without anyone seeing him. I got zip from the janitor, likewise the chaplain, who says he was in his office for part of the afternoon." He nodded in the direction of the dead girl; a team from the medical examiner's office was bending over her. "She's only dead three, maybe four hours, according to the body temp, when the janitor found her."

Since body temperature fell one to two degrees Fahrenheit per hour after death, on average, undoubtedly one of the first things the ME team had done was to measure the girl's temperature.

Lee said, "That means he brought her in here in broad daylight, and yet no one saw him."

Florette frowned. "How could he do that? Wouldn't someone have seen him?"

Lee considered the question. "Somehow, he must have found a way to sedate her."

"For a while," Florette added. "She obviously struggled once he got her here."

"Maybe she didn't even look like a person at all," Morton suggested. "Maybe he brought her in a bag or container of some kind."

"That would make sense," Lee agreed.

"I'll do a complete sweep of the building and see if we can come up with anything," Florette said. "I also want to talk to your primary on the Bronx girl. . . . what's his name? Detective Butts?"

"That's right," Chuck said. "We tried to reach him, but his daughter says he took his wife to a matinee, and he's turned off his cell phone."

"Well, give him my number and tell him to call me as soon as he can."

They all looked at the dead girl, her skin already turning bluish white as the blood drained away. The carved words stood out against the pale skin. *Hallowed be thy name.* The wounds were the color of dried rust.

"I suppose the brass could establish a task force on this guy, right?" Florette said.

"They might," Chuck answered.

"In that case, Detective Butts would be the primary from now on," Florette said, looking down at his polished shoes, and Lee could sense the reluctance in his voice. He understood the way the system worked, but once cops got a case, they didn't like to let go—especially when they were homicide detectives, and especially when the victim was a young girl. Lee had noticed the white knight types were drawn to police work, and often ended up in homicide. Seeing women in distress was likely to press every button they had. The fact that the women were young and attractive would just raise the stakes for the white knight cops—they wanted to come to the rescue of the princess, to kill the dragon and claim the prize.

Lee glanced at poor Annie again, lying so still in the midst of all the activity around her, as the CSI and ME teams continued with their work. This princess was dead, and there would be no prize, no hand given in marriage to the hero who tracked down this dragon.

"I'll just have to wait to see how they handle it, but I'd guess a task force is likely, yeah," Chuck said.

Florette took a deep breath and put his little notebook in his pocket. "Okay. Well, I don't have to tell you that I'd like to be on it."

"Yeah, sure," Chuck answered, "if I have anything to say about it."

Florette wandered over to speak with the CSIs on the other side of the room, and Lee took the opportunity to draw Chuck aside.

"There's something else I should tell you," Lee said.

"What's that?"

"I . . . I think someone took a shot at me tonight."

"What?"

Lee told Chuck about the bullet that narrowly missed him, and Chuck called the commander of the Ninth Precinct to send someone over to dig out the bullet.

"We'll do a ballistics test on it. It could give us something," Chuck said. "And you'll need protection."

"Oh, come on—" said Lee.

But Chuck cut him off. "It's not up for debate."

"Okay," Lee answered. "It doesn't really fit the profile, though. I wouldn't expect someone like this killer to be a shooter. It could be completely unrelated to the case."

He thought about mentioning the text message on his cell phone, but he saw Detective Florette heading their way and decided to wait.

Florette walked up and stood beside them, hands in his pockets. "This guy is really sick, isn't he?" he said to Lee.

"Yeah," Lee replied. "He's really sick."

"So now we've definitely got a multiple on our hands," said Chuck.

"What we have here," Lee said, "is a serial killer."

Chapter Twenty-two

Everywhere he went, he felt people were looking at him, judging him. There was no forgiveness, no redemption. He knew that as well as he knew every inch of his bedroom ceiling, having stared up at it all these years while lying on his bed, hoping that his mother wouldn't call him—no, please don't—but then she always would, asking him to kneel beside her on the hard floor, smelling the odor of floor wax and hair spray that permeated her bedroom.

But the Master understood him, and one day, he promised, he would find Samuel a girl who would embrace him and forgive him for all his wickedness. They were so young, so innocent, soft as young birds, with smooth skin and eyes as wide as the blond meadows that surrounded his boyhood home. He often thought of that house in Iowa, the rows of cornfields stretching off into the horizon, and the feel of his father's hand in his as they headed for the barn to bring out the big green tractor.

He never really understood why his father left, except that men are evil by nature, and that they all leave sooner or later. And now there was just Queens, and the sound of trucks on the Long Island Expressway at night, and his mother's footsteps upstairs as she wandered the house like a lost soul searching for redemption. *The Lord loves you, Samuel—find your salvation in Jesus.*

Rage bubbled up from deep inside him, boiling in his stomach and constricting his throat, choking him. Maybe it was as his mother had said, that if she had never had a child, his father would not have left. He imagined scenarios that might have been if he had never been born: his mother and father together, driving in the car with the wind blowing in the open windows, his mother laughing, her head thrown back—not that tight laugh he knew now, but a softer, happier sound, like the tinkling of wind chimes. One of the girls had laughed like that, a gentle, rolling sound, like the bubbling of a brook. He imagined making a woman laugh like that someday . . . a sound that she would make only for him, in response to his touch. . . . *Women like that are sluts, Samuel— they'll corrupt you, you'll see!*

He shook his head to try to erase the voices in his head, but it was no use. He was tired, so tired. . . . Spread out on the table in front of him was a small collection of silver and gold crosses on their delicate chains. He selected one with a tiny diamond in its center and smiled. His mother would like this one.

Chapter Twenty-three

The sad-eyed priest beckoned to him from the other side of a long, winding river. Lee longed to cross the river and be with the priest, but the current was strong and he was afraid of being sucked downstream. The priest opened his arms and smiled, and just as Lee was about to jump into the water—

The phone rang. Lee pulled himself out of the world of his dream, threw off the covers, and grabbed the receiver, glad to be rid of the image of the sad-eyed priest, relieved to be in his own bedroom.

"Hello?"

"It's me." It was Chuck. "We got a hit on the girl in Queens. Some kids came forward to say they thought they knew her. They're at the station now."

"Be right there."

At the station, Lee followed Chuck and Butts down the hall to Interrogation Room Three, still rubbing sleep from his eyes, a cup of coffee in his hand.

Through the one-way glass he could see them: three East

Village types, two boys and a girl. They were young, and probably even younger than Jane Doe Number Five. Two of them, the girl and one of the boys, were gothed up to the max—black leather, purple spiked hair, bloodred lipstick, their skin pierced with enough hardware to set off metal detectors in any airport. Lee counted five rings in the boy's nose alone.

The third kid was less outrageously dressed. Slim and small-boned, he wore a simple buckskin jacket over blue jeans and no makeup, and sported a single nose ring. His hair was brown and combed straight back, rather than spiked up into points like the other boy's hair, which resembled the crown on the Statue of Liberty. He looked more nervous than his companions, too, glancing at the door every few seconds, as if he expected it to open and disgorge a monster into the room.

The other boy was larger, solidly built but soft, with bits of baby fat poking out between his leather vest and metal-studded black leather pants. Judging by his pale eyebrows and lashes, Lee figured that his hair was probably naturally blond, but it was hard to tell what was hidden under all that purple dye.

His forearms showed evidence of recent wounds—not needle tracks, Lee thought, but the small slashes left after "cutting"—a process where kids would nick themselves with sharp knives, sometimes a dozen or more cuts at a time. It was fashionable among the goth crowd right now, but it reeked of despair, a desperate attempt to numb feelings more painful than physical discomfort.

He looked at the girl to see if she too was a cutter, but her arms were covered by the sleeves of her lacy black sweater. She was tall, with dyed jet-black hair. Her lipstick was the color of dried blood, and her mouth turned downward at the corners in a habitual pout. Her eyes were ringed with black eyeliner, so that she resembled a surly raccoon. Under all the makeup, Lee imagined she was probably quite pretty. She wore a hard expression, and both boys looked as though they took orders from her. The smaller boy had a sharp, intelligent face, whereas the bigger one looked to be the muscle of the organization. Beauty, brains, and brawn, he thought, watching them. There was usually a leader and followers in groups like this, and the girl was clearly the leader.

The girl was staring at a photo of Jane Doe Number Five. Pushing it away from her to the other end of the table, she frowned at her companions.

"Look, you're good with kids," Chuck said to Lee. "Why don't you handle this one?"

"Okay." Lee looked to see if Butts was feeling any resentment, but if he was, he wasn't showing it.

He and Butts and Chuck entered the room together, Lee moving slowly but with purpose, keeping his face as blank as possible. If he read these three correctly, the best thing he could do was to play his cards close and let them come to him. They watched him warily as he sat in the only vacant chair, a scarred green plastic affair with a crack in the seat. He smiled at them.

"Hi," he said, "thanks for coming in."

"Look, we just want to help you catch her killer, okay?" the girl said, as though he had challenged her in some way.

"Okay," Lee answered, not reacting to her belligerent tone. "We appreciate that."

"Here's the deal," she said, leaning forward. Lee tried not to look at the dark line where her breasts met under the lacy shirt. "You don't ask who we are, and we tell you everything we can. Deal?"

Lee glanced at Chuck, who nodded.

"Deal." Their desire to remain anonymous meant they were probably runaways. Petty thieves too, maybe, drug users possibly—but mostly they were just scared kids.

"Okay," the girl said. Her voice was husky, smoky as her

kohl-lined eyes—whether from too many cigarettes or drugs, he couldn't tell.

"You have to understand our culture," the girl said. "We stick together, right?"

"I can appreciate that," Lee replied. "I'll be grateful for anything you can tell us."

"Okay." She took a deep breath and looked at her companions, who sat watching her. "She turned up about a month ago at a rave in an abandoned building on Avenue C. Told us her name was Pamela. No last name, just Pamela. Then she turned up one night at CBGB around midnight. Wasn't that it, Scott?" she said to the larger boy.

CBGB (Country, Blue Grass, and Blues) was a legendary music club on the Bowery, home to many punk and heavy metal bands in its thirty-year history. Lee's apartment on East Seventh Street was just around the corner.

The larger boy shrugged uncomfortably, as if trying to loosen something from his shoulder. "Yeah, around then." His voice shook and jumped a little, as though it had only just broken. Lee wondered how old he was.

"How was she dressed? What did she say?" Chuck asked, but his eagerness made the girl more wary. She flicked a strand of black hair from her face.

"She was dressed like a nice girl—middle class, all that. I don't think she's from around here."

"What makes you say that?" Butts asked.

"Her accent—it was different. I don't know how, but different."

The smaller of the boys spoke. "New England. She was from New England."

Both Chuck and Lee turned to study him. He didn't really seem like he belonged with the other two. There was also an air about him, a thoughtful, refined quality, as though he were a scholar moonlighting among truckers.

"You sure about that?" Lee asked.

"Freddy's good with accents and stuff like that," the girl said.

"New England," he repeated. "I have cousins up there. I recognize the accent."

"Okay," Butts said. "New England's a pretty big place. Can you narrow it down, give us a state, at least?"

Freddy frowned. "Uh, New Hampshire—Maine, maybe. Not sure about that."

"What else can you tell us about her?" said Chuck.

The girl bit her lip. "Well, she didn't do drugs or anything, right, Scott?"

"Yeah," he said, looking at his shoes. "Went to a rave with us but wouldn't drop any E. Said she'd heard of kids dying after taking it."

"E?" said Lee. "What's that?"

"Ecstasy," said Butts. "It's a big rave drug."

"She ever mention friends, family, anything back home?" Chuck asked.

The three kids looked at each other, as if they were trying to decide how much to reveal.

"She said one time that her folks didn't understand her," the girl said. "But hey, take a number, right?"

"So she didn't give any specifics?" said Butts.

Scott replied without taking his eyes off the girl. "Told me one time her dad was mean, and mom was a wimp."

"No mention of friends or towns or last name?" Lee asked.

Freddy shook his head. "I got the feeling she didn't want to be found . . . like she was hiding out."

"For sure," the girl said. "She was hiding out. I asked one time what it was like where she came from, and she said she didn't want to talk about it."

"She have a boyfriend or anything?" said Butts.

Again the three of them exchanged a glance.

"Not really," said the girl. "Had sex with a couple of guys. Had a weakness for losers. Nothing serious."

Scott averted his eyes, and the other two avoided looking at him. Scott clearly had been one of her sex partners—the question answered was whether he was the *last* one.

"What about jewelry?" Lee asked. "Did she wear anything special?"

"She hardly wore any—kind of stuck out, actually," said the girl. "But we accepted her even if she looked different."

"That's real big of you," Butts muttered. Lee and Chuck glared at him.

"She did wear something around her neck all the time," Freddy said. "A little silver cross, I think. I remember because someone asked if she was Catholic, and she said no, her grandmother had given her the necklace."

Lee felt the blood rush to his head.

"Are you sure about that?"

"Yeah," Freddy replied. "It was real pretty. Never saw her without it."

Lee looked at Chuck, who was biting his lower lip.

"Is that right?" he said, looking at the others.

The girl picked at her fingernails. They were long and pointed, with tiny death's-head emblems on each nail. "Yeah. I saw the cross. At first I thought it was like, ironic, you know, but she wasn't really the ironic type."

Lee turned to Scott. "Did she wear it during sex?"

The boy's face turned a mottled, boiled-lobster red, and Lee felt sorry for putting him on the spot.

"Yeah," he answered in a barely audible voice.

"Can you describe it exactly?"

"Uh, silver . . . just plain silver, that's all." He held up his thumb and forefinger. "About this big."

"Okay," said Chuck. "Anything else you can tell us?"

The kids looked at one another, and all of them shook their heads.

"If you think of anything—anything at all—you can call

us day or night," Chuck said, handing them each a business card. "You've been really helpful," he added, escorting them out the door. "Thanks again."

The girl stopped and looked at him. "Whatever. Just catch that guy, okay?"

"Don't worry, we will," Chuck replied.

Just then Chuck's cell phone rang.

"Morton here," he said, leaning against the wall. He looked exhausted; Lee could see the toll the investigation was taking on his friend.

After listening for a moment, Chuck said, "Are you sure?" After another pause, he said, "Okay. Thanks anyway," and hung up.

"What is it?" Lee asked.

"That was Delaney from the Ninth Precinct. He sent his guys over there right after I called, but they couldn't find the bullet."

"Are you sure it was the right lamppost?"

"Oh, it was the right one—had a deep dent in it. But the bullet was gone. Looks like the shooter got there first and dug it out himself."

"Christ," Lee said. "Whoever this is, he's good at covering his tracks."

"He's got to slip up sooner or later."

Lee wished he shared his friend's confidence. His cell phone beeped, and a shiver shot through him as he fumbled to dig it out of his pocket. Another text message:

I'm watching her too.

He stared at it, then handed the phone to Chuck.

"What's this about?" Chuck said after reading it.

Lee told him about the text message of the day before.

"Your sister?" Chuck said, puzzlement on his squarely handsome face.

"What else could it be about? Laura was wearing a red dress when she disappeared."

"But no one knows that except—"

"Exactly. How did he find out?"

"And is this even the same guy?" Chuck said. "How do we know these messages are from the . . . the killer?" He resisted using the name Butts had chosen for the killer. He thought "the Slasher" sounded lurid and distasteful.

"We don't," Lee answered, but in his mind there wasn't much doubt.

"I'll see what we can do about tracing the messages," Chuck said. "And starting tomorrow, you'll be under surveillance."

What neither of them said was that if the Slasher was talking about watching his sister, it meant that Laura was still alive.

Chapter Twenty-four

"Who among us can say he's never had a violent fantasy?"

John Paul Nelson looked over the assembly of students, who looked back at him uncomfortably, as if he had just accused them personally of being criminals.

Lee sat in the back of the lecture hall, watching as Nelson surveyed the young faces, blank as unformed clay. It was Monday morning, and today the heat was on with a vengeance. Hisses of steam erupted at irregular intervals from the radiators lining the assembly room walls. As soon as the lecture was over, Lee planned to give Nelson Chuck's urgent invitation to join their investigation. He had tried to reach Nelson by phone the day before without success—sometimes, he knew, Nelson would turn off both his phone and answering machine.

"Anybody?" Nelson continued, a smile struggling to break through the corners of his mouth. "So you've all had a violent fantasy at one time or another in your life, then. Good— then you'll be able to follow what I'm about to say next." He picked up the remote and aimed it at the slide projector.

One click and a familiar face appeared on the screen: the

hangdog, boyish features of Jeffrey Dahmer, with his sad, basset hound eyes and splotch of blond bangs. A murmur floated up from the crowd and dissipated, smokelike, when Nelson turned to face them.

"I see most of you recognize him. Ask yourselves: what separates him from us?"

The blond girl snaked an arm tentatively into the air.

"Yes?" Nelson said.

"Uh . . . nothing, sir."

"Nothing? You mean you don't have an answer?

She cleared her throat and pushed a strand of straight pale bangs from her eyes. "No, sir; I mean 'nothing' as in nothing separates us."

"That's an interesting point of view. Would you care to elaborate?"

The girl shifted in her seat and tightened her grip on her notebook.

"What I mean is that they're more like us than us than they are different from us. I mean, they're different in degree but not in kind, you might say."

Nelson raised his left eyebrow. "Nicely done, Ms. Davenport—I couldn't have put it better myself."

Lee smiled. For all his arrogance, Nelson was always ready with praise for students who asserted their own opinions. Lee had never really studied Dahmer's face before, but now, seeing him closely, he looked lost, so lost, like a little boy abandoned by his parents—which, of course, he was.

Nelson cleared his throat. "Mr. Dahmer was not an alien, a scientific oddity, an exotic species of some kind—a mutation, a marsupial, or a manta ray."

He paused and looked at Ms. Davenport, who gazed up at him with rapturous devotion.

"Alike in kind," he mused. "I want you all to consider Ms. Davenport's felicitous phrasing. We are all alike in kind—even the most degraded, despised, or dispossessed."

He walked back to the slide projector and picked up the remote again. A click and Dahmer's face disappeared and was replaced by a colorful illustration. Two interwoven strands—one red, the other blue—climbed like vines around one another, twisting in and out in perfect symmetry.

"This is what we all share: DNA, the double helix, the structure of life as we know it. Or perhaps this is only the starting point, and everything we are cannot be reduced to ink stains on a piece of paper." He clicked again, and a symmetrical, dark-on-white design appeared—a black splash of ink that Lee recognized immediately as a Rorschach blot.

"What is this?" Nelson asked, stroking his chin. "A butterfly? Or maybe an anvil? Or do some of you see a manta ray? Or a uterus? How about a dead body? If you do see a dead body, are you a serial killer in the making? Or maybe the serial killer is so repressed that he's the one who sees the butterfly?"

He seated himself on the edge of the desk and swung his right leg back and forth. "Flaubert famously said, 'Madame Bovary, c'est moi.' In order to write about a character, a writer insinuates himself into the character's mind—slips into his skin, as it were. The criminal profiler must do the same, like the actor who becomes the character he plays."

The theater had certainly lost a gifted actor when Nelson turned to a career in psychology. With his forceful personality, resonant voice, and charisma, Lee thought Nelson would have been a natural for the stage.

"For most of the repeat offenders we have come to know as serial killers, fantasy plays an enormous role. Often, their very identity represents a kind of fantasy: Ted Bundy, the concerned citizen, political activist, and loving friend; or John Wayne Gacy, the community organizer, Rotary member, and friendly clown who performed at children's parties. These were facades created to hide a darker personality the offender wishes to keep hidden from society."

He paused to let this sink in and drank from a bottle of Evian water on his desk. Lee thought Nelson looked tired, the lines under his blue eyes deepened. He leaned against the desk again and crossed his arms.

"R. D. Laing said that the more identity *is* fantasy, the more intensely it is defended. Doesn't that make sense? If you *know* who you are, then there's no need to defend against an attack—real or imagined—because you're secure in your knowledge. But even though the subject knows on some level that his false self is unreal, the alternative is unthinkable: not just death, but complete annihilation.

"The subject can't see that maybe his false self could be replaced by a real, authentic one. His tragedy is that he can't see what lies beyond—to him it appears to be an endless void in which he wanders like a zombie, a creature ostracized from human society, doomed to walk the earth, empty eyes staring vacantly out of a face with no mind, a body with no soul.

"And so he defends this false identity with all the ferocity of a lioness fighting to save her cubs—because his instinct for self-preservation tells him to."

Ms. Davenport raised her hand. "So are you saying in effect that with these people, there's 'no there there'?"

Nelson smiled. "Pithy as usual, Ms. Davenport." He turned to the rest of the class. "Ms. Davenport here has summed up my whole complex theory in a few words—but essentially, she has it. The shell the offender constructs for the outside world is no more 'real' than the fantasy life he lives in private."

He leaned forward, and his face was very earnest, almost vulnerable. "Most of us take our identities for granted. You, Ms. Davenport, for example. Let's say you're the first child, the smart one, the organizer, efficient and responsible. Your mother and your siblings could always count on you, and you knew that about yourself before you remember having language. Knowing this about yourself gave you a certain sense of security in the world."

Ms. Davenport blushed, a deep purple that spread from the base of her neck to the thin blue veins on her forehead.

Nelson continued. "I don't know anything about Ms. Davenport's family, of course. But let's just say she had a younger brother who was the family clown, the funny one, a little irresponsible maybe, but he could always make people laugh, and that gave him some security, a sense of who *he* was.

"My point is that we all take these things for granted—by the time we can verbalize *who* we are, we already have a sense of it from the way other people relate to us, and the way we relate to them.

"But for the person who goes on to become a serial offender, this is not the case. He is lacking a basic sense of who he is, and consequently has a sense at times *of being nobody at all.* He feels impotent and powerless. So he creates a fantasy world that is that exact *reverse* of what he perceives to be reality: a world in which he is omnipotent, is all powerful, and has total control over others. This control most often involves violent sexual fantasies—again, the exact *reverse* of what he perceives on another level as reality: total *rejection* of him by women (or men, if he is homosexual).

"Jeffrey Dahmer cut off his victims' heads and put them in his freezer *so they wouldn't leave him.* That level of desperation is directly related to the level of rage these criminals express against their victims—who are often substitutes for people in their lives who did in fact harm them. So, for example, a vicious killer of women could be acting out rage toward his emotionally abusive mother."

Nelson looked out over the room of upturned faces. "What's the difference between a killer's signature and his MO?" Nelson inquired, leaning back on his heels. "Yes, Ms. Davenport?"

"The MO is short for modus operandi—the way a killer

usually operates—but it can change. The signature refers to the repetitive ritualistic acts, often unnecessary for the commission of the crime, but which are necessary to the killer in order for him to receive emotional or sexual satisfaction from his crime."

"What might constitute a signature, for example?"

The skinny blond boy with the raspy voice shot up a hand. "Yes?"

"Things like postmortem mutilation or the way the body is posed—those could be signatures, for example."

"Right again." Nelson smiled. "A signature is deeply significant to the killer—and to the criminal profiler—because it arises out of some unconscious drive or obsession, and does not change in its basic essence, though it may evolve."

A dark-haired boy in the front row raised his hand. "Evolve? What do you mean by that?"

"Well, for example, the posing of the body may become more elaborate, more detailed—the Boston Strangler's, the Green River Killer's, and Jack the Ripper's victims all had certain similarities, but in all these cases the rituals escalated and become more ornate as time went on. This represents the killer becoming more at ease with what he does—he feels freer to act out his fantasy in increasing detail. Or, in a mentally ill, disorganized killer, it can represent the increasing pressure of his mental illness."

Nelson glanced at his watch. "Okay, that's it. Don't forget to do the reading I've assigned for our next class."

As the students filed out, Lee walked up the side aisle to where Nelson stood gathering his notes and slides. When Nelsen looked up and saw his friend, he smiled, but his smile faded when he saw Lee's expression.

"Oh no," he said. "There's been another one?"

"I'm afraid so. Chuck wanted me to ask—do you think you could—"

"He wants me to consult?" Nelson sounded as though he

was trying to hide his pleasure at being asked to join the investigation.

"If you're not too busy."

"Of course not." He paused and studied Lee, his freckled face serious. "How do you feel about my coming on board?"

"I'd be honored. And I have a feeling we're going to need all the help we can get."

Chapter Twenty-five

Detective Leonard Butts looked around Chuck Morton's office as though he had found himself in the den of a small and rather dirty burrowing animal. He studied the chair nearest him as if calculating the number and severity of diseases he might contract by sitting in it, then lowered himself into it with an air of resignation. Lee glanced at Chuck to see if he noticed Butts's attitude, but if he did, he didn't react. Morton walked over to his desk and perched on the edge of it, his muscular arms folded. Nelson sat in a chair in the corner, a paper cup of coffee held between his freckled fingers. Detective Florette sat in the opposite corner, looking like he had stepped straight off the cover of *GQ*—blue striped Brooks Brothers shirt with French cuffs, black Givenchy loafers polished to a glossy sheen. They had all been waiting, somewhat uncomfortably, for Butts to appear.

"Well?" Nelson said. "What have you got?"

Morton picked up a manila envelope from his desk and tossed it to Nelson, who caught it with his left hand.

"Brooklyn," Morton said, rubbing his eyes. "She was found

Saturday. Same MO—strangulation, mutilation, left on the altar."

Nelson raised his left eyebrow, which could signal anything from surprise to disgust. Nelson looked at the photos in the file and then turned to Lee.

"You went to the crime scene?"

"Yes. There was a difference this time: there was evidence of a struggle—a lot of it."

Chuck rubbed his forehead wearily. "This time the pathologist said the wounds were ante-mortem."

Nelson raised an eyebrow. "So now he's torturing them before he kills."

"Yeah."

"That means either he's restraining them physically or chemically," Nelson mused. "Is the tox screen in yet?"

"Nope," said Detective Butts.

Nelson stared at him.

"Detective Butts is the primary on this case," Morton said, "since the first vic turned up in his precinct. I'll be overseeing the investigation from here, but for day-to-day details go to him."

Detective Butts shifted in his chair, a look of satisfaction on his broad, pockmarked face.

"Mmm," Nelson said, placing the photos on Chuck's desk. "What do we know about the victims?"

"The first one we know for sure was his was Marie Kelleher," Butts replied with a glance at Lee. "A sophomore at Fordham. Nice Catholic girl, religion major, steady boyfriend, no known enemies."

"Yeah, right," Nelson muttered. He looked down at the stack of photographs. "What about this girl?"

Detective Florette held up the crime scene report. "Annie O'Donnell, twenty-one years old, a senior at Brooklyn College, philosophy major. Ditto with the nice Catholic girl. Boyfriend—not so steady, but seems like a nice kid."

"So he goes for nice girls," Nelson remarked, staring out of the grimy windows at the gray February sky. "If this Jane Doe Number Five—"

"Pamela," Lee said.

"Right. If she's his too, she's probably a nice girl as well."

"Okay," said Morton to Lee. "What can you tell us so far?"

"Well, first of all," Lee said, "these fantasies have been in place for a long time—way before he committed his first murder."

Detective Butts stared at him. "So now you're a mind reader?"

"Okay, Detective, that's enough," Chuck snapped. He turned to Lee. "How do you know that?"

"In part because it's usually true of serial killers, but here in particular the crime is very specific, very ritualized. There's been a lot of forethought and planning—it's not in any way an impulse killing." He glanced over at Nelson, who nodded his approval.

"Okay," said Morton. "What else?"

"He's likely to have a history of arson, abuse of animals, maybe a few arrests for Peeping Tom type activities—maybe even stalking. On the other hand, he may have no criminal record at all."

"That's not much of a help," Butts muttered.

"We can infer a lot from the way he leaves the victims. He displays them in a very specific way—"

"No kiddin'," Butts muttered under his breath.

"—but it's not for us."

"Really?" Florette said. "Then who *is* it for?"

"If we knew that we'd have him," Nelson grumbled.

"He's motivated by rage," Lee said, "but it's directed at God as much as at women. He defiles these women *before God*, so he's taunting God as much as he's taunting us."

Butts leaned forward in his chair, which creaked on its ancient hinges. It was an old-fashioned office chair on rollers, the kind of heavy oak furniture common in the 1930s. Chuck's desk sergeant had brought it into the office to accommodate the extra people. "What about hair, fiber, prints on the second girl?" he asked.

Morton shook his head. "Nothing."

"But she put up a fight this time," Florette pointed out.

"Not only that, but he brought her to the church conscious this time—last time he just used one as a dump site," Butts added.

Chuck picked up the glass paperweight on his desk and tossed it lightly from one hand to the other. "We're pretty sure he's wearing gloves."

Lee frowned. "Lack of forensic evidence means he's knowledgeable in the field of criminal investigation."

"Right," Nelson agreed, leaning against the dirty radiator, which hissed at him in protest. "Probably reads detective magazines. Maybe even has fantasies of being a cop. You might look through your files to see who's applied but been rejected in the last few years."

Morton groaned. "That could take forever. Do you realize how many inquiries we have in a given year?"

"Hey, maybe he *is* a cop," Butts suggested. When the rest of them stared at him, he said, "Look, I just don't think we should entirely eliminate the possibility. Some of those guys are pretty weird, lemme tell you."

"Detective Butts has a point," Lee said. "The worst thing we can do right now is to close off any options."

"What I don't get," Florette said, "is why there's no sign of sexual molestation. I mean, the knife is very phallic—"

"But a phallic substitute," Lee pointed out. "Since there's no sign of penetration, I think he could be a virgin."

Nelson raised an eyebrow.

"He's spent his life converting any sexual thoughts he

might have toward women into religious impulses," Lee continued.

"Until he decides to kill them," Florette pointed out. ·

"Which would mean we're dealing with someone who is extremely withdrawn in his personal and social life," Lee continued. He turned to Nelson. "He might have fantasized about being in law enforcement, but I doubt he ever acted on those fantasies. He'd be too much of an introvert." ·

Nelson grunted. "Maybe." He took a sip from a paper coffee cup, made a face, and put the cup back down on the desk.

"Not only that," Lee went on, "but from a geographic point of view, it's a very odd profile."

"What do you mean?" said Florette.

"Well, usually killers choose victims within a certain radius of where they live—places where they feel comfortable. But these two locations are miles away, in different boroughs."

"So maybe he has a job that allows him to travel," Florette suggested. "Some kind of work having to do with churches."

"Or it could be an attempt to cover his trail so we can't use geographic profiling on him," Lee mused.

"That would indicate tremendous sophistication about crime investigation on his part," Nelson pointed out.

"What about the person who took a shot at you?" Chuck asked Lee. "Isn't it possible that's—"

"What?" Nelson growled, turning to Lee. "You didn't tell me about that."

Lee told him about the incident on Third Avenue. "But there may not be a connection," he added. "I don't see this guy as a shooter."

"Yeah, that would really change the profile," Nelson agreed.

"What else you got?" Butts asked, getting up to stretch his stubby legs. "Isn't there *anything*?"

"He doesn't fit neatly into any particular category of killer," Lee said, "which makes it harder to get a fix on him."

"But that's not that unusual," Nelson said.

"I'd call a sexual killer who's a virgin pretty damn unusual," Butts grumbled, plopping back down in his chair.

"That's another part of the puzzle, isn't it?" Florette responded, straightening his immaculate starched cuffs.

"Right," said Nelson. "With a guy like this, at some point sex and violence become linked in his mind—"

"—and to religion," Lee added.

"There's another angle on the altar motif," Florette pointed out. "It's where couples are married."

"Good point!" said Butts. He tossed an empty coffee cup toward the wastebasket and missed. With a groan, he heaved his bulky body out of his chair, plucked the cup off the floor, and deposited it in the basket.

"Yes," Lee agreed. "And I think there's little doubt that he's Catholic, since both bodies were found in Catholic churches."

"I'd agree with that," Nelson said, "but I'm not sure I go along with the virgin thing. He could just be sexually inadequate—impotent, maybe."

"What else can you say about him?" asked Chuck.

"He's likely to be of a similar socioeconomic level as his victims, a middle-class Catholic—which is one reason they'd feel comfortable around him," said Lee.

"But he's a virgin, huh?" Butts said. "So how old is this guy—thirteen?"

"Well, he's obviously arrested emotionally, but I'd put him in his early to mid twenties," Lee replied, "close to the victims in age."

"Right," Nelson agreed. "And he lives with—"

"With his mother or another female relative," Lee finished for him.

Chuck looked at Nelson, who was searching through the coffee cups on the desk for one that still had coffee in it.

"Of course, his chronological age could be older," Lee mused. "For example, if an offender spends time in jail, he can emerge after a number of years at the same emotional age as when he was incarcerated."

"You mean like Arthur Shawcross," said Nelson.

"Exactly."

Florette leaned back in his chair and frowned. "The Genesee River Strangler?"

"Right," Lee replied. "He was incarcerated for fifteen years for murder, and when he got out of prison he went right back to killing—with pretty much the same maturity level as when he went in."

"Jeez," Butts said. "So we could be lookin' for a middle-aged guy after all?"

"It's possible," Lee admitted.

"Shawcross was pretty stupid, though," Nelson pointed out. "This guy is much smarter."

"What about his method?" Chuck said. "Strangulation is a very up close and personal way to kill someone. I mean, there's rage there, but it's a pretty controlled rage."

"I know this is a stretch," Lee said, "but I think there's also a clue in the way he strangles them."

"Slowly, you mean?" Butts asked.

"Well, yes. I think there's significance to it."

"He wants to hold the power of life and death in his hands as long as possible," Nelson said.

"Yes, there's that," Lee said, "but I think it's also something to do with breathing."

"What do you mean?" asked Chuck, fishing a few bottles of water out of the small refrigerator next to his desk.

"Well, maybe he has trouble breathing—a chronic condition of some kind. I know it sounds odd, but he's suffering along with them even as he kills them."

"What kind of chronic condition?" Butts said, holding out his hand for a bottle of water, which Chuck tossed to him.

"I don't really know . . . bronchitis, allergies . . . asthma, maybe. He's too young for emphysema," Lee said.

"Interesting," Nelson mused, "but a bit thin on evidence, don't you think?"

"I told you it was a stretch. There's something else," Lee added.

The others turned to him expectantly.

"I know what he takes from them."

"Really?" Nelson asked, leaning forward.

"He takes the crosses they wear around their necks. Her boyfriend said that Marie always wore hers, but it wasn't on her body. And the same thing with Pamela, according to her friends. I'll lay odds that Annie O'Donnell wore one too."

"Taking jewelry from the victim is not at all uncommon," Nelson pointed out, taking the bottle of water Chuck offered him.

"He didn't take just *any* jewelry," Lee said. "He took a cross. I think it's significant. It may relate to the victomology—how he chooses his victims."

Butts took a swig of Poland Spring and frowned. "Yeah? How so?"

"He's after good Catholic girls who wear crosses around their necks."

Lee's cell phone beeped, indicating he had a text message. He fished around for it in his pocket, his heart pounding.

When he read the message, though, it simply said:

Hey, Boss, when can we meet?

Relief flooded his veins like a sweet river. It was only Eddie. He had completely forgotten Eddie was trying to reach him. He was a little surprised to see Eddie sending text messages—it didn't seem like his style—but he was glad to hear from him.

"Okay," Butts was saying. "So all we have to do is find a loser who fantasizes a lot and lives with his mother. Why don't we just go hang out at a Star Trek convention? You know what we got on this guy? We got bupkes—that's what."

Nelson smiled at him, but it wasn't really a smile—it was a challenge.

"Well," he said, "we'll all just have to work harder, won't we?"

Chapter Twenty-six

Chuck Morton walked down the long cold corridor of the city morgue, his footsteps sharp as gunshots. Of all his duties as a cop, he hated this one the most. As he approached the middle-aged couple at the end of the hall, huddled together, desperately clinging to one another, he recognized the body language. He'd seen it more times than he cared to remember. He took a deep breath as he got closer. The woman was transfixed on the plate-glass window in front of her, but the man turned his head toward him as Chuck approached. On his face, ravaged by worry, was written an unspoken plea Chuck had seen too many times: *Tell me this isn't happening—isn't it possible you've made a mistake*? Chuck looked through the window at the sheet-draped body on the steel gurney and braced himself for the inevitable flow of grief that would follow.

"Mr. O'Donnell?"

"Yes?" His voice was wary. He was tall, with thick sandy hair.

"I'm Detective Chuck Morton. We need you to—"

The woman interrupted, her voice shrill with pain. "It

can't be her! Not Annie—who would want to hurt her?" She clung to her husband's arm, as if that were the only thing preventing her from collapsing onto the floor. Her eyes searched Chuck's face for any hint of reassurance. Her curly dark hair—just like her daughter's—was in disarray, and she looked as if she hadn't slept for days. Her skin was pale, and under the green glow of the fluorescent lights it was a pasty, unhealthy color.

"I'm so sorry, Mrs. O'Donnell," he said. His voice felt disembodied, as if it were coming from someone else. "But we need you to identify your daughter."

The husband turned to his wife. "Look, Margie, if you'd rather not, I can—"

"No!" She cut him off sharply. She turned to Chuck. "I'll stay with my husband."

Chuck nodded to the medical examiner's assistant, who had been waiting next to the body. He was a young Asian man with thick dark glasses. His straight black hair, plastered to his skull, gleamed wetly under the fluorescent lights. He pulled back the sheet, revealing the girl's face. Chuck was relieved to see that he avoided showing any of the rest of her mutilated body. Those details had not been released to the public or to any of the parents.

There was a sharp intake of breath from Mrs. O'Donnell, and silence for several moments—and then it started, a low, keening wail that began at the bottom of the scale and slid up to the high notes in one long gliding crescendo.

"No-o-o-o-o! *No-o-o-o-o!* Not my Annie, not my girl, my baby, not her! No-o-o-o-o!"

Chuck looked at Mr. O'Donnell, who had folded his wife in his arms as if she were a child. He stood there, rocking her, whispering to her, while Chuck watched miserably, hands at his sides. He hated the sheer senselessness of it all and the impotence he felt, but most of all he hated being a witness to these people's grief. It felt like an invasion of their privacy, as if they were being violated all over again. It ran counter to his own deep longing for privacy, his reticence toward any public display of emotion.

He laid a hand gently on the man's shoulder.

"I have to go—stay as long as you like, and someone will see you out. I'm so sorry."

O'Donnell looked at him with glazed eyes, clearly in shock. Morton knew this, but he also knew there was nothing more he could do for them now—except to find their daughter's killer.

Chuck's cell phone rang.

"Excuse me for a moment," he said, grateful for the interruption, and ducked around the corner to answer it. "Morton here."

"Chuck, it's Lee."

"What's up?"

"There's a new twist—"

"What is it?" Chuck said in a lowered voice. The last thing he needed was the victim's parents to overhear his conversation.

"The priest found blood in the communion wine."

"*What?*"

"The priest at Saint Francis Xavier went in to prepare for the service tomorrow, and when he went to fill the communion wine carafe, he noticed something odd about it. Turns out there was blood in it."

"Oh, Jesus. So CSI never vetted that—"

"Well, they searched the whole church, but that room was way in the back, and it was locked, with no signs of tampering. I mean, they can go back and dust for prints, but if he didn't leave them at the crime scene, I doubt he got sloppy when he tampered with the communion wine."

"Good lord. Send it to the lab for DNA analysis to find out if it's her blood."

"Butts already did that." There was a pause. Then, sounding reluctant, Lee added, "You know what this means."

"What?"

"He's evolving."

Chuck clicked off his cell phone and looked around at the shiny, antiseptic walls of the morgue, his forehead burning with rage. For the first time, he thought of the killer by the name Butts had picked out for him. *You sicko,* he said under his breath. *You goddamn psychopath Slasher . . . I'm coming for you, ready or not.*

Chapter Twenty-seven

The city sat in Sunday morning stillness as Lee and Nelson sat with Detective Florette in Chuck Morton's office studying crime scene photos. The traffic in the street below was reduced to a sluggish crawl, with none of the usual impatient honking or screeching of brakes, just an occasional engine starting up or the sound of an empty truck rattling by.

Chuck and Detective Butts had not yet arrived, and the three men sat in a lopsided circle around Chuck's desk. On the desk were the case files for Marie Kelleher, Annie O'Donnell, and finally, Jane Doe Number Five—or Pamela, as they now knew her. No one had come forward with a full identification of her yet.

After poor Annie was found, the Queens detective in charge of that investigation had grudgingly admitted there might be a connection and forwarded the files over to Chuck.

"Blood in the communion wine? Talk about gothic," Nelson said, draining the last of a day-old cup of coffee. He made a face as he swallowed the last of the bitter brew. Lee had just finished filling them all in on the latest development in the case.

"How long will it take to get the DNA back?" Nelson asked.

"Usually that kind of thing takes weeks," Lee replied, "unless they put a big rush on it."

"Does it really matter whose blood it is?" Florette asked. "I mean, for your profile of this guy?"

Nelson shrugged. "Not really—unless of course it's his blood. But I think we can safely assume it's hers."

"So this is part of his signature?" Florette said.

"Yeah," Lee answered. "And it means it's evolving, which is not necessarily a good thing."

"The tox screen on her blood came in negative," said Florette. "That means he's restraining her physically—so he has at least average strength."

"Not necessarily," said Nelson. "He could blindside her in the initial attack, knocking her unconscious before he ties her up."

Lee shifted uncomfortably in his chair. He realized he had been hoping the tox screen would be positive—at least if the victims were drugged, there was a chance their suffering would be dulled.

"There are some chemicals that wouldn't remain in the system long enough to show up in a tox screen," Chuck added.

"Some," Nelson agreed. "But he would have to have access to them."

"Okay, so he's getting close enough to them to attack them suddenly," said Florette. His deep, rich baritone sounded more like the cultivated voice of an FM classical announcer than a police detective. "If he's not alarming to his victims right away, maybe there's something about him that disarms them—that appeals to them, even."

"That's why killers like Bundy are so terrifying," Nelson said. "It's their appeal—he was killer, con man, and fantasy date all rolled into one."

"I'll tell you something else about him that is just like Bundy," Lee said.

"What's that?" Florette asked, sitting up a little straighter.

"Have you noticed the similarities in the victims?"

"You mean, they're all nice conservative Catholic girls?"

"No," Lee answered. "It's more specific than that."

Nelson looked at the photos spread out in front of him. "Oh, God—I didn't see it before, but you're right!"

"Right about what?" Florette asked.

"The hair," Nelson replied. "Remember how Bundy always chose women with straight dark hair, parted in the middle?"

Florette frowned. "I don't have quite the same expertise you—"

Nelson interrupted him. "His victims all resembled a woman who had broken his heart—"

"But wasn't that a common hairstyle in the mid seventies when Bundy was operating?" Chuck pointed out.

"Fair enough," Lee said. "But the point we're trying to make is that there's a physical similarity between this guy's victims too, or at least there seems to be. They all have dark curly hair, cut short."

"You're right," Florette agreed.

"I think we should open our minds to another possibility," Lee suggested.

"What's that?" Florette asked.

"That there is more than one person involved."

"Oh, come on, Lee—" Nelson began.

"Just hear me out—"

"Doesn't this kind of killer work alone?" Florette asked.

"Yes, but occasionally you find them working in pairs," Lee replied. "A stronger, more dominant type with a submissive partner—Charles Ng, for example."

"He was the exception that proves the rule!" Nelson retorted irritably.

Charles Ng was one of the most sadistic and horribly deviant serial killers who ever lived—and a lot was known about him, because he videotaped his crimes. His sidekick Leonard Lake was the weaker but equally culpable partner in their rampage of kidnapping, torture, and murder of men and women in California in the 1980s.

"What if he was the 'assistant' or sidekick to a rapist say, five years ago—and he's since graduated to his own crimes?" Florette suggested.

"I actually think the nature of these killings indicate there could be two perpetrators working together," Lee said. "There is evidence of arrogance *and* gentleness—"

"What's 'gentle' about these crimes?" Chuck asked.

"The killer is someone who didn't seem threatening to his victims, which means he was probably shy and unassuming—"

"Or smooth and convincing, like Bundy," Nelson interjected.

"Then there are the physical difficulties of one perpetrator doing this all by himself," Lee went on.

"Yeah," Butts agreed. "It does seem kinda tricky."

"The girls were all low-risk victims who were left in public places," Lee continued. "And the carving is both arrogant and incredibly risky. At least one perpetrator is controlling and organized, with a sophisticated knowledge of forensic investigation."

"It's perfectly believable that it could be the work of one person," Nelson argued.

"If there are two killers," Lee continued, "we could expect the more submissive partner would be exhibiting odd behavior as the stress begins to get to him. People around him would notice this."

"What about the other guy?" Florette asked.

"If he is in a relationship of some kind, he would be controlling and possibly violent—though not necessarily physically violent. But he would certainly be manipulative and controlling. He might have a history of petty crimes: shoplifting, breaking and entering, that kind of thing. But he might not have a criminal record yet, depending on how old he is— or how lucky."

"What about these mysterious text messages you've been getting?" Chuck asked, changing the subject. "Do you think they're related?"

"I don't know," Lee replied. All attempts to trace them had been unsuccessful so far.

"What text messages?" Nelson asked. "I didn't hear anything about that."

The door was flung open, and Detective Butts stormed into the room, brandishing a newspaper over his head as though he were going to swat someone with it.

"What the hell is this?" he demanded, slapping the paper down on Morton's desk.

Nelson's eyes narrowed and hardened, as they did when he was dangerously irritated. Butts was oblivious to Nelson's mood, however; his square body was rigid with rage.

"Look at what these pansy reporters wrote! Where the hell do they get off writing this kind of crap?"

Lee looked down at the paper, its headline screaming out alarm:

Slasher Continues to Terrorize City
Police Baffled

"For Chrissake, talk about yellow journalism!" Butts fumed, shoving a chewed cigar stub into his mouth.

Florette snorted. "Well, what do you expect from the *Post*?"

"That's all we need, to have a goddamn panic on our hands!" Butts threw himself into the beat-up chair in front of the window and stared out moodily.

Lee looked down at the headline, and read the first paragraph of text. "*The killer is not content to merely kill, but must mutilate his victims in order to achieve his sick satis-*

faction . . . " He looked at Butts. "Where did they get this? This information wasn't released to the public." What he didn't say was that it was curious that the press had picked up on the nickname Butts himself had chosen for the killer.

"Who knows?" Butts replied. "They're goddamn vultures—scavengers makin' money off these girls' deaths."

"Well, if you put it that way, we are too," Florette pointed out.

Butts chewed viciously on his cigar, nearly biting it in two.

"It's not the same thing! We're workin' to *solve* this thing. Our job is about protecting people."

"Well, we're not going to get very far if someone keeps leaking things to the press," Lee pointed out.

Butts got up and tossed what was left of his cigar in the trash basket next to Morton's desk and sat in one of the captain's chairs scattered around the desk. "It probably was one of the geeks in the morgue, or maybe a CSI did it. Who knows? Could be anyone."

Chuck walked into the room, his face grim.

"We've got trouble," he said, sitting behind his desk. "Walker's lodged a formal complaint against you," he said to Lee.

Butts smacked the arm of his chair with his closed fist. *"Bastard!"*

"What does this mean for the investigation?" Lee asked.

Chuck picked up the glass paperweight from his desk and held it in both hands. "It's hard to say. Internal Affairs will have to evaluate the complaint and decide what to do about it."

"Can they take me off the case?" Lee asked.

Chuck put the paperweight down and put his hands in the air in a gesture of helplessness. "They can do anything they want."

Butts blinked, his homely face slack. *"Anything?"*

The relationship between Internal Affairs and the other

members of the police force was like the relationship between a prison warden and the incarcerated: watchful, wary, and mutually distrustful. Visitors from IA were as welcome in precinct houses as an infestation of head lice in an elementary school classroom.

The phone on the desk rang, and Chuck answered it.

"Morton here." He listened briefly and then he said, "Really? When? Where are they now? Okay, thanks."

He hung up and exhaled. "Jane Doe Number Five has been identified. Her parents just called and ID'd her photograph from our Web site."

Lee rose from his chair. "Who is she?"

"Name's Pamela Stavros. She's a runaway from New England. Parents are flying down from Maine today."

"Okay," Chuck said, "let's go over what we have." He read from aloud from an autopsy report on his desk. "Two of the autopsies indicated the presence of semen. One girl was on the pill, the other was found still wearing her diaphragm. The third girl used a condom. In each case there was sexual conduct shortly before her death, but no evidence of rape. In the case of Marie Kelleher and Annie O'Donnell, the boyfriends admit to having sex with the victims the night before they were found dead."

Lee stood up, his face rigid. "He watches them."

Chuck stared at him.

"You mean . . . ?"

"He watches them have sex—but he can't stand the feelings it stirs in him, so he has to kill them."

"So since they're the source of his arousal," Nelson said, "they have to die?"

"But that's not how he sees it. Somehow he manages to rationalize his acts."

"Maybe he sees himself as their savior, rescuing them from the sin of carnality?" Florette suggested.

"Yes, yes. That would make perfect sense," Lee agreed.

"Look, the mayor and the DA are both coming down hard on us," Chuck said, "so we're going to—"

"Round up the usual suspects?" Nelson suggested dryly.

"Bring in a few more known sex offenders for questioning," Morton finished, ignoring him.

They had already completed interviews of half a dozen known sex offenders. Nelson disdained to be present at any of these interviews, which he deemed a waste of time and taxpayers' money, but Detective Butts was keen on them.

"Go ahead," Nelson said. "But it won't do you any good."

"Yeah?" Butts challenged. "And why's that?"

"Because you won't find him that way."

Butts blew air out of his nostrils and rolled his eyes.

Chuck looked at Lee. "You agree?"

"I'm afraid so," he replied. "He'll have a history of abusing animals, maybe setting a few fires, but chances are he wasn't caught."

"I checked with VICAP again for crimes similar to this UNSUB," Florette said, flicking an invisible speck from his immaculate shirt. He seemed to enjoy using anagrams whenever possible. VICAP stood for Violent Criminal Apprehension Program and UNSUB was shorthand for Unknown Subject.

"VICAP could be useless for a guy like this," Nelson responded. "Up until now, he could have been flying under the radar."

"Oh, that's just *great*!" Butts said, biting off the end of a cigar and spitting it in the trash can. He frowned, the pockmarks on his forehead merging. "You said this was a sex crime."

"Like I said, this guy will probably have a history of cruelty to animals," Lee said. "Also possibly voyeurism and fetishistic behavior, maybe some arson—but arsonists are hard to catch, so he may not have any criminal record."

"Fetishism—you mean like a fixation on shoes or women's underwear, somethin' like that?"

"Right. And that isn't illegal."

"Not yet, anyway," Florette remarked glumly. "Though if this administration had its way—"

"Also, wouldn't that kind of behavior tend to be pretty private?" Chuck asked, turning to open a window. The frigid February air felt good as it rushed into the room.

"Right," said Lee. "He's a voyeur, obviously, but that too can be hard to spot, especially if he's careful. He's not breaking and entering to get his victims, so he's abducting them outside their homes."

"That means less chance of leaving forensic evidence behind," Chuck pointed out, bending down to pick up some papers the wind had blown off his desk.

"Exactly," Nelson said. "And the wide dispersal of victims means he's comfortable in a large geographic area."

Lee pointed to the map on the wall, placing his finger on the red tack indicating the location where Pamela Stavros's body had been found.

"One of the reasons it's important that we include Pamela Stavros as the first known victim is that most likely this is the borough where the killer lives."

Butts frowned again. "Really? How do you figure?"

"Well, he's most likely to live nearest to his first victim," Nelson said. "It's where he feels most comfortable—closest to home. After that, he's more likely to branch out, but statistically, he will kill for the first time close to home."

"He may have other attempts in his past, where he tried but failed to abduct a girl," Lee pointed out. "You should send that to the media for possible leads."

"Right," said Chuck.

"Isn't there usually a stressor of some kind that sets these guys off?" Florette asked.

"Usually, but not always," Lee replied.

"Like what?" Butts asked.

"Oh, it could be anything—loss of a job, death of a parent, being dumped by a girlfriend. Something like that . . . an event that a normal person could handle, but which sends these guys over the edge."

"Look, Annie O'Donnell's funeral is day after tomorrow," Chuck said. "I was thinking—"

"One of us should be there?" Nelson interrupted.

"Returning to the scene of the crime," Florette murmured, running his elegant fingertips over the arm of his chair.

"Some criminals get a lot of pleasure from observing the results of their crimes," Lee observed.

Butts frowned and kicked at the wastebasket. "That always really fries me, you know."

"Detective Butts," Nelson remarked, "I'm sure that we're all equally upset by these events, but do you think it's really necessary to express yourself constantly on the subject?"

Butts blinked twice, and his mouth moved like a fish gulping for air.

"All right, that's enough," said Chuck. "Let's focus."

"I'd like to cover the funeral," said Lee.

"Do you believe the UNSUB is likely to make an appearance?" Florette asked, removing a pair of glasses from his breast pocket and cleaning them with a crisp white handkerchief.

"It's not unusual for them to show up," Nelson replied.

"Okay," Chuck said. "You've got the funeral, Lee."

"But if he already took a shot at Lee—" Nelson protested, but Lee cut him off.

"We don't know whether the shot was even intended for me."

"Right," Chuck agreed. "And no one is likely pull out a gun at a daytime funeral in Westchester. It's not the same thing as shooting at someone on Third Avenue at night. Detective Florette, I'd like you to start an investigation of the churches involved so far—find out what, if anything, they have in common."

"Right," Florette said, rising from his chair. "I'll get right on it."

Lee looked around the room at the others. The mood had visibly darkened. Butts slumped back in his chair, forgetting all about picking a fight with Nelson. Somehow, putting a name to Jane Doe Number Five didn't help things. Now they had a name to go with a victim, but they still didn't have a killer.

Chapter Twenty-eight

Annie O'Donnell's funeral was held in Hastings, one of the quaint Westchester towns dotting the Hudson Valley like puffballs after a spring rain. Lee took Metro North from Grand Central, catching the 12:15 local train on the Harlem Line, arriving in Hastings in forty minutes flat. He had convinced Chuck to remove the plainclothes cops who had been tailing him, as their presence at the funeral would be too conspicuous. The train station was down by the water, but it wasn't far to the church. He walked up the long road that curved inland from the river. Hastings was perched on the bluffs that rose from the banks of the Hudson, its waterfront buildings looking down over the moody currents of the great river. Clouds swung low over the sluggishly moving gray water, and seagulls swooped low over the river's opaque surface, searching for fish.

The church was a modest white clapboard affair, not very grand by Catholic standards. Except for the sepia tones of the grass on the church lawn, black and gray dominated the landscape. The drab February sky hung low over the mourners, not even a suggestion of sunlight filtering through the flat gray cloud cover. The monochromatic setting, the dark suits of the mourners as they stood in a little clump outside the white wooden church, all reminded Lee of a scene from a black-and-white film. A shiny black hearse was parked in the driveway, waiting for the slow, stately crawl to the cemetery.

The ceremony was just ending as Lee arrived. As he walked up the flagstone path, one of the mourners emerged from the church carrying a bouquet of red carnations, bright as a splash of fresh blood against her black dress.

A solitary crow perched atop a low branch of a black oak, observing the scene with its head cocked to one side, its bright eyes sharp as pine needles. The tree's trunk was darkened by the recent rain, the rough black bark still visibly damp, tiny droplets of water tucked into the deep crevices. The crow gave a low, hoarse caw and took off from its branch, ascending rapidly into the dun-colored sky in a flurry of flapping wings.

Lee watched it rise and disappear over a copse of trees as a light mist fell on the already soggy ground. The small clump of journalists looked miserable, huddled under their huge black umbrellas, cameras tucked under their raincoats. He studied them. Most were young, probably greenhorns still on probation with their cranky, overstressed bosses. None of them had the look of established stars or even up-and-comers—this was hardly a plum assignment, covering the funeral of the unfortunate victim. The real stars would get to cover the discovery of the body, police press briefings, that kind of thing.

Lee watched the mourners leaving the church, searching for any unusual aspect of appearance or behavior that stuck out—anything that didn't quite fit. He didn't know exactly what he was looking for, but hoped he would recognize it when he saw it.

He scanned the crowd of mourners. Their faces were suitably solemn, some swollen and red-eyed from grief, most of them pale and pasty in the feeble sun. A tall, sandy-haired man with handsome Irish features emerged from the church, supporting a slight, black-haired woman on his arm. She wore a long black veil, but the devastation on her face was clear even through the gauzy material. Obviously they were Annie's parents. The daughter took after her mother, with her wavy black hair—the so-called Black Irish, whose curly dark hair was a remnant of their Italian conquerors of centuries past. Annie's mother had the same delicate white skin as her daughter, though, bespeaking her Northern European ancestry.

Her father had the kind of Irish good looks Lee saw all over New York City: square, broad forehead, deep-set blue eyes, his prominent jaw jutting out beneath a thin, determined mouth. His ruddy, wind-burned skin was the complexion of someone who spent his time out herding sheep on the moors instead of working at an accounting firm. He had the big, blunt hands of a shepherd, not an accountant.

The rest of the crowd was varied—friends and family, as well as neighbors and schoolmates. A dozen or so young people of college age gathered in a little group to one side. As the O'Donnells made their way down the church steps, the crowd parted for them, people stepping respectfully aside as the couple moved slowly toward the waiting cavalcade of automobiles. When Mrs. O'Donnell saw the hearse, she stumbled and lost her footing, collapsing forward. Half a dozen hands came up to steady her, and she continued on her slow pilgrimage. Her husband tightened his grip on her arm, his face a tight mask of grief and anger.

The family climbed into the limousines the funeral home had provided, as everyone else dispersed toward their own cars, leaving the journalists alone on the wet sidewalk in front of the church. Lee studied the mourners, but he couldn't see anything unusual about them. They all looked grief stricken, and everyone seemed to be there with at least one other person. Lee was quite certain that the killer, if he came, would be alone. There were a few young men who fit the age and physical profile, but they were with girlfriends or families, or were part of the group of Queens College students. Lee looked over the students, but it was highly unlikely that the Slasher was a college student, let alone one of Annie's classmates.

The television journalists stood around delivering their spiels into the cameras. Others were scribbling earnestly in notebooks, while a few more lit up cigarettes, hunched under raincoats pulled over their heads, shielding their matches from the rain. Lee turned to go—and then, out of the corner of his eye, he saw a figure standing apart from the rest of the press corps.

A thin young man in a dark blue raincoat stood leaning against a Douglas fir. Even under the bulky coat Lee could see that he had narrow shoulders, and his protruding wrists suggested a scrawny, underfed physique. He had long, thin neck and a prominent Adam's apple, but his head was bent over a notebook, so Lee couldn't see his face. There was something unsettling about him, the hunch of his shoulders perhaps, that reminded Lee of a vulture perched on a tree limb.

The man lifted his face to look at the column of departing cars, and Lee saw the delicate, almost feminine features—on a girl they would have been considered pretty. His face had a haunted quality, with sunken hollows beneath his cheeks and dark circles under his eyes, as though it had been a while since he'd had a good night's sleep. He looked about nineteen, but was probably twenty-five or so, Lee guessed. His most striking feature were his golden eyes, yellow as lamplight—wolf's eyes. Watchful and wary, they gleamed like gemstones in his pale face. Lee couldn't make out the name on the press pass hanging from the lapel of the blue raincoat, and he didn't want to stare. So far the young man hadn't noticed him. As he was watching, the man pulled something white from his pocket and put it to his mouth. At first Lee had the impression it was a pack of cigarettes, but then he realized the object was an inhaler. His stomach tightened as the stranger gave the plunger a single, well-practiced push, inhaled deeply, held his breath, then exhaled.

Lee's pulse raced as the man shoved the inhaler back into his pocket. *He's asthmatic!* Lee's palms began to sweat, and he tried not to stare at the man as he formulated a way to get closer to him without arousing his suspicion. He would approach and ask for a cigarette—no, that wouldn't do, when there were several journalists puffing away just a few yards from him. Something that wouldn't arouse suspicion, something. But as he was trying desperately to think of something, the man folded the notebook and put it into his coat pocket.

He looked around, until his eyes met Lee's, and a look passed between them. Lee couldn't be sure, but he thought it was a look of recognition on the other's part. The man's eyes locked with his, and—was it his imagination?—he gave a slight nod, as if to say, *Yes, it's me.* The ghost of a smile flickered on the pallid face. *He knows who I am,* Lee realized. The man pulled his coat around his lean body and strode rapidly around the side of the church.

Lee took off after him, but he was forced to go around a group of elderly mourners coming out of the church. Then, as he approached the gaggle of journalists, a short, balding man stepped forward.

"Excuse me, but aren't you with the NYPD?"

Taken off guard, Lee stared at him.

"Well, I—"

"Yeah, you're the profiler, right? The one who lost his sister?" the man said. "My buddy wrote the story about you a couple of years ago. I recognize you from your picture."

Lee groaned. He had been the unwilling subject of a

"human interest" story when he started working with the police department; someone at the city desk had gotten wind of his appointment, remembered his sister's disappearance, and decided it would make a good story. It did make a good story, but Lee did not enjoy the attention and publicity that followed.

"Are you working on this case?" the man continued, and then, without waiting for an answer, "Do you have any comments?"

The others, smelling blood, crowded around him, shouting out questions:

"How's it going?"

"Any leads?"

"What have you figured out about the Slasher?"

"Will he keep killing until you stop him?"

"I'm sorry," Lee said, "but I can't comment on an ongoing investigation." Standard fare, and he didn't suppose they would swallow it.

They didn't.

He struggled to push through them, murmuring apologies, but they trailed after him, sticking to him like so many leeches in black raincoats. He hurried around to the back of the church, turning the corner of the building just in time to see an old, dark-colored car peel around the bend in the road. He couldn't read the license plate, and he didn't know cars well enough to place the make of this one. It wasn't a late model, and he thought it was American—but he couldn't even be sure about that. Black or dark blue, dented left rear fender— that was all he could see.

The reporters crowded around him, barking out their questions.

"Do you think he'll strike again?"

"Are you any closer to solving it than you were?"

"Who else is on the special task force?"

"Are you going to bring in the FBI?"

When they saw that Lee wasn't going to give them anything, they broke up, peeling away one by one, tucking their notebooks into raincoat pockets before heading off to expense account lunches at local restaurants.

Well, if it is him, at least now I'm sure he owns a car, Lee thought. But he had been fairly certain of that already. Everything about this guy fit the profile—right down to the inhaler. Lee pulled his coat collar up to his ears and shoved his hands deep into his pockets. The rain was coming down harder now, cold little needles stinging his bare skin. He walked briskly toward the train station as the heavens let loose a torrent intense enough to wash clean the transgressions of an entire generation of sinners.

Chapter Twenty-nine

Later, back home in his apartment, Lee looked out the window at the softly falling rain. He thought about his earlier conversation on the phone with Chuck, who had been less than thrilled with his report of his visit to the funeral.

"Damn reporters—they're like goddamn locusts! I can't believe you couldn't even get a license plate number."

Lee had no good reply. He didn't feel comfortable vilifying the press, but he had to admit that they had gotten in his way.

"How do you suppose he got a press pass? Just forged one, I guess?"

"Probably."

Chuck was exasperated when Lee admitted that he didn't manage to read the name on his press pass.

"It was probably a pseudonym anyway," Lee pointed out.

He had seen the department sketch artist, just in case. Lee had made a vow to himself that he would not forget the lean, ascetic-looking face with the striking yellow eyes and high cheekbones, the Cupid's-bow curve of his mouth. He had looked like a lost little boy, until he smiled—and then he looked like a hungry wolf. The resulting sketch was pretty good, though it failed to convey the feeling Lee had of the twisted personality behind that smile. Butts had already shown the sketch to the victims' families, but none of them recognized him. That didn't surprise Lee—the killer wouldn't be anyone they knew. There was no one who resembled him in the VICAP files, either—again, not surprising. Although Lee still couldn't help feeling he had seen him before . . . but where? Try as he might, the memory remained shadowy in his mind.

Lee watched as raindrops gathered in rows on the windowsill, silent silver sentinels standing briefly shoulder to shoulder before sliding to the ground. *Why do we bother?* he thought. Why fight the same wars over and over, make the same mistakes, slaughter and enslave our fellow human beings? What was the point, really, if we weren't going to evolve as a species? Why should each generation drag themselves through the same tired territory as the one before, if mankind as a whole was not getting wiser, kinder, more enlightened? The mind-numbing repetitiveness of human history was exhausting.

He felt the old darkness descending, and stood up, forcing his mind away from this train of thought. He needed to monitor thoughts like these before they gained momentum. Depression was like an underground fault line in his emotional life, and he tried hard not fall into that long, slippery slide to the bottom. The wrong thought, a sudden flash of insight, morning sunlight coming in the window in a certain way—anything could set off an episode.

He forced himself to concentrate on the case files awaiting him on his desk. Just as he sat down at his desk, his cell phone beeped. He picked it up and looked at the screen: NEW TEXT MESSAGE. He forced himself to breathe more slowly as he scrolled down to see the message:

That was a close call. Better luck next time.

He put the cell phone down. *Better luck next time*. Now he was certain that not only had the Slasher posed as a journalist at Annie's funeral, but he had also sent Lee the messages about his sister. But how could he know details that were never released to the press? It was troubling . . . very troubling.

Lee started to dial Chuck, but as he did, his phone rang. He picked it up.

"Hello?"

"Heya, Boss. Whaddya know—I finally reached you!"

"Hi, Eddie."

"So what's up?"

Lee hesitated. He wasn't sure how much he should tell Eddie. After all, he wasn't part of the official investigative team. But ever since those dark nights at St. Vincent's, Eddie had been a confidant, confessor, and therapist all rolled into one.

"I think I saw him today."

"Jeez. Really?"

"Yeah. I'm pretty sure."

"How d'you know?"

"I don't really want to go into detail over the phone."

"'Fraid someone might be listening in?"

"No, not that." The truth was that Lee wanted to get back to work.

"Hey, you eat yet?"

"Uh, no."

"Okay, listen—meet me at the Taj in ten minutes, huh? I'll tell you what Diesel and Rhino have turned up."

The Taj Mahal was Eddie's favorite Indian restaurant on East Sixth Street, and it was exactly a block and a half from Lee's apartment.

Lee glanced at the clock above his desk. Six-thirty. He would have to eat sooner or later.

"Okay."

"Right. Ten minutes. See you then."

Lee left a message for Nelson on his home phone (Nelson didn't own a cell phone—he considered them a sign of the Apocalypse), and called Chuck on his cell. Chuck didn't answer, so Lee left a message for him too, threw on a coat, and left for the Taj Mahal.

When Lee arrived, Eddie was already seated, tucking into a basket of pappadam—paper-thin, crispy Indian bread studded with peppercorns. Like most of the other restaurants on Sixth Street, the Taj Mahal was small—long and narrow. Its walls were festooned with a dizzying assortment of decorative lights: colored fairy lights, red-hot chili pepper lanterns, and strings of Christmas lights. All of the Sixth Street restaurant owners seemed to have the same notion of interior decoration. It was always Christmas on Sixth Street. You could see the street from blocks away, flashing, sparkling, glittering, glowing. Lee had tried to come up with a theory to explain the phenomena—some kind of relationship between excessive lighting and spicy food, perhaps. He often imagined the money flowing into the coffers of Con Edison as a result of all of this unbridled luminatory enthusiasm.

Eddie was seated at his favorite table in the far corner, underneath a billowing canopy of purple cotton fabric. He waved to Lee as he entered.

"How's it goin', Boss?" he said, popping a piece of golden, crispy pappadam into his mouth. Eddie was in a good mood. But then, Eddie was always in a good mood in public—or pretending to be.

"Okay," Lee said, taking a seat across from him. "How are you doing?"

"Oh, just great. You know me—I always land on my feet."

Lee knew that wasn't true; a suicide attempt had put Eddie in the bed next to his at St. Vincent's. Eddie had slashed both wrists and lay on his bed in an SRO hotel, waiting to die. He hadn't bled out, though, when his neighbor at the Windermere Hotel found him. When Lee met him, his wrists were still heavily bandaged, and he was on daily doses of Haldol.

Lee must have glanced down at Eddie's wrists involuntarily, because Eddie looked at him sharply.

"Somethin' wrong, Boss?"

"No, I was just thinking."

"Yeah? About what?"

"About how circumstances bring people together. I mean, if you hadn't been my roommate at St. Vincent's, we wouldn't both be sitting here."

It was only after Lee played his words back in his head that he realized the implication of what he had just said: one or both of them might be dead.

"Coupla nut cases, that's what we are. I'll have the vindaloo, extra spicy," Eddie said to the approaching waiter without missing a beat.

The waiter wrote on his notepad and turned to Lee. "And you, sir?" He was a slim, handsome Indian man with very dark skin and a thatch of glistening black hair.

"I can never resist a good chicken kurma," Lee said, closing the menu. "Thanks."

"Very good, sir," the waiter replied. He picked up the menus and withdrew into the kitchen. Indian waiters were always so courteous they made Lee think of the days of the British Raj, when exaggerated manners and politeness covered a desire to murder the occupying white regime.

After the waiter had gone, Eddie leaned into Lee, his voice quieter.

"You, uh, been having them again?"

"What?"

"You know—urges." Eddie meant suicidal thoughts, but he never used those words, as if saying them would make it too real.

"No, not lately—thank God," Lee answered. He looked at Eddie. "How about you?"

"Naw . . . I'm fit as a fiddle!" Eddie responded a little too vigorously. "Strong as an ox, this boy."

As if to prove it, he gave a sharp smack to his stomach with his open hand. His belly, while thick, did look hard. Lee didn't believe him, though, and sensed an even greater restlessness in Eddie today—a disquieting, reckless energy.

"Are you taking your lithium?"

"Sure I am!" Eddie shot back, a little too fast. Lee was concerned, but didn't want to press his luck. Something told him that if he lingered on Eddie's mental health, his friend would shut down completely. Eddie was a great listener, and they had shared many things during that bleak week in St. Vincent's. Eddie was comfortable playing the role of confidant, but getting him to talk about his own problems was another thing. He liked being in control—in fact, he had let his bipolar disorder deteriorate because he enjoyed the manic phases too much. During that week in St. Vincent's, Eddie had talked about the feeling of freedom, energy, and power, the sweet illusion of omnipotence. It was seductive, and it wasn't hard to see how someone like Eddie could get used to weathering the depressive phases of his disease just so he could get back to the heady whirlwind of the manic state.

"Look, I think I got somethin' for you," Eddie said as he wolfed down the last of the pappadam.

"So you said."

"Oh, not that thing I called about the other day—that turned out to be nothin'. But this I think is really something."

"What is it?"

"A guy. A guy who may have seen somethin'."

"Yeah? This guy—who is he?"

Eddie looked around the restaurant as though checking for spies, but the only other customers at this hour were a young couple holding hands at the far side of the room. They whispered in the low, intimate tones of lovers, heads bent over the table, their hair shiny in the reflected glow of a thousand tiny lightbulbs.

"This guy is homeless, okay? Hangs out mostly in Prospect Park. Wouldn't make a great witness in court, but—well, you talk to him. See what you think."

"How did you find him?"

Eddie leaned forward. "Remember Diesel and Rhino?"

Lee laughed. "*Remember* them? You're kidding, right?"

Eddie grinned, displaying his crooked, yellowing teeth. "Okay, I guess you don't forget them too easily."

"No, you don't. They found him?"

Eddie shoved an entire samosa into his mouth. He chewed once, then swallowed. Lee was reminded of a crocodile—a smiling, yellow-toothed crocodile. "Yeah. They been sort of stakin' out the church, you know? Watchin' it to see who comes, who goes. And this guy's been there a couple a nights in a row. Goes to the soup kitchen on weekends."

"Okay," he said. "Let me know when and where."

Eddie's homely face spread into another broad grin. "Okay, Boss—you got it."

Chapter Thirty

They found him sitting on a bench not far from the Prospect Park Boathouse. That part of the park was usually busy, but today few people gathered near the marshy pond at the back of the boathouse. The man was long and thin as the reeds lining the banks of the lake. His stringy gray hair was tied back with a red sock, and he wore the matching sock on his left hand, with holes cut in it so that his fingers poked out. His bony right hand was bare, and the fingers twitched spasmodically from time to time.

His clothes were decent: a sturdy pair of brown corduroy trousers fastened with a leather belt, tied in a knot because the buckle was missing. Blue and green flannel shirt, also in good shape, over a long red undershirt, clumsily tucked into the pants, bits of it still poking out. A forest green down parka in good condition, wool socks, and leather Docksiders with thick soles completed his outfit. Either someone was taking care of him or he had hit a thrift store jackpot, Lee thought—either way, he was glad the man was warmly dressed. Being homeless wasn't any picnic even in the best weather, but it could be especially brutal in February.

He watched Lee and Eddie approach with a wary frown.

"Hiya," said Eddie. "Remember me?"

"Sure I remember you. You were here with your two body-guards." The man scrutinized Lee. "This guy doesn't look so impressive. What happened to the other two?"

Eddie laughed. "This is my weekend bodyguard."

The man's frown deepened. "No offense," he said to Lee, "but you don't look very scary."

"I'm not."

"My friend's name is Lee," Eddie said. "And I'm—"

"No, don't tell me," the man interrupted. "Larry. Elmer. Pete. Elijah."

"Eddie."

"Right, right—Eddie. I remember now. My friends call me Willow," he said to Lee. Then, with a chuckle that was more like a hiccough, he added, "My enemies don't call me. You won't tell them you saw me, will you?" he asked, his eyes searching Lee's face. His eyes were watery and blood-shot, but radiated a sharp intelligence.

His face was as long and thin as his body, with cheeks so sunken that they made his protruding buckteeth look even more prominent. His eyes were dark and deeply recessed in their sockets, and Lee didn't know if they were red-rimmed from booze, lack of sleep, disease, or just general ill health.

"Hey, don't worry," Eddie said. "We won't tell anyone. Here—we brought you somethin'." He dug a carton of Marl-boros out from under his jacket. Willow leapt up from the bench and snatched them up eagerly, his eyes gleaming.

"Thanks! How d'you know my brand?" he asked as he tore away the cellophane wrapping and dug out a pack. He ripped it open and extracted a cigarette, examining it, peer-ing at both ends. "Gotta check for microchips," he said, placing the cigarette in his mouth. He pulled a stainless-steel lighter from his pants pocket and lit the cigarette, sucking on it so deeply that Lee imagined his cheeks touching inside his mouth. He exhaled a plume of blue-gray smoke and smiled blissfully. The expression sat oddly on his lean features, making his face even more grotesque.

"Oh, that's better," he said, taking another deep drag before settling back down on the bench. The hand holding the cigarette was still, resting on his bony knee, but the other one danced about nervously. He picked at the green chipped paint on the bench, and that seemed to calm him somewhat. His eyes roamed the park, as if trying to spot potential spies and saboteurs. The only people in sight, though, were a young mother rolling a baby in a stroller, and an old man walking a decrepit Boston terrier. Owner and dog shuffled along, both of them arthritic, the dog's bulbous eyes cloudy with age. The man was wrapped in a red wool scarf under his parka, and the dog wore a little red wool coat made from the same material.

The pair didn't escape Willow's roving gaze. "Look at that!" he said. "Like master, like dog." He muttered something under his breath and took another drag of the cigarette, pulling at it with his whole body. He held in the smoke and then let it snake slowly out through his nostrils.

Eddie sat next to him. "So you told my friend that you had something for us? Some information—something you saw."

"I see a lot of things," Willow said, almost to himself. "I see a *lot* of things."

"Yeah, I know," Eddie replied. "But there was somethin' in particular you saw that we was interested in, remember?"

Instead of answering, Willow dug another cigarette from the pack and lit it with the first one, which he tossed over his shoulder. Lee's hopes sank—this man was a washout, a dead end. He had come all the way out to Prospect Park to watch a homeless schizophrenic smoke himself to death.

But then, to his surprise, Willow nodded. Looking around

one last time, he lowered his voice even more. "Okay, I'll tell you what I saw, right?"

"Right," Eddie said.

"If you promise not to tell the Feds. CIA, FBI—they all want to get me, you know?"

"Yeah," Eddie assured him. "Don't worry, we won't tell anyone."

"Plant microchips in your brain, that's what they do when they get you, you know. Did you know that?"

"I heard something' about it, yeah," Eddie said. "Now what was it you saw?"

"Well, it was this guy, you know, and what was weird about it was that he was taking trash *into* the church. I thought that was odd. Thought maybe he was one of the ones after me— I'm always on the lookout."

"Right, right," Eddie encouraged him. "This is All Souls Church, right?"

"Yeah."

"When was this?" Lee asked.

"Well, it was last Saturday night. I know 'cause that's the day they have their soup kitchen, and I always go. Well, sometimes they throw stuff out later in the day, so I was just poking around, you know—nothin' illegal."

"No, of course not," Lee reassured him.

"So it's Saturday evening and there's really no one else around, and then I see this guy."

"What he look like?" Eddie asked.

"Little guy—runty, you know? Like if he was a pup in a litter they woulda drowned him. Only they didn't, 'cause there he was."

Lee had the uncomfortable thought that it might have been better for everyone if someone had drowned the man they were pursuing.

"Runty like how?" said Eddie. "You mean deformed or something?"

"Naw, nothin' like that. Just small—short, you know—and skinny. Not as thin as me, maybe, but pretty damn skinny, I'll tell you."

"Did you get a look at his face at all?" said Lee.

Willow shook his head, loosening the sock holding his gray ponytail. Lee didn't want to think about what might be living inside that greasy nest of hair.

"Not real well—too dark. No moon that night, and one a' the street lamps was burned out—has been for a while. But I did see the light across the street shine on his forehead. He had a big forehead. High, y'know, like his hair is receding."

"This trash can he was carrying," Eddie said, "did it seem like it was full?"

"Yeah, that's the other weird thing," Willow said, scratching his head. "Who brings a full trash can *into* a building, you know? Weird."

"Did you see him bring anything back out?" Lee asked.

"Nope. I saw a guy light up on the corner, bummed a smoke from him. Didn't see anything after that."

"Do you remember how he was dressed?"

"Mmm . . . dark clothes. Raincoat sort of like the ones the Feds wear, except this guy was no Fed—not well enough fed for that. Hey, that's not bad," he said, smiling broadly, displaying a mouth badly in need of dentistry. Several teeth were chipped; others were missing altogether. "Not well enough *fed* for a *Fed*—hey, not bad." He gave a chuckle, a low rumbling sound of phlegm rattling in his lungs.

"Anything else?"

"Oh, yeah—there was one thing."

"What?"

"His breathing. It was wheezy, you know? Like a guy who's been smokin' too long—except he didn't light up or nothin'."

"Do you think you could identify him from a police sketch?"

Willow picked at a scab on his chin. "I don't know. Maybe. What's in it for me?"

"Okay, look," Lee said, "you've been really helpful. Is there anything we can get you—some food, a place to sleep?"

Willow held up the carton of cigarettes. "More of these?"

"Hey, look," Lee said, pulling five twenty-dollar bills from his wallet. "If I give you this, will you promise to spend some of it on food and shelter?"

Willow took the money and counted it. "You made a mistake, man—these are twenties."

"It's not a mistake. I want you to have them. But please buy some decent food for yourself, will you? And maybe a room at the Y?"

"Y-M-J-A," Willow sang softly as he stuffed the money into his shoe. "I can stay at the Y-M-J-A. Da da da da da da, I can get anything I want, at the Y-M-J-A." He looked at Lee. "I'm Jewish—get it?"

"Yes," Lee said. "I get it. You will? Promise?"

"Sure!" Willow sang out, but his attention was drawn by a passing jogger, a well-built young black man in red spandex.

"Now *he's* a Fed," Willow whispered. "You see? They've found me already—they move fast, lemme tell you." He began singing again. "Who needs a bunker in Iraq-aq-aq-aq-aq-aq?" He sang to the tune of the Billy Joel song, "Movin' Out." "If that's what's movin' in, I'm gettin' out."

Without saying good-bye, Willow stood up and wandered off in the direction of the boathouse.

Eddie looked at Lee. "Well, I guess that's all she wrote."

"Yeah," Lee said. "Listen, how can I reach you?"

"You can't," Eddie replied. "I'll call you."

Lee wanted to protest, but he knew there was nothing like pressure to drive Eddie even further away. And, as they walked out of the park, he was busy thinking about why someone would drag a trash can into a church in the middle of the night.

Chapter Thirty-one

Surely his mother wouldn't object to his spending time with this girl. She was so slight, so frail, more like a little bird, really, than a girl. A little sparrow—yes, that was it. She was exactly like a tiny, underfed sparrow, and he longed to take her in his arms and feed her until she fell asleep, contented and safe in his gentle embrace. It was nothing lustful; it was more like the feeling you might have toward a beloved pet, a desire to take care of them, to nurture them the way you might a puppy, or any helpless creature. What could be the harm in that?

He screwed his face up and put his hands over his ears, as if that would drown out the voice in his head, but the voice burrowed all the way through to his eardrums, making him dizzy. The memory of that first awful humiliation played like a tape in his head, from beginning to end.

Sam-u-el! How could you do that? How could you touch that nasty, nasty creature, that filthy little harlot? How could you do that to me—to Him? Do you want to make Jesus cry? Do you?

The wooden figurine of Jesus on the cross above her bed

looked down on him, disappointment carved into the wooden face. The tortured eyes implored him—him, Samuel—for help as if he could ease Jesus's suffering.

Sam-u-el! Look at me when I'm talking to you! Did you think Jesus wouldn't see you, wouldn't know what filthy thoughts you were thinking?

He didn't think his thoughts were filthy, but maybe he was wrong. His mother had said that the Devil disguises thoughts sometimes, to fool the sinner—maybe his heart was full of lust after all. He thought about the girl, so thin, so pale, her bones fragile as a bird's. Even her delicate little pointed chin had a beaklike quality. It didn't feel like lust, or what he thought of as lust, but how could he argue with God? Even worse, how could he argue with his mother?

He had to make the voice stop before his head burst. He had to make God happy, and he knew of one way to do that—thanks to his Master. He looked at his watch. It would be dark soon, and then his work could begin.

Chapter Thirty-two

"Oh, yeah, he'd be just a *dream* in court," Butts said, rolling his eyes.

He was sprawled in one of the chairs facing Chuck's desk. Lee sat across from him in the matching one. They were in Morton's office the next day, comparing notes. Chuck was perched on the windowsill, arms folded. Nelson sat in the captain's chair behind the desk, his fingertips drumming the arm of the chair. Detective Florette sat in a straight-backed chair in the corner, his posture as disciplined and rigid as the starched cuffs of his immaculate white shirt.

"A lot of credible sources make lousy witnesses in court," Chuck pointed out. "You know that as well as I do, Detective Butts. We both cover the Bronx, for Christ's sake."

"Excuse me, Mr.—uh, *Willow*, is it?" Butts continued. "Can you tell me who, if anyone, in this courtroom is an informant working for the FBI? Oh, I see—that man in the long black robe? And how do you know that? Oh, because of the microchips they planted in your *brain*?"

"All right, Detective, knock it off," Chuck said wearily.

"Obviously this guy isn't usable in court. The question is, is it a lead we can work with?"

Nelson shrugged. "He may turn out to be the only eye-witness we have so far."

"Unless that really was the Slasher that Campbell saw at the funeral," Butts pointed out.

"I don't see how it could have been anyone else," Florette pointed out. "That last text message seemed pretty conclusive."

By now they had all been told about the text messages Lee had been receiving; there was general agreement among them that the killer was probably sending the messages about Laura, though Chuck remained skeptical.

"You said this Willow character didn't get that good of a look at this guy, right?" Butts asked.

"Right," Lee agreed.

"But you did—assuming it was him," said Nelson. "Any hits on the families with the sketch of the guy you saw?"

"No. None of them recognized him."

Chuck picked the police artist sketch up from his desk and held it aloft. Even now, looking at it sent a shiver up the back of Lee's neck. The artist had captured the intensity of his stare, the look of both loss and danger in his eyes.

"Why don't you take the sketch to this Willow character, and ask him if it looks like the man he saw?" Chuck asked.

"All right," Lee replied, "but he said it was too dark to make out any of the man's features." What he didn't say was that he had no idea how to get in touch with Eddie—Eddie always called him, usually from a pay phone on the street. Lee had never mentioned Eddie by name, nor did he say how they had met. He referred to Eddie as "a reliable informant." No one had pressed him for more information. Everyone in law enforcement had their sources, and they weren't often choirboys.

"Let's say we identify the guy that this Willow fellow saw as being the same guy you saw at the funeral—and let's assume he is the UNSUB," Florette said. "You said before that chances are he could have a record, but maybe not?"

"Right," Nelson said. "Sexual killers often begin with break-ins, burglaries, that kind of thing—and sometimes they're Peeping Toms before they 'graduate' to more serious crimes."

"He's already graduated," Chuck pointed out.

"And do you think those text messages came from him?" Butts asked.

"I think it's likely," Lee answered. "Otherwise, the timing does seem too coincidental."

"How about your idea that there's more than one perp?" Florette asked.

"Yeah, what about that?" Chuck asked.

"I still say that's an incredible long shot," Nelson protested. "It's just not—"

The phone on Chuck's desk rang. He grabbed the receiver.

"Morton here." He listened, his face darkening. "No, I don't have any comment on the case."

He slammed down the receiver. "Damn press—they're all swarming around like flies on honey." He sank down in his chair and leaned rested his elbows on the desk. "Look, I don't have to tell you that forensic evidence on this case is not exactly piling up, so we have to try different angles. What about the churches?" he said to Florette. "Any luck there?"

"Well, staff interviews haven't gotten us much—no one saw anything unusual, that sort of thing. Detective Butts and I have been looking into the congregations, but that's taking a while."

"Right," Butts agreed. "So far no one fits the offender profile. And no one recognizes the sketch of the guy Lee saw."

"We've also been looking for something these churches

had in common," Florette answered. "Maybe something that links them in some way."

"And did you find anything?" Butts asked.

"Nothing obvious, other than they're both Catholic churches. But then we looked into all the programs going on at the churches—most of them have lots of meetings, you know, support groups and the like."

"Right," Nelson said. "There's a support group for everything these days. Mothers Who Lactate Too Much, Adult Children of Republican Parents—you name it."

"But most of those groups are anonymous," Lee pointed out.

"Exactly," Florette replied. "So there's not much we could do there—at least for the time being. We'd have to have a lot more evidence linking this guy to membership in one of the groups."

"Which we don't have," Butts pointed out, extracting a battered cigar from his pocket.

"Right," Florette said. "But then we started looking into the charitable works the church is involved in—feeding the homeless, that kind of thing."

"We know that Marie Kelleher volunteered at her church once a month," said Butts.

"Any leads there?" Nelson asked.

"Our first thought was that maybe he works for one of these organizations," Florette replied.

"Okay," Chuck said. "Definitely stay on that—we'll check all the employees you can dig up against the profile we've got so far."

There was a knock on the door.

"Who is it?" Chuck asked.

The answer was curt and businesslike. "Internal Affairs."

"Oh, for Christ's sake," Chuck said, opening the door. "This is not a good time."

"It's never a good time for IA," Butts muttered.

The man was tall and stern-looking, with an impassive, long-jawed face. He reminded Lee of a cross between his grade school principal and Abraham Lincoln.

"Dr. Campbell?" he said, looking at Lee.

"Yes?"

"Lieutenant Ed Hammer, Internal Affairs. I'm investigating the matter of a brutality complaint by a Mr. Gerald Walker, who was being interrogated in this facility on—"

"Yeah, we know who he is," Chuck interrupted. "Get to the point, please."

"Were any of you present during the interrogation?"

"I was," Butts said. "And I can tell you—the guy is a class-A creep."

"That may be, Detective . . ."

"Butts."

The man checked a notebook he was carrying. "Detective Butts, would you like to tell me why you haven't returned any of my phone calls?"

"I got more important things to worry about. Let me tell you something, Lieutenant Hammer: this guy was askin' for it. I woulda whaled on him myself in a minute."

"So you saw Mr. Campbell abuse the suspect?"

"Abuse, my ass!" Butts snarled, his cratered cheeks reddening. "He barely touched him."

Lieutenant Hammer looked at Lee. "Is that how he got the black eye?"

"Look, *Lieutenant*," Butts said, biting out the words, "Walker is a crybaby as well as a wife beater."

"Will you come down to our office and make a statement?"

"You bet!" Butts snapped back, grabbing his coat.

Chuck waved Butts back to his chair. "Just a minute, Detective." Then he stood up and crossed the small space between himself and Hammer, putting his face very close to Hammer's.

"Look, Lieutenant Hammer, I appreciate that you are just trying to do your job, but both Dr. Campbell and Detective Butts are important members of our investigative team. I promise I will have Detective Butts make out a statement and send it to your office. I don't need to tell you that our work is vitally important to the security of the citizens of this city. For every minute of our time that is wasted, another woman could die."

Hammer sighed. "Yes, Captain Morton, I understand that. But, as you say, I have my job to do, just as you have yours. We would also like to get a formal statement from you."

"Fine," Chuck said coldly without breaking eye contact. "I'll fax one over tomorrow. Give me your number."

Hammer scribbled a number in his notebook, ripped the page off, and gave it to Chuck, who stuffed it in his pocket.

"And now, if you'll excuse us, we have work to do."

"I'll expect your statements by oh eight hundred hours tomorrow," Hammer said. "You too, please, Dr. Campbell." And with that, he left.

There was an awkward silence; then Butts muttered, "Oh-eight-hundred hours my ass! Who the hell does he think he is, Goddamn Patton?"

"Never mind," Lee said. "I think we should all get him our statements as soon as possible."

"I agree," Chuck said. "But let's forget it now, okay? Can we get back to the case at hand?"

"The Catholic angle is interesting," Florette suggested. "You definitely believe we're dealing with a religious fanatic here? I mean, he's not faking it or something?"

"I don't know if the killer is trying to set up an insanity plea or not, but the religious fervor is real," Lee ventured.

"Really? Why?" Florette asked.

"Leaving the bodies in churches is risky and difficult—he could have easily been caught, and he's too intelligent not to know that. And the carving is even more risky. It's an important part of his signature, what he needs to get emotional satisfaction."

"Yeah? So now we know what drives him, how does that help us nab him?" Butts asked.

"You know, *Detective*, if you spent less time criticizing the profiler and more time working with him, you might be closer to catching this guy." Nelson's voice oozed sarcasm.

Butts frowned and crossed his arms. "Yeah, and if pigs had wings, they'd fly."

"All *right*!" Morton interrupted. "I know this is frustrating for all of us, but let's remember we're on the same team and stop sniping at one another. Knock it off." He fixed a stare on Butts until the burly detective sighed and looked away. Morton turned his gaze on Nelson, who smiled.

"I couldn't agree more, Captain Morton," he replied.

"Well," Butts remarked, "this guy is bound to slip up sooner or later."

Nelson looked at the detective as though trying to determine what species he belonged to.

"The question is," he said acidly, "what do we say to the parents of the next victim? That we decided to wait until he 'slipped up'?"

Butts's pockmarked face turned purple, and he clenched his plump hands into fists. "Look, I wanna catch this guy as badly as you do! Anyone who says otherwise is—"

"All *right*!" Chuck shouted. "Will you both cut it out? We have work to do!" He pointed to a map of the five boroughs tacked up on the wall. "Now, the red thumbtacks indicate where he's struck already."

"Bronx, Queens, Brooklyn," Florette said. "So far he's going borough by borough."

"Could that be a coincidence?" Chuck asked.

"No," Lee replied. "This guy is compulsive and orderly—obsessively organized. No," he said, looking at the little row of tacks, "I think it's all part of a pattern. He's staking out his territory."

"I agree," Nelson said. "However, the question is, what's next? Is he going to come to Manhattan, or cross down to Staten Island, leaving Manhattan as the final jewel in his crown, as it were?"

"You're right," Lee agreed. "There's no way of knowing."

"Why don't we put out a public warning telling girls in those two boroughs not to go out alone?" Butts suggested.

Nelson bit his lip. "We tried that during Son of Sam. It didn't work then, and it won't work now. People are going to do what they're going to do."

"Of course we'll issue a warning," Chuck said, rubbing his eyes.

"It won't do any good," Nelson said. "This guy is patient. The only way we stop these killings is to stop *him*."

"Right," Lee agreed. "He'll wait—sooner or later he'll find someone who fits his profile."

"So he's profiling his vics the way you're profiling him?" Florette asked.

"Pretty much, yeah," Lee answered.

"Man," Butts said. "That's creepy."

Nelson smiled. "Detective Butts, I must agree with you there. Creepy is exactly what it is."

As they filed out of the office, Nelson took Lee aside.

"What is it?" Lee asked, seeing the troubled look in his friend's face.

"I'm worried about you, lad. You look tired. Maybe you should take a leave of absence for a while, get some rest?"

"I'm fine," Lee replied.

"Well, you don't look fine. Are the text messages getting to you? They must be very upsetting."

"I'm fine—really. And I need to see this case through to the end."

Nelson's face was stern and grim. "The end may be more than you bargained for."

"Thank you for your concern, but I'll be all right."

"Well, at least be careful, please?"

"I will. I promise."

But even as he said the words he knew that being careful might not be enough—for him or for the Slasher's next victim.

Chapter Thirty-three

The park was empty, just the way Willow liked it. His only companions this morning were the Canada geese who had stopped to rest on their early migration back north after their annual Florida vacation. That's how he thought of it: a Florida vacation. His mother had gone to Florida, but she had never come back. He imagined her flying overhead, honking at him, her voice harsh as the cry of the speckled geese waddling around the boat pond. He sat on his bench and watched the geese pecking at the lumpy brown earth, tattered from the snow and ice of winter.

Rubbing his hands together, Willow looked around the park in satisfaction. Today was a good day. The voices hadn't come at him yet, with their whispering and taunting, driving him to wander and fidget and talk to himself, just as they drove other people away from him.

In his more lucid moments, he knew how he must appear to them, and why they shunned him. He might be crazy, but he wasn't stupid. In fact, his mother once told him he had an IQ of 150. *Near genius level*, she had said. *Near genius level . . .* well, fat lot of good it had done him. His meds—when he remembered to take them—couldn't entirely block out the voices that reminded him who was after him. The CIA, the FBI, and occasionally aliens who posed as joggers or young mothers—or sometimes even their kids.

Paranoid schizophrenia, that's what they called it. They could call it whatever they wanted—they could call it a pig in a poke, for all he cared.

Christ, he needed a cigarette. He rummaged in his pockets, but all he found were bits of string and fast-food wrappers. Chicken McNuggets, his favorite. He liked to keep things in his pockets because it helped to keep him warm.

He rubbed his hands together again and looked up to see a man approaching him.

"Hey, got a cigarette?" he called out.

The man smiled.

"In my backpack—but I left it in the woods."

That struck Willow as odd, but he shrugged.

"Shouldn't leave it there. Someone might take it."

"Come with me, and I'll give you one."

"Okay." Suspicious, Willow frowned. "Hey—you don't work for the FBI, do you?"

The man looked surprised. "Good heavens, no—in fact, they're after me. Don't tell them you saw me, okay?"

Willow winked at him. "Don't worry. Your secret is safe with me."

"I knew I could count on you. Now, how about that cigarette?"

Willow got up and followed the man toward the thicket of woods on the other side of the jogging path.

Behind them, the geese continued their search for scraps to eat along the banks of the pond. When the sound of strangled gasps came from the wooded area, they didn't even look up.

Chapter Thirty-four

Straining at the seams like a dowager in an overstuffed dress, Chinatown had for years been expanding into adjacent districts, encroaching on the border of Little Italy to the north and the court district to the south. It was perhaps the most vibrant—and most chaotic—of all Manhattan neighborhoods. When Kathy Azarian called Lee to say she was in town for the evening, and suggested they meet, it was the first place he thought of.

They met at Chatham Square and wandered the crooked, narrow streets until dusk. Chinatown lay in a jumble all around them, spread out like a web woven by a drunken spider. There were no right angles—everything was twists and turns, streets as crooked as the orderly grid of Midtown was straight. There was mystery around every corner, behind the opaque steamed windows of noodle houses, squeezed through the narrow doorways of dim sum parlors, with their platters of succulent, sticky dumplings visible through grimy picture windows. Lee had always loved the dimly lit doorways of the curio shops, the pharmacies and herbariums, with their imponderable supply of green tea cures, shark fin soup, and musty boxes of rare, unpronounceable herbs. Chinatown wasn't just another neighborhood—it was a separate universe.

Lee had gone down there in the early days after September eleventh, and felt as though he were wandering onto the set of a disaster film. It was all unreal, the once-familiar streets now a scene of unbelievable devastation. Below Canal Street, three out of every four people were in uniform: the National Guard, with their military camouflage gear, looking ready for combat; state troopers, tidy and crisp in blue and gray, with their Smokey the Bear hats; and of course New York City cops, everywhere. They roamed the streets in their starched blue uniforms and heavy black shoes, wary but full of purpose.

And of course there were the firemen, worn and weary but lit from within, caught in the incandescent glow of heroism, trudging to and from the scene of horror in their thick rubber boots and coats, courageous faces smeared with sweat and grime.

Downtown in the days that followed, the night air was yellow with soot and tiny particles from the explosion, and the streets and sidewalks were covered with a dusting of light gray debris. As he biked through it, Lee was reminded of films he had seen about nuclear devastation. The whiteness felt like a nuclear winter. Dismounting, he had wheeled his bike down as far as the intersection of Liberty and Nassau. He was surprised they allowed him to get so close—he had a clear view of Ground Zero. Once again, he was reminded of a movie set. Huge mercury lights threw their yellow glare onto the remains of the doomed buildings, writhing metal that looked like the weathered ruins of ancient castles, twisting up from the earth as though they had stood there for centuries.

Everywhere, workers came and went. Relief workers in their dusty overalls, grimy kerchiefs tied around their heads, leaned against office buildings or sat on the steps, their white dust masks hanging around their necks. Young cops gathered on street corners, shifting their weight from one foot to the other, poking at piles of debris with their billy clubs. The air was suffused with a golden mist that you could smell and taste, and it was incongruously, cruelly beautiful.

Now back in Chinatown again, this time with Kathy beside him, dusk deepening into twilight, Lee still felt the terrible sadness, but this time it was mixed with a new emotion: hope. They walked in silence for the most part, stopping occasionally to admire a piece of ornate carving in a shop window, or inhale the aroma of roasted duck coming from a noodle shop. He tried to keep his mind off his current case, but the newspaper headlines kept running through his head.

Slasher Continues to Terrorize City
Police Baffled

The sight of Kathy, standing in the neon light coming from the window of a Vietnamese restaurant, made his heart give a little leap. Her curly black hair had captured the light in a faint halo, and a single lock fell onto his forehead. He stared at her, mesmerized by the power of a few stray strands of hair.

"Do you want to go in here?" she asked, looking back at him.

"Sure, this is fine. I've never been here, but it looks good."

They walked down the steep, cracked steps and into a steam-filled foyer, moisture condensing on the glass door of the restaurant. A middle-aged Asian woman conducted them to a table in the corner by the window and handed them large menus covered in red plastic. The woman was impersonal and businesslike as they settled into their seats.

As she handed them the menus, Kathy said, "Thank you. Do you have Saigon beer?"

The woman's face broadened into a smile. She looked at Lee.

"Two?"

"Sure, why not?"

As the woman left, he turned to Kathy. "You made her happy."

"I think it's because I asked for Vietnamese beer instead of Chinese."

"And you even knew the brand name."

"Well, they do have Vietnamese restaurants in Philadelphia, you know."

Lee laughed, surprised at how easily the sound left his body. He hadn't laughed much lately. "Let's not get an intercity rivalry going this soon."

"Okay. Just figured I'd establish my territory early." She bent her head to look at the menu, and the same lock of dark hair fell onto her forehead. Lee's stomach lurched again. He looked down at the menu, but he wasn't very hungry tonight.

It was a quiet Sunday night, and there were only a few other customers in the place, all of them Asian. Nelson always told him that was a good sign in Chinatown, and meant the food was decent, or at least authentic.

Kathy looked up from the menu. In the lamplight, her eyes were the color of the Hudson River on a cloudy day. "What do you think of chicken with lemongrass and chili?"

"Sounds good to me." The truth was, it could have been sawdust, and he would have said the same thing.

"Okay, let's get that. And how about this mushroom appetizer? Does that sound good?"

"Sure."

In the end they settled on another entrée, something involving noodles.

"So," she said, putting her elbows on the table and leaning toward him, "how do you like what you do?"

"It can be very frustrating, but it feels like what I should be doing—right now, at least." He thought about telling her about the Internal Affairs investigation, but didn't want to spoil the evening.

"I know what you mean," Kathy said. "That's the main thing—not that work is easy, but that it feels right for you, somehow."

"You know, a lot of people think what I do is 'soft science.' They don't respect it much."

She gazed into her teacup as if seeking her answer in the dark liquid within.

"And what do you think?"

Lee smiled. "You sound like Dr. Williams."

"Oh. Is she . . .?"

"My shrink—yes."

Again she lowered her eyes, as if it wasn't proper to say the words.

"That's one of the things I like about bones," she said. "There's nothing 'soft' about them. They're so clean, so smooth—the last thing to surrender to the decay process. You know that properly preserved, they can last indefinitely? They're kind of heroic."

"I never thought about it that way."

"A lot of times bodies are found when only the bones are left, as the last physical reminder that this once was a human being. If it weren't for bones, even more crimes would go unsolved."

Somewhere, deep in the woods perhaps, Laura's bones were waiting for him—for someone—to discover them.

The woman came back with two beers and poured them into tall thin glasses, all the while smiling at Kathy.

"You've made a friend," Lee said after the woman had gone.

She looked around the restaurant. "It's different here now, isn't it?"

"Yeah," he said. "There was this feeling, in the weeks

afterward, that's hard to describe exactly, but it was a kind of camaraderie—a feeling that we were all in this together."

"I know what you mean. It was sort of like that in Philly, too."

"And we all thought that there might be more attacks coming too—we didn't know what to expect. Where were you when it happened?" he asked.

"I'm ashamed to say. I was in the Caribbean."

"Why be ashamed?"

"I was snorkeling in St. Thomas when we heard the news. I guess I wanted to be back here—to help in some way, you know. And instead there I was, forced to stay an extra week at Crystal Beach. Poor me—another week of fried conch, Tecate beer, and palm trees."

"What was it like there? How did people react?"

"Disbelief, at first, and then shock. Just total, utter shock. I remember sitting around the bar that night. There was no television, but someone had brought out a radio, and we were all huddled around it, listening."

She looked at the raindrops gathering on the window-pane. "It's ironic, actually. One of the main selling points of this resort was that you could 'get away from it all'—you know, no TV, no phones in the rooms. We were all there because we wanted to be cut off from the rest of the world. And then this terrible thing happens, and we sit there together in the bar—I guess there were a dozen or so guests and about half that many staff—and we just sat and listened to that damn radio all night. By morning we were all on a first-name basis with each other. It was like instant bonding, you know? Like in wartime—our country had been attacked."

"So you were all Americans?"

"One couple was Canadian, and there were two elderly English ladies traveling together. We all thought they were lovers, but they were very 'discreet' about their relationship. We called them Gertrude and Alice when they weren't around."

"As in Gertrude Stein and Alice B. Toklas?"

"Right."

The waitress brought steaming plates of food and set them down on the table. Kathy poured hot sauce on her chicken—a lot of hot sauce. Lee was amazed when she took a bite and swallowed it as though it were nothing.

"Up until that night everyone had been drinking piña coladas, margaritas—frozen drinks with fresh fruit and little paper umbrellas—but that night we all ordered scotch and whiskey and gin, straight up. People weren't drinking to have fun anymore; they were drinking to calm down. It was kind of surreal. All we could pick up on this little radio was this local station that was getting a feed from the BBC. The announcer sounded really upset. It was startling to hear this very formal, stiff-upper-lip-type Englishman almost lose it on the air."

She took a long drink of her beer and motioned to the woman for another one.

"But at least we were spared the pictures that night. Thank God for that. No one slept very much, but at least we were spared the pictures."

"Who were you traveling with?" Lee asked, feeling an unwelcome flicker of jealousy.

"My dad. We both love to snorkel. I'm an only child, and since Mom's been gone, I guess we sort of depend on each other, you know?"

She looked at him, her eyes serious. "Do you think that's weird?"

"No, I think it's sweet."

She reached for the noodle dish, almost knocking over her beer. She was a bit of a loose cannon, he thought. In spite of her scientific training and precise manner in professional settings, away from her work she had an open, childlike demeanor. When she talked there was a force behind the words, a passion for the minutia of life that made him want to drink up her words.

A thought flashed into his head, unbidden: *In the midst of death, there is life.*

He couldn't remember where he had heard it, but as he looked at Kathy Azarian's glistening, eager face, he understood what it meant.

Chapter Thirty-five

They lingered over dinner until they were the last patrons in the restaurant. Lee pushed food around on his plate and managed to eat some, but his stomach felt as twisted as the jumbled heap of rice noodles in the house special dish.

Kathy had a healthy appetite, though, expertly plucking food from her plate with her chopsticks, placing it between her startlingly white teeth. She pierced a piece of pineapple with one chopstick and put it in her mouth.

"Mmm, I like it when they give you fruit for dessert." She glanced at Lee's plate. "You didn't eat very much."

"My appetite comes and goes." What he wasn't ready to tell her was that for six months after Laura's disappearance, he had hardly eaten at all, living mostly on liquid protein drinks.

"Hmm," Kathy said. "We need to put some weight on those bones."

She thinks I'm too thin. Still, he thought the use of "we" was promising.

"Oh, I can eat like a horse sometimes," he said. "Don't you worry."

"You know better than to tell a woman you can eat a lot without gaining weight, right?"

"Yes, I think I know that much," he said, laughing. He felt grateful for her presence—it lightened him and made his heart quicken.

Lee looked around the restaurant. The other customers had long since left, and the staff sat around one of the round tables, rolling wontons. He thought they were trying hard not to glance at him and Kathy.

"Well," he said, "we're keeping these poor folks up. We should pay and get out of here."

He began to take out his wallet, but Kathy laid a hand on his wrist. "This one is on me."

When her fingers touched his skin, he felt the heat exchange between them, and wondered if she felt it too. If she did, she gave no sign, pulling her own wallet out of a small black knapsack. She selected a credit card and waved it at the waitress, who nodded and returned with the bill.

"Thanks," Lee said as they walked up the crooked narrow steps and into the nearly deserted street. Since September eleventh Chinatown had suffered. The formerly robust flow of tourist dollars slowed to a thin, anemic trickle. The mayor himself was making frequent pleas to people to go down to the struggling community and spend whatever they could afford.

They stepped out into a misty evening. The temperature had soared twenty degrees in the past twelve hours, bringing with it a soft dusting of rain. The droplets hung suspended in the air, as if not quite heavy enough to fall to the ground. The yellow neon lights of a teahouse across the street were surrounded by halos, round rings of layered light shimmering like ripples on a pond.

"It's really so beautiful that it's painful, isn't it?" she said.

Oh, yes, he wanted to say. *From where I'm standing, at least*. But he just said, "Yes, it is."

They strolled in the direction of the subway. Parts of Chinatown still had the grim, gray look of a war zone. Shopkeepers were still dusting soot off their stacks of rice dishes, mahogany Buddhas, carved jade bulls, and brightly colored paper birds.

"I felt guilty, you know, not being here when it happened."

"What could you have done?"

"As it turns out, nothing. My work is only just starting. I'm part of the body identification team." Her sigh was a deep, ragged sound. "Complete remains are almost unheard of—mostly it's bits and pieces. Most people just disintegrated."

They both stared at the traffic on Canal Street for a moment. Lee glanced at his watch, surprised to see how late it was.

"Are you returning to Philly tonight?"

"Yeah. I'm seeing my dad tomorrow. He's preparing a presentation for the Vidocq Society, and he wants my help."

"Wow," Lee said. "Your father is a member?"

"Yeah. Going on ten years now."

The Vidocq Society, based in Philadelphia, was named after François Vidocq, the brilliant eighteenth century French criminal who became a detective later in his life. The society was devoted to solving cold cases that people from all over the world brought to them. Membership was by invitation only, and Lee thought there wasn't a forensic professional alive who wouldn't consider it an honor to join the group. All the members were prominent in their respective fields.

"How often do they meet?" Lee said.

"Once a month, in the Public Ledger Building. It's an interesting place, very old-world, with thick Oriental rugs and big, heavy drapes—sort of Edwardian, really. The kind of place Sherlock Holmes's brother Mycroft would have liked.

When I first saw it, I imagined that's what Mycroft's club would look like."

"You're a Conan Doyle fan?"

She gave a lopsided little smile. "Isn't everyone?"

"So your father's a member of Vidocq—that's impressive. Is he an anthropologist too?"

"He's a forensic toxicologist."

"Is that what got you interested in forensics?"

"Sort of."

"I'm sure he's proud of you."

"I guess. You know how fathers are, though."

No, Lee thought, *I don't*, but he said nothing.

He walked her down the subway stairs and stood with her by the turnstiles as she waited for the train. On Sunday evenings they didn't run very often, and Lee found himself wishing the train would never come.

They stood next to each other, their bodies at an angle, half facing the tracks, half facing each other.

He glanced at Kathy. What was it she'd said? *Bones are heroic.* Kind of a mystical notion—though there was nothing mystical about her. With her brisk, short haircut, black leather knapsack, and firm, determined chin, Kathy Azarian was not an ethereal person. In a world where planes drop out of the sky, towers crumble and fall, and young woman are snatched abruptly from their lives, Kathy had a solid, three-dimensional presence that was reassuring.

Standing close to her, he could feel a connection between them like a current. He looked around the subway station, which was practically deserted. Contentment settled over him like a blanket, and he could have stood there all night, next to her, waiting for a train that never came.

But soon the number-nine local train came clattering into the station, its headlights snaking around the corner like the yellow eyes of a mythic beast.

"Okay," Kathy said, feeding a token into the slot. "I'll see you soon—you have my number."

At the last second, before sliding through the turnstile, she turned and planted a kiss on his neck. She seemed to be aiming for his cheek, but she was so much shorter than he was that, in her haste, she missed and caught his neck instead. Her lips were soft and warm, and caught Lee by surprise.

He turned his head to reciprocate, but just then the train rattled to a halt, the doors slid open, and she slipped through the turnstile and made a dash for the nearest car, stepping inside just as the warning bell sounded. The doors closed, the train rumbled out of the station, and Lee was left alone, staring at an empty platform. But his heart felt full, and his head was light. For the first time since his sister's death, since 9/11, since all the horrors of the past weeks, he could imagine what it was like to feel whole again. He headed toward the stairs leading up to the street. It was such a beautiful night he had decided to walk the mile or so back to East Seventh Street.

His attackers seemed to come out of nowhere.

He never saw the first blow coming. It was a sucker punch—a karate chop to the base of his neck—and it sent him stumbling forward. He turned to face his assailant, but another blow caught him from behind, this time to the kidneys. He went down on his knees, hard, only to find he was being lifted to his feet by strong hands, to be hit again—and again. Most of the punches were body blows, for which he was oddly grateful—he hated being hit in the face. But they hurt just the same. The jabs were hard and short and quick, the work of professionals. He never got a chance to throw so much as a single punch.

The two men made quick work of him, hitting him swiftly and soundlessly. It was all over in less than two minutes. They left him crumpled on the subway platform, leaning against the wall, dazed and bruised.

The only thing he could be sure of later was that they were both stocky, both wearing ski masks covering their faces, and he was pretty sure they were both white. Other than that, they could have been anyone.

He heard the sound of rapidly retreating footsteps, and then sank into darkness.

Chapter Thirty-six

Evelyn Woo was tired. Her feet ached, and her back was stiff. The only thing on her mind was a hot bath and a glass of warm plum wine before dropping gratefully into bed.

At first glance she thought the man lying on the subway platform was one of the drunks she had seen dozens of times after her late-night shift. She was a good worker, and her boss liked her, but Evelyn was always among the last to leave the Happy Luck Restaurant, and she hated the late-night subway rides to the small Chelsea apartment where she lived with her boyfriend, a medical student at NYU. She would start medical school next year, but meanwhile she was holding down two jobs to save money. Her father's cousin owned the Happy Luck, and she got to take home lots of free food every night, so that made the job worthwhile.

She passed by the man, the bag full of takeout cartons swinging at her side. He moaned and tried to sit up, and she glanced down at his face. It was a handsome face—for a Round Eyes (the derogatory term her uncle used for Caucasians)—and there was something about his eyes that made her look twice. She stopped walking and stared at him. Clearly, he was not a drunk—he was well dressed and well groomed. His mouth was bleeding, though, and she could see dark bruises on his cheeks.

"Are you okay?" she said, keeping a safe distance.

The man raised his head and gestured to her. She stepped closer.

"Please," he said. "Can you help me?"

Later, she would recall that she thought it was odd he refused to go to a hospital; instead he asked her to help him to a cab. She didn't hear the address he gave the cabbie, but she remembered those eyes—the wounded look in them stayed with her for a long time afterward. It also occurred to her later that before 9/11 she might not have helped him, but now—well, things were different now, she told her mother and all her cousins. Now we all have to look out for each other.

Chapter Thirty-seven

"For God's sake, Lee, will you stop this nonsense and go see a doctor?" Chuck Morton said as they walked through the labyrinth of hallways in the building housing the medical examiner's office. Their heels rapped sharply on the shiny polished floors, echoing down the tiled basement corridors.

"I'm all right," Lee said as they rounded a corner on the way to the lobby. Overhead fluorescent lamps cast a sickly yellow glow on his face, and Chuck wondered if he looked as bad as his friend under these lights.

"Well, you don't *look* all right," Chuck replied, casting a sideways glance at him. He had just about had it with Lee Campbell's bullheadedness. Underneath his anger was worry, of course—but he was damned if he was going to show it.

"You could at least take a day or two off," he muttered.

"Not right now. I need to see these people. I need to get a sense of whether they're on the level or not. You know as well as I do that I should be here at this meeting."

Chuck clenched his fists, digging his fingernails into his palms. Lee was right, but he really didn't feel good about seeing his friend up on his feet after the attack of the previous night. The two mysterious assailants, obviously professionals, had worked quickly and efficiently, Lee had said—and they had taken nothing, not even bothering to stage the attack as a robbery. They had even worn gloves, minimizing the possibility of gathering DNA evidence. It was obviously a message—but from whom? The whole thing gave him the creeps.

"I'll tell you one thing," he said. "That's the last time you go anywhere without a tail. From now on counter-surveillance is twenty-four-seven."

They rounded another corner and pushed open the door to the foyer, where Pamela Stavros's parents were waiting for them. They were the only people in the dingy waiting room, with its collection of mismatched plastic yellow chairs and dying spider plants crowded together on the dusty windowsill, thin and straggly in their cracked green pots. The only other living creature in the room was a fly trying vainly crawl up the dirty windowpane, buzzing feebly as it slid back down. Some places give the impression of having gone downhill, while others look as if they gave up before ever trying. The waiting room in the ME's office was one of those places.

The Stavroses were blunt, plain people who were obviously in shock. Theodore Stavros was a square, stolid man with meaty arms and legs, and sported the buzz-cut, flattop hairstyle he had probably worn since he was a boy. It looked like you could bounce a quarter off the meticulously mowed top of his head. He held his wife protectively to his side. Her face had sunk into a doughy middle age, though Lee could see that the delicate features must have once been pretty.

"I know this is very hard for you," Chuck said to the couple as he led them back through the corridors toward the exam room that held their daughter.

It was the second time Lee had been there in a week, and he still couldn't bear the smell of formaldehyde seeping into the halls from behind the closed and bolted metal doors lining the corridor. His head ached, and his ribs hurt with every breath, but he clenched his jaw and tried to keep his face impassive. After reporting the attack on him to the Chinatown precinct commander, he had fallen asleep, slept eleven hours, and woke up feeling like hell. But he had insisted on being here today, and here he was.

"You don't have to do this if you don't want to," Chuck told Mrs. Stavros. She looked at her husband and pressed her trembling lips together.

"She'll get through it," Mr. Stavros replied. "Let's get this over with." His accent was as flat as the Maine coastline. He glided over his *r*'s like a seagull swooping over the frigid coastal waters of New England.

As they entered the room with the wall-to-wall compartment containing all the unidentified corpses, they found a young technician waiting for them. He was Asian, with thick black hair and a delicate pair of wire-rimmed glasses. Lee was reminded of the sweet-faced Asian girl who had helped him the night before. He didn't even know her name. The technician nodded at Chuck and Lee, waiting as the little group assembled themselves in the room.

Mrs. Stavros made a gurgling sound that was like a stifled sob. Lee glanced at Chuck, who looked embarrassed and miserable. Chuck had never been relaxed in social situations where the rules of conduct were not clearly spelled out. As a policeman, he had entered a society full of rules, regulations, and prescribed behavior. In college, it had been Lee's job to smooth over social situations with a joke or a witty remark—he had been the charmer, while Chuck was the serious one.

The Stavroses stood still as stone, their faces rigid and swollen with unshed tears, as the medical technician pulled out the tray with their daughter's body. Once again Lee was struck by the spotless, shining metal and the pristine whiteness of the sheet covering Pamela's body. Chuck nodded, and the technician lifted the sheet, exposing the girl's face. It was untouched, white as chalk, but dark purple strangulation marks were visible on her neck.

Mrs. Stavros gasped and buried her face in the crook of her husband's thick arm. Chuck gave another brief nod to the attendant, who replaced the sheet and slipped the body back into the freezer unit. Mr. Stavros hid his wife's face from the terrible sight.

"It's her," he said brusquely, as if he was angry with Chuck for bringing him here. Lee had seen this displaced anger before, and he felt sorry for his friend. These people were so filled with grief and rage, and they vented their frustration on the only person available: Chuck Morton. Lee knew it was hard on his friend. As precinct captain, Chuck was used to giving orders and being obeyed, but to Pamela's parents he was simply the bearer of bad news.

The four of them walked in silence back through the hallways toward the building entrance. Lee knew that the Stavroses' anger would make it harder for him to do his job. They would resist his questions, and maybe even refuse to answer them. As they entered the lobby of the building, he decided to take a stab at a pretty obvious sales tactic.

"Would you mind answering a few questions that will help us catch your daughter's killer?" he said, leading them to a row of scuffed yellow plastic chairs in the corner of the room.

Mr. Stavros turned around to face him. "Catch him? *Catch him*? I'll help you fillet, boil or fry him," he said, spitting the words out. "Better yet, you lead me to him, and just leave the rest to me, huh?"

Theodore Stavros was a big man, solid as a slab of granite, and Lee felt the physical threat as Stavros hovered over him, his small blue eyes shot through with burst blood vessels and rage. He had an abrupt realization: Ted Stavros was an alcoholic. He wondered that he hadn't noticed it before—

the ruddy cheeks, the bloodshot eyes, the slight tremor in his powerful hands. Probably at his wife's insistence, he hadn't had a drink today, but he sure as hell looked like he needed one.

Lee looked at the timid, frightened expression on Mrs. Stavros's face, and he suddenly realized what Pamela had been running from. This was not a happy family. Ted Stavros was a man who could get nasty. Violence leaked from his pores like sweat; barely concealed rage was evident in the way he held himself, in the tightness of his mouth, the deliberate flatness of his voice. For a teenage daughter, it was probably terrifying.

"Wh-what do you want to know?" Mrs. Stavros asked, sitting in one of the chairs.

"Do you have any idea who Pamela's friends were, who she saw here in New York?" Chuck asked.

Mrs. Stavros shook her head. "No. She, uh, didn't tell us where she was going. We didn't even know she was in New York until we . . ." She tried bravely to master her emotions, but her voice gave out.

Her husband finished for her. "Until we saw your Web site. She had a 'boyfriend,'" he continued, pronouncing it as though he had said "cockroach." "He was a creep, a two-timing junkie, but she was hooked on him."

Garbage in, garbage out, Lee thought. *We all follow patterns we're familiar with*, he wanted to say, *and your daughter is no exception*. But he said nothing, and arranged his face in a mask of sympathy and concern.

"So you think she came here with him?" Chuck asked.

"I dunno," Stavros replied. "He wasn't from around here—and he turned up back in town a couple of weeks ago, saying he had nothing to do with her disappearance."

"Did you believe him?" said Chuck.

Ted Stavros looked away, a slight smile prying the corners of his mouth upward. Lee could picture the scene: Stavros threatening the young man, or worse.

"Yeah, I guess," he said. "I gave him every chance to change his story." Lee silently translated his comment. He had given the boyfriend a severe beating, and when the terrified kid stuck to his story, even under torture, Stavros believed him. However bad the boyfriend was, Lee thought, he wasn't as bad as the father. Stavros seemed pleased with himself.

He looked at Mrs. Stavros. What he had taken before as behavior caused by severe grief he now saw as telltale signs of a battered spouse. Her shoulders rolled inward, as if she was afraid of taking up too much space. She looked at her husband constantly, checking with him before she said or did anything, as if she feared incurring his displeasure. *Classic submissive behavior*, Lee thought, and he felt sorry for this once-pretty woman who was shackled to this oafish bully, bonded by their shared history—and now, their shared grief.

"One other question," he said. "Was your daughter religious?"

Ted Stavros frowned. "What's that got to do with anything?"

"No, not especially," his wife answered. "We're Greek Orthodox, but she wasn't exactly fervent or anything."

"Did she wear a cross around her neck?"

Mrs. Stavros seemed surprised by the question. "Yes, as a matter of fact, she did. Remember?" she said to her husband, who was still frowning. "The jade one Nana gave her for Christmas one year?"

"Oh, yeah," he said. "Right. She liked it a lot—always wore it." His face softened as if he was about to cry.

"Jade?" Lee said. "So it was green?"

"Yes. I don't suppose we could have it back?" Mrs. Stavros asked timidly. "It was a gift from her grandmother."

Lee exchanged a glance with Chuck and then looked at the woman sympathetically. "I'm very sorry, Mrs. Stavros. We'd be glad to return it to you, but we don't have it."

Her eyes widened. "You don't? Then who . . . ?" She left the question dangling.

"I hope someday we can give you the answer to that question," Lee said as Chuck escorted them out into a leaden February twilight.

Lee's real question had been answered, however: Pamela Stavros was, without doubt, the first known victim of the killer everyone now knew as the Slasher.

As they stood at the curb waiting for a cab, Mrs. Stavros stared down at the tips of her sensible brown Hush Puppies. There was nothing flamboyant or vivid about her, as if anything colorful about her had been extinguished long ago.

"So, um, did she suffer much?" she asked quietly.

"No," Lee replied gently. "The attack would have been sudden—it all happened before she realized what was going on."

"So she didn't fight back, get in a few swings at the bastard?" Mr. Stavros hissed, his bulldog face reddening.

"There wasn't time for that," Lee answered. What he didn't add was that there was time for her to realize she was being strangled, to look up into the last face she would ever see—the face of her killer.

Mrs. Stavros let out a sigh—a thin, hopeless sound, like air escaping from a balloon. Lee felt sorry for this quiet woman whose one source of comfort had been snatched from her.

"So if she didn't fight back, that means the killer's got no marks on him either," Ted Stavros remarked, displaying more intelligence than Lee would have credited him with.

"Right," said Chuck.

Had she fought back—scratching, biting, maybe—there might be DNA samples of his skin under her fingernails. But they had no such forensic evidence. In fact, they had zip— nothing at all. They might as well be chasing a ghost.

Chapter Thirty-eight

"So you're determined to play this out and not go to a doctor?" Chuck demanded as the two of them walked south on First Avenue. They had put the Stavroses in a cab, then headed downtown toward the Ninth Precinct. The sky was a dull gray—a typical February day in Manhattan. Even the trees looked cold, their bare black branches thrust upward in supplication to the unforgiving heavens.

"Look," Lee replied. "If it'll make you feel better, I'll go. But I don't think anything's broken."

"You don't *think* anything's broken," Chuck said with disgust. "Jesus Christ. What *is* it with you, Campbell? This isn't a goddamn rugby game!"

"Let's just say I've had enough of doctors and hospitals for a while."

That shut Chuck up. Neither of them really wanted to talk about Lee's nervous breakdown right now.

"Have you heard anything from the guys at the Chinatown precinct?" Chuck asked as they passed a row of food vendors lining the eastern side of First Avenue in front of Bellevue Hospital. People were lined up outside the carts, smoking cigarettes, talking, counting their money as they waited for their souvlakis, hot dogs, and shish kebabs.

"I don't think they really have much evidence to go on," Lee answered. "I'll go down and make a full report later today."

"Yeah," Chuck said, stepping aside as a small boy escaped from his mother's grasp and lurched toward him, arms outstretched. She ran after him, her pretty face lined with stress. She smiled at them apologetically as she scooped up her son.

Both Lee and Chuck knew nothing would come of the report, but they had to go through the motions anyway. "It does sound like they were professionals," Chuck said. "I wonder how long they were following you."

"I don't know. They chose a good time to attack: it was a Sunday night, and the platform was deserted."

"Yeah," Chuck agreed. "Look, I wouldn't blame you if you wanted to take some time off—you know, maybe get some rest."

"Are you taking me off the case?"

Chuck paused as an ambulance rattled past them up First Avenue, lights flashing, siren screaming. "No," he said. "I just think that—"

"Good," Lee interrupted. "Then let's talk about the case, okay?"

"I'm just worried about you. Whoever did this to you—"

"Whoever did this to me does *not* fit the profile of the Slasher."

Chuck frowned. "So you don't think there's a connection?"

"I don't know," he answered as they continued walking.

"I was trying to think why he would target you in particular. I guess because you saw his face."

"Could be. Or maybe there's no connection." Secretly Lee believed there was a connection, but he wasn't about to say that.

"So you don't like the boyfriend for Pamela's death?"

"Nope."

The two of them walked along for a while, passing Twenty-third Street, where a long line of people were waiting for the crosstown bus. They all had the look of middle-of-the-week workday weariness, with tired eyes and sore feet.

"Could it be a copycat, maybe?" Chuck suggested.

"No," said Lee. "I'm more convinced now than before that this is our guy's work. If the missing necklace weren't enough—"

"Granted, that's a bit of a coincidence," Chuck agreed, "but she could've lost it anywhere. She could have sold it, had it stolen."

"Come on," Lee said, sidestepping a dog walker with eight or ten different breeds in tow. "We never released that information to the press. Don't you think that's too much coincidence?"

The dog walker paused to let a black Labrador retriever relieve himself on a hydrant. The other dogs followed suit, eager to deposit their calling cards, in the mysterious language of dog communication.

"I don't know," Chuck said. "I feel like I don't know anything anymore."

"Think about it," said Lee. "She was found in the crucifixion pose, just like others. The only difference was that she wasn't in a church."

"And she wasn't mutilated."

"No, because he didn't feel comfortable where he was. He didn't feel he had enough time. Or . . ."

Lee looked down the avenue. From where they stood he could see long gray plume of smoke snaking skyward from the still smoldering ruins. The odor was sharper today: the thin, acrid smell of defeat.

"Or what?" Chuck said.

"He keeps refining his signature—like the blood in the wine, which is a whole new thing. Did the DNA tests of the blood turn up anything yet?"

"It's all hers. Not surprising, I guess."

"The thing I don't like about it is that he's becoming *more* organized, instead of less," Lee said. "That means that instead of falling apart, as some killers do, he's actually gaining more control as he goes."

"Have you seen that Willow guy again?" Chuck asked as they dodged a gaggle of schoolchildren. The students were about seven—just Kylie's age, Lee thought. They walked hand in hand, three abreast, followed by a harried-looking teacher. The tassel on her striped Guatemalan wool hat swung back and forth as she lunged after the children, her arms full of papers and notebooks.

"Uh, no—not yet." Lee had waited for Eddie to contact him, but so far had heard nothing from his friend.

"Did you get your statement in to Internal Affairs?"

"Yeah. I did that right after the guy showed up in your office."

"Jeez," Chuck said. "Doesn't all this sort of—*get* to you?"

Lee looked at him. "Chuck, these days, *everything* gets to me, okay?"

"Okay, okay. Don't bite my head off. I was just asking."

"Look, here's how it is for me: this is awful stuff, but it's something I can *do*, something that I have some *control* over, you know what I mean? I can't control what these guys do, but I can help catch them—and that gets me up in the morning. And for a while, that was the hardest part of the day. Still is, I guess."

Chuck stopped walking and shoved his hands in his pockets. "Look, I know you've been through a lot," he said, staring at the traffic barreling noisily up First Avenue. "I just—well, I guess I worry about you sometimes, you know? I mean, I don't want to get weird on you or anything, but you aren't looking all that great these days."

"Really?" Lee said. "You *think*?"

This struck them both as funny for some reason, and they burst out laughing. A thin brunette in a tracksuit frowned as she approached them, as if she thought they were laughing at her. She had a tight little ass and was power walking with Heavyhands weights, and her face curled up in contempt as she passed them without breaking stride. That just made them laugh even harder. The more they tried to stop, the more impossible it was. Tears spurted from their eyes like buttons popping from a shirt, and they were forced to stop walking, totally immobilized by unrestrained, hysterical laughter. Lee leaned against a parking meter for support, and Chuck collapsed on the steps of a deli, holding his stomach. Lee's stomach ached too, but he still couldn't stop laughing.

Passing pedestrians looked at them, frowning, as if they disapproved of such levity so soon after the worst tragedy in the city's history. It wasn't levity, though, Lee knew. The laughter had an out-of-control, frantic quality. The tension of the preceding days had risen to such a level that the only thing left was to release it in a torrent of explosive laughter. It hurt him even to breathe, and laughing was agony—but there was no stopping it. He hugged the parking meter, hanging onto it like a drunken man, while Chuck sat doubled up on the concrete stairs of the deli.

After a couple of minutes, they both ran out of steam at the same time. Lee wiped the tears from his eyes as Chuck got to his feet and stumbled to stand next to him.

"What was *that*?" he asked, his voice hoarse.

"Well, I guess that would be what folks in my line of work might call a catharsis."

"What the hell were we laughing about?" Chuck said as

he straightened his tie and ran a hand through his short blond hair.

"Nothing, really," Lee answered, letting go of the parking meter. It was one of the old mechanical types, and the white-on-red lettering said EXPIRED. "That was just a physical release to a buildup of stress."

"I just suddenly completely lost control," Chuck said. "That was *weird*."

"Our bodies had had enough stress, and found a way to release the tension."

"Okay," Chuck answered. "You're the doc."

Chuck's comment reminded Lee of Eddie Pepitone, and he wondered how Eddie was getting along. He made a mental note to call him. He also wanted to talk to Willow again, to bring him the police sketch and see if he could get a positive ID of any kind.

"So you don't think there were others before Pamela?" Chuck asked. They walked side by side down First Avenue as the lights in the shop windows went on one by one. Inside the restaurants lining the avenue, waiters were lighting candles, turning up the dimmer switches on the chandeliers, staving off the coming sense of isolation as dusk settled over the city.

"It's possible, but I don't think so. The placement of her body was hurried, unlike the later crimes, where a lot of care and planning took place. It was risky, too, to leave the last two where he did, and this guy is no dummy. He was aware of the risk. With Pamela, though, he shows all the hallmarks of spontaneity. It's as though he was in more of a hurry. Her killing might have even been unplanned."

Lee looked in the window of Ryan's Irish Pub, at the row of regulars hunched along the bar, necks lowered over their drinks, the red in their eyes measured by the number of shots in their glass. He wondered how Nelson was doing.

"Why does a guy like this just suddenly start killing?" Chuck was saying.

"There's usually a precipitating stressor, something to make him crack when he did."

"You mean like losing his job or breaking up with his girlfriend?"

"Yes, except not those things. I seriously doubt he's ever had a real girlfriend, and I don't think this stress was job related."

"Why not?" In the dim light, Chuck's blue eyes were opaque topaz.

"Call it a hunch, I guess. No, it's something else with this guy—something related to control and his feelings of frustration and impotence."

They walked for a while, then Lee said, "Did you hate leaving Princeton when you did?" He needed to know if Chuck was holding on to resentment because Lee got to graduate—resentment that might compromise their work together.

In front of them, a line of people waited for the M15 bus. They were hunched against the cold, hands in their pockets, scarves wrapped tightly around their necks. This had been a cold winter, and everyone looked worn out by the gray skies and chill winds of February.

Chuck stopped walking.

"Yeah," he said. "Yeah, I guess I did."

"You had a choice to make, and you chose being a good son."

"Yeah, I know. It still didn't feel good."

"The right choice doesn't always feel good."

Chuck kicked at a stone on the sidewalk. "I resented you for a while, for being able to finish. But then I looked at what you didn't have that I did."

"Like a father."

"That, and other things."

"You mean Susan."

"Yeah."

There was a pause, and then Chuck said, "Tell me something, Lee—did she really leave you for me?"

"You know she did," he lied. "Why do you have to ask me?"

"Sometimes I wonder, that's all. She's so . . . how can I put it? I wonder how much she really needs me."

"From what I can tell, she dotes on you."

"Well, she's got me jumping through hoops, that's for sure." He patted his flat stomach. "Even got me on a low-carb diet, for Christ's sake. Oh, hell, Lee, I love her and I always have, and maybe I'm a fool for it, but damn it, there it is. She's still every fantasy I've ever dreamed of."

"That's great, Chuck. I think that's just great." Susan Beaumont Morton was a woman who thrived on worship—without it, Lee suspected, she would dry up and blow away like a discarded seedpod.

Lee's cell phone rang.

"Hello?"

"Hey, Boss." Eddie didn't sound good.

"Eddie, what's up? I've been waiting for you to call."

"Bad news."

"What's wrong?"

"It's about Willow. He's dead."

Lee stopped walking. "What happened?"

"I found him floating in the boat pond in Prospect Park."

"Did he drown?"

"No, Boss, he definitely did not drown."

"What, then?" Lee glanced at Chuck, who was looking at him anxiously.

"He was carved up."

"Oh, God."

"What?" said Chuck. "What is it?"

Lee waved him off. "What kind of carving?" he said into the phone.

"It was from the Bible, Boss. It was—"

"No, don't tell me. It was *Thy kingdom come, thy will be done.*"

"Yeah."

"Goddamn it."

"It was him, right, Boss?"

"Look, Eddie—"

Chuck tugged at his sleeve, and again Lee waved him off.

"Sorry about all this, Boss. I guess the Slasher got to him before we could."

"It's not your fault. Eddie, do me a favor? Be careful, huh?"

"Sure, sure. Don't worry about me, Boss—I'm the original Iron Man."

"Just be careful—please?"

"Sure, Boss. Sure."

"Okay. Call me soon."

"Right. Will do."

Lee put the phone back in his pocket and looked at Chuck.

"It's Willow—Eddie found him in the boat pond."

"Damn." Chuck smacked his forehead with his closed fist, his face red. "Goddamn it. And was it—?"

"Yeah. He took his time. He took the trouble to carve the next part of the prayer on poor Willow just so we would know it was him."

Chuck's fair complexion reddened even more. "Bastard! He's taunting us."

"Yeah. He's having a good time with all this—and he's beginning to feel invulnerable. But that's what's going to make him screw up eventually."

The key word there, Lee knew, was "eventually." The thought of yet another victim felt like too much to bear right now. They walked in silence for a while, and then Chuck said, "You know, without any forensic evidence, trying to find this guy really is like looking for a needle in a haystack. I mean, no offense, but there's really only so much profiling can give us."

"I know," Lee replied. "I wish we had some hair, fiber, prints—*anything*."

"Which borough do you think he's going to do next?" Chuck asked

"I wish I could say," Lee answered.

He didn't say what they were both thinking. By that time, it might be too late, and someone else would die.

Chapter Thirty-nine

At some point Lee realized that sex with Kathy was inevitable.

Maybe it was when she laid her hand on his as they sat squeezed next to one another in that crowded Madison Avenue café. Or perhaps it was the glance they exchanged at the bagel shop on West Seventy-second Street, as he set the bagel down between them . . . the plump brown circle of dough, toasted and crisp on the outside, soft and yielding on the inside. Lee felt a rush of warmth to his cheeks as he thought about entering her. Would she too be soft and yielding, under her crisp exterior? Once the thought blossomed in his head, it sent out tendrils, runner vines that spread throughout his brain, crowding out other thoughts.

He found everything about her absurdly charming: the way she curled her index finger around her coffee cup; the way she stood with her weight balanced on one hip, arms crossed over her chest; her habit of running her tongue over her teeth when she was concentrating; the resolute set of those square little shoulders; the languid curve of her upper lip; the way one black curl fell onto her forehead. Kathy Azarian had engaged his heart from the first.

He had no idea if she felt as strongly as he did, and he didn't want to ask, in case the answer was no.

Her invitation to come back to her friend's Upper West Side apartment where she was staying was almost casual, another step in the delicate dance the two of them had been performing ever since they met.

"I'm house-sitting for her for the weekend, and she won't be back until late Sunday."

She smiled, and the dimple on her chin puckered and blossomed.

And so they found themselves, later that afternoon, lying in bed at her friend's apartment, on a green plaid bedspread, the late afternoon light creeping across the opposite wall, forming shadows and patterns that her friend's two gray kittens attacked in little hops and leaps.

When at last his mouth found hers he didn't want to move on, but lingered as her strong little pointed tongue felt the insides of his cheeks. He ran his tongue over her perfectly white teeth, imagining them shining in the darkness of her mouth, waiting for his tongue to discover them. It had always amazed him that this act of intimacy was necessary to continue the species—for one body to actually enter another. Surely there would have been easier, safer ways. Instead, Nature had given them this gift, this miracle of flesh on flesh.

The back of Kathy's neck smelled tart and fresh, like winter flowers—carnations, maybe, or narcissi? Her body was so slight that he was afraid he might crush her, but the space between her hip bones tautened and trembled when he ran his lips over it. Her breasts were small but prominent, and perfectly round, like two cupcakes, her nipples sweet as ripe cherries.

He postponed the moment of entry as long as possible, until his body ached to thrust into her, and he gave in, sinking into her wet, unknowable darkness. She took him inside her, and he could feel her body pulling him in. It seemed as natural a fit as a hand inside a well-worn glove. As he entered her he thought of the deep, soft soil of furrowed farm fields stretching out between the white and green trimmed houses of his childhood.

He looked down at her face. She smiled at him through half-closed eyes, and again the dimple on her chin blossomed. He had wondered what her face would look like in the heat of passion, and now he knew. Her dark skin was flushed, her lips full and open.

He drove deeper inside her. She moaned and dug her nails into his back.

Being inside her was like being at the center of the earth. He had experienced good sex that was simply a physical connection, a mutual satisfying of needs—but this was different. He felt engulfed, surrounded, and he surrendered gratefully, wanting her to suck out all the pain of the last few years.

It was still amazing to him that these beautiful creatures, women, could be touched and smelled and licked and entered.

She breathed harder and harder, until her breath was coming in hoarse gasps and she moaned underneath him. He loved the feeling of power it gave him to make her moan like that, as she writhed and cried, "Oh, oh, oh *God*," her slim body twisting like a snake beneath him, perspiration collecting on her upper lip, in the hollow of her neck. He wanted to know things no one else knew about her.

The aftermath of his orgasm was like the descent of the winter sunset outside the lace curtains, as daylight slipped slowly into night, separating into a pastel palette of colors too subtle and delicate for the robustness of a summer's evening. He watched the shades of winter twilight, watched as the day seemed relieved to let go and enter the long slide into night. They lay wrapped in the green plaid bedspread as the light outside the window faded, a tangle of arms and legs and cat hair.

He braced himself against the sadness that followed. It surged up inside him, just under his breastbone—soft, wet, and full. It pulled at his throat, closing off his airway, until he cleared it with a deep sigh.

She looked at him, alarmed. In the dim light, her eyes were the color of spruce needles: greenish blue, opaque as storm clouds.

"What's the matter? Are your injuries bothering you?"

"No."

"What was that sigh about, then?"

He wasn't sure how it would sound, to speak of the sadness that always settled upon him after sex. He was afraid she might take it the wrong way.

She rolled over onto her side, her breasts pressed together to create a narrow valley between them. He thought of losing himself in that valley, of sliding in between the heavy softness of those breasts, nestling there forever like a small, furry animal. Her nipples were deep red, almost brown.

"Is it the sadness?" she asked. The question was so unexpected he was caught off guard. She smiled and leaned up on one elbow, her breasts brushing against her arm. "Do you get it too—the sadness that comes afterward?"

He looked away. He had never discussed this with anyone. "Sometimes, I guess."

She reached over and traced a straight line down his forearm with her little finger. It made him shiver. "I've often thought that this might be why the French called orgasm 'a little death.'"

He couldn't think of anything to say. He had always believed his reaction to be peculiar to him alone. Talking about it felt more intimate than sex itself.

She retraced the line on his arm in the other direction.

"It's probably a biochemical reaction of some kind. I wouldn't worry about it."

Her scientific bluntness made him laugh.

"That's a relief. I'll call off the existential angst patrol."

She laughed and flopped over onto her back. Her breasts were the whitest part of her body, but they were still darker than his skin.

"I just didn't know anyone else felt it."

"You never talked about it with anyone?"

"No." He didn't want to know whether or not she had.

"It's really an odd thing, when you look at it—sex, I mean," she said.

"How so?"

"Well, I suppose nature has made it arduous and difficult for the male for a reason—another form of natural selection, I guess."

"So how is making it hard for computer geeks to get laid good for the species?"

She punched his arm. "That's not what I'm talking about. I mean that it requires a certain amount of . . . stamina. If it weren't a fairly athletic activity, then anyone could mate, and that would be bad for the species."

"I just love it when you talk science." He ran his tongue over the outer rim of her ear, tasting the mixture of sweat, ear wax, and lavender.

After the third time he slipped into a deep, stuporous sleep. Murky images drifted in and out of his dreams, sluggish and bulky as whales, sinking just beneath the reach of his conscious mind. He awoke to a bright dawn seeping through the white curtains and the comforting sounds of pans clattering in the kitchen. For a few minutes he lay there on his back, eyes closed, listening to the city coming to life around him. The sound of traffic was picking up momentum on Amsterdam Avenue, and he separated the various sounds in his head: the low diesel rumble of the M11 bus, the rattle of delivery vans as they lurched from one pothole to another, the clatter of metal security gates being raised as shopkeepers opened their stores for the day.

The two gray kittens entered the room and attacked his feet under the covers. The cats waged a continuous campaign of attacks and counterattacks, flinging themselves upon each other in a series of short leaps and hops, and then went instantly from full battle mode to licking themselves.

Contentment crested over him like a wave. The kitchen sounds were replaced with footsteps. Already, he thought, he could identify her walk, light and quick. She appeared at the doorway, wearing a green terry cloth robe knotted loosely around her waist, so that the upper part of her inner thighs was visible, dark and inviting where the robe came together. The smell of coffee floated in through the open door.

As she entered the room, the cats skittered out of it, brushing her ankles as they dashed off after each other.

Kathy laughed. "Those two—they're like teenagers cruising down Main Street. They're just looking for action, and pretty much anything will do."

Lee smiled. "They put on a pretty good show. But then, so do you."

She cocked her head to one side. The black curls, uncombed, grazed her shoulder.

"Coffee?"

He stretched his arms out to her.

Chapter Forty

The next day Lee took a long-promised trip to drive to his mother's house to pick up his niece and bring her back to town with him for a visit. Chuck had insisted he take the weekend off, and he even though he disagreed with his friend, he had no choice but to obey.

Fiona Campbell lived in the same house where Lee and Laura were born, in a tiny village nestled deep in the Delaware valley. She had lived there since the first day of her ill-fated marriage, and she intended—or so she often claimed—"to die there, by God,"—which was more of an oath than an appeal directly to the divine.

When Lee arrived to pick up his niece, Kylie was on the front lawn waiting for him, standing on Turtle Rock, the big round boulder he and Laura used to pretend was a giant tortoise. Sometimes it was a whale, a pirate ship, or even a magic carpet, but most often it was a turtle. The boulder rose from the earth in a single graceful arc, its smooth gray hump of a back perfect for straddling, or standing on, or jumping from. Once, years ago, his mother had contemplated having the boulder removed from her lawn, but Lee and Laura made such a fuss that she'd dropped the idea.

His niece was dressed in a pink and white snow parka, with matching pink sneakers and a pink ribbon tied around her blond hair. Pink was Kylie's favorite color, followed by purple. Unlike his mother, with her stern Scottish Presbyterian spine, Kylie was all girl, soft and sweet, but with a streak of mischief.

Lee got out of the car. "Hi, there, pastel girl."

Kylie made a face and balanced on one foot. "Why are you calling me that?"

"Is today a No Teasing Day?" Lee asked, scooping her up off the boulder and putting her on his shoulders. He managed to keep her from seeing his face—at least for now.

"Maybe," she said, putting her hands over his eyes. Her fingers smelled of lemons.

"Guess who!"

"Uh, let me see. Pastel girl?"

"Ugh!" Kylie gave a grunt of mock frustration. It was a sound Laura used to make when she was faking exasperation.

"Where's your grandma?" he asked, holding on to her ankles so she wouldn't fall as he walked toward the house.

The house was built in 1748, the large, irregular river stones held together by white masonry. Most of the wide, hand-hewn floorboards and ceiling beams were original, and the ceilings were low—only about eight feet high—and always made Lee feel a little like stooping.

"Mom?" he called, as he pushed open the heavy oak front door. The front hall smelled of eucalyptus and apples and ancient wooden beams. The walls were painted a creamy off-white, adorned with rather masculine hunting prints.

"Hello, Mom!" he called again.

"Fiona!" Kylie shouted.

"You don't have to shout—I'm right here," his mother said,

coming around the corner from the dining room. She had perfectly good hearing, but some of her friends had bought hearing aids, and she was sensitive on the subject. Physical weakness would not be tolerated when you were a Campbell.

"Uncle Lee's here!" Kylie cried, rushing to wrap herself around her grandmother's legs.

Fiona Campbell gave Kylie's head a perfunctory pat before extracting herself from her granddaughter's embrace, like a cat stepping over a wet spot on the floor.

Fiona Campbell had the kind of square, strong-jawed good looks that were not exactly pretty, but her high, firm cheekbones, as she put it, "held age well." Her skin had a healthy, ruddy glow, and with her clear blue eyes, straight nose, and firm, determined mouth, she was a handsome woman. Lee had once suggested to her that she try modeling for the cover of magazines for seniors, and she had dismissed the idea with a contemptuous wave of her hand. He wasn't sure whether the contempt was aimed at the idea of modeling or the notion that anyone would think of her as a "senior." She talked about the "old ladies" at her church as if they were an alien species.

Fiona exchanged the necessary kiss on the cheek with her only son and then looked at him closely.

"What on earth happened to you?"

"I had an accident."

"Good lord! What on earth?"

Kylie looked up him too, squinting in the dim light.

"You have a black eye, Uncle Lee!"

"I ran into a door," he lied. "It was stupid."

Kylie was satisfied with this explanation, but his mother was not. She raised an eyebrow at him, but he shook his head and glanced at Kylie. His mother took the hint and changed the subject.

"So where are you two going today?" she asked.

"Can we go to Jekyll and Hyde? *Please,* can we?" Kylie asked.

"Sure," Lee replied.

Kylie turned to her grandmother. "It's the *coolest* place!" She hopped from foot to foot, humming to herself.

"Well, mind you don't stay up too late," Fiona said.

"We won't, we won't!"

"Okay, we'd better be off," Lee said, twirling the car keys in his left hand. He had a tendency toward ambidextrousness, a trait Fiona claimed was inherited from his father.

"Would you like a cup of tea before you go?" his mother said.

Lee glanced at his watch. "No, I don't think so. It's kind of a long drive."

"Very well. Off you go, then," she said briskly, whisking the two of them out the door after brushing her lips across their cheeks.

"Who's that?" Kylie asked when she saw the dark sedan parked out in the road.

"Oh, that's my own personal guard," Lee replied, nodding to the plainclothes cop behind the wheel.

"Cool," Kylie said, waving to him.

Lee decided to take River Road—he liked the view as it twisted and wound along the Delaware. As he headed toward the river through the farm fields, he rounded a familiar turn in the road. There, ahead of him, was McGill's Hill. A wide, steeply sloped incline, it was the prime sledding venue for everyone within miles. People came all the way from Doylestown to sled there. The hill humped steeply at the top; then a sharply angled grade bottomed out into a concave, bowl-like base, followed by a football field's worth of flat land all the way to the creek that snaked through a smattering of trees.

McGill's Hill was an exhilarating ride. The top was so abruptly humped that the sled left the ground, only to return with a thump on the fast downhill slope before rising into the air again at the bottom. After clearing the spoon-like hollow, it was straight across the flatlands to the creek. If the creek was frozen, and if you could manage the sharp turn, you could glide along the ice for a while. The trick was not to hit any of the trees lining the bank. He had seen more than one concussion suffered when head met tree trunk, and had banged his own head once or twice trying to make the treacherous turn.

McGill's Hill was a mecca still popular among local children, who zipped down the hill on everything from plastic bags to fancy hand-steered toboggans—and they still tried to make the dangerous turn, hoping to eke out just a little longer ride.

A thin dusting of snow clung to the brown grasses on the hill's slope, and Lee was reminded of a mocha cake with vanilla frosting. A lone terrier trotted along the crest of the hill, sniffing energetically at the base of a tree before depositing his calling card, casting a short shadow in the feeble February sun. A young woman followed at some distance, carrying a rolled-up leash and reading a book, not paying any attention to her surroundings.

Lee had to stifle an impulse to stop the car and tell her to be more careful. The sight of a woman alone in an isolated area always brought up these feelings for him now. Laura had loved sledding on McGill's Hill.

"Does your grandmom take you there to sled?" he asked Kylie, who was sitting next to him, her eyes half closed, lulled by the motion and warmth of the car.

"Sometimes," she answered. "And she likes to be called Fiona, not grandmom."

Lee smiled. He didn't know what his mother's latest little quirk was about—not about her age, surely. She told anyone who would listen how old she was—usually after asking them to guess first. Then she would beam proudly when they guessed ten or fifteen years too low, as they usually did. Once a very young black waitress had gotten it right on the nose, and Fiona had been in a bad mood all during the rest of the lunch.

"Trying to insult me!" she'd muttered as she picked at her salmon mousse. "She'll be lucky to look half this good when she's my age!"

"Well, you did ask her to guess," Lee pointed out, but that didn't pass muster either.

"I don't care—it's just *rude*, that's what it is!" she insisted.

"Never mind, Mom. We all look the same to them," Lee remarked, but the joke had gone so far over her head he could hear the rushing of wind as it passed.

He had left an especially big tip in case the girl had overheard anything his mother had said.

He looked over at Kylie, whose eyelids were sliding shut, her head resting against the windowpane, her breath forming a cold little spot of mist on the glass. She was a pretty child, with her father's coloring—blue eyes and blond hair. He breathed a silent prayer for her safety to gods he didn't believe in, an empty benediction without the power of faith behind it. Things that were mysterious in his childhood were mysterious to him still. Life's big questions remained unanswered, and he had no faith that would ever change.

Chapter Forty-one

Kylie slept during most of the drive back to the city, but as they neared Jekyll and Hyde, she woke up and began craning her neck for a better look at the restaurant.

"There it is!" she shrieked as the car shot up Sixth Avenue.

Jekyll and Hyde was a theme restaurant aimed at out-of-towners and the Harry Potter crowd—seven- to twelve-year-olds. It occupied all four floors of a curiously stubby building on Sixth Avenue and Fifty-eighth Street, snuggled tightly between towering banks and office buildings. The ornate sign on the neo-Gothic façade was in crimson lettering dripping like spattered blood.

The Jekyll and Hyde Club

Actors roamed the restaurant's four floors dressed in a variety of roles straight out of grade-B horror films—the mad scientist, vampiric hostess, dotty professor, lusty chambermaid—while grotesque statues of gargoyles and skeletons spoke and moved. The creepy portraits in ornate gilded frames lining the walls had eyes that really did follow you around the room.

As they walked toward the restaurant, Kylie bounced from foot to foot and chanted softly to herself. "Chicken *nug*gets, chicken nug-gets."

Kylie adored fried chicken strips, but Lee's mother refused to buy them for her, calling such food "rubbish."

They stepped into the building and were absorbed into the heavy Gothic atmosphere of the restaurant. Red velvet wallpaper lined the walls, and thick Victorian drapes blocked out any shred of sunlight that might sneak in through the floor-to-ceiling French windows. The club was in a state of eternal twilight, with only the flickering of thin yellow flames from gaslights to illuminate the patrons as they wandered through the dim, spooky hallways.

A cadaverous actor dressed as a vampire met them at the door and escorted them up the stairs to the second floor. They were seated at a table in the corner, underneath a portrait in an ornate gilt frame. The face in the picture was of a middle-aged man with heavy features, and he wore a fur-lined red velvet cape and hat, suggesting a nineteenth-century courtier. The man's eyes, under their heavy brows, actually moved. Lee supposed this was done by remote control. Perhaps there was one person on the staff whose job it was to move the eyes in the paintings. As he and Kylie sat down, he saw the eyes follow their movements.

Kylie saw it too. "Look!" she squealed. "He's watching us!"

"Yes," he replied, looking around the restaurant. He had the disquieting feeling that they were actually being watched. But the place was filled mostly with families, the children squirming in their chairs, watching the costumed staff work the room, weaving in and out of the tables as they chatted with customers.

Kylie nudged Lee in the ribs. "Here comes the professor."

Lee turned to look as the actor playing the mad professor

approached their table, coattails flapping. Sinister instruments protruded from the pockets of his white lab coat, which was splattered with suspicious-looking red splotches. His hair was teased into a spiky disarray, and his rumpled lab coat suggested someone who, more often than not, slept in his clothes.

"Hello there," he said in a fake-sounding English accent. "What's your name?"

Kylie leaned back in her chair and looked up at him. "Kylie."

The professor raised an eyebrow. His face was angular, with high cheekbones and deep-set eyes. Under the character makeup, Lee could see that he was young, probably in his early thirties.

"Kylie? What kind of a name is *that*?" he barked hoarsely. Lee wondered if his voice was overworked from talking over the music and the din of the customers, or if it was naturally raspy.

"It's a *nice* name," Kylie replied, thrusting her chin forward in a challenge.

"A nice name? A *nice* name?" the professor bellowed. "Did you hear that?" he said, addressing a nearby table, occupied by a family with towheaded, pink-cheeked children. "What do you think?" he said, descending on one of the boys, a stout lad in a green Pokemon T-shirt. "Do *you* think Kylie is a nice name?"

The boy blinked and looked at his mother, a plump woman with a face as innocent as a cornfield. She looked embarrassed. She gave a weak little smile and poked at her penne primavera.

"Well?" the actor demanded. "Speak up, boy!"

"Uh, sure—I guess," the boy said at last.

"You *guess*? Could you *be* any more indecisive?" The professor looked at Kylie. "Looks like I didn't pick a very brave lad to defend you."

The boy looked at Kylie, who laughed. Relieved, he smiled. "Yes, it's a nice name!" he declared, crossing his arms over his plump chest.

"I don't know what's happening to our young people today," the professor lamented in exaggerated tones, pulling out a plastic scalpel from the pocket of his lab coat. "Maybe I should dissect one of you to find out, eh? What do you think?" he asked Kylie. "Should we cut up your friend here and see what makes him tick? What do you say?"

"No, leave him alone!" she answered, trying to grab the scalpel, but the professor was quicker. Moving out of range, he replaced the instrument, ran a hand through his fright wig of a hairdo, muttering to himself as he moved on to the next table.

"Young people today," he said, shaking his head. "I just don't know."

Kylie smiled at the boy and then leaned her head on Lee's arm. "He's funny. I'm hungry. Can I have chicken nuggets?"

"You can have whatever you want."

"You won't tell Fiona?"

Lee leaned in and whispered in his niece's ear.

"She won't hear it from me."

Kylie picked up her silverware and began drumming on the tabletop.

"Chic-ken nug-gets, chic-ken *nug*-gets."

The mother at the next table shot a look at them, disapproval stamped on her bland face.

Lee wrested the fork and knife from Kylie.

"Look, the show is starting," he said.

The lights around the stage flickered, and a puff of white steam shot up from the fog machine as the slab bearing the body of Frankenstein's monster rose up from its underground home. The whirr of the hydraulic lift was drowned out by the thundering bass line of the music piped through the sound system loudspeakers. Colored strobe lights danced across the monster's inert form, slashing through the haze of stage fog, cutting it with long ribbons of yellow and blue shimmer.

The music was replaced by the equally loud voice of the MC.

"And now, ladies and gentlemen and everything in between, it's showtime! Please direct your attention to our stage at the front of the restaurant."

"I have to go to the bathroom," Kylie said.

"Okay. Hurry back or you'll miss the show."

She slid down from her chair and headed toward the back of the restaurant. Lee watched her until she turned the corner into the foyer. He considered following her, but didn't want to embarrass her. Kylie was only six, but she was stubborn and independent, and resented being fussed over.

When the waiter came, Lee ordered chicken nuggets and Thai stir-fry for himself, then turned his attention back to the stage, where the mad professor hovered over the supine body of his monster. Jets of steam billowed up from the fog machine and hung clustered around his head. The scientist released a burst of maniacal laughter and turned, laying a hand on a large wall switch, preparing to turn on the "electricity" necessary to animate his horrible creation.

Lee wondered if Mary Shelley realized what she had stumbled onto that night she set her troubled dreams down on paper—the creation of life from death, inert matter transformed into a living, sentient being. Did she know that she, too, had created a "monster" when she wrote *Frankenstein*, and that 150 years later the story would spawn endless imitators and retellings?

"And now, behold!" the professor cried, whipping the sheet from the body with a single sweeping motion. The lights shuddered and went black for an instant, then came back on to a blue background with a single scarlet spotlight on the monster, who sat up stiffly, arms outstretched. The children at the next table watched, their eyes fixed on the monster— the child abandoned by the parent who gave him life.

Lee was sorry Kylie was missing this part. *Come to think of it, hadn't she been gone too long now?* A thin river of panic welled up inside him.

He got to his feet and walked to the ladies' room, trying to control the panic that seared the lining of his stomach like vinegar. He knocked on the door and, receiving no answer, opened it and called inside.

"Kylie! Kylie! Are you in there? Kylie!"

There was no answer. He turned and headed for the restaurant's front entrance. Adrenaline raced up his spinal cord, filling his head. He felt as if he were drowning. *Oh, no—first Laura, now her! This can't be happening!*

He lost the ability to think clearly. He forced himself to breathe as he rounded the corner into the hallway. There, inspecting the various mugs and T-shirts for sale, was Kylie. Relief flooded Lee's bloodstream and made his knees soften and go weak. He stumbled and almost toppled over.

He grabbed her by the shoulders and shook her.

"What is it?" she whimpered, frightened. He wanted to slap her, to scream at her, to hug her, all at the same time.

"Kylie, *never* go off without telling me!"

"But I was only looking at the T-shirts."

He didn't want to frighten her, but the words came out harshly.

"*Never!* Do you understand?"

Kylie's lower lip quivered, and tears gathered at the corners of her eyes.

"I won't run off—I was right *here*," she said as a tear slid down one cheek.

"Do you *understand*?"

Kylie let loose the righteous tears of one wrongly accused.

"*I wasn't running away!*" she wailed, choking on the words as her throat thickened with tears.

"I couldn't stand to lose you too!" he said, hugging her to him. "Can't you understand that?"

She greeted his words with a long, loud wail that caught the attention of a couple of women as they came out of the ladies' room. One of them wrenched Lee away from Kylie and planted a well-aimed slap across his face. The other one hoisted Kylie into her arms.

"Is he hurting you, poor thing?" she said, wiping the girl's tears with a red polka-dotted handkerchief. Lee stared at the red dots, imagining them to be drops of blood. *Circular blood spatter patterns indicate dripping as opposed to flung splatter.*

The other woman looked as if she was about to hit Lee again. She was tall and hefty, with shoulders like a linebacker and a helmet of thick, gray-streaked hair. Lee backed away from her, bumping his ribs painfully against a pay phone on the wall.

"I'm her uncle," he said to the woman holding Kylie. She was shorter than her friend, but also thickly built, with fat wrists and ankles, and a plump, dimpled double chin. Both women were wearing the kind of polyester pantsuits only seen on out-of-towners. The shorter one's was geranium red. The linebacker's was marigold orange.

"You may be her uncle, but that doesn't give you the right to engage in child abuse!" the taller one said, squaring off again as if just waiting for an excuse to hit him again.

"It's okay," Kylie said.

"The victim always protects the abuser," the shorter one said, folding her flabby forearms over her formless bosom.

"He was just upset because he didn't want me to disappear like my mommy," Kylie said.

Both women stared at her.

"What?" one said.

Lee considered telling them about his work with the NYPD, but since he had no badge and no gun, felt it would be unconvincing. Instead, he explained about his sister's disappearance.

"Just leave us alone, please," he begged.

With a sniff, the polyestered protectors of justice relented, albeit reluctantly, and retreated back to the dining room, leaving Lee and Kylie alone in the hallway.

"Look, I'm sorry I got upset," he said to her. "It's just—"

"I know," Kylie replied. "Fiona says when you act strange it's because of Mommy."

And what's her excuse when she acts strange? he thought, but said nothing.

"When do you think she'll come back?" Kylie asked.

Her voice was calm, matter-of-fact, as though she were asking when her mother would return from the grocery store. The question put Lee in an impossible position. If he answered it, he would be lying. But if he disagreed with the premise—that his sister was still alive—he would be going up against his mother. Kylie was much too young to be burdened with the disagreement between him and Fiona. He also would be doing his best to shred any lingering hope that Laura could still be alive and might return some day. He bit his lip and took the coward's way out.

"Tell you what, Kylie, why don't we go back in and see if we can catch the last part of the show?"

Kylie took his hand in hers.

"I know why you were being weird. You didn't want to lose me—right, Uncle Lee?" she said as they passed a grinning skeleton hanging on the wall. The skeleton wore a crimson fez and a matching bow tie.

He felt his throat thicken. "That's right. I didn't want to lose you."

Chapter Forty-two

When they left the restaurant, there was no sign of the plainclothes officer who had been tailing him. Lee figured his shift had ended and the cop who was supposed to relieve him hadn't shown up. He should have called it in, but he was glad to be alone for a change. He drove along the dark country lanes in rural New Jersey as Kylie slept in the backseat. He had promised his mother to bring her back that night so she could go to a school fair the next day. It was a long drive to make at night, but he didn't mind. It gave him a chance to think.

The dark sedan was upon him before he registered what was happening. It seemed to come out of nowhere, its headlights on full high beams, so close behind his car that they reflected into his rearview mirror, blinding him. At first he thought it was his surveillance protection, catching up to him, but when the driver remained close, high beams on full, he realized it wasn't a cop behind him.

"Christ, what *is* it with these people?" he muttered as he adjusted the mirror.

His first thought was to pull over and let the car pass him, but that thought was shaken out of his head when he felt the jolt. The sickening realization came instantly: the other car had hit him.

There was no doubt in his mind that it was intentional.

His hands gripped the steering wheel tighter, squeezing it hard as sweat oozed from his palms.

"Oh, God," he said under his breath. "*Goddamn it*." This time it was more of a prayer than a curse.

The car hit him again—harder this time. He heard the crunch as the bumpers met, metal against metal.

In the backseat, Kylie stirred and woke.

"Uncle Lee? Are we there yet?"

He took a deep breath and tried to will the panic out of his voice.

"No, honey—go back to sleep."

Another bump, this time sending his car into the opposite lane, so that he had to fight to control it.

Kylie's voice came from the backseat, wide awake now, sounding as panicked as he felt. "Uncle Lee, what's going on?"

He had no idea what to say to her, how to explain that there was someone trying to kill them both.

"Go back to sleep, okay? Everything's going to be fine."

Even as he said the words he could feel how hollow they were. Everything wasn't going to be fine.

The headlights glared into his side mirror, the beams bouncing back into his face. He squinted and rolled down the window, pushing the mirror away. A blast of cold air hit his face. He heard the engine behind him rev, and braced himself for another jolt. Instead, the headlights disappeared, and he saw the car pull up next to him. The two-lane road twisted and wound through the Jersey countryside, the solid double yellow line indicating that passing was forbidden. Even at this time of night, he knew, this was suicidal behavior. There was no way for the other driver to see an oncoming car before it was too late.

"Jesus," he said under his breath. His leg trembling, he rammed his foot down hard on the accelerator. The little Honda jerked and shifted into first gear, spurting ahead of the car next to him.

"Uncle Lee," Kylie whimpered, "what's happening?"

"There's a crazy driver following us," he replied, trying to sound casual. "Maybe he's drunk or something."

This was a route he had driven countless times, from the day he got his license at the age of sixteen, and he knew every twist and turn in the road. He had often joked that he could drive it in his sleep. It was the one advantage he had over his unknown pursuer, and he prayed that it would count for something now. If the other driver managed to pull in front of him, Lee knew, he could almost certainly force Lee to stop. If Lee attempted to pass him, he could force Lee off the road.

He pushed the gas pedal to the floor. The Honda's engine revved, and the car pulled ahead of his pursuer. The Honda's engine was small but efficient, and had good pickup speed. Lee offered a silent prayer of thanks to Japanese engineering.

The headlights reappeared behind him once again, and he heard the other car's engine gun as its headlights got closer. He prayed that the other car was not a more powerful machine than his four-cylinder rental Honda.

The road lay in front of him, a dark, curling ribbon of concrete. Ahead of him loomed McGill's Hill, curved as the back of a whale, barely visible in the darkness.

He gripped the steering wheel and leaned forward.

"Okay, you bastard," he muttered, "let's see how you like this."

With an abrupt twist of the wheel, he pulled off the road and headed for the stream at the bottom of the hill, his headlights on full beam. The car shuddered and shook as it hit the uneven ground, bumping and jerking along the frozen earth. He could hear Kylie whimpering in the backseat, but he gritted his teeth and drove on at a steady speed. Seeing the frozen stream—shallow enough to be frozen clear through, he knew from experience—he steered the car toward it.

His tires slid onto the frozen stream. The car fishtailed, then righted itself. He pressed the accelerator steadily, in search of what traction was possible with the car's front-wheel drive.

The sedan continued its pursuit, weaving as its tires hit the ice.

Lee's headlights picked up the copse of trees at the bottom of the hill, the grove of poplars so dangerous to generations of sledders. The stream was at its deepest point there, and on the other side of the trees was a deep ditch—invisible at night. He gunned the engine and then jerked the wheel all the way to the right, just missing the first tree. With the wheels spinning in the thin layer of snow covering the ground, he turned the car in a tight circle and avoided the ditch.

His pursuer was not so lucky.

Lee heard the crunch of metal as the other car glanced off the first tree. He glanced out of the rearview mirror just in time to see the car land headfirst in the ditch, tires spinning uselessly in the air.

Anxious as he was to know the identity of his pursuer, his instinct to protect his niece was stronger. He knew that if the driver was wearing a seat belt, he might be only mildly injured. He longed to go back for a look at the license plates, but what if their pursuer had a gun? He couldn't take that chance. He turned the Honda in a tight circle and headed back to the road. A wave of nausea threatened to overcome him as he pulled back onto the road, but he took deep gulps of the icy air coming in through his still open window and sped off into the night.

Kylie had grown very quiet in the backseat, so when he had gone a mile or two, he looked back at her to see if she was all right. She sat staring at him without speaking, her hands clutching the stuffed dinosaur he had bought for her earlier.

"Kylie? Are you okay?" he said.

"What happened to the other car?" she asked. "He hit the tree. Is he going to be all right?"

"I don't know, honey, but I'm going to call the police as soon as I can so they can go rescue him."

"Why did you go off the road like that?"

Because he was trying to kill us.

"Well, I just wanted him to stop following us."

"Why was he following us?"

"I think he must have been drunk or something."

Kylie began to cry. "But what if he died?"

"Don't worry, Kylie—it's going to be all right. The police will take care of him. Everything's going to be all right."

But the more he said the words, the less he believed them. Someone was after him, and he suspected that whoever it was, they wanted him off the case—very, very badly.

Chapter Forty-three

Lee drove for a while without looking back, taking side roads and detours. When he was certain that he wasn't being followed, he pulled off the road to call the police. After dialing 911 and reporting the accident, he started the Honda's engine up again. He was worried about his family's safety. The attack had taken place in their backyard this time, and he couldn't be there to protect them constantly.

Kylie had fallen asleep in the backseat again—with the emotional resilience of childhood, she had forgotten her panic, accepting Lee's explanation that the whole thing was just the crazy actions of a drunk driver. He had no intention of telling her the truth.

As the engine turned over, he was seized by an uncontrollable wave of shivering, and had to turn off the car again for a while to calm down. He realized that all he knew about the other car was that it was a dark sedan—any other details were lost in a blur of action and decision making. He couldn't even say how many people were in the car. It could have been more than one, for all he knew, though he didn't think so.

Every instinct in his body told him that the pursuer was one man and one man alone.

When he arrived at Fiona's house it was three in the morning. The grandfather clock in the front hall ticked loudly as he tiptoed in through the front door, Kylie in his arms. Surrounded by the familiar smell of apples and old wood, Lee had trouble imagining the threat they had both just survived—here, at his mother's everything felt so familiar, so comfortable, and so safe.

He closed the heavy door behind him quietly and carried Kylie upstairs to her bedroom. She hardly stirred as he laid her on the bed, removing her shoes and socks and tucking her under a thick layer of blankets and quilts. Fiona Campbell kept a watchful eye on the thermostat, and the house was cold at night. "A cool room at night is better for you than a stuffy one," she would say. "A bit of fresh night air never hurt anyone."

Lee was exhausted but wide awake, so he went down to the living room and lit a fire. He then took out his cell phone and dialed the state police headquarters, located in Somerville, about twenty minutes away. He had a feeling that the state troopers would find an empty car down by the stream, but he wanted the car held and checked for evidence: blood, DNA, anything that could help identify his pursuer. He gave his name to the sleepy operator who answered.

"New Jersey State Police. How can I help you?"

"Hello, this is Lee Campbell of the NYPD. May I speak with your shift commander, please?"

"That would be Lieutenant Robinson. Just a minute, please."

"Robinson here." The voice was deep, educated, probably African American. Lee hadn't had much contact with Jersey troopers, but they had a reputation for being fierce and efficient.

Lee explained the situation as calmly as possible, emphasizing to Lieutenant Robinson that he didn't know if the attacker was related to the case he was working on, but that he suspected there was a link. Robinson listened, then asked if Lee and his niece were all right.

"We're fine, thanks—just shaken up a little. I'm at my mother's house, and if it's all right with you I'll come by tomorrow to have a look at that car."

"Fine. I've already spoken with the troopers who found it—it's right where you said it was, but it's empty. There's a trail of footprints in the snow leading away from the car out to the road, but that's where they disappear."

"How many sets of prints?"

"One. A man, by the look of it. Medium-sized feet— about a size nine, Trooper Edwards said. Guess we should take a cast of the prints, if there's a possible connection to a murder suspect."

"I would appreciate that very much."

"And we'll do a trace on the car, of course. Doesn't look like a rental."

"Thanks."

"You're sure you're okay now?"

"Yeah, fine—thanks."

"Okay, then, we'll see you tomorrow."

"Right."

Lee hung up and stared into the fire. The flames licked greedily upward, as if they wanted to fly straight up the chimney and into the night. The pointed tongues of flame reminded him of pitchforks, and, listening to the wind whistling through the house's ancient eaves, he imagined he was hearing the howls of the damned.

Chapter Forty-four

The trip to Somerville the next day was disappointing. The car had been reported stolen earlier that day, and the owner, a well-respected local doctor, was beyond suspicion. He also wore a size-eleven shoe.

No blood was found inside the car, at least not in the preliminary search, but it was being sent to the state crime lab for further analysis. Lee doubted they would find anything—the driver, whoever he was, had probably worn gloves.

The first thing Lieutenant Robinson did was to put a twenty-four-hour guard on Fiona's house, much to her disgust. Lee also called Kylie's father, over his mother's protests, and asked him to come stay with them for a while, which he did gladly. Lee tried not to alarm him unduly, but George Callahan was a kind man, and his concern was obvious. He offered to take Fiona and Kylie over to his house, but Fiona was having none of it. She called the whole thing "silly," insisting that Lee had simply had an encounter with a drunk driver.

"It's true what they say about Jersey drivers, you know,"

she said, both eyebrows lifted in disdain. "They are a dangerous lot."

Lee wasn't interested in his mother's opinion, and insisted on the safety precautions. The state trooper was to accompany Kylie to and from school, at least for a while.

When Lee told Chuck Morton about the attack, he insisted on meeting as soon as Lee was back in the city.

By the time Lee left New Jersey it was nighttime, and a late winter storm was blowing in. Lee returned to the city just as the storm slammed into the coast with a vengeance. He barely made it to the car rental place in the Village. A foot of snow had already fallen by the time he headed out for his apartment on foot.

When he got in, he phoned Chuck on his cell phone to say he would come by first thing in the morning. He wasn't going out again tonight. Chuck was already on his way back to his house. If he delayed his departure from the city any longer, he might end up having to spend the night. Everyone was saying this was going to drop a load of snow on the area—possibly up to three feet.

Lee sat at the piano playing a Bach prelude as he listened to the storm moaning as it swirled around the low-lying buildings of East Seventh Street. The old tenement building creaked and shuddered as the wind whirled around the edges of the windows, gusting and howling like a living thing, a demon in search of souls to capture.

He stopped playing and stared out the window at the trees across the street, which were bending and swaying so violently he thought they might snap. *Demons. Lost souls*. Lee wasn't sure he believed in the existence of souls, but what was this killer if not a lost soul?

The phone rang, jolting him out of his reverie. He picked it up.

"Hello?"

"Can I—uh—see you?" Nelson's voice was ragged, shaky.

"What's the matter?"

"It's Karen. I need—"

It was as though he were straining his words out through a sieve, trying to hold back the emotion behind them. Lee knew that it was barely three months since his wife's tragic death. He also knew all about grief. Just when you thought the worst was over, it could come back at you like the kick of a shotgun.

He looked outside at the gathering snow and sighed.

"I'll be there in twenty minutes."

Lee pulled on his waterproof hiking boots and walked to the liquor store on Third Avenue. He picked out a bottle of Glenlivet single malt, then found a brave cabbie with snow tires. Traffic was light on Park Avenue, and the cabbie crossed Central Park through the 68th Street transverse right behind a snowplow, pulling up in front of Nelson's building on 73rd Street.

John Paul Nelson lived in a penthouse apartment of the Ansonia Hotel, a splendid, ornate Rococo building on the southwest corner of 73rd and Broadway. Rising proudly over the confluence of Broadway and Amsterdam Avenue, the Ansonia stands at one of the great crossroads of the city. The Seventh Avenue line spits out its passengers at the subway stop in the traffic island that bifurcates Broadway as it splits in two before reuniting and continuing on its northwesterly journey, while Tenth Avenue, reborn as Amsterdam—its name a reminder of the city's Dutch heritage—shoots straight uptown, slicing through the Upper West Side, neatly bisecting the neighborhood, equidistant from its two great parks, Riverside and Central Park.

Nelson opened the door when Lee knocked. He looked exhausted and lost. His auburn hair was uncombed. He was unshaven and wore an old blue flannel shirt over rumpled chinos. He waved Lee to a seat on a couch strewn with books and magazines.

"Sorry about this. Just, uh, make a place for yourself."

He plucked a few books off the end of the sofa and put them on the floor. Nelson's apartment, like his office, was a place of controlled chaos, comfortable clutter. When she was alive, Karen had managed the mess, keeping it under control, but since her death, things had deteriorated. There were books and periodicals all over the room—Lee wondered how it was possible for anyone to read as much as that. The books were on everything from archaeology to philosophy, physics to natural history.

Nelson stood in the middle of the room, running a hand through his untidy hair. After one look at him, Lee decided not to mention the incidents of two nights ago. Nelson would find out about the mad car chase soon enough.

"What can I get you?" Nelson asked.

It was only then Lee remembered the bottle of scotch in his hand.

"I didn't remember if it's your brand or not," he said, handing it to Nelson.

"If it's alcohol, it's my brand," he replied, and Lee regretted buying an expensive single malt.

But when his friend returned with two cut-crystal glasses and handed one to Lee, he was glad. The scotch had a piney, musty flavor, like open woodland and fireplaces in the fall.

"Really nice of you to spring for the good stuff," Nelson said, settling down in a tattered blue armchair. His Irish setter, Rex, emerged from the kitchen, padded over to him, and sat at his feet, sniffing the air. Nelson reached down and scratched the dog behind the ears.

"Thanks for coming over," he said, taking a swallow of scotch. "I guess I didn't want to be alone. Funny, it kind of caught me off guard . . ." He stared at his glass for some time before speaking. "I just can't help thinking that if I loved her better, she wouldn't have died."

"She was very sick, you know."

Nelson looked down at Rex's silky head. "I know. My logical mind tells me that, but I feel that if I had loved her better, she wouldn't have been able to leave me."

"It wasn't like she had a choice—"

"I *know*! I've told myself that a thousand times over, but what I fear more than anything is that Karen really didn't want to live enough. That she just . . . gave up."

"My God," Lee said. "You've got to stop punishing yourself over her death. Take it from someone who knows."

Nelson looked at his glass, and then at Lee. "How did you do it?"

"I don't think we ever get over missing the people we lose. We just learn how to live with the loss."

"I still can't accept that I had no control over it."

"It isn't uncommon to feel guilty in a situation like this."

"Yes, yes, I know," Nelson answered, some of the old impatience creeping into his voice. "It's just that—well, when it comes right down to it, I guess we don't think of ourselves as 'other people,' do we?"

"No, I guess not."

Nelson slumped in his chair and stroked Rex's shiny golden fur. They matched almost exactly, master and dog—Nelson's curly rust-colored hair was just a shade or two darker than the dog's burnished red-gold coat. Rex leaned into his master's leg, a blissful expression on his big, friendly face. The dog was Nelson's perfect mirror image, a kind of reverse alter ego, as sweet and outgoing as Nelson was sour and mistrustful. Lee knew his friend's behavior was a mask for an almost unbearable sensitivity, but few people saw through the mask. Lee had been allowed a glimpse of this, and over time Nelson had opened up to him—but he was one of the few. Karen was another, of course, but now she was gone.

Nelson broke the silence with a cough—the deep, rattling hacking of a lifetime smoker. Lee looked at him sternly. The whole apartment smelled of clove cigarettes.

"When is it you're going to quit smoking?"

"For God's sake, Lee, one thing at a time! I never smoked around her, you know," he added. "Not even before she—"

"I know," Lee answered. "I know you didn't."

"It was pretty funny, leaving my own apartment to smoke out on the street like some furtive teenager. We used to laugh about it," Nelson said, smiling, and then his smile slid away. His face fell, and a sob raked his vocal cords, making a harsh sound. He regained control after a moment, though, and took a deep breath.

"It's funny how so many other fears seem to spring from the basic fear of abandonment, isn't it?" he said.

Lee looked into his glass of scotch, the tawny liquid catching the light refracted by the cut-crystal glass. "Yeah. You know, that's even true for . . ." He broke off without finishing the thought, and looked away.

"What? True for who?"

"I was thinking about the case."

Nelson sat back in his chair. "I'm listening."

"I just didn't think it was right, under the circumstances—"

"For God's sake, man, you've piqued my curiosity now!" Nelson roared. "And do you think I want to spend all night moaning about Karen's death? Please—distract me!"

"Okay. It's not that big a deal, really. I was going to say that for him it's also about abandonment."

"For the Slasher?"

"Yes. Control, yes—but the roots are fear of abandonment."

"But what does it get us—or where does it get us, I should say, that we haven't already been?"

"He can't even allow himself to experience normal sexual impulses toward women. I think they may be irretrievably locked for him now—sex, religion, and death—to the point where, in his mind, they represent the same thing."

"And there's the sadomasochistic aspect of Catholicism: the suffering Jesus, bound and bloody on the cross."

"And Mary—always depicted as young and beautiful—looking up at him with adoration in her tear-swelled eyes."

"You know, you're right," Nelson said. "I never thought about it. If Jesus really is thirty-three when he dies, then Mary has to be at least in her fifties, right?"

"Right. And this is in a sun-drenched climate before Botox and face-lifts, or even decent dental care. She's going to *look* her age."

"But she's always depicted as young and beautiful—as if she were his sister rather than his mother."

"Right," Lee agreed. "Even more confusing for a young man who's having trouble escaping a clinging mother."

Nelson took a long swallow of scotch. "The less said about Catholic mothers, the better."

Nelson had said very little about his own mother to Lee over the years, and always seemed to steer clear of the topic.

"Which borough do you think will be next?" Nelson asked.

"Chuck asked me the same thing. I wish I had an answer." Nelson stared out the window.

"How do we do it, Lee? How do we sift through the mountains of misery life throws up at us and keep going?"

"I don't know," Lee said. "Some of us don't."

"Yes, but most of us do, that's the amazing thing," Nelson said, rising from his chair to pace restlessly, hands shoved into his pockets. "You know, Karen talked about ending it all as her disease got worse, in spite of her faith. I even talked about helping her. In the end, though, we cherished every last moment together, even when it was really hard. But that's different, isn't it? I mean, anyone with a terminal illness is going to think about ending it, even if they don't act on that, right?"

"I'm sure anyone would at least consider it—unless their faith prevented them from it."

Nelson snorted. "Faith. One of mankind's greatest lies. Do you know I still have the cross she wore? She had her faith right up until the end. I think I envied her that, even though I never shared in it."

The phone rang. Nelson grunted, balanced his drink on the arm of his chair, then rose to answer it.

"Hello?" There was a pause, and then he said, "Who is this?" Another pause, and then he hung up.

"Who was that?" Lee asked.

"That was really strange," Nelson replied, shaking his head. "All I heard on the other end was music playing."

"What kind of music?"

"It was an old Rodgers and Hart song, actually—one I recognized."

"Which one?"

"'Manhattan.'"

"Oh, God," Lee said. He sank back his chair. "Good lord . . . so he knows you're on the investigation."

"Obviously."

"Your number's unlisted, right?"

"Right."

"Caller ID?"

Nelson glanced at the receiver. "'Unavailable.' Probably using a phone booth somewhere. We can track it, but I doubt it'll give us much. If he's smart—which he is—it won't be anywhere near his home."

"Well," Lee said after a moment, "at least we can stop wondering which borough is going to be next."

Chapter Forty-five

The wind took the barren black branches of the trees and swung them back and forth in a kind of mad dance, a tango of bad weather to come.

They didn't *know* they were being bad, these soft-eyed girls with their white hands and even whiter throats—little lambs, really, innocent white lambs with their trusting, open faces. They trusted him, and why shouldn't they? He was there to save them, after all, to make sure their souls went up to heaven, instead of down *there*, that horrible place his mother kept talking about, where demons ate your flesh and you lived in eternal damnation.

He walked along the creek bed, stepping carefully on the stones so as not to get his feet wet. He tried to shut out the sound of his mother's voice in his head, but it was to no avail.

Samuel! Sam-u-el! Are you listening to me? They'll tear at your flesh, and you'll be forever damned—trapped down there in eternal torment! And do you know what the worst thing of all will be? You'll never get to see Jesus again! You'll be eternally banished from His presence. Think about it, Samuel. Never *to see Jesus again, never to look upon His divine presence!*

He did think about it. It would be too bad, he supposed. But then again, it might be a kind of relief. Jesus' eyes were so sad, so tormented. Samuel felt bad just looking at the carved figurine of Jesus, garishly painted blood dripping from His side, on the cross above his mother's bed. It was as if Jesus were begging Samuel to come save Him from torment, but he couldn't. He wanted to, but Jesus was already dead—they had already killed Him. And yet, somehow, here he was, hanging above his mother's bed, his beautiful doelike eyes begging for mercy—begging him, Samuel, for deliverance, for release from his agony.

Well, Samuel couldn't do anything about Jesus, but he could help those girls. He could release them, point them the way to eternal salvation.

He smiled. It had to be right, what he was doing, because it felt so good. He was delivering them from sin and temptation—and yes, evil. *Deliver us. Deliver us.* The words rang a tattoo in his head, rhythmic as a pulse. He sniffed at the air like a bird dog on a scent. The wind was blowing in from the river, carrying the smell of salt air and fossilized sea creatures. *Forgive us our trespasses.* Tonight he would get to work.

Chapter Forty-six

Sophia wanted a cigarette. She knew she shouldn't smoke, but she desperately, dreadfully needed a cigarette. She sat at the desk in her dorm room trying to concentrate on the book in front of her: *Film Analysis* by R. L. Rutsky and Jeffrey Geiger.

Her mother had said she was crazy to think she could make a living working on "those Hollywood movies," as she called them, but her father had glowed with pride when she was accepted into NYU as a film major.

"She has a talent, Loretta—you'll see," he had said to his wife, squeezing her to him, her round little body plump as a ripe peach.

"You should be glad she's staying close to home," he continued, looking out at the garden in front of their two-family house in Queens. "She'll be able to come over for dinner."

Sophia wished she were going away to college, but NYU was a really good school and she was grateful to be accepted into the film studies program there.

Now, sitting in her dorm room with most of her classmates asleep around her, she tried to concentrate on the book on her desk, but the words blurred and danced on the page in front of her. All she could think of was how much she longed for a cigarette.

Finally she gave up. Moving quietly so as not to disturb her sleeping roommate, she grabbed her pack of Marlboro Lights, pulled on her boots and overcoat, and slipped out of the room.

The fresh snow was silent and glistening in the street, soft and white and pristine, not sullied yet by the soot of engines and the pollution of the city. Sticking a cigarette in her mouth, she realized she'd forgotten her matches. She shivered, drew her coat tighter around her, and headed through the snow toward the deli on the corner of La Guardia Place.

The street was deserted, and the street lamps cast pools of light onto the softly falling snow. The flakes swirled and danced under the lights; caught up in the magic of the night, Sophia almost didn't see the man standing in the shadows of the NYU dormitory building. Seeing her, he took a step toward her.

"Need a light?" His voice was soft, his face still half in shadow.

"Sure—thanks."

It was the last thing she ever said.

Chapter Forty-seven

When the phone rang at seven the next morning, Lee awoke instantly, the sharp stab of sound pulling him out of bed. He grabbed the receiver.

"Hello?"

"Lee, it's Chuck."

"Oh, God—another one?"

"Yeah."

"Where is it this time?"

"Old St. Patrick's. You know it?"

"On Mulberry?"

"Right."

Old St. Patrick's Cathedral was a beautiful landmark building nestled between Mott and Mulberry Streets, at the intersections of Chinatown and Little Italy. Lee had never been inside, but had walked past it countless times. It was a fifteen-minute walk from his apartment.

"I know where it is," Lee said. "Jesus."

"I'm on my way," Chuck said, "but you'll probably get there first."

"Right. Any instructions?"

"No—just don't let anyone move anything until I get there."

"Right."

Lee pulled on some clothes and hailed a cab in under five minutes. He was there in less than ten. He showed his ID to the uniformed cop on duty and went in the side door.

The scene at Old St. Patrick's was depressingly familiar: the same group of investigators dispersed around the church, the same hushed voices and dimly lit interior. The early-morning rays of the rising sun crept tentatively through the circular stained-glass window at the back of the church.

Lee walked past the crime scene technicians, who were just unpacking their equipment, and approached the altar, to look upon the face of the latest victim. He steeled himself for the sight of her naked, mutilated body, but he couldn't prepare himself for what he saw.

There, on the altar, lay the torso of a young woman. Her head was still attached, but that was all; her limbs had been severed, and were nowhere to be seen. On her dismembered torso were carved the words *On earth as it is in heaven.*

Lee absorbed this information in one terrible moment—then, turning away, he vomited. The members of the CSI team glanced at him, then continued with their work. This was obviously not the first time they had witnessed this reaction to a crime scene. Within seconds, a young woman from the CSI team headed toward him with a rag and a bucket, hastily gathered from the mop closet.

As she cleaned up after him, Lee forced himself to look at the victim. As he expected, she had the same short, curly dark hair as the others, though her skin was more of an olive hue. Her lips were fuller, her body—what there was of it—more womanly and developed. His head began to spin, and, fearing he was going to be sick again, Lee turned away.

"Sophia," said a deep voice behind him. "Sophia Lo-Bianca."

Lee turned to see Detective Florette approaching from the back of the church. Though without his usual jacket and tie, he wore a crisp white shirt, creased trousers, and polished brown loafers. Lee wondered if the man had a full-time valet.

"NYU student, film major," Florette said, frowning.

Lee stared at him. "How did you get all that?"

Florette indicated a young man in a clerical collar sitting in the back pews of the church.

"Father Joseph. Knows her because she sings in the choir here."

Florette looked down at Sophia—or what was left of her—and shook his dignified head.

"Nasty business. What do you make of this?"

Lee gritted his teeth, determined not to be sick again in front of the elegant detective. "I'll know more once we find the rest of her."

Florette laid a hand on his shoulder. "Come with me."

Apprehension gathering in his churning stomach like a sour storm cloud, Lee followed the detective to the back of the church. There, underneath a stained-glass window depicting Death terrifying a group of people, he saw a leg. He looked around for a blood trail, but there was none. That meant either the Slasher had cleaned up, or she had stopped bleeding by the time he cut her up, which meant she was already long dead—thank God. He took a deep breath and looked at Florette.

"There's more," he said, and led Lee to the other side of the church, where, on the basement stairs, they found another leg—and then an arm, and finally, under a statue of Mary holding Jesus, the other arm.

Florette gave Lee a few moments to process what he had seen, and then he said, "Does it have significance—the placement, I mean?"

"I think it does, probably a religious significance, but I'm not equipped to interpret it." He wished with all his heart

Nelson were here—he would know what to make of all this. He was a lapsed Catholic, but he had absorbed all the symbolism and church history.

Lee looked over at the priest, still huddled in a corner pew. "Can he stick around for a while?"

"I'll ask him," Florette answered, and walked over to the priest.

Chuck arrived shortly afterward. When he saw what the Slasher had done to poor Sophia, his face grew crimson right up to the roots of his blond crew cut.

"Jesus," he said. "Bastard," he added through clenched teeth, though the epithet hardly seemed strong enough.

Lee and Florette filled him in on what they knew. Nelson wasn't answering his phone, and Detective Butts was with his wife's family out in the middle of New Jersey. There wasn't much for them to do. The CSI team had things under control, as usual, and after interviewing the priest again, all they could do was watch as poor Sophia was processed and bagged, piece by piece, and taken off to the ME's office. Lee noticed a smell in the air, something he couldn't identify. It was sweet, and it lingered in his nose even after they left the church. It seemed somehow familiar, but maybe it was just the aftereffects of all the years of burning incense.

As they were leaving he remembered the last murder, and pulled aside a CSI technician, a young man with bad skin and neatly trimmed blond bangs.

"Test the communion wine for blood," Lee instructed him.

The tech looked at him, puzzled. "Why would there be—"

"Just do it, okay?" Lee said.

"Christ," Chuck said as they stood on the steps of the church watching the dark blue medical examiner's van drive away. "We've got to catch this bastard." He glanced at his watch. "I've got a meeting in half an hour—let's meet this afternoon in my office."

Lee went home and showered, then called Nelson, but he still wasn't answering his phone.

That afternoon at Chuck's office, none of them looked well rested, having been awakened by the early morning summons. Butts had driven in straight from his in-laws' place, and looked as ragged as the rest of them. Nelson was still unreachable, so they started without him.

"Is there any news from New Jersey?" Chuck asked Lee, taking usual his seat behind his desk.

"I spoke with the state troopers in Somerville this morning. They processed the car thoroughly, but the only prints they found were from the doctor and his family. The only thing they have is the footprints in the snow."

Chuck frowned. "Without a suspect in custody, they're worthless. And I chewed out the cop who was supposed to be tailing you that night—turns out he had a family emergency, but that's still no excuse."

"What's this all about?" Butts asked.

Chuck filled him and Florette in on Lee's wild car chase.

"We think there might be a connection," he added.

Frowning, Florette cocked his head to one side. "According to your profile, that doesn't sound at all like this guy."

"I know," Lee agreed. "That what's so disturbing about it."

Butts's homely face crinkled in concern. "Do you think you oughta be—I mean, maybe you should—"

"Look, we can talk about that later, okay?" Lee interrupted. "Right now, let's deal with what we do know, okay?"

"Okay," Chuck said. "What do you make of this new twist?"

Lee frowned. He wished Nelson were here to help him.

"I suspect there's a significance to the placement of the body parts, but I don't know enough to explain that. I do think he's—"

"—becoming more confident," Florette finished for him.

"Yes, that's true—but he could also be unraveling. Some serial killers fall apart after a while. The strain of being chased gets to them, and they become sloppy and reckless. Bundy fell apart completely at the end, butchering several residents of a sorority house and leaving behind all kinds of evidence, including an eyewitness who survived. And Gacy began to break down after being conspicuously trailed by the police for a week."

"So that's good, right?" Butts said.

"Not necessarily. It also makes him more dangerous, more unpredictable."

"So what now?" said Chuck.

"Well," Lee answered, "we have to hope that he's getting overconfident."

"Pride cometh before a fall," Florette murmured.

"Something like that," Lee agreed. He looked out the window at the sunless sky.

As he walked from the subway to his apartment, Lee's cell phone rang. The Caller ID said Fiona. That was odd—she hated cell phones, and never called him on his.

"Hello?"

"Lee?" His mother sounded upset—her voice was shaky.

"What's wrong?"

"It's Groucho. He's . . ." Her voice shook, and he could hear a muffled sob.

"What happened?"

"I don't know. I couldn't find him last night, and today I found him underneath the willow tree." Another muffled sob, and then she came back on the line. "I don't know if I'm imagining things, but I think he was poisoned."

"Have Stan take him to the vet for an autopsy."

"Am I being silly? I know he's just a cat, but—"

"No, you're not being silly! How's Kylie taking it?"

"She's very upset. She's with her father today."

"Okay. Now listen carefully. You call Stan and have him

take Groucho to the vet for an autopsy—and let me know the results, okay? Then you go immediately to George's and stay there."

"But—"

"Please! Do as I say—for God's sake!"

"All right," she answered meekly.

"I'll call you in an hour to see if everything went all right. And for God's sake let the police escort know where you're going in case you get separated, will you?"

"Yes, dear. What do you think . . . ?"

"I don't know. But please don't take any chances."

"I won't. I'll be all right. Stan's here with me."

"Good—keep him with you." The more people he could surround his family with, the safer they would be.

I'll take Manhattan . . .

The Slasher, whoever he was, didn't make empty threats.

Chapter Forty-eight

The results from the vet in Jersey were exactly as Lee had expected. The cat had indeed been poisoned—arsenic, mixed in with canned tuna fish. *"Poor Groucho. He never could resist tuna fish,"* Lee's mother had said on the phone. There was no way to determine who had done it, of course—but Lee didn't have much doubt. He urged Fiona to stay at George's and not leave the house unless she was accompanied by a policeman.

Their meeting in Chuck's office the next day had a desultory feeling. There didn't seem to be any way to stop the Slasher—in fact, he seemed to be hitting his stride. Chuck sent out a notice to all precinct commanders in Manhattan to be on alert, but none of them thought it would do any good. The level of vigilance was already high citywide after the attack on the World Trade Center.

Long after darkness closed in on the city, Chuck sent them all away. The mayor had called a press conference for the following day, and he had to meet with the mayor that night to catch him up on their progress—or lack of it.

As everyone was leaving, Chuck beckoned to Lee.

"Got a minute?"

"Sure—what's up?"

Chuck looked down at his shoes.

"I'm worried about you."

"Look, Chuck, I—"

"No, please—just hear me out, okay? I was willing to believe on some level that the attack in the subway might be unrelated to this case, but after the incident in Jersey, I've been thinking long and hard about this, and we've got to face it, Lee: he's after you now."

"But why me in particular?"

"That's what I've been asking myself, and I don't have any answers. But it's getting too dangerous for you. I wish you'd just—"

"I know what you're going to say. Now let me say something. I *need* this case, okay? If we allow him to win, I'll never be able to get over it. Besides, we don't know for sure that whoever is after me is really the Slasher."

Chuck folded his arms. "No, we don't. But what do you think the odds are?"

"I don't know—just like I don't know how he knows the details of my sister's disappearance, or even if he does. But I have to be the one to find out. You can see that, can't you?"

Chuck looked down at his shoes again. They gleamed like a new penny.

"For God's sake, Lee, put it all together. The gunshot, the text message, the—"

"Look, just give me a couple more days, okay?" Lee said. "Please—I'm begging you."

Chuck bit his lower lip and looked out the window at the darkened city. "Okay, okay," he said. "Christ, even in school you could always get your way in the end. I'll let you stay—but for God's sake, Lee, be careful, will you?"

"I promise."

What neither of them said was that all the vigilance in the world couldn't keep the Slasher from making his next move.

Lee went home and played the piano for two hours straight. He spent the entire first hour thrashing through a Bach partita he was working on. It was gritty, sweaty work—the Devil himself had taken up residence in the left-hand passages. What was really irritating was that he could just imagine Bach himself playing the damn thing without so much as a minute of practice.

"Goddamn genius," he muttered as he grappled with a knotty modulation. No matter what he played, though, the same song kept intruding, running through his head: *I'll take Manhattan . . .*

He made a pot of coffee and drank it until his teeth ached, as he looked through his case notes. After several hours of this, he had to stop, but he was too caffeinated to sleep, so he turned on the radio. A Verdi opera was playing, and he wasn't in the mood for tremulous tenors and overwrought sopranos, so he tried television.

He watched the Turner Classic Movies's rerun of *Gaslight* for a while, but Charles Boyer's sadistic, tormenting husband routine irritated him. If only villains announced themselves so baldly, he thought. If only their evil intentions were so obviously displayed. He wanted to grab Ingrid Bergman and shake her, lovely as she was, scream at her to wake up and realize what was going on.

"Trying out a little projection, Campbell?" he muttered as he changed channels restlessly. *Well, it's always easier from the outside looking in, isn't it? Everything is easier—spotting people's neuroses, destructive patterns, self-delusions. Much harder to spot your own. Physician, heal thyself, indeed.*

There was nothing else good on the television, so around 2 A.M. he sat down at his computer and logged on to the Internet. The moment he typed in his password, an instant message appeared in the upper left-hand corner of his monitor. Lee's chest tightened when he saw the name on the screen: Holyman.

Hello there. What's the matter, can't sleep?

He took a deep breath and typed a reply:

I like being up late. What about you?

I'm what they call a night owl, I guess. What do you know— that's something else we have in common.

Do I know you?

No, but I know you.

Tell me what else we have in common.

We both have a fascination with death.

I hadn't realized that.

But it's so *obvious*.

Maybe you're right.

Humor him, Lee thought. *Try to draw him out.*

The only difference is that I've held the power of life and death in my hands, and you haven't.

Really? What do you mean?

You know what I mean.

Okay.

So how is it going?

How is what going?

The investigation, of course. Too bad about the cat.

Anger flooded Lee's body, making his stomach tighten. *So he* was *behind Groucho's death.* He decided not to give the man the satisfaction of a response.

How did you get my screen name?

Oh, please. Ask me something harder—like how did I manage to abduct a coed from a crowded campus.

Why did you do that to Sophia?

If you were any kind of decent Catholic you'd know.

I know what you took from them. Why did you take what you did?

There was a pause, and then the reply came.

I'm disappointed in you.

I'm sorry to hear that.

You have no idea what it feels like, to hold another person's life in your hands.

Tell me.

Do you think that'll give you another piece of the puzzle you need to catch me?

Not really. I'm just curious.

Curiosity killed the cat.

I'll take that chance.

Like your sister? Did she take chances?

Lee leaned back in his chair. This man was trying to get him—but had told him nothing important, except that he had done his research about Lee's family. He counted to ten and typed.

Why do you do it?

He tells me to do it.

Does it get easier or harder?

Easier. Much easier. The first time was the hardest.

Don't you feel bad for the women?

No. I just think of where they're going. I'm sending them to God—away from this world of sin and on to God. It is a great privilege, really.

But killing is forbidden by the Bible.

I am a Servant of God. He *tells* me who to kill.

Lee wondered if this was just a put-on. Was he saying this to set up an insanity defense later? *I hear voices from God ordering me to kill, Your Honor.* David Berkowitz—a.k.a. Son of Sam— had tried it, claiming his evil impulses were the result of urgings from the neighbor's rottweiler, but the jury hadn't bought it. Later he confessed the dog voice thing had occurred to him after his second killing. Berkowitz was highly intelligent, and so was this man.

Lee decided to go fishing, to play along. Maybe he'd find out something.

How did you know about my sister?

It was in all the papers.

Not the detail about the dress.

Oh, that.

How did you find that out?

Finders keepers.

Lee wondered if Holyman had something to do with Laura's death. He doubted it—though Laura fit the victim profile, it had been over five years since she disappeared. He wouldn't have taken five years between killings—unless, of course, he was in prison for something else. What, though? This was not the kind of person who would be a "common criminal"—definitely not drugs or alcohol. He tried a tactic to appeal to the man's sense of isolation.

I do understand you, you know.

Nobody understands me.

I do—I swear it. I know what it feels like to be you.

If you did, you'd know what I'm going to do next.

I do know.

You think you'll get me to tell you that way?

I don't need you to tell me.

Reverse psychology—that's so pathetic.

You seem to know something about psychology.

I know all I need to know.

Really? What's that?

I'll be striking closer to home next time.

What's that supposed to mean?

You figure it out. You're the one with the degree.

We're a lot alike, you and I, don't you think?

Nice try. See you later.

The message box read,

Holyman *has logged off.*

Lee bit his lip and stared at the screen.
I'll be striking closer to home next time.

Chapter Forty-nine

The mayor stood on the platform, the sun reflecting off the bald spot on his head. Camera crews jostled with each other to get the best angle, the closest shot. People in the crowd craned their necks and stood on tiptoe, climbing up onto the bases of street lamps, straining to see better. Chuck Morton stood behind him and to the left, next to the Manhattan DA and the police commissioner. The police presence on the street was heavy. Patrolmen dotted every corner, and there were still a few National Guardsmen roaming around in their military outfits.

There was an oddly festive atmosphere in the air. Ice cream vendors wheeled their carts down Park Row, men selling brightly colored helium balloons plied their way through the crowd, and there were pretzel and hot dog vendors on every corner, all of them doing a brisk trade. After a cold, dark February, the temperature had shot up to nearly sixty degrees. Lee could smell coconut oil, bringing with it the incongruent memory of summer days at the beach. He and Butts stood at the edge of the crowd, near the iron gate leading into the park.

Lee couldn't help thinking of the scene at public hangings, or the crowd that surrounded the guillotine as Madame Defarge calmly knitted her way through the carnage. *Knit one, purl two.* He suspected most of the people here didn't believe they were in danger from the Slasher, and that they were just attracted by the event itself. *Oh, look, Harriet, the mayor's giving a press conference open to the public. Let's grab the kids and head on down.* After 9/11, people seemed to gather in groups in public more often, as if there truly *was* safety in numbers.

"What do you think?" Butts said, sucking on a salted pretzel. "Is this guy full of it or what?"

"Well," Lee said, "I guess we'll see."

The mayor raised his arms, and the buzzing in the crowd subsided. He looked out across the rows of expectant, upturned faces, eager for him to lead them once more, to recite magic words of comfort, once again restoring order out of chaos. The crowd grew silent, and Lee could hear the rushing of the wind through the caverns of lower Manhattan, picking up speed as it crossed over the flat expanse of New York Harbor, to wind its way through the twisted labyrinth of downtown skyscrapers.

A gust of wind lifted a tuft of the mayor's thinning hair, and he put a hand up to stop it, then seemed to forget all about his hair as the shifting wind brought with it the thin, acrid smell of smoke from the still smoldering ruins a few blocks to the south. The mayor hunched over the microphone and tapped it. There was a buzz, a short, high-pitched burst of feedback, and then silence as the sound crew adjusted their dials. The mayor cleared his throat, and the crowd leaned in to hear his words.

"My fellow citizens," he began, adjusting the mike stand, "this has been the most trying time in this great city's history. The events of five months ago proved that New York is indeed the greatest city in the world."

He paused for the wave of applause that rose from the crowd below, cresting upward and echoing off the narrow streets. "Now, once again, we are challenged by another kind of terrorism—this time violent actions of a lone, mentally disturbed individual. But this great city survived the worst attack ever on American soil, and we will not be cowed by the evil deeds of a single, psychotic individual!"

Again the pause for applause. The mayor removed a stringy strand of hair from his forehead and placed it back on this top of his head. He knew where the applause breaks were in his speech, and his audience didn't let him down—they clapped long and hard, with a few cheers and whistles sprinkled in.

"And so," he continued, "I am creating a special task force to oversee the apprehension of the man known as the Slasher."

More applause. Lee looked at Chuck, standing behind the mayor, his normally impassive face grim. He shifted from one foot to the other, coughed, and looked away. *He's not enjoying this*, Lee thought. It was clear that his friend did not like the mayor. He wondered if the mayor knew this. If he did, he was too professional to show it.

After introducing everyone, he stepped back and clapped a hand on Chuck's shoulder. Lee saw Morton stiffen at the gesture. He managed to force out a stony smile, but Lee wasn't fooled. The mayor didn't seem to notice, though, and Lee concluded that he hadn't gotten where he was by paying attention to every little slight. Like most successful politicians, the mayor had control over his emotions in public. He managed somehow to look both serious and hopeful.

"I am confident that Captain Morton will be successful in leading the elite task force to the successful capture of this heinous criminal."

"Elite task force, huh?" Butts muttered under his breath. "Wait till the wife hears that one."

"What does this mean for us?" Lee asked Chuck later, as

the three of them walked uptown, passing the Chinese merchants piling empty wooden crates and bags of garbage on the narrow curb of Mott Street, the fading sun casting a golden glow over the jumble of streets and alleyways.

"Not much. More paperwork, more of City Hall breathing down my neck, but it's really just a political gesture. He doesn't want the FBI barging in, for one thing, and so he's fluffing up his feathers and strutting around the yard a little."

"Politics," Butts said, kicking at an empty carton.

"I think I'll leave that up to the mayor," Chuck said.

"I just hope he does right by us," Lee remarked.

"What I want to know is where the *hell* is Nelson?" Chuck fumed. "Does he do this often?" he asked Lee. "I mean, just drop out of sight like this?"

"Since the death of his wife his behavior has been pretty unpredictable," Lee replied.

Chuck kicked at a discarded soda can on the sidewalk in front of him.

"Well, he really picked a bad time to go on a bender, if that's what he's doing."

Lee looked over his shoulder at the thin trail of sunlight dipping in and out between the buildings. He was afraid something had happened to Nelson, but he didn't want to say that to Chuck, who had enough to worry about right now. But he knew he needed to fill Morton in on what happened last night.

"The killer contacted me last night—or at least I think it was him," he said.

Chuck stopped walking.

"What? How?"

Lee told Chuck and Butts about the instant messages of the previous night, including the threat to "strike closer to home" next time.

"Wonder what he meant by that?" Butts mused.

"I've been trying to figure it out. Maybe he meant closer to me?"

"But he just *did* Manhattan," Butts pointed out.

"Or maybe he means *his* home," Chuck suggested.

"But that wouldn't make sense in terms of the patterns of most serial killers. His first victim would be the one closest to his residence. Besides, the message was meant for me."

"Jeez," said Butts, shaking his head as he stepped over a wayward garbage bag on the sidewalk.

"Can we trace him, do you think?" Lee asked Chuck.

"I'll check with the folks in the Computer Crimes Division, but I think there are ways he can hide his trail, if he's smart."

"Plus, we don't know for sure if this is him," Butts said. "Could be a copycat, a wannabe."

"True," Lee agreed, but in his heart he didn't believe it.

"I'll send the guys in Computer Crimes over later to check out your machine and see if they can trace the source of the messages," Chuck said.

"Did you get the test results from the communion wine yet?" Lee asked.

"Yeah," Chuck said. "The report came in this morning: zip, nada."

"No blood?"

"Not even very much wine. It was a pretty watered-down Zinfandel, according to the lab. That's it."

Lee couldn't decide if the Slasher was trying to throw them off, or if he was just becoming more disorganized, as the dismemberment of poor Sophia might suggest.

"What about your contact who put you in touch with that homeless guy? Anything from him lately?" Butts asked.

"No, he seems to have gone underground." The truth was that Lee was worried about Eddie too. It was unusual for him to be out of touch for this long.

But when Lee returned to his apartment, there was a message on the machine from Eddie.

"Hey there, Boss Man. Good news! I may have a real break in the case. I'll call back later. So long for now." Lee wished Eddie would call his cell phone, but Eddie hated cell phones. He didn't like answering machines either, and only grudgingly left messages on them.

Feeling relieved that Eddie was okay, Lee sat down at the piano and warmed up on a few jazz standards before tackling a new Haydn sonata. The left hand was a series of octave arpeggios, and soon the back of his hand ached from the prolonged stretching. After thirty minutes or so he took a break and poured himself a Rolling Rock. A favorite aunt of his had always kept a few cold ones for him at her house, and he bought them in memory of her.

Standing at the kitchen counter, he looked out the window, across the yard behind his apartment into the lighted windows of the neighboring building. A middle-aged couple was sitting at their kitchen table, having dinner. The man lowered his head and said something to the woman, who threw back her head and laughed, the overhead light shining on her upturned face.

Next time I'll strike closer to home.

What the hell did that mean? *Closer to home . . . whose home?*

He took a drink and felt the cold liquid slide down his throat.

Closer to home . . .

Suddenly it hit him: Closer to home *did* mean Lee's home, but not Manhattan—it was his family that was in danger! He felt like kicking himself for not realizing it sooner.

He picked up the telephone and dialed his mother's number. She answered after three rings.

"Hello?" She sounded irritated and a little sleepy. She often fell asleep watching the local news, though she would never admit it.

"Hi, Mom—it's me."

"Oh, hello, dear. Isn't it a bit late to be calling?"

Lee looked at the ceramic clock over the stove, a present from Fiona on one of her many trips to Mexico. The design was a sunburst in primary colors, with a Mayan-style face mask in the center. The time was twelve minutes after ten.

"It's not that late, Mom. It's a little after ten."

"All right," she said. "Is this something that can't wait until tomorrow? I've been up since six." That was so like her—since he had caught her asleep, it was important now for her to save face by telling him now how early she had risen.

"No, it can't wait. Is Kylie at her dad's house?"

"Of course. He picked her up when he went off shift at eight."

"Why aren't you there too? I thought I told you—"

"Don't worry," she said. "Stan's with me."

"Did they get back safely?"

"What do you mean?"

George Callahan lived about fifteen minutes away from Fiona, in Lambertville, a nearby town along the Delaware River.

"I mean, did they get back to his house okay?"

"I don't know—I suppose so. Why do you ask? What's going on?"

Lee debated as to how much he should tell her.

"I just want to make sure Kylie is okay."

"Why wouldn't she be?" He could hear suspicion creep into her voice.

"Mom, would you do me a favor?"

"What?"

"Would you make sure your burglar alarm system is turned on?"

After Laura disappeared, Lee had bought his mother an elaborate, state-of-the-art alarm system, but she rarely used it.

"Why?"

"Will you just do that for me?"

"Stan already turned it on. I wish you'd tell me what's going on."

"Look, just do it—okay? Please? I'll explain later."

Her heard air escaping from her nostrils. His mother always sighed through her nose—a tight, disapproving sound.

"All *right*. You know those policemen are still watching us all the time, don't you?"

"They're watching me, too, Mom."

"Then you know how it feels."

"I'll call back tomorrow, and we'll talk about it, okay?" He was anxious to call George's house to see if everything was okay there.

Another sound of escaping air, a thin hissing noise. "Very well. But I wish you wouldn't be so *mysterious* all the time."

"Look, I'm sorry. I'll call you tomorrow." To press her any more now would just backfire. "Good night. Talk to you tomorrow."

"Very well. Good night, Lee."

He hung up and speed dialed George Callahan's number. George answered on the first ring.

"Hello?" He sounded cheerful—probably on his third beer. George wasn't a heavy drinker, but he liked to knock back a few after a week of double shifts at the hospital.

"Hi, George, it's Lee."

"Heya, fella. How are you doing?"

"I'm fine. I—uh, I was wondering how you guys are doing?"

"You mean Bunny and me?" George called his daughter Bunny, and had ever since she was a baby. Lee couldn't remember how it had started—something to do with bunny pajamas Laura had given Kylie on her first Christmas, just like the ones Laura had as a child. "We're fine, just great. I'd let you talk to her, only she's in bed now. School day tomorrow, you know."

"Sure, sure. So she's okay?"

"Fine. Hey, listen, don't worry. The cops are still keeping an eye on us."

"Good, good. Is your alarm system on?"

"Yeah, sure. Any breaks in the case?"

"Not yet, but we're working on it."

"You'll get him. I know you will. Hey, let's have a cookout at my place one of these days, huh?" George said. He loved entertaining, and liked to fire up his barbeque and grill steaks.

"Sounds great."

"Good. It's a deal, then."

"Sure, sure." Lee wasn't about to tell George the whole story, any more than he would tell his mother.

"Okay, then, buddy, I'll see you soon." Lee heard the sound of a sports broadcaster in the background, and could tell George wanted to get him off the phone so he could watch the sports news.

"Right. See you soon," Lee said.

"I'll tell Bunny you called."

"Great, thanks. 'Bye."

"So long."

Lee hung up and stood in front of the collection of faded snapshots of his sister on the refrigerator. In one, the sun glinted off her dark hair, showing the copper highlights—more evidence of their family's Celtic ancestry. Her grin was wide and lopsided, and she held a border collie puppy in her arms, a present from George Callahan. After Laura's disappearance George had given the dog away. Though he never said so, Lee thought that he couldn't stand the daily reminder of her absence. He knew that ever since Laura's disappearance, George watched his daughter very carefully—and as an emergency room worker, he knew what people were capable of.

He went back into the living room, where the piano stood, waiting for him. It was close to eleven now, though—too late to play without disturbing the neighbors. He ran his fingers lightly over the keys, looking the pages of a Bach partita open in front of him. Tomorrow he would make time for Bach.

Back in the kitchen, he looked out the window at the couple across the way having dinner. They had finished now and were doing the dishes together. The woman stood at the sink, head down, washing dishes, and the man came up behind her and put his arms around her waist, hugging her body to him. It was a simple gesture, but it conveyed both protectiveness and possession. What happened, Lee thought, when protection faded and only possession was left? He closed the window's bamboo shades and left the room.

Somewhere, out there in the darkness, was a man with evil on his mind. The phrase ran through his mind, over and over, stuck in a never-ending loop of numbing repetition: *Closer to home . . . closer to home . . .*

Chapter Fifty

The girl was slim and long of body, with willowy light brown hair. She walked with the loose-limbed grace of youth, and the satisfaction of being alive. She was not pretty, with small, pale eyes, a long prominent nose, and thin mouth, but her features were clean and wholesome and oddly aristocratic. Her face radiated kindness and honesty. She was the kind of girl you'd want as a best friend, the kind of girl men might not fall in love with right away but would feel drawn to. Samuel knew, down deep, that such a girl could never want him. . . . And he longed for her, for her carefree body that moved so freely and easily—her aliveness and unself-conscious enjoyment of physical existence. He tried to imagine feeling that way, but if he ever had, he couldn't remember it.

He watched her sitting on the park bench for quite a while, until she stood up and stretched, arching her back and throwing her head back, exposing her throat. It was the sight of their exposed throats that excited him the most: moist, white, supple, arched in passion. The naked curves of this bare flesh were more alluring to him than breasts, erect nipples, or tender thighs. The sight of a woman's bare throat made his eyes glaze over and his heart quicken in its bony cage, as if it wanted to burst out of his body.

After she had left the bench, he went over and sat on the spot where she had sat, warming the green-painted wood with her soft bottom. Samuel could smell faint traces of her shampoo—lily of the valley. He knew his floral scents—his mother had taught him well. He thought of his mother, digging in the dirt, her back to him, her bottom in the air, waving it at him, taunting him.

He felt the anger inside him, a tiny nugget of hardened rage, smoldered and condensed, shrunken like a piece of anthracite fired to its most hardened form. It hovered there at the core of him, shiny and black and smooth, nestled at the very center of his being. There was a time when it had hurt him, when its sharp and unpolished edges tore at his soul, chafing him no matter which way he turned—but he had nurtured it, until eventually it became his constant friend and companion. He turned it this way and that, gazing upon its shiny surface, noticing with admiration how it seemed to absorb all the light around it, drawing him down into its darkened depths.

Gradually he had come to accept his rage not as an enemy, but as a friend. It had things to teach him, and he was determined to listen. He learned to love its hard, unforgiving surface and dark beauty. The outside world would always be a bewildering, disappointing place, but he could draw into himself and know that his rage would be there waiting for him, an unpolished gemstone in the dark center of his soul.

Underneath the park bench, a fly struggled in a spiderweb. He smiled as he watched the spider approach its struggling prey, all nicely wrapped in the deadly grip of the spider's web. In eating the fly, the spider was simply doing its job. Just as he, in his late-night missions, was doing his job. A spider, he knew, can feel the tiniest vibration on its web—a signal that another meal has landed. Then, carefully, the spider will approach to inject venom in its hapless victim. He too felt a vibration on his web, and he was going to do what he could to trap his victim.

Chapter Fifty-one

The next day, Lee, Nelson, Chuck, and Detectives Butts and Florette sat in Chuck Morton's office, discarded coffee cups littering the surfaces of the room. The five of them now comprised the officially appointed members of the mayor's "elite task force." Butts and Florette also had a couple of sergeants and patrolmen at their disposal, as needed.

Nelson had responded to Chuck's phone calls—and, without apology or explanation, had turned up at the meeting, looking tired and thinner, but sober.

"What's with this whole 'elite task force' business?" Butts said, biting deeply into a sugared doughnut. "And why does it rate a press conference?"

"Politics," Chuck replied. "The mayor wants to let people know he's in control and on top of things."

"All right, so what about the instant messages the killer sent to Lee?" Nelson asked. "Any chance of tracking them?"

"Nope," said Chuck. "It's a cold trail. According to the computer whiz kids in the Computer Crimes department, the address and information on the account were bogus."

"He certainly knows what he's doing," Florette remarked with a frown. He was dressed elegantly as usual, with a gray silk tie over a striped blue and white shirt with French cuffs.

"What about leaving a trail from where he logged on?" Lee suggested.

"Holyman logged on from different locations all over the place, including public libraries," Chuck answered.

"So he's used every means available to protect himself," Florette said.

"Yep," Chuck agreed. "And so far it's worked."

"So our guy is basically a ghost," Butts remarked. "A face without a name."

"Okay, what about the online conversation between this guy and Lee?" Chuck said. "Did anyone have a chance to study it?"

"I did, yes," Nelson said.

"Does it tell us anything?"

"I don't think it adds anything to the profile, other than he's educated and articulate—but we knew that already. He's ballsy, but that's not news either."

"Right," Florette agreed. "Even if he knows his way around a computer, he has to know he's taking a chance getting in touch like that."

"The guys in Computer Crimes were reluctant to admit defeat. They wouldn't even tell me exactly how he did it," Chuck said. "Said they don't like to give out that information."

"Maybe they don't want people knowing there are ways of getting around their tracking techniques," Florette suggested.

Chuck indicated the series of crime scene photos spread out on the large poster board that had been set up in his office.

"All right, what about the placement of Sophia's body?" Chuck said. "Any thoughts on that?"

There was a silence as they studied them; then Nelson said, "I know what he's doing. It's so obvious—I can't believe I didn't see it immediately."

"You want to share it with us?" Chuck said. He sounded irritated; Lee didn't think he'd entirely forgiven Nelson for his long unexplained absence.

"It's the *Via Dolorosa*—the Stations of the Cross," Nelson replied.

"The what?" Butts said.

"There are fourteen Stations of the Cross, each representing a moment in Christ's final hours. The idea is to meditate on the major moments in Christ's suffering and death. It's especially popular among Roman Catholics, and it's also called the *Via Dolorosa*, or Way of Sorrow."

"How do you figure that's what's behind it?" asked Butts, the fat wrinkles on his forehead folding over each other. His face never resembled that of an old bulldog so much as when he was looking thoughtful.

Nelson pointed at the wide-angle shot of her leg, in which the stained-glass picture of Death was clearly visible. "The first station of the cross is Christ being condemned to death." He pointed at the second photo, in which Sophia's arm was placed underneath the cross at the back of the church. "The second station is Christ receiving the cross. And this," he said, pointing to her other leg, which was positioned on a set of steep stairs leading down to the basement, "this is the third station, in which Christ falls for the first time."

"And this one?" Florette said, pointing to the final series of photographs, in which Sophia's other arm had been placed at the feet of a pietà.

"That's the fourth station," Nelson replied. "Jesus meeting his mother on the way to his death."

"Jesus," Chuck said, wiping sweat from his forehead, even though the room was quite cool. "What does this tell us?"

"Well," Nelson said, "the good news is that as his rituals get more bizarre and obsessive, his daily behavior may start to draw attention to itself. The bad news is that the killing is more frenzied, and that makes him more dangerous."

"I still think there could be two offenders at work here," Lee commented. "This new twist in the signature—"

"Oh, come on, Lee! If you learned *anything* from me, it's that a signature is perfectly capable of evolving!" Nelson interrupted irritably.

"I know," Lee answered. "I just think—"

"Do you think he had something to do with Laura's disappearance?" Nelson said, changing the subject.

"My instinct tells me no. Because of the five-year gap, and also because it would be just too strange a coincidence."

"But then how did he know about the red dress?" Florette asked.

"Maybe he knows the guy who did it?" Butts suggested.

"Okay, let's shift focus," Chuck said, turning to Florette. "Have you dug up anything on the churches?"

"I checked with the volunteer programs at all the churches, and none of the volunteers are screened. Some of them have a sign-in sheet, but they don't really check up on anyone."

"Sign-in sheets," Butts said. "Does that include names and addresses?"

"Optional," Florette replied. "But I thought it might be useful to have a look at these."

He pulled a pile of papers from his briefcase. "Now, here are the sign-in sheets for the past few weeks—or at least all the ones I could get hold of. Fordham doesn't keep theirs for more than a few days, but Saint Francis Xavier does, and Old St. Patrick's adds the names to their mailing list. We got lucky at St. Patrick's—they hadn't yet updated their mailing list, so they hadn't thrown it out yet."

He spread the sheets, half a dozen crumpled pages, stained and covered with handwriting, out on the desk.

Lee looked over the first sheet of names, from Saint Francis Xavier Church. Nothing stuck out. It was about evenly divided between men and women, most of whom did not include their addresses or phone numbers. He picked up the second sheet. At the bottom, someone had signed in as "Samuel Beckett."

He handed it to Nelson. "What do you make of this?"

Nelson peered at the list and frowned. "Very funny."

"Can I see that one for St. Patrick's, please?" he asked Butts, who was studying it.

"Okay," Butts replied, handing it to him.

Lee looked at the list. The names were different from the one for Saint Francis Xavier, except for one name: Samuel Beckett. Same handwriting, delicate and almost feathery. Not "manly" handwriting. Maybe the handwriting of a mama's boy?

He handed the sheet to Chuck.

"Samuel Beckett, like the playwright?" Chuck said. "This guy trying to be funny?"

"That's what I was wondering," Lee answered.

"This is definitely strange," Florette agreed. "I was wondering what you'd make of it."

"If this is our guy," Nelson said, "it would fit it with the whole idea of this being a game to him. He'd get a kick out of signing in as a playwright known for his gloomy existentialism."

"Waiting for Godot," Florette murmured. "That's sort of what we're doing."

"Yeah," Chuck agreed.

"So he could be using this volunteering to look for victims," Butts said.

"Right," said Nelson.

"I'll run the name through VICAP, see if we come up with anything," Chuck said.

"And we should also find out how many people with that name live in the five boroughs. Check up on each of them," Florette said.

"Right," Chuck agreed. "I'll get the sergeant on it."

"There's something else about him doing all this volunteer work," Lee suggested.

"What's that?" Butts asked.

"Someone who has a lot of time on his hands. Not only does he volunteer a lot, but he does it all over the five boroughs."

"Right," said Chuck. "So maybe he's wealthy, or at least well off?"

"Or self-employed," Nelson suggested.

"Right," Lee agreed.

Butts studied the sheet in his hand. "Do you think it's possible this name is a clue to his identity in another way?"

"What do you mean?" Chuck asked.

"Well, like maybe it's partially right—an anagram, or something like that."

"That's good," Lee said. "That would fit in with his personality."

"I'll run it through an Internet program on anagrams," Florette said. "It's not that great on proper names, but it might give us something."

"Good idea," said Chuck.

The phone rang, and Chuck picked it up.

"No comment," he said after a moment. "I have a suggestion, though. Why don't you stop wasting the department's time, so we can do our job?"

He hung up, his face red, and stalked out of the office. They could hear him through the closed door, chewing out the duty officer for putting the call through.

"But I didn't know it was a reporter," they heard the cop say. "He told me he was—"

"I don't *care* what he told you!" Chuck bellowed. "Next time use your head!"

Lee looked out the window at the bright splash of sunlight on the windowsill. Even as the days were growing longer, everyone's temper was getting shorter, as they all realized that time was slipping away.

Chapter Fifty-two

When Lee returned to his apartment later that afternoon, the first thing he did was sit down at the piano. The sight of the notes on the page comforted him. Music was a language he had spoken since childhood, a language of sound and rhythm and color. It went directly to a part of him that was beyond the reach of words.

He began a Beethoven sonata, enjoying the pure physical pleasure of his fingers on the keyboard. He played the adagio movement first, lingering on the graceful phrases, the swell and rise of the melodic line. Then he plunged into the allegro passage, channeling his rage and frustration through his fingertips onto the keys. He couldn't help thinking about what Nelson had said. There were fourteen Stations of the Cross, and the Slasher was only up to number four.

During the dark days, there were times when music alone could reach him, when it was the only thing that passed through the wall of his depression, to lift him back into life.

He was dimly aware of the sound of the phone ringing, but he blocked it out and continued until he finished the sonata. Then he rose, went to the answering machine, and listened to the message.

The minute he heard Diesel's voice, he knew something was terribly wrong. He listened to the message in a fog of impending horror. He was vaguely aware of hearing the words "Eddie . . . subway train," and "killed instantly."

No, not Eddie . . .

He dialed the number showing on his caller ID. Diesel answered after one ring.

Fifty minutes later he was sitting in McHale's, nursing a pint of Saranac Amber, waiting for Diesel and Rhino to show up. The beer, with its dark, nutty flavor, reminded him of Eddie. Maybe the demons that had plagued him since the war—the napalm-scarred corpses of his nightmares—really had come to call on him one final time, luring him down onto the subway tracks. Even Eddie's chattiness was just another camouflage for his pain. In his tales of wartime horrors, he always appeared to leave something out. Lee had the sense that things happened in Vietnam that even now he couldn't come to grips with.

But suicide? Lee didn't believe it. Something else was at work.

When Diesel and Rhino arrived, Diesel's eyes were red rimmed. Rhino wore dark glasses, his white skin pasty in the weak light coming in through the grimy windows. They both slid into the booth across from him without a word. They were both wearing dark jeans and very white T-shirts under black leather jackets.

"Sorry," Diesel said. "I had a few people to call—you know, to tell them."

"What happened?" Lee asked. Their phone conversation had been brief, confined to the where and the when, leaving out the uncomfortable question of why.

Diesel shook his head. "I don't know yet. It's only been a

couple of hours so far. They haven't even released his name to the press yet."

"How did you find out?"

Diesel leaned back in his chair. "I have a few contacts here and there."

As usual, Rhino did not speak. He took off his glasses, cleaned them carefully, and put them in his jacket pocket. His hands were surprisingly delicate for such a powerful-looking man. Lee noticed that his eyes, too, were bloodshot.

"You want anything?" Lee asked them.

"Let us get this round," Diesel said as Rhino rose from his seat and headed for the bar.

"Thanks," Lee said. He could use a second drink.

"Eddie didn't even like riding the subway," Diesel said. "Always said he hated standing on that yellow warning track."

Lee leaned forward. "Do you think he jumped?"

"Absolutely not. I know Eddie could get low—it wasn't any secret that he suffered from ups and down—but right now he was in an up phase." He picked up a beer coaster and ran his fingers lightly over the edges. "Could have been an accident, I guess. He had just won a lot of money, and he was probably excited about it. He may not have been paying attention because of all the money he'd just won—maybe he was thinking about that."

"But you said he hated standing on the warning track. Why would he even be close to the edge like that?"

"That's what I can't figure out."

Rhino returned with three glasses of very cold beer. Lee drank half of his in one gulp, and felt the bubbles rise to his head.

For the first time since Lee had met him, Rhino spoke.

"I think someone got to him." His voice was oddly thin and high, like the upper reaches of a woodwind instrument—a reedy oboe or clarinet.

"You mean someone pushed him?" The minute Lee spoke the words, he knew that was what he had been thinking all along, in the back of his mind.

Rhino's pale eyes narrowed. "No way a guy like Eddie falls onto a track—or even jumps. It's not his style."

Lee turned to Diesel. "Do you agree?"

Diesel nodded slowly. "I can't figure it any other way." He took a long drink and wiped his mouth delicately with a cocktail napkin.

"Did Eddie have any enemies that might have—I mean, he did gamble, right?"

"Yeah, but he didn't owe his bookie, and he'd just won big at the track."

Lee frowned. "He told me he was clean—that he'd given it up."

His companions exchanged a glance.

"Eddie didn't always exactly tell the truth," Rhino said, looking down at his beer glass.

"This guy you're after," Diesel said, "is he capable of something like that?"

"Oh, he's capable of just about anything."

"But I thought he killed women."

"Yes, but a murder like this would be different. It would be to protect himself from getting caught. But how would he know who Eddie is?"

"I don't know," Diesel said. "But maybe he tailed him into the subway and waited for his chance."

"But why? What did Eddie know? That's a big risk to take."

"Yeah, it is. I don't know what Eddie knew, because I hadn't spoken to him for a couple of days. But maybe this guy had been watching him."

"Okay," Lee said to the pair sitting opposite him, "I'm going to need some information from you."

"Anything you want, you got it," Rhino replied.

"Right," said Diesel. "If this guy did Eddie, we want to help you any way we can."

Lee shivered as another thought came into his head. For the first time it occurred to him that whoever wanted him off the case might very well be someone he knew.

Chapter Fifty-three

The SRO desk clerk was a thick, lumpy man with a face that looked like it had been hewn from an oak tree with a rusty ax. His cheekbones were set at different heights, giving his whole face a lopsided look, and his nose was flattened and crooked. Lee realized he was looking at a boxer's face. The man's clothes and haircut belonged to a different era. They reminded Lee of gangster films of the '30s and '40s.

"Excuse me, I wonder if you could help me," Lee said as he approached the desk.

The man looked up from the sports pages he was reading. "Sure, Mac, whaddya need?" Even his voice was straight out of a B movie.

Diesel and Rhino had given Lee the address of the West Side flophouse where Eddie lived, but they didn't know the manager's name. This guy had night staff written all over him, though, and a couple of twenties later Lee was seated on the bed in Eddie's room, going through his things. Word had already gotten around about what happened to Eddie, and the clerk insisted on watching while Lee went through his friend's possessions. He stood in the doorway fingering a cigarette, as if he couldn't wait to go outside and smoke it.

It was a dismal room, the stale smell of desperation clinging to the peeling wallpaper, and Lee felt ashamed that he hadn't known how close to the edge his friend was living. Any offers of help had been politely rebuked. Eddie had a way of appearing to be able to take care of himself. A single bed and an unpainted pine dresser were the only pieces of furniture, a green braided rug the only touch of comfort.

He looked through the contents of the dresser: half a dozen shirts, a couple of pairs of pants, socks and underwear, and a couple of sports jackets. The rest of Eddie's possessions were unremarkable—pens, paper, and other simple office supplies, a few cans of soup, a box of crackers, several decks of cards, well thumbed and grimy—but one thing caught Lee's eye. It was a racing form dated the day Eddie died. In the first race, a horse's name was circled in red pen: Lock, Stock, and Barrel. Lee looked at the night clerk and held up the form.

"Can I keep this?"

The man stuck the unlit cigarette behind his ear. "You can keep all of it, Mac. Poor Eddie won't be needin' it now, I guess. Unless he had family somewheres, but I don't think so."

"Did he seem depressed in the last few days?"

The man cocked his lopsided head to one side. "Naw, that's the thing—he seemed really happy, y'know? Told me he'd bet on a sure winner."

Lee held up the racing form and pointed to the circled name. "This horse?"

The man squinted to read the name and shook his head. "Don't know. Just said he had a feeling his horse was gonna win. Never saw him after that. Poor guy. He was a good egg, you know?"

Lee slipped the clerk another twenty before leaving, because the man seemed to feel sorry for Eddie. As he stepped out of the building, hot tears clouded his vision. He took a deep breath and headed out into the night.

The next stop was Eddie's bookie—another bit of information he managed to get out of Diesel and Rhino. He didn't know what he expected to find; he only knew that he owed it to Eddie to try and find out anything he could.

The apartment was in the ground of floor of a five-story walk-up, one of the rows of brick tenement buildings the lined the forties and fifties from Eighth Avenue to the river. The long, narrow "shotgun" apartments (so named because you could fire a shotgun at one end and the bullet would pass straight through to the other end) were once crammed with poor migrant families—and more recently, struggling actors and writers. But now you could buy a house in New Jersey for the price of a one-bedroom co-op on West Forty-seventh Street.

The building showed all the signs of a neglectful landlord. The hallway was drafty and badly lit. The walls were an insipid shade of pale yellow, and hadn't seen a paintbrush for years, and the tile floor was chipped and stained. Lee knocked on the door of apartment number 1C and waited. After a moment the metal peephole cover slid open.

"Yeah?" The man's voice was wary, hoarse.

"Hi. I'm Eddie Pepitone's friend."

"Yeah?" There was an echo, as though he was inside a cave.

"He made a bet with you the other day. Lock, Stock, and Barrel—trifecta in the third race."

"Yeah? So?"

"What happened? In the race, I mean."

"His horse won."

"I need to know if he spoke to you about it."

"So why don't you just ask him?"

"I can't."

"Why not?" The voice was suspicious.

"He's dead."

There was a long silence. Lee heard the sound of something frying inside the apartment. The smell of rancid oil floated out into the hallway.

"Who are you?" The voice was tighter, accusatory.

"I just want to talk to you for a minute."

There was the sound of a chair scraping over a bare floor, then the sound of many dead bolts being unlocked. The door opened a few inches, restrained by a metal chain. Lee got a whiff of bacon grease and fried potatoes. A bloodshot eye peered out at him.

"You a cop?"

"No," Lee lied. "I'm just a friend who wants to find out who killed Eddie."

"Shit," the man said. "So you weren't shittin' me? Somebody iced Eddie?"

"That's what I think. I just need to know one thing: Did he talk to you about his horse coming in?"

"Yeah. Two days ago. Said he was comin' over for the money. Never showed up—I figured something came up, y'know? How did he die?"

"He was run over by a subway train."

"Hey, I heard something about an accident on the news tonight. Shut down the whole A line for hours, they said. I thought it was a suicide or something. Didn't know it was Eddie." There was a pause, and then he said, "Hey, how did *you* know?" His eye squinted through the crack in the door, studying Lee hard. "You sure you're not a cop? You're startin' to smell like a cop to me."

"Look, I have no interest in closing you down—just tell me when it was you talked to Eddie last, okay?"

"Let's see . . . Monday. Race was Sunday. He calls me up

first thing Monday, says he's coming over. Never showed up.
I figured he'd show up sooner or later. It was a nice sum, five
thousand smackers. Horse was a real long shot." His eye narrowed again. "Hey, you haven't come for the dough, have
you?"

"No—keep it. I'm sure you can use it."

The man whistled softly through the gap in his front
teeth. "Shit, man. I don't feel good about Eddie dyin' or nothing, you know."

"Neither do I."

"He was a good customer and a straight-up guy, far as
gamblers go, anyway. Hey, wait a minute—on the news they
said it was an accident. So are you sayin' it wasn't no accident?"

"That's what I'm trying to find out. How did Eddie choose
which horse to bet on?"

"Funny you should ask. Eddie was superstitious, y'know?
He always had these weird reasons for bettin' on a horse."

"Yeah? Like what?"

"Oh, I dunno. One time a coupla years ago my daughter
had a baby, you know, and Eddie bets on a horse that has the
same name as the baby. That kinda thing, you know? I think
he had some kinda idea that the universe was givin' him
messages or something. I know it sounds weird, but sometimes the horses came through for him. He did okay, he
really did."

Lee held up the racing form with the name "Lock, Stock,
and Barrel" circled. "Any idea why he'd choose this horse?"

The man peered at it. "No. Wish I did. All I know is he
seemed sure about it."

"Okay," Lee said. "Thanks. Thanks for your help. I appreciate it."

"But I didn't really help you."

"Oh, yes, you did," Lee replied as he hurried down the
dingy hallway and out of the building.

Chapter Fifty-four

"Eddie Pepitone didn't kill himself," Lee declared as he walked into Chuck Morton's office. It was just after eight o'clock the next morning, and Chuck was still on his first cup of coffee.

"Whoa there—back up a second. Who is Eddie Pepitone?" Chuck said, putting down his coffee.

"The guy on the subway yesterday. The 'accident' on the A train—held up the trains for hours. Did you hear about it?"

"Of course—everyone did. But no one saw him being pushed."

"Well, I think he was pushed."

Chuck's blond eyebrows shot upward in surprise. "What do you mean? How do you know?"

Lee tossed the racing form onto his desk.

"He had just won five thousand dollars and was on his way to his bookie's place to get it."

"I don't follow you."

"Eddie was a friend of mine. We were at St. Vincent's to-gether—he was my roommate."

"Oh, Jeez, Lee, I'm really sorry. But what are you say-ing?"

"I think the Slasher got to him."

"Why would he—"

"Because Eddie was helping me in the investigation."

"Helping you? Why wasn't I in on this? Who was this guy?" Chuck Morton's face reddened, and the cords on his muscular neck stood out.

"Eddie is—was—a guy with some unusual friends. His help was strictly unofficial."

"Unofficial or not, don't you think you should have let me in on it?"

Lee rubbed the back of his neck. The room suddenly seemed stuffy and overheated.

"Eddie wasn't always on the straight and narrow side of the law."

"So *what*? You think all the cops on the force work with squeaky-clean informants? Come on, Lee, you know better than that!"

"He didn't like cops."

"What about you?"

"We met under special circumstances. Look, do you want to hear what I think about his death or not?"

"Okay, okay!" Chuck sat in his chair and twisted the phone cord between his fingers, tapping his other hand on the desk irritably.

Lee told him the story of Eddie's involvement in the case.

"So he was the one who led you to that homeless guy?"

"Right."

Chuck got up from his chair and came around to lean on the front of the desk. "And you think he was pushed? Couldn't he have tripped and fallen? It happens, you know."

"No," Lee interrupted. "Eddie was afraid of subway trains. He would never have been waiting so close to the tracks."

"And suicide is out because he'd just won all this money."

"Right. Not only that, but I think the name of the horse he bet on is a clue."

"A clue to what?"

"To what he was going to tell me."

"So what are we going to do about it?"

"Well, the first thing you can do is to add another name to your list of victims when we catch this son of a bitch."

"Yeah—right."

"Look, Chuck, I could be wrong, but I don't think so. And if we can find out what Eddie knew, we could be that much closer to catching this guy."

Chuck rubbed his immaculately shaved chin. "Maybe he didn't know anything. Maybe this guy was just trying to send you a message by killing your friend."

"I thought of that, but I don't think so."

"He's one sick bastard." Chuck laid a hand on Lee's shoulder. "You sleep last night?"

"Not much."

"Look, I want to catch him just as much as you do," Chuck said. "Now, why don't you go home and get some rest? You look awful. Come back this afternoon, and we'll have a meeting with everyone. I'll call you if I find out anything—I promise."

As usual, Chuck was right. Lee was too tired to function, having been up half the night trying to unravel the mystery of what Eddie might have known. He went home, took a Xanax, and fell into a dead sleep.

He awoke to the wail of a car alarm in the street outside. The sound pierced his head and jolted his entire body into a state of alert. His stomach ground and twisted, and he felt the old, familiar warning signs of an attack. His head began to swim, as his mind began to cloud up, and his breathing became rapid and shallow. For days now he had awakened with his stomach clenched hard as a fist, a tight knot of tension that dissipated only gradually as the day wore on. His head was pounding, and his neck was sore, oddly stiff, as if he had pulled a muscle or something.

Stop this, he told himself. He tried to concentrate on slowing his breathing as he opened he eyes and saw the calendar on the wall above his bed. March fifteenth. *Beware the Ides of March.* It was exactly five years since his sister had disappeared, slipping silently away from the world of the living like a drowning swimmer sinking into the recesses of the deep-blue ocean waves, leaving no trace behind.

She must have left *some* trace—they just hadn't been able to find it yet, he told himself, but they would, they *had to*— he needed to believe that. And yet, with every passing anniversary, the hope receded a little more.

The front door buzzer rang. Lee threw the covers off his body and sprang out of bed. His neck was so stiff he could hardly move his head. A wave of nausea rose up from his stomach as he headed for the door. Then he felt the blackness descend as he crossed the bedroom into the living room. He managed to call out, "Who is it?"

He heard the response as if in a dream.

"It's Butts."

But then the blackness draped itself over him, enveloping him like the wings of a great dark bird, bringing him to his knees. He struggled feebly toward consciousness, then surrendered to the pull of oblivion.

Chapter Fifty-five

He awoke to the sound of muffled, far-off voices. The air smelled of rubbing alcohol and lemon-scented disinfectant. He could hear the low whirr of machinery, and footsteps sounded in the hall outside—the faint sucking sound of rubber soles on polished floors, the sharper click of leather heels, mingling with the rattle of carts being rolled along, and the occasional burst of laughter. Further down the hall, a phone rang insistently.

Even with his eyes closed, Lee knew that he was in a hospital. He postponed the moment of returning fully to consciousness, knowing that when he did, he would have to interact with the people attached to the voices all around him.

Meanwhile, footsteps came and went. The jumble of voices and machinery hovered in the halls. Lying in a state of semi-consciousness, eyes closed, he could distinguish between the steps of the visitors—clipped, quick leather shoes—and the soft, rubber-soled sound of the nurses as they moved from room to room, checking charts, dispensing drugs, taking temperatures.

He had the odd sensation that something was sitting on his chest. A large animal—a bear, perhaps. Yes, that was it—a bear was sitting on his chest. He wanted to ask the bear to move, and moved his lips to form the words, but he couldn't make any sound come out.

Bits of conversation drifted down the hall: ". . . excellent dental plan . . . she's a nice girl . . . you want something from the cafeteria?"

Some pieces of conversation didn't make much sense. ". . . number of Jews in Madison, Wisconsin." He tried to figure out why someone would be talking about the number of Jews in Wisconsin.

He focused on the bear again. It was just sitting there, draped over him, its paws on his shoulders. He didn't mind it being there, except that it was so heavy. He wanted to say something to the bear, but he couldn't move his mouth or even open his eyes. He could smell its fur—a damp, musty aroma like rotting logs and summer mushrooms—and he could feel its warm breath on his cheek. He felt the bear wished him well, that it was there to protect him in some way.

His own experience with bears was minimal. He had seen them in the wild only twice, once through a canopy of leaves too thick to make out anything other than a bulky, dark brown shape. The other time, the bear stared at him across a stream with eyes so wary and watchful that it was hard to resist anthropomorphizing the animal. He remembered feeling as though the creature was studying him with an almost human intelligence—that it was seeing *into* him—but he dismissed the thought as fanciful.

He tried to raise his arms to push the bear away, but he wasn't able to move them. He fought to open his eyes, but the effort was enormous—something kept pulling him back down into unconsciousness. He finally managed to open his eyes a little bit, but all he could see was a large white blur. The blur moved, and he realized it was the bear. He was surprised that the bear was white . . . a polar bear, maybe? But what would one be doing so far south? He was puzzling over the question when the bear spoke.

"How are you feeling?"

The voice was deep and resonant, just what you might expect from a bear. It sounded British. Were there bears in England? He tried to concentrate, to focus his thoughts. He tried to answer, but all that came out was a hoarse croaking sound, like the scraping of metal over concrete.

He tried again. This time his voice responded: "I'm okay . . . thanks." He wrenched himself away from the pull of sleep and opened his eyes. The bear came into focus, and to his surprise, it was wearing a white lab coat. A crooked blue and white plastic label on the lapel of the coat read: DR. PATEL.

"I'm glad you're back with us," said Dr. Patel.

Still confused, Lee looked around the room for the bear. Where had it gone?

Dr. Patel spoke again. "Mr. Campbell?"

"Yes?"

"Do you know where you are?"

Lee didn't answer at first. He was busy sorting out this new information. So Dr. Patel was the bear after all. Or, rather, there *was* no bear; he had just thought there was—but why? The effect of drugs, maybe?

"What did you give me?" he asked, his voice groggy.

"I'll be glad to review your chart with you later," Dr. Patel replied. "Do you know where you are?"

Lee looked around the room, and was struck by its familiarity. The pasty yellow walls had ancient stains showing through successive coats of paint like old scuffs on hastily polished shoes, and the crookedly hung landscape prints were bland reproductions of obscure paintings.

He realized he was back in St. Vincent's. What he didn't know was whether it was the psych ward or not.

He squinted up at the doctor's face. "St. Vincent's."

Dr. Patel's face brightened.

"Good," he said, like a teacher bestowing praise upon a promising student. "Very good."

Lee felt pleased with himself, and sank back into oblivion.

When he awoke again the light outside his window had faded into a twilight gray, and the blinds had been partially drawn. A suspended plastic bag dripped clear fluid into an IV line in his left arm. To his great relief, his right arm was unencumbered. He cleared his throat, startling the young nurse who was studying his chart at the foot of his bed. She let go of the chart and looked down at him. Her eyes were honey colored, just a shade lighter than her hair, which was the color of winter wheat, and very straight. It was pulled into an untidy ponytail fastened at the nape of her neck. She was very young, with a pointed chin and a sweet, heart-shaped face. The sound of his voice had startled her, but she tried to cover her surprise with a professional manner.

"Mr. Campbell, you're awake." She looked at him as if that were impossible. "How do you feel?"

"Well, let's see. Sort of like I've been run over by a large vehicle, then thrown down several flights of stairs, and finally, been used as a punching bag." His neck was so stiff he couldn't move his head, and his whole body felt heavy and exhausted. "Is this the psych ward?"

She looked puzzled. "No, of course not."

Relief flooded over him like rainwater. "Good. That's good. So what's wrong with me?"

The young nurse lowered her eyes. "I'd better let the doctor explain that to you."

"Okay, can I see him—or her?"

The whole conversation seemed to take place underwater—

dreamlike, through a dim haze. The nurse looked at him wistfully and walked out into the hall. Her expression puzzled Lee—was he really that sick, or was he misreading something else for pity? He sank back into sheets smelling faintly of bleach and closed his eyes. He dreamed of swimming in the indoor pool at his high school, where the aroma of Clorox pervaded the air.

When he opened his eyes again, Dr. Patel was standing beside his bed. He wore the same crooked name tag, and he looked tired. He had a dolorous, basset hound face with sad dark eyes and a sagging jaw line. His skin was very dark, and his heavy lips had a bluish tinge.

"Do you know why you are here, Mr. Campbell?" he asked. His voice was very British, very correct, with only a graceful twist of his *r*'s and slight roundness of vowels to suggest his Indian origins.

"I'm sick?"

"What can you remember?"

Lee tried to think, but all he could recall was being at home. There was some bad news, very bad news. He remembered hearing Butts's voice outside his door, then falling—sinking?—to his knees on the living room rug.

"Eddie," he said.

Dr. Patel looked puzzled. "Eddie? Who's that?"

"I think I can help you, Doctor," said a familiar voice behind Patel.

Nelson stepped forward into view. He didn't look good. His blue eyes were rimmed with deep purple circles underneath them, and his skin was mottled and dull looking. He looked exhausted.

"You gave us bit of a scare, lad," he said, leaning over the bed. The smell of alcohol oozed from his pores.

"So who is Eddie?" Dr. Patel demanded, his voice petulant.

"He was a good friend who died," Nelson answered.

Dr. Patel reached for Lee's wrist to take his pulse. He looked overworked and impatient, but held his personal feelings in check behind a firm professional façade.

"Are you my doctor?" Lee asked.

"I'm Dr. Patel, your neurologist."

"Neurologist?"

"You have an infection of the brain," Dr. Patel continued. "For a while it was touch and go, but we believe we now have it under control."

The first thing Lee felt was relief. *It wasn't depression*—an infection he could handle. He looked up at Nelson, and he wanted to tell him not to worry, that this was far better than mental illness, but he couldn't think of how to communicate that.

He caught the nurse looking at him again as she fiddled with an IV line. Was that longing in her eyes, or just compassion?

"We're treating you with a series of wide-spectrum antibiotics," the doctor continued, "and so far you've been responding well. How do you feel?"

Like my head has been used as a paperweight, Lee wanted to say, but he just shrugged.

"Fine."

Nelson snorted. "Okay, how do you really feel?"

"Not bad," Lee lied. The truth was that no matter how much his head throbbed, no matter how weak and confused he felt, it was better than those endless, mind-numbing days of depression, when his soul felt as if it were on fire, and consciousness itself was an unbearable burden.

"How's the investigation going? What have I missed?"

"Very well, that's enough for now," Dr. Patel intervened. "You mustn't wear yourself out."

"How long have I been here?" said Lee.

Nelson and Patel exchanged a glance.

"How long?" Lee demanded.

Finally Nelson spoke.

"Three days."

"*Three days?* What the hell was going on for three days?"

"You collapsed in your apartment three days ago with a cero-spinal meningitis," Patel said, his voice very clipped and brisk.

"Cero—what?"

"It is a brain fever, usually bacterial. You remained in a coma for three days, from which you have now awakened."

Lee looked at Nelson.

"It's true, lad," Nelson said softly.

Lee shifted his gaze to Patel. "Bacterial . . . so it's not contagious?"

"No."

"When can I get out of here?"

"Let us not be in too much of a hurry, now," Patel cautioned. "You have been very ill, you know. You are responding well to the antibiotics, but—"

"But I'm working on an important case—"

"Lee," Nelson interrupted, laying a hand on his shoulder. "Chuck is concerned about you. We all are."

That sounded like a prelude to bad news.

"What? What is it?" Lee demanded, feeling panic rising in his throat. "What's happened? Was there another victim?"

"No, no, nothing's happened," Nelson reassured him. "It's just that—" He paused and looked away.

"He's not taking me off the case?" Lee could hear his voice tightening, becoming shrill.

"Please," said Dr. Patel. "Please do not become agitated—"

Nelson rubbed his left eyebrow and looked away from Lee. "Chuck thought you could use some rest."

"I just *had* three days of rest, for Christ's sake!"

"I know, I know," Nelson replied.

Dr. Patel attempted once again to intervene. "Now, I really *must* insist—"

"But Lee, you almost died! Did you know that?"

"Well, I'm here now, aren't I?"

"Gentlemen, please!" Dr. Patel's voice now held an edge of panic.

"Let me talk to Chuck," Lee pleaded.

"You can try," Nelson said, "but I don't know—"

"Now you really must be leaving!" Dr. Patel practically shouted, taking Nelson by the shoulders. "If you are not leaving I will be calling security to have you removed!"

"All right, I'm going," Nelson growled. "Chuck will be by when his shift is over. You can talk to him then," he called over his shoulder as the doctor pushed him out of the room.

Patel returned to Lee's bedside after Nelson was in the hall. "You must not be getting so upset," he said, checking Lee's pulse. "It really is not advisable."

"Sorry." Lee's temples were pulsing with pain, and his body ached with exhaustion.

Dr. Patel frowned. "I am going to be blunt with you, Mr. Campbell. If you do not allow your body time to heal, you cannot hope to recover. If you attempt to hurry the process, you could very well end up in hospital again—or worse. Do you understand what I am saying to you?"

Lee looked away. "Yes," he said, trying to stifle a yawn. "I understand." But what he was thinking was how quickly he could talk them into letting him out of this place.

Chapter Fifty-six

By that evening Lee's head had stopped pounding. He awoke as the sun was setting, feeling ravenous. He turned his head to see Chuck sitting next to his bed, flipping through a magazine. Dr. Patel stood at the foot of the bed, studying his chart.

"I'm starving," Lee said.

"Okay." Chuck replied. "What do you want?"

"A cheeseburger."

Morton smiled. "That's got to be a good sign."

"You're not out of the woods yet," Dr. Patel said glumly. He seemed to think that throwing cold water on their hopeful mood was his unpleasant but necessary duty.

"Is he allowed to eat?" Chuck asked.

"If he feels hungry," the doctor replied gloomily, as if Lee's appetite were a dismal sign.

"Okay," Chuck said, rising and tossing the magazine on the chair. "I'll be right back."

"Hey, has anyone called my mother to say I'm okay?" Lee asked.

"She was here earlier, while you were asleep. She'll be

back tomorrow. Oh, and Dr. Azarian stopped by too," he added. "She said she'd come by later."

He darted out the door, followed by a gloomy-faced Dr. Patel.

Lee's stomach took a little hop of anticipation at the mention of Kathy's name. He longed to talk to Chuck about her, but the subject of women was a strained one between them, since things turned out the way they had with Susan. On the rebound from Lee after college, Susan Beaumont had gravitated to Chuck for many reasons, both good and bad. Lee knew this because she had told him as much after a few too many glasses of eggnog at a Christmas party a few years ago. Marrying Chuck was another way to stay close to Lee, she had said. Instead of feeling flattered, as she had perhaps expected, he reacted with guilt and dismay. He begged her never to repeat this to anyone—least of all Chuck—but he had no idea what went on between them in private. He prayed she had taken his advice. She wasn't an unkind woman, just a chronically immature one.

Susan Beaumont was exactly the kind of woman Chuck Morton was drawn to: one who seemed to need protecting. Lee thought she was an emotional vampire, but Chuck needed to be needed, and like every man who saw Susan, he was floored by her beauty—the kind of effortless, shimmering beauty that struck other women as unfair, and left men helpless and weak-kneed before her. Susan Beaumont Morton was the kind of woman who wore her good looks so casually and yet so consciously that it was hard for anyone—man or woman—to think of anything else when talking to her. But Lee sensed Circe's touch in Susan from the beginning, and just hoped she had been kind to Chuck, who still adored her after all these years of marriage, with an eager devotion Lee found touching. Chuck had always been in love with her, and Lee hoped that she had come to care for Chuck the way he deserved.

She needed things Lee couldn't give her—things he suspected no one could give another person, but Chuck Morton's mission in life regarding women was unchanging ever since Lee had known him: rescue, protect, and serve. Lee knew Chuck's protectiveness extended to him as well, and he was touched by it. He could tease Chuck about that, but he would never tease his friend about his relationship to women. Chuck believed to this day that Susan had left Lee for him. Lee allowed him to believe this fiction because it was easier on everyone—or so he hoped.

But Kathy Azarian was different. He had dated more beautiful women, others besides Susan, but no one who touched him quite the way Kathy did. Was it the way she wrinkled her forehead when she was thinking hard, or the way she pursed her lips to one side, the single lock of curly hair that fell over her eyes? It was that and more—the sound of her low, throaty voice, the slight lisp in her speech, the way she wrapped her fingers around his arm as they walked, a hundred little things and yet no one thing in particular.

As if in answer to his thoughts, there was a soft knock on the door, and Kathy's face appeared between the parted curtains in the hall outside.

"Come in!" Lee called, and struggled to sit up in bed. The effort caused a wave of dizziness.

Kathy entered the room and sat on the chair Chuck had vacated. She put a hand on Lee's arm. Her fingers were cool and soft.

"How are you feeling?"

"Not bad. Hungry."

"That's a good sign." He could tell she was trying to camouflage any concern she felt, so as not to frighten him.

"I'm going to be fine," he said.

"I never doubted it for a minute," she replied too quickly. "Oh, I brought you a proper suitcase," she said, holding up a leather satchel. "For when you come home. It's a girl thing," she added with a laugh. "We love shoes and suitcases—very Freudian, right?"

"Right," he agreed. Just having her in the room cheered him up.

"Oh, and I also brought you something even more useless," she added, digging through a tan rattan shoulder bag on her lap.

He watched her, noting the familiar renegade curl of dark hair falling over her eyes. The mystery of desire was part of the greater mystery that Lee had come very close to during his descent into depression. In the midst of damnation, he had sensed the possibility of salvation. And maybe this was why he felt he could relate to the tortured soul of this young killer, caught as he was in the cycle of damnation. There were no maps showing the way through the dark thicket Lee had found himself in. But he had learned that salvation and damnation were very close, the line separating them thin as the band of winter twilight separating earth and sky.

"Here it is," Kathy cried triumphantly, pulling a dog-eared piece of newspaper from her bag. "This week's Tuesday crossword puzzle in the *Times* is all about forensic science. I thought maybe we could do it together."

"Okay," he said. "I'm not that good at crossword puzzles. I don't do them often enough. My mother's a real whiz. Does double crostics."

"Well, this is only Tuesday's puzzle, so it shouldn't be too hard."

"Good."

She handed it to him, and he studied it. The title was "Criminology." He looked at the first clue: "FBI Profiling guru." There were seven spaces. "Ressler," he said. "Robert Ressler. Or it could be Douglas—John Douglas."

"You bite your left lower lip when you're concentrating," she said. "Did you know that?"

He looked up. "I never thought much about it. Here," he

said, handing the newspaper back to her. She took it, but let it fall in her lap.

"Oh, hell," she said. "Damn."

"What? What's wrong?"

"*Damn.*"

"*What?* What is it?"

She tossed the newspaper on the bed in a gesture of surrender. "I'm in love with you."

A laugh burst from his throat, taking him by surprise. She cocked her head to one side and raised her right eyebrow.

"That's funny?"

"Well, it was the way you said it."

She smiled only on one side—it was her rueful look, the nearest expression she had to looking apologetic.

"Maybe you just feel sorry for me," he suggested.

"I didn't *mean* anything by it, really. It's just that—well, I wasn't planning on it right now." She looked irritated, but her voice was soft.

He laughed again. It felt good, like something inside him was unfreezing. "Sorry to upset your plans."

"You don't laugh very often, you know."

"I know. I used to—before."

"Oh. Right." Her face went slack, then assumed a holding pattern, as if she wasn't sure what the proper expression was.

"I guess it means I'm feeling better," he said, then winced at how much the tone of forced cheer reminded him of his mother. *God, get a grip, Campbell.*

"Are you?" she asked. "Feeling better, I mean?"

"Yes, much." He looked around the room. "It's weird to be back here again. I haven't been here since—"

"Right. Is that—uh, is that better?"

"That? Yes. I mean, it comes and goes at times, but mostly I'm better."

She smiled. "Oh, good. I've never had . . . that"—(funny how both of them were reluctant to say the word "depression")—"but I've had friends who did. I didn't realize how bad it was until one of them committed suicide."

Lee swallowed once, hard. "How did she—" he began, then realized he didn't want to hear the answer.

"He, actually. Carbon monoxide. Sat in his car in the garage with the engine on. His mother found him."

"How old were you?"

"It was a few years after college."

"Close friend?"

"Close enough that I asked myself for years afterward what I could have done or said to change things. I didn't even know he was depressed—we'd sort of lost touch, I guess. I found out from mutual friends."

"I'm sorry."

She looked out the window and put her right forefinger to her forehead. "I don't know why I'm telling you this. I'm sorry—after what you've been through."

"Well, I *am* a trained psychologist," he said. "If people can't talk to me, who can they talk to?"

She smiled at his attempt to lighten the conversation.

"What I learned from that was how . . . irreplaceable everyone is. Once you lose someone, that's it. There's really no replacing them."

"That's true. I just never thought of it exactly that way."

Chuck returned with hamburgers from the coffee shop next door. Lee thought he saw a flicker of irritation on his friend's face when he saw Kathy.

"Hi," Chuck said, "nice to see you again."

"Yes," Kathy replied. "Good to see you too."

Fortunately, Chuck had bought three hamburgers, so they each had one. Lee liked the way Kathy ate, with a hearty, unself-conscious appetite. But as soon as they had finished, Dr. Patel appeared, wagging his stethoscope at them.

"Time to rest," he said sternly, herding Chuck and Kathy out of the room.

"Does he ever sleep?" Kathy whispered to Lee as she kissed him good-bye.

"He's a resident," he whispered back. "They never sleep."

Dr. Patel did one more quick check of Lee's blood pressure and pulse, nodded grimly, muttered something to himself, made a notation on the chart at the foot of the bed, and left the room. Lee lay back on the pillow, feeling an odd sense of contentment. Sleep dragged at his eyelids, and he sank into its dark and welcoming arms.

Chapter Fifty-seven

The church was vast and empty, its dark marbled interior cold as the grave. A chill wind swept over Lee as he walked down the long corridor toward the altar. The pews were empty, but he could hear whispering, tongues slithering over consonants like so many snakes. The click of his heels on the hard stone floors was like a rhythm track underneath the wall of whispering. He couldn't make out what they were saying, but felt that they were talking about him in the dimly lit chapel, illuminated only by flickering votive candles lining the walls. He strained to see them, but saw only rows of empty pews stretching out before him, silent wooden sentinels.

He walked on. The corridor stretched out before him, and the altar seemed to recede as he approached it. The whispering was behind him now, and he strained to make out the words, but the voices blended into a hissing like the sound of raindrops on a tin roof. A single white light shone down upon the altar as he as-

cended the steps. The whispering got louder, thickening the air like the buzzing of cicadas.

There, on the altar, Laura was waiting for him. She lay on her back, her hands folded over her spotless white communion dress. Her eyes were closed, her face peaceful in death—and there was no doubt in his mind she was as dead as the dried flowers lining the steps of the altar. Lee studied her face, waiting for the roses to bloom in her cheeks once again, to replace the gray pallor of death. Her hair surrounded her pale face like a dark halo, falling in crisp ringlets on her shoulders. Laura had always been proud of her hair—thick, black and shiny as polished river stones.

He felt sadness, but no horror. To his surprise, he also felt relief. He had always known she was dead, but now here was proof, and she was at peace. Instead of a rotting, mangled corpse cast off in a ditch somewhere, exposed to the elements, and eaten by wild creatures, she was perfectly preserved, pristine as a bride, her beauty intact forever. He was glad—glad for her and for his mother, who could now accept the reality of her death.

He bent to kiss her dead cheek, but as he did, her face morphed and changed before his eyes—into Kathy Azarian's face. A fist of fear grabbed his heart, squeezing the breath from his body. He sank to his knees, blind terror wrapping itself around his brain, pressing down on him so that all of his senses began to fade. He struggled to see, to hear, to feel, but a cloud of unknowing draped itself over him, dimming his senses. He tried to cry out, but his vocal cords had turned to dust, dry as the dead flowers surrounding the altar.

He awoke to middle-of-the-night stillness. It took him a few moments to realize where he was. The phones at the nurses' station had stopped ringing, and he heard the soft whirr of machinery from the ICU unit down the hall. He was flooded with an overwhelming sense of relief that his dream was just that: a dream.

The room was dark; the only source of illumination was the light seeping through the smoked glass door panel. The venetian blinds on the window next to his bed were closed, blocking out even the light from the street lamps. As his eyes grew accustomed to the dim light, Lee had a strong sense of a presence in the room with him. He peered into the far corner of the room, where a straight-backed chair sat against the wall. At first glance Lee thought maybe someone had thrown an overcoat across the chair, but then he realized the dark figure on the chair was a person. He thought could just make out a man seated in the shadows—unmoving, as still as if he were made of stone.

He knew who it was.

Lee's hand twitched, and he almost reached for the call button to summon the nurse, but something stopped him. Curiosity, maybe—or perhaps an instinct to submit to whatever fate held in store for him. The figure in the corner sat very still. Lee reached over and pulled the string on the Venetian blinds, letting in light from the street outside. As he did so, a gleam of moonlight reflected off the high, pale forehead. The room was still too dark to get a good look at his face, but he could tell that the man was thin and pale.

Lee ran his tongue over his parched lips. "How did you get in here?" he croaked.

His visitor laughed nervously. "I'm very good at getting into places—but you should know that by now." The voice was young, high pitched, and raspy, and there was a soft wheezing sound when he breathed, as if his lungs were worn and tattered bellows, stiff and dried with age. Lee couldn't resist feeling a sense of triumph. *So I was right about the asthma.* He also had the feeling he had heard the voice before, but where? In their brief encounter in Hastings, no words had been exchanged between them.

"What do you want?"

"What does anyone want? Money, power, immortality— but I'm not interested in those things."

"What are you interested in?"

"Love. Like the love I feel for God: unconditional love and devotion."

"Is there a difference? Between love and devotion, I mean?"

"I guess it depends on who you are. But there's really no such thing as unconditional love—not in this life, anyway."

"So why are you here?"

His visitor leaned forward in his chair. "To let you know that He tells me to do what I do."

"God, you mean?"

"Yes. It's His work I'm doing."

"Aren't you afraid of getting caught?"

"The righteous cannot afford to feel fear."

"But don't you feel it anyway? To know all those people are out there looking for you?"

The pursuer becomes the pursued.

"I have God to protect me."

"Is that what you think? That He'll keep you from getting caught?"

"Until His work is finished, yes."

"What about the girls? Don't you feel bad for them at all?"

His breath became more hoarse. Lee heard the wheezing from deep within his chest, lungs struggling to pull in enough air.

"I have to save them."

"From what?"

"Eternal damnation. I always ask their forgiveness, but it must be done."

There was a pause. "I don't want to kill you too, you know. I feel close to you."

"Why do you keep going?"

"I couldn't stop if I wanted to now. You should know that." The voice was half ironic, half sincere.

"Why don't you turn yourself in? Then you could rest— you could finally be at peace."

His visitor inhaled, making the deep, rattling sound of congested lungs.

"I don't think so. Why is it that cops always seem to think people are going to go for that one? Has anyone in the history of law enforcement ever actually fallen for that?"

Another pause.

Then Lee said, "Why did you have to kill Eddie?"

"I'm afraid I don't know anything about that. And now I have to go—I have an appointment with death," he said, rising from the chair. He was out the door before Lee could find the call button. As the door clicked closed behind him, Lee imagined he was already on his way to Seventh Avenue, perhaps slipping into a stairwell to avoid being seen in an elevator.

Lee shivered and stared out the window as the moon slid behind a looming cloud. He wouldn't forget that voice. It carried the buried rage of a life gone sour. He couldn't shake the feeling he had heard the voice before, but he couldn't quite place it.

To his surprise, Lee recognized some of himself in this man. Like most civilized people, Lee was forced to swallow his rage—but this man had given into it, punishing innocent young women for the sins of a careless and indifferent God.

Chapter Fifty-eight

Chuck Morton arrived the next afternoon with Detective Butts in tow. Butts was even more rumpled than usual, and he looked around the room uncomfortably, scratching the back of his neck. After a brief greeting, he lurked at the far side of the room, inspecting the idle hospital machinery at the end of the empty bed across from Lee's.

"We just came by to see how you were doing," Chuck said, but Lee sensed that was not the real reason for their visit.

"I'm ready to get out of this place," Lee replied.

"Do you really think that's a good idea?"

"They can't keep me here against my will."

"Don't you think you should listen to your doctor?"

"Aw, what do doctors know anyway?" Butts interjected, lowering his bulk into one of the plastic chairs and fanning his face with a packet of sterilized towelettes.

Lee began to get out of bed.

"Look, there's no need to punish yourself because we haven't caught this guy yet," Chuck said.

"I'm not punishing myself," Lee answered, even though he knew Chuck had a point.

"Okay, fine," Chuck replied. "Don't you think you should listen to your doctor anyway?"

Lee looked at his friend. He seemed ill at ease.

"Hey, I'm dyin' for some coffee," Butts declared. "You want some?"

"No, I'm fine," Chuck replied.

"Uh, sure," said Lee. "Sounds good."

"I'll be right back," Butts said, leaving the room as though he couldn't wait to get out.

"I don't think he likes hospitals," Lee remarked.

"Yeah—right," Chuck answered, but he sounded distracted. There was an awkward pause, and then he put a hand on Lee's shoulder.

"Look, Lee . . ."

Something in his tone of voice caused a thin trickle of dread to seep into Lee's veins.

"What is it? Was there another victim?"

Chuck avoided looking at him. "No, it's not that."

"What, then? What's wrong?"

Chuck bit his lip and studied his shoelaces.

"The mayor's been hounding the DA, you know, and he's been coming down hard on us."

"So? What are you saying?"

"Well, they're pressuring me to bring in the Feds."

"You mean bring in an FBI profiler?"

"Yeah."

"I'm all for it—if they can spare the manpower."

"And you really need to rest—"

"Look, Chuck, I'm fine now! I'm ready to go—"

"No, you're not. Dr. Patel says you should stay in bed for at least another week."

"Dr. Patel is a professional pessimist."

"The thing is, we don't have the manpower available we once did, since—"

"I know—we're all stretched thin since September eleventh. But even if the FBI can spare someone, you'll need help filling them in. I'm getting out of here right now."

Lee struggled to get out of bed, but Chuck kept his hand on his shoulder.

"Come on, Lee, don't be like that."

"Like what, Chuck? Like *what*? What am I supposed to do? Stay in bed and take my medicine like a good boy? To hell with that!"

Lee pushed Chuck's hand away and struggled out of bed, fighting not to show the dizziness the sudden activity caused him. He dug his clothes out of the bureau next to his bed and stuffed them into the leather satchel Kathy had brought him.

Chuck smacked a hand onto his own thigh. "I *knew* it—I knew this was too close for you!"

Lee wheeled around to face Chuck. "Do you want to know how close it is? Do you? He *came* to me last night!"

"What do you mean?"

"He was *here*—sitting in that chair!"

"What are you talking about? Did you have some kind of fever dream or something?"

"No, I was as clear as day. He got in somehow."

"What? How?"

"I don't know how! He probably just walked in." Lee's head throbbed, and he had to sit on the bed.

"The bottom line here is that you're really not well yet."

"Oh, don't start with that again, for God's sake!"

"Would you just slow down for a minute and think what you're doing?"

"We're moving too slowly already!" Lee pulled on his shirt so violently that he ripped the sleeve. "Shit!" he said. "God*damn* it!" He picked up a shoe and threw it as hard as he could across the room.

As he did, he looked up to see his mother and Kylie standing in the doorway to his room. Kylie's eyes were wide with amazement, and his mother looked as though she had just swallowed a gnat.

"Well," Fiona Campbell said frostily, "it looks as though someone is having a bit of a temper tantrum."

"Uncle Lee, those are bad words," said Kylie.

"Yes, they are, Kylie," he replied, "very bad words."

Butts returned with two cups of coffee and an enormous cheese danish.

"I thought you might be hungry, so I—" He stopped, sensing the tension in the air. "What's the matter? Something happen while I was gone?"

"Well," Lee's mother said, "this is awkward, isn't it?"

Chapter Fifty-nine

Half a dozen apologies later, Fiona was persuaded to take Kylie shopping, while Lee and Chuck went back with Detective Butts to Chuck's office.

When they got there, Nelson and Florette were waiting for them. Nelson did not look happy.

"The *Feds*?" he bellowed. "The goddamn *Federales*? What the hell do you want to bring them in for?"

"It wasn't my idea," Chuck pointed out.

"Good God!" Nelson fumed. "You'd think they have enough on their hands right now, with all their recent screwups!" His eyes were bloodshot, and his cheeks were lit up by a map of tiny red veins. It was clear to everyone in the room that he was not sober.

"Look," Lee said, "why don't you get some rest? You don't look so good."

"I don't look so good? *I* don't? You should take a look in a mirror, laddy—you look like something the cat dragged in."

"Okay, okay," Chuck said, placing a hand on his shoulder, "calm down."

"I am perfectly calm," Nelson replied.

"I think we can use all the help we can get," Florette remarked. He was dressed in a dapper green suit with matching tie; his shoes were shined to a gleaming sheen. Next to him, Nelson looked ratty and scrappy, like a bar brawler ready to go.

"Well, then, why doesn't someone *do* something about it?" he muttered. "Why all this goddamn pussyfooting around?

Butts stepped forward. "I think the first thing that someone should do is to send you home. You're not—"

But he never got a chance to finish his sentence. Nelson growled and threw a punch at him. He was too drunk to make contact, though, and ended up flat on his back on the other side of the room.

"Oh, you wanna get into it?" Butts said. "Come on— bring it on! I'm ready for you."

"Stop it!" Chuck barked. "All right, that's it," he continued, kneeling beside Nelson. "We'll take a little break and start up again in a few minutes." He pulled Nelson to his feet. "What's the *matter* with you?"

"I'll tell you what's the matter with me," Nelson answered. "This damn psycho has us all by the short and curlies— *that's* what's the matter with me.

"This isn't helping things," Chuck said. "Why don't you go home until you can sleep this off?"

Nelson looked at Lee, who said, "I think you know Chuck is right."

It took more convincing to get Nelson to leave. After he had gone, a pall settled over the room. They were all emotionally exhausted, and Nelson's behavior reminded them how close to the edge they all were.

"All right," said Chuck. "Let's just try to concentrate for a moment, can we?"

"I know how Dr. Nelson feels," Florette said, adjusting his already perfectly centered silk tie, "but don't you think a fresh set of eyes might be a good idea at this point?"

"I'm surprised they've got anyone to spare, with all the antiterrorism work they're doing right now," Butts remarked.

"I trained with some of these guys at Quantico, and they're terrific, but it'll take time to bring them up to speed." Lee said.

"What you said before is right," Butts pointed out. "The bottom line is getting this guy off the street as soon as possible."

"Yeah," Lee agreed. He went to sit down, felt faint, and almost fell.

"Hey," Chuck said, "maybe someone else should be going home right about now."

"I'm fine," Lee replied tersely.

Butts squinted at him. "Is there any chance that your infection was caused by—by something that was done to you?"

Lee stared at him. "What do you mean?"

"Could he have—I mean, can someone cause that kind of infection in another person?"

"I think that's unlikely," Florette interjected. "I was a med student as an undergraduate, and I never heard of a case of bacterial meningitis that was the result of deliberate contamination. It's not—"

"Okay, so let's move on," Chuck said, coming around to lean on the front of his desk. "Did you have any luck tracing Samuel Beckett?" he asked Detective Florette.

"Not really. We looked into the handful of people with that name, but no one came even close to the profile—an old retired sailor on Staten Island, one rich, middle-aged French businessman on the Upper East Side, and a would-be playwright using it as a nom de plume in the East Village, most definitely gay."

"Any follow-up on how he got into the hospital room at that hour?" Chuck asked Butts.

"One of the night nurses found a discarded orderly jacket in a broom closet, but there are no workable prints on it,"

Butts replied. "Probably wore gloves again—God knows there are plenty of those in a hospital."

"Yeah, and he's too smart to discard those in the hospital," Lee remarked. "He would know that prints can be lifted from the inside of latex gloves."

Chuck looked at his watch. "Look, it's late. Why don't we all get a few hours of sleep, and meet first thing tomorrow morning?"

"Okay," said Butts. "My wife's gonna be real shocked to see me—says she hasn't seen me for so long that she's forgotten what I look like. Which, in my case, maybe isn't such a bad thing," he added with a rueful smile.

They all headed out for their various subway trains as the city settled into early evening stillness. A few clouds punctuated an otherwise clear night sky, and there was a smell of fresh earth in the air.

Lee and Florette took the express train downtown together as far as Times Square.

"You know," Lee said as the local stops flashed past the windows, "there's got to be some key to this whole thing."

Up on the walls of the subway car was an advertisement for horse racing at Belmont Park, a speeding thoroughbred with a jockey leaning low over its muscular neck. As Lee looked up at the picture, an idea slowly formed in his mind.

"Oh, my God—that's *it*! A *key*."

"What?" said Florette.

"Eddie," he said. "The racing form—that was the key!"

"What key?" Florette asked, still confused.

He explained his idea to Florette as the stops continued to rush by.

Half an hour later, he was on East Seventh Street, headed for his apartment. The minute he got inside, he dialed Chuck's number in New Jersey. After two rings a woman answered.

"Hello?"

It was Susan, her voice low and liquid, smooth as olive oil. Lee had seen her once since her drunken Christmas party confession, at one of the 9/11 police funerals, and he had done his best to avoid her then. He considered hanging up, and rejected the idea—knowing Susan, she would have caller ID, and hanging up would only make things worse.

He took a deep breath. "Hello, Susan." He tried to sound natural, and ended up sounding completely forced.

"Hello, Lee." She stretched out the *l*'s, rolling her tongue over the consonants sensually, like a cat stretching itself. "Long time, no see." It was an accusation, an implication, and an invitation. Lee wondered if she was faithful to Chuck.

He took another breath and swallowed hard.

"Is Chuck around?"

"Yes, he's in the basement working out. Just a minute—I'll get him."

She put down the receiver, and he could hear the click of her heels as she crossed the kitchen floor. Since being married to Susan, Chuck had become devoted to his weight routine, buffing his already athletic body to a burnished movie star musculature. If he didn't exercise regularly, he was given to thickening around the middle—unlike Lee, whose appetite came and went, Chuck had been renowned at Princeton for his eating ability. He once ate four dozen Maryland crabs at a seafood festival, and Lee had seen him down a sixteen-ounce steak.

Susan had kept her looks, too—she worked hard at it. Hours at the gym, Botox, implants, micro this, retinol that—her body was a project. Within a week of giving birth to her son, according to Chuck, she was doing crunches in front of *Oprah* reruns. She'd get her beauty any way she could have it. From a bottle, a box, or a scalpel—it was all the same to her.

Susan came back on the line. "He's coming," she purred.

"And don't be such a stranger—come out and see us sometime. It doesn't always have to be about business, you know."

Oh, yes it does.

Chuck came on the line. "Hello?" he said, sounding out of breath. Lee imagined him standing on the immaculate kitchen floor, toweling off, being careful not to get a drop of sweat on the perfectly waxed floor.

"Listen, Chuck, I have an idea."

"Yeah?"

"I know it sounds crazy, but I think Eddie's racing form may hold the key—"

"What racing form?"

"Eddie Pepitone called me before he died to say he had an idea about the killer's identity."

"And?"

"He had just won some money on a horse called 'Lock, Stock, and Barrel.'"

"So?"

"Eddie was a superstitious guy. I think he bet on that horse because of something he knew—or thought he knew—that he wanted to tell me."

"What would that be?"

"Well, you know how this guy has been getting into the churches so easily?"

"Yeah. But some of the churches told us they often leave doors open."

"I know. But remember how he got into the hospital the other night with no problem?"

"Right."

"And got into the locked room where they kept the communion wine with no sign of a break-in?"

"Yeah?"

"Well, this may sound far-fetched, but what if he has an expertise that helps him do this?"

"Such as?"

"Well, what if he's a locksmith?"

"Hmm. You mean as in 'Lock, Stock, and Barrel.' That's not bad. It's worth a shot, anyway."

"We agreed that he was probably self-employed, right?"

"Right."

"So what if he actually *owns* a business?"

"Okay," Chuck said. "We can put Florette's men on it right away."

"I rode the train down with him."

"Yeah? And?"

"He liked the idea. I suggested we draw a radius to begin with of a mile around that church in Queens. That will be the most likely place—assuming he works not far from where he lives."

"Okay. We can start calling places by about eight a.m."

"I'll be in your office at eight sharp."

"Okay." There was a pause, and Chuck spoke softly, as if he didn't want someone in the room with him to hear. "Lee?"

"Yeah?"

"You okay?"

"Yeah. I'm going to bed now."

"Okay. Do that, all right?"

"Sure. I may call Nelson first, but—"

"Oh, let him sleep it off. He acted like a total jerk."

"I know. He's in pain, though."

"Yeah, right. Aren't we all?"

"Yeah. Sure."

"Bed, Lee."

"Right. Good night."

"Good night."

There was a click on the line, and Lee imagined Susan wrapping her arms around Chuck, luring him to bed. *Well,* he thought, *one man's meat is another man's poison.*

He put on a CD of some vocal music by the Estonian

composer Arvo Pärt, and looked out the window at the fading light as the voices of the choir floated around him in the air, singing cluster chords in soft, spooky tones. The days were getting longer now, and on warm days he could smell a hint of spring in the air. He knew he was supposed to rejoice in the opening of buds and the quiet greening of the trees, and yet all he felt was wistfulness.

He longed for a retreat into darkness, to sink into the womb of winter, instead of having to claw his way into the light. The longer the day, the more he felt the pressure to solve this case, and the growing impossibility of his task shook him to the core.

He could not know that was something he had in common with the man he pursued.

His mother rejoiced in the sunlight, of course; in fact, she took Lee's journey into depression as a rebuke to her very existence. When she asked about his mental health—which she did rarely—she danced around the topic as though it might bite her.

The phone rang. He picked it up.

"Hello?"

"Hi, it's me." It was Kathy. "Just called to say good-bye."

"Why?"

"I'm going back to Philadelphia tomorrow. The Vidocq Society monthly meeting. My dad invited me, remember?"

"Oh, right. Sorry—I forgot."

"No problem. My place is being renovated, so I'll be staying with my dad. I'll call you."

"Okay, great."

"How are you feeling?"

"I'm fine."

"Well, make sure you get enough rest," she said, sounding unconvinced.

"I'm going to go lie down right now."

"Okay. I'll talk to you later in the week."

"Right."

"I'll miss you."

"Me too."

After they hung up, he looked out the window at the Orthodox Ukrainian church across the street. A ray of moonlight fell on the huge round window above the door of the church, lighting up the colors of the stained glass like a kaleidoscope.

He was reminded of the sun glinting off the windows of the World Trade Center, windows that would never reflect light again, and of the three thousand souls that lay buried in the debris. The sheer arbitrariness of the attack still stunned him. *But for the grace of . . . God? Fate? Nature?* What would you call it if you'd rejected traditional Christian notions of faith? *A leap of faith*—more like a dive, a plunge into the abyss. And yet, he thought, surrender could be sweet—so sweet that intelligent, educated young men had surrendered themselves, or so they imagined, to the will of Allah.

He wondered what was in the minds of the hijackers as they carried out their implacable plan. For, he was convinced, it was not so different from what was in the mind of his own Holyman, the Slasher.

Chapter Sixty

He looked around the restaurant in Grand Central Station. These were all nice people, surely, with families and mortgages and dogs they had gotten from rescue shelters— scruffy terriers with sweet, lopsided faces, sporting red bandanas, who liked to chase Frisbees in the park on Sunday afternoons. They were the kind of people that advertisers targeted on television: middle-class families looking to upgrade their dishwashers, their laptops, their life insurance policies. They had aging parents in managed-care facilities they were concerned about, college tuition to save up for, IRA accounts to roll over.

But *he* existed outside of their world. His was a half-lit netherworld of dark drives and even darker deeds. He glided in and out of their cheerful daytime lives like a ghost, an unwelcome visitor whose mission was to disrupt their daily ordinariness to satisfy his appalling fantasies.

If he could not be one of them, then he would live to remind them of that, to let them know they were not safe—not in their fortified SUVs, their multiplex houses with the elaborate security systems, or their fabulously expensive office buildings with the Japanese fountains and designer furniture fresh from the showroom. He would strike wherever they lived, worked, or played. He would invade their safety like a virus, a worm, a bacterium. They could not know his world, but he would know theirs.

He glanced at his watch—it was time to leave. His train would be boarding for Philadelphia soon.

Chapter Sixty-one

Lee promised himself that he would call Nelson right after he had a short nap on the couch. His head had been pounding now for hours, his neck was stiffening up, and he felt nauseous. He took one of the pills Dr. Patel had given him, and tried not to think about the doctor's face when he announced his intention to leave the hospital. He lay down on the couch and pulled the green afghan, the one Laura knitted him when she was sixteen and he was on his way to his freshman year at Princeton, over his legs. As he drifted off, he saw a thin ray of moonlight reflecting off the silver wind chimes Kylie had given him last Christmas.

He awoke to a ringing bell. In his dream it was the wind chimes ringing, but when he regained full consciousness he realized it was his phone. He threw off the blanket and staggered over to the phone.

"Hello?" His voice was slurred, ragged.

"Lee?" It was his therapist.

"Oh, hello, Dr. Williams."

"Are you all right?"

"Uh, yes, I'm fine."

"I'm sorry to call you on a Thursday evening, but I was becoming concerned about you. You've never missed an appointment and then not called."

Thursday! His weekly appointment with her was on Wednesday afternoons, and he had completely forgotten about it.

"I'm sorry. I was in the hospital."

"What's wrong?"

He could hear the concern in her voice, underneath the patrician professionalism.

"I'm okay now."

"Was it . . . ?"

"I had an infection of the brain. Bacterial meningitis."

"That can be very serious. Are you sure you're all right?"

"Yes. I was just asleep, that's all. I'm sorry I didn't call you."

"Never mind. I'm just concerned about you."

"Look, I'd like to reschedule, but I think we're closing in on this guy."

"The Slasher, you mean? That's wonderful."

"Yes." He tried to sound hopeful and positive, but knew he had failed.

"You feel conflicted about it."

He stared out into the blackened sky. The stained-glass window on the Ukrainian church now reflected only pale lamplight.

"Maybe you identify with him. You told me that you believe he has an absent father and controlling mother."

"Yes, but—"

"So in some ways, you may feel that his rage is your rage."

A terrible thought crowded itself into his mind. Though he was, in every way, luckier than this young man, Lee realized that he felt an unwelcome emotion.

"It sounds awful, but I think I envy him just a little."

"What do you envy about him?"

"Because I have to swallow my rage, and he gets to act it out."

"So you wish you could be like him?"

He took a breath and held it. "Yes. I wish sometimes I could just be a murderer."

There was a pause, and Lee heard the click of call waiting.

"Dr. Williams, will you excuse me? There's another call coming in, and I really should get it."

"Of course. Why don't you just call me when you're ready to see me?"

"I will. Thank you for understanding."

He clicked the receiver button and picked up the second call. It was Nelson, and he sounded stone-cold sober.

"I am *so* sorry. Can you ever forgive me for acting like a damn fool?"

"Of course," Lee answered.

He filled Nelson in on his theory about the locksmith store.

"That makes sense," he agreed, "because he would probably have a van with the company logo on it—a perfect way to transport the bodies."

"And a place to do the killing away from prying eyes."

"Yeah, that too," Nelson said. "So what did he say to you in the hospital?"

"He went on about being a servant of God, that kind of thing."

"Anything else?"

"Not really—mostly how he was on a holy mission."

"So he's a true believer."

"Looks like it." The sound of the killer's voice was still fresh in his ears, and Lee continued to have the feeling he had heard it before—but where? An image popped into his head of Nelson lecturing in the crowded classroom, and then it struck him. The voice belonged to the thin young man at the far end of the hall—whose face he had never seen.

"Do you have a listing of all the students signed up for your class?" he said.

"Why do you ask?"

"Do you remember that thin blond boy with the raspy voice?"

"Let's see . . . I think so."

"Who is he?"

"I don't recall his name offhand, but he said he was doing a makeup class or two because he missed a lecture in Dr. Zellinger's class."

"I think that's him."

"You mean *him?*"

"Yeah—I think he's the Slasher."

"Oh my God. If you're right, then he could have posed as building maintenance, or even picked a lock on a side door."

"Sure," Lee answered. "The main security gate at John Jay is up front, but no one guards the side entrances."

"So he's been watching us all this time."

"That explains how he knew who I was—and you too."

"Damn. So we had him *under our noses* all that time! Goddamn it!"

"Let's just focus on getting him, okay? I'll see you first thing tomorrow morning."

"Right."

After he hung up, Lee looked at the Seth Thomas clock on the mantelpiece, a gift from his mother. It was ten o' clock.

He looked out the window one last time before going to bed. He could feel the Slasher, out there in the darkness, waiting for him, waiting,

"I'm coming," Lee whispered. "Ready or not, here I come."

Chapter Sixty-two

By 8:30 the next morning all the members of the task force were seated around the table in the conference room, a pile of phone books scattered over the big oval table. Florette and his sergeant sat at two computer terminals, doing their search online, while the rest of them leafed through the Queens phone book.

"Not too many locksmith shops will have Web sites, I'd think," Chuck said, peering over their shoulder.

Florette turned to look up at him. "Maybe, but you never know."

"What are we lookin' for, exactly?" Butts sneezed as he dialed a number. He was coming down with a cold, and his pockets bulged with tissues.

"Names and addresses of the owners," Lee replied.

"How will we know when we find the right one?"

"We won't," Nelson growled from the corner, where he sat, sucking at an unlit cigarette, a phone book balanced on his lap. He was looking more cheerful than the previous day, since as it turned out, the FBI was too swamped to send anyone for at least a week.

"We'll just start within a three-mile radius of the church, and go outward from there," Lee said. "Assuming that he lives near his shop—"

"Which is a pretty big assumption," Butts sniffled.

"Which, I was just going to say, is a pretty big assumption."

"Hey," Butts said, "do you remember the day that first girl died, and a locksmith showed up at the church? Claimed there was a broken lock in the basement?"

"Yeah," Lee answered. "It turned out there was a broken lock, but no one seemed to know about it at the time."

"You think that was him, coming in to check on his handiwork?"

"I think it's likely. He's been close to the investigation all along, it seems, in one form or another."

"Too bad we didn't detain him for questioning then."

"How could we know?"

"Yeah," Butts said. "I guess you're right. Still, it really burns me that he was right there—"

"Never mind, Detective," Chuck Morton said. "Let's concentrate on the task at hand."

They sat for about twenty minutes, dutifully collecting names and addresses of owners, when Lee chanced to put in a call to a place called Locktight Security Systems. It had a big ad splashed over half a page in the Yellow Pages.

We make sure that you stay safe—it's our business!
All the latest technology in locks and security systems

Lee dialed the number. A kid answered—unenthusiastic, bored.

"Locktight Security."

"May I please speak with the owner?"

"Uh, he's not here right now."

"When will he return?"

"I dunno, really."

"What's his name—can you tell me that?"

"Uh, sure, I guess. It's Sam. Sam Hughes—or Samuel, he likes to be called."

"And he lives in . . . ?"

"Queens. Not far from here. Can I ask who's calling?"

"I'm an old friend. I'll try back later—thanks."

He hung up and sank back in his chair.

"What is it?" Chuck said, noticing him. "You got something?"

"I'm not sure. Remember how we kept seeing the name 'Samuel Beckett' on all those church volunteers lists?"

"Why, did it come up again?"

"Not exactly. Guy's first name is Samuel, though. I just have a feeling. Let me try something."

He called back, and when the boy answered, did a passable stab at an upper-class British accent.

"I say, my good man, I'm trying to get in touch with Mrs. Hughes, Samuel's dear mother, old school chum of hers. He lives with her, I believe?"

There was a pause. Lee was afraid the kid wasn't going to buy his act. But then he snickered.

"Yeah, sure he does. Guy's pushing thirty, and he still lives with his mother."

"I see. Do they still live on the same street—oh, what was it . . . ?"

"Lourdes Street."

"Yes, of course! Number—"

"Number 121."

"Right. Thanks ever so much. Cheerio."

He hung up, to find everyone staring at him.

"Cheerio?" Nelson said. *"Cheerio?"*

Lee made a face at him. "I was improvising." He looked at Butts. "Want to go out to Queens and check this out?"

Butts muffled a sneeze in a wad of Kleenex. "Yep—you bet!"

* * *

Fifty minutes later, Lee and Detective Butts emerged into the diffuse glare of an overcast sky, the sun struggling to assert itself through a thick gray cloud cover. Lourdes Street was a few blocks from the subway, right across the street from St. Bonaventure Catholic Church.

The Queens neighborhood had the smell of defeat. The houses were depressing little boxes with peeling paint, crumbling bricks, and cheap aluminum siding, stained and battered with age, overlooking cramped lots with rocky lawns—if you could call them that—of crabgrass and overgrown weeds. The occasional lawn ornament—mostly plaster dwarfs and religious figures—only reinforced the aura of hopelessness.

The same attitude of resignation was stamped upon the faces and slumped shoulders of the residents, who shuffled along the ill-kempt sidewalks, heads down, eyes focused on the cracked slabs of concrete, probably to keep from tripping and breaking their necks.

"This is it," Butts said, pointing to a little white house crammed between its equally undistinguished neighbors. Like many of the other properties, it was surrounded by an ugly chain-ink fence. Number 121 was a little neater than some of the others. The walk was swept, and a small concrete pond was adorned with a white plaster Virgin Mary, perched next to a statue of a fawn drinking from the pond.

The front gate on the chain-link fence creaked when they opened it, and their footsteps clicked loudly on the concrete path leading up to the house. When they reached the front door, Lee lifted his hand to knock, but saw that the door was cracked open. He pushed on it, and it swung forward on well-oiled hinges but then stopped, as though something was blocking it. There were no lights on inside the house, and no sign of life within its whitewashed stucco walls.

"Mrs. Hughes?" he called out through the opening.

No response.

He called louder.

"Mrs. Hughes? Are you there?" He rapped the door sharply with his knuckles. He was burning to burst into the house, but they had no search warrant, and the last thing they needed was to have the whole case thrown out of court.

"I don't think anyone's in there," Butts said, shifting his weight back and forth on his feet. He, too, looked impatient and anxious.

"The door is open," Lee said, "do you think we should—"

But at that moment he realized what was blocking the door. As his eyes adjusted to the dim interior, he could make out a pair of woman's shoes—still attached to their owner. She lay partially out of sight, in the small front foyer, but even in the darkened room, Lee could see her feet, her legs, and—was that blood?

He turned to Butts. "We're going in. Cover me."

"I don't think we should—" Butts began, but that was all he managed to get out.

Lee didn't wait for Butts to pull his gun. He pushed against the door with his shoulder, and it gave.

What he saw made him catch his breath.

The dead woman in front of him was nude, just like the rest of the Slasher's victims. But there was no neat positioning of the body with the arms spread out evenly from her shoulders. Instead, she lay splayed out on the floor, her hands flung above her head, a jagged scar where her throat had been cut. A dark rivulet of dried blood snaked crookedly from her throat across the white linoleum floor.

"Jesus," Butts said softly, behind him, looking around the room. Blood spatter was everywhere—on the floor, the walls, the furniture, even the ceiling.

The victim was slight of build—*like her son,* Lee thought—

and, unlike the other victims, she was middle-aged, but slim and trim, what was once called "well-preserved."

On her chest had been carved the words, *Deliver us From Evil.*

He was looking at a textbook example of overkill. In addition to slashing her throat and carving on her chest, the killer had ripped her clothes from her body, and they lay in tatters around her. Her limbs were splayed out in every direction. It's possible she had fallen like that, but Lee thought it more likely that the killer was making a point by leaving her this way. He had staged every other crime scene, and would probably have staged this one—unless he was falling apart completely now, which was also possible.

He knelt and felt for a pulse, but knew there was no point. Her dead eyes stared reprovingly at the ceiling. The expression on her face was of shock and disbelief, as if she could not fathom what could cause this depth of violence from her own flesh and blood.

Lee straightened up to face Butts, who was staring down at Mrs. Hughes.

"He finally killed the person he meant to kill all along," Lee said.

"So we finally got our guy," Butts remarked.

"Except that we don't have him yet," Lee reminded him. He touched her dead hands. Rigor mortis had already begun to set in, indicating the time of death was probably some hours earlier.

"Do you think it means anything that he skipped over part of the prayer?" Butts asked, looking down at the body. "I mean, should we be lookin' for more vics to turn up?"

"Judging by this, he's spinning out of control, becoming more disorganized. I think he's on the run."

Bundy had gone on the run at this point, fleeing all the way down to Florida, where his killing became unhinged—

he attacked five young women on his final, orgiastic night of slaughter.

"I'll call it in," Butts said, getting out his cell phone.

"Okay," said Lee. "I'm going to look around." There was a slight chance Samuel was still here—*very slight,* Lee thought, given the circumstances. The killing of his mother represented the culmination of his violence, the final—and most authentic—act of retribution in what had until now been symbolic slayings. This would make him more vulnerable, but also far, far more dangerous.

Lee stepped from the foyer into a small but tidy living room adorned with religious icons. He caught a flash of white disappearing around the corner—a cat, probably. He looked around the room. Statues of Joseph and the Virgin Mary graced either side of the mantelpiece, and one wall had a kitschy portrait of Jesus looking heavenward with tragic, soulful eyes. But the most striking icon was the heavy gold cross above the fireplace. A suffering carved Christ was nailed to it with what looked like real nails, and he was dripping blood from every pore. The carving was so realistic that it made Lee's flesh crawl. The furnishings evoked a Victorian parlor—dark furniture covered with fringed antimacassars and lace doilies.

"Okay," Butts said, lumbering into the room, "they're on the way. Hey—look at that, will ya?" he said.

Lee followed his gaze. There, sitting on a small round table, next to an old-fashioned dial telephone, was a white plastic inhaler, the kind used by asthmatics. Next to it was a slip of note paper. Lee picked it up and read the hastily scrawled handwriting.

Amtrak → Philly 3:35 pm Penn Station

He glanced at his watch. The train had left from Penn Station an hour ago.

"Philly?" Lee said. "Why would he go to Philly?"

"Here," said Butts. "Take a look at this." He thrust another crumpled receipt in front of Lee, this one for the Adam's Mark Hotel, just outside downtown Philadelphia.

Lee stared at the receipt. Suddenly his ears were ringing, and there was a roaring sound in his head. He realized why Samuel Hughes was going to Philadelphia.

Next time I'll strike closer to home.

He's after Kathy. Panic rose in his throat, choking him. He grabbed Butts by the arm, dragging him to the door.

He wasn't sure what he said or did, but somehow he managed to get Butts out of there. They rushed down the street, the stubby detective trundling a few years behind him as he sprinted toward the subway. There were no yellow cabs cruising this neighborhood, and he reasoned that an express train would be faster anyway.

"What's goin' on?" Butts asked, panting as he tried to catch up with Lee. "You trying to give me pneumonia or something?"

"I've got to get to Philadelphia!" Lee called back over his shoulder.

"How are you gonna find him in a place like that?" Butts yelled as they charged down the steps to the train, dashing through the turnstiles just in time to catch an express headed for Manhattan.

"Okay," Lee said as they threw themselves down onto the plastic seats, panting heavily, "listen carefully. I'm going straight to Penn Station. I want you to contact Chuck Morton and tell him that I've gone after Samuel Hughes, and that he's our man."

"Oh, *man,*" Butts said, struggling to breath through a sudden coughing fit. "Have you gone loco on me? How do you figure to find this guy in goddamn Philadelphia?"

Lee told him what he feared—that Hughes was going

after Kathy now—and that that was the reason for his trip to Philadelphia.

"Oh, jeez," Butts said. "Let me come with you!"

"No, I need you to talk to Chuck first, and explain everything. Then maybe he can get in touch with the cops in Philly and get me some backup. It's tricky, though. We don't really have anything concrete on this guy, so they might not want to stick their necks out. And he might not want to risk asking them, either. They may all think I'm crazy."

"Okay, okay," said Butts. "Where are you gonna be?"

Lee gave him the addresses of Kathy's father's house, and the Vidocq Society.

"If you can, call both those places and leave a message for her or her father to stay put until I arrive. There's no guarantee he'll show up either of those places, though," Lee said, looking at his own cell phone. The battery only had one bar left on it. He turned it off—he wouldn't be able to charge it again before reaching Philadelphia.

"So what do you think he's gonna do?"

"I don't really know."

And that was what frightened him most of all.

Chapter Sixty-three

The Adam's Mark was the kind of hotel built for conventions and large groups of people. Easily accessible from I-95, it stood twenty-five stories high, a hulking monolith on the outskirts of downtown Philadelphia. After catching a cab from the train station to the hotel, Lee walked into the lobby and told the young desk clerk he was there to see Samuel Hughes. To his surprise, Samuel was registered under his own name.

The lobby was full of fantasy and science-fiction fans—large, oddly dressed people with pasty skin and pale, intelligent faces. Some wore medieval tunics and tights. Others wandered about dressed in jeans and T-shirts with dragon emblems on them. One nerdy-looking man with greasy black hair wore a vest covered with buttons with sayings like MY MOTHER IS A KLINGON, and MY OTHER CAR IS A MILLENNIUM FALCON.

The desk clerk refused to give Lee the room number until he presented his ID, showing his identity as a civilian consultant to the NYPD. It looked exactly like the ID a cop might carry, except that the background was red instead of blue. Fortunately for him, she was too young to know that this position gave him no legal authority—and, in any case, the NYPD had no real jurisdiction in Pennsylvania. She dispatched a porter with a master key to follow Lee to the room.

When their repeated knocks on the door received no answer, the bellboy unlocked the room to let Lee inside. Lee thanked him and sent him away with a ten-dollar tip. He didn't know what he would find inside, but he didn't want anyone else around when he found out. He pushed the door open, stepped inside onto the plush carpeting, and closed the door behind him.

The first thing that hit him when he entered the room was the smell of death—and fear. The air was heavy with the scent of panicked sweat. It was dark inside, and his first impression was that he was alone in the room.

But then he saw, silhouetted in the yellow light of the street lamps coming in through the window, the body hanging from the wooden rafters.

It swung back and forth, moving in the air currents created when Lee entered the room. He switched on the overhead light, and looked at the face. It was indeed the same thin, ascetic young man he had seen at the funeral in Westchester. An overturned footstool lay on its side underneath his feet. By all appearances, he had hanged himself from the strong oak beams that straddled the ceiling of the room.

Technically, Lee knew, he should call the hotel security staff and alert them, but instinct told him that something wasn't right. He didn't know what it was yet, but *something*. He moved around the room, careful not to touch anything—to keep the crime scene pure, but also to avoid leaving evidence that might lead to him needing to explain later why he was there.

Crime scene—the phrase popped into his head, even though at first glance it appeared to be a suicide.

Lee approached Samuel's body. Unlike the girls he had left in the churches, who looked so lifelike even in death, Samuel looked *dead*. There was no color in his face—it was the sickly color that comes when all the blood has been drained away from the skin, leaving a grayish white pallor. The eyes were wide open, and Lee felt an accusation in the stare of those dead eyes, as though Samuel somehow blamed him—for what?

The suicide note was short and to the point:

```
I have done many bad things, and I am
sorry for everyone that I hurt. It is best
this way--I can't hurt anyone else.
I love you, Mother.
                    --Samuel
```

The first thing that struck Lee as odd was that it was typed. Who types out a suicide note? Did he write it before he left for the convention? If so, why go to Philadelphia to kill himself? And why did he *type* the note? Presumably, he could have used the computers in the hotel, but why go to the trouble of *typing* the note? Why not just write it by hand on hotel stationery? And why did he tell his mother he loved her when he had brutally killed her hours earlier?

The questions swirled around Lee's mind as he worked his way through the room, taking note of everything he saw. A suitcase of clothes lay open on the bed. He looked through the clothes, all neatly packed—underwear, socks, shirts, enough for three days. Another puzzle. Why take clothes for three days if you planned to kill yourself the night you arrived?

A musty, sweet odor hung in the air. It smelled familiar, but he couldn't place it.

He went over to the body to examine it more closely. Samuel was fully dressed, in black slacks and a pressed white shirt, with conservative oxfords and argyle socks. *Why hang yourself wearing shoes?* He tried to think of seeing any photos when he was enrolled at John Jay of people wearing shoes when they hanged themselves, but couldn't think of any.

He examined the footstool that lay beneath the body. When he stood it up, it was not tall enough to reach Samuel's feet. Lee felt a surge of adrenaline through his veins. Samuel could have looped the rope through the rafters without the help of the stool, but if he had hanged himself standing on the stool, it would have to be at least tall enough to reach his feet.

There was no doubt in Lee's mind now that this was a staged crime scene. Someone had killed Samuel and then tried hard to make it look like a suicide—but not hard enough. The details didn't add up. Either the murderer lacked knowledge of forensics, or he was in a hurry.

Lee went over to the suitcase full of clothing. Perhaps it held a clue, something to help identify the murderer. He searched the clothes, but found nothing helpful. Seeing the hotel phone on the bedside table, he punched the *Speaker Phone* button, and, on an impulse, hit the *Redial* button.

The musical pattern of the numbers was so familiar to him that he didn't even have to wait for the voice mail to pick up. In an instant, everything became horrifyingly clear to him. In a flash, he saw every misread clue, every wrong turn in the road, every false lead. He knew now what the musty, sweet scent in the air was.

His hand trembling, he put the receiver back in its cradle.

Depression began to tug at him, seeping into his stomach like poison, threatening to spread upward, turning his limbs to stone as surely as if he had seen Medusa herself.

"*No!*" he muttered through clenched teeth, fighting it off with all his might. "*Not this time you don't!*"

He took a last look around the room. There was nothing more he could do for poor Samuel. He would leave the crime scene untouched for the local police to ponder.

He had to go, now—before it was too late.

Chapter Sixty-four

Dr. Azarian's house was not hard to find. A handsome Edwardian brick structure in an affluent neighborhood, it stood at the end of a short stone walkway. The front gate was open, and Lee went through it and up to the front door. The house was dark, though, and the blinds were drawn. He stood on the front stoop and peered inside. There was no sign of life—no sound, no movement. He walked around the house and looked in all of the windows. He found no sign of forced entry, no indication that anyone was inside. He glanced at his watch. It was only five o'clock, and the Vidocq Society meeting would not start for several hours yet. Kathy and her father could be anywhere.

He had an idea. Forcing himself to breathe against the rising panic in his chest, he turned from the door and stumbled out into the street. A little old lady bundled up in a blue woolen coat was pushing a shopping cart loaded with groceries down the street.

"Excuse me!" He was afraid his voice came out too high, too urgent. Not wanting to alarm her, he kept his distance several feet away.

The woman looked up, startled, her body already tightening in response, her eyes apprehensive.

"Excuse me," he repeated more softly, "do you know where the nearest Catholic church is?"

That seemed to relax her a bit, but her eyes were still wary. She wore garish blue eye shadow, and black mascara was caked thickly on her lashes, giving the impression of a wrinkled, wizened Kewpie doll. Then her face spread into a smile, and she lifted one gloved hand from the handle of her shopping cart and gestured north along the street.

"There's one just four blocks up," she said. Her voice was thin, like a shredded nylon cord. "I prefer St. Michael's, of course," she continued, her tone conspiratorial. "Father Paul is very young, you know, but he gives a wonderful sermon."

But Lee was already running in the direction she had indicated.

"Thank you," he called over his shoulder.

By the time he reached the church he was out of breath, more from fear than exertion.

The church was a heavy, neo-Gothic monstrosity, built during an era when labor was cheap and building materials plentiful. The main chapel loomed over the street, and various gray stone outbuildings sprawled from beneath its buttresses like chicks under the wings of a great stone brooding hen. A clunky sign, made out of the same gray masonry, sat on a little square of grass outside the church.

**Welcome to St. Mary's
Come Worship With Us
And Celebrate the Glory of God**

Lee dashed up the shallow front steps, but the heavy wooden front doors were locked. He raced around to the side of the church, where a single door faced the side street. When he turned the brass handle, the latch clicked, and the door opened inward.

He pushed open the heavy oak door. It was dark and quiet inside, the only light coming from flickering votive candles along the far side of the chapel. A deep animal instinct warned Lee that he was in danger, but his feelings for Kathy propelled him forward.

He crept forward into the semidarkness of the chapel. The air was heavy with bayberry incense. He felt his breathing thicken, and tried to clear his throat without making any sound. He thought he heard a scurrying sound at the back of the church, and he froze, his heart thumping wildly in his chest.

He took a few steps toward the noise, and a strange sensation crept from his fingertips up his forearms, as if ants were running up his arms. He shivered and took a few steps toward the choir loft, the burnished mahogany pews glimmering in the dim light.

As he rounded the corner of the pews, he heard a rustling sound over his right shoulder. He wheeled toward it, but too late. A flash of light blinded him; then a heavy object crashed down on the back of his head. He felt himself falling, and then the blackness closed in around him, cradling him in its dark embrace.

He awoke with the feeling that he was floating above the ground, but as his body regained sensation he realized that he was tied to the heavy wooden cross above the altar. He struggled to move, but he was bound firmly. His arms ached, and his head throbbed. Kathy was stretched out over the altar, and a dark figure in a black robe was bent over her. She was wearing a long white dress. He recognized it as a choir robe.

"Stop it!" Lee cried out as loudly as he could to the figure bending over her. "Leave her alone!"

The man looked up, and Lee saw the face of his mentor and surrogate father, John Paul Nelson.

Nelson smiled up at him. "Nice touch, the robes, don't you think? I found them hanging in the vestibule."

Lee looked down at his mentor through bleary eyes. "Please, don't. I—I understand you."

"Oh, please! No one 'understands' me!"

"No, you're wrong—I do, I swear it."

"Nice try, Lee." Nelson's voice was harsh, the vowels twisted into diphthongs, consonants sharp as the prongs of a garden rake.

Lee pulled on the ropes binding him, trying to wrest free.

"Why did you have to ignore me?" Nelson said. "I begged you—*begged* you—not to take on this case! I tried to protect you. Even all that rubbish about your sister—that was to throw you off—but you just had to persist, didn't you? My God, I never wanted it to come to this!"

Lee craned his neck to peer at Kathy, trying to see if she was still breathing.

"Oh, she's still alive," Nelson said. "I don't kill them all at once, you know . . . press and release, press and release. You'd be surprised how long you can keep someone alive throughout slow strangulation. But then you know that, don't you? You know a lot of things about me—except the things that count."

"Why? Why did you do it?"

"Well, my dear old dad *was* a member of the Westies, after all. You could say violence runs in our family. If you'd bothered to actually profile me, you'd see I have a tidy little history of violent behavior. I'm just very good at hiding it."

"But the women . . . why . . . ?"

"Oh, come *on*, Lee! Haven't you ever wondered what it felt like? Not just to study them from a distance—but to actually *be* a killer?"

Nelson's face was eager, his eyes shining in a way Lee had never seen before.

"Why did you have to kill Eddie?"

Nelson snorted. "That's obvious, isn't it? He was getting too close." He sighed. "I sent you so many warnings, and you ignored them all."

Lee groaned and struggled to free himself, but the ropes binding him were firmly tied.

Nelson watched him. "You know, I never imagined that sailing class at summer camp would be quite so useful," he said. "It just goes to show that you never know what's going to come in handy. I learned quite a few nifty knots. Of course, you have to have a mind for it. Fortunately, I do have a knack—for knots, puzzles, mazes of all sorts."

He looked up at Lee with an expression of mock sympathy. "I thought you were a puzzle solver yourself, but you seem to have come up a bit short this time, I'm afraid."

Lee tried again to wrench himself free, but the ropes only cut more deeply into his flesh. His head was pounding, and his whole body ached.

"Save your strength," Nelson said. "There's no point in wearing yourself out."

A drop of sweat from Lee's forehead fell on Kathy's face, and her eyelids fluttered.

"Come to think of it, what's a Christ figure without a little stigmata?" Nelson said, and seized the ornate Greek cross on its long pole. He raked the sharp edges savagely across Lee's ribs, slashing a wound in his right side. Lee couldn't help crying out in pain.

"There, that's better," Nelson said. "More like the real Christ on the cross."

Lee groaned and fought to remain conscious.

"Does that hurt?" Nelson snarled. "I didn't invite you here, you know."

"Just—let—her—go," Lee pleaded, the words forcing themselves from his throat. "I won't turn you in—I won't tell anyone."

Nelson snorted. "And if I believe that, I'll bet you have a bridge in London for sale too."

He crossed himself and kneeled at the altar.

"Bless this act of deliverance, oh Heavenly Father, as I deliver the soul of your servant into your care."

He looked up at Lee, who was running out of strength, panting from the effort of trying to free himself.

"I don't believe in God, of course, but I like saying the words all the same."

Lee felt the blackness threatening to close in again.

"You know, you should feel honored to witness her transformation," Nelson said, his voice sarcastic. "That's what *he* thought. Poor Samuel—what a nutcase. He thought he was saving them from sin—sending them to God. Poor deluded idiot."

"Why did you do it?" Lee gasped.

"Why did I strangle nice Catholic girls who never did me any harm?"

Lee nodded weakly.

"You'd be surprised how easy it is. After a while, you develop a taste for killing—you actually get to like it. And the Biblical carving was a nice touch—my idea, of course, but Samuel took to it, and did a nice job of it, I thought, didn't you?"

Nelson's eyes were the eyes of a fanatic. He didn't so much look at Lee as right through him. It was like being looked at by a sleepwalker. His calm was more terrifying than an outpouring of raw fury might have been.

"But—*you*?"

"Oh, don't be so *naïve*, for God's sake!"

"But *why*?"

Nelson's face darkened with rage.

"Because they didn't deserve to live and serve God after He took Karen away from me!"

"Oh my God," said Lee. "It was Karen's death—"

Nelson laughed—an ugly, grim sound, like a rock hitting water.

"Yes, that was my 'precipitating stressor'—classic textbook case, eh? Except who would have thought the pursuer would become the pursued? Now, if that's not irony, I don't know what is!"

The pursuer becomes the pursued. . . . the phrase repeated itself in Lee's foggy brain as Nelson leaned over Kathy's motionless body, his red hair reflecting the single overhead altar light. There was a tiny bald spot on the top of his head, the scalp pink and bare, and Lee was reminded of the tiny pink feet of a litter of newborn mice he had seen as a boy. The color had struck him at the time as sickly, and now, as he tried to keep from passing out, the pink bald spot seemed to shift its shape and grow in size. . . . *Can this be it, then?* he thought. *This is really what death is?* He felt an odd peacefulness settle over him, as if he were watching the entire scene from very far away, through a thick layer of gauze.

"I'm sorry about her, I really am," Nelson said. "Everyone will think that Samuel did it, of course. He *did* do some of them, you know—once I convinced him of the rightness of it."

"You used him," Lee said, pushing through the fog in his brain.

"I realized early on I needed a fall guy—a patsy, as they so colorfully call it in old movies. He was a good student, one of my best. Little did I know how good he'd turn out to be, actually," he added, pulling on a pair of surgical gloves. "That was the only real gamble I took—but it worked out in the end."

"Samuel's dead," Lee said. "You killed him."

"I knew you'd track him down sooner or later."

"Christ, you even smoked a cigarette while he died!"

"Ah, yes—the clove cigarettes. That is a rather distinctive odor, I suppose. But I couldn't very well let him live, could I? Any more than I could let you live—or her, for that matter."

Nelson leaned lower over Kathy. Lee saw the glint of metal, and saw the knife descend over her body.

With tremendous effort, Lee shook himself out of his stupor. He felt a roar well up in his throat, and gathered all his strength to rock his body forward. He felt a screw on the wall behind him give way, and he paused for breath, then gave one last desperate lunge forward. There was a crunching sound as the screws tore away from the masonry wall. The cross teetered for a moment, then thundered down over the altar. Nelson stood frozen, as if he didn't believe what was happening, then tried to dodge out of the way—but it was too late. The heavy wooden cross came crashing down on him.

The last thing Lee was aware of before he lost consciousness was Nelson's body folding underneath him like a puppet whose strings have suddenly been severed.

Chapter Sixty-five

Darkness . . . more darkness . . . hands lifting him up . . . flashing lights . . . people scurrying about everywhere . . . then he opened his eyes to see Chuck Morton's face looking down at him. They were in the back of an ambulance. Lee was lying in a stretcher, his friend crouched over him.

"Kathy—" he began, but Chuck cut him off.

"She's going to be fine."

"Where is—?"

"She's already on her way to the hospital."

A paramedic fiddled with an IV bag next to him. The ambulance was sitting behind the church, its doors still open. The paramedic didn't look unduly alarmed, so Lee figured he'd be okay.

"What about Nelson? Is he . . . ?"

Chuck shook his head. "Pronounced dead at the scene. You're lucky he broke your fall. You landed right on top of him. Broke his neck."

Instead of relief, Lee felt a deep sadness. That was no way for a life to end, not even such a twisted one.

"How did you know where to find me?"

"I just went where I figured you would go."

Behind Chuck, Lee heard a familiar voice speaking. "We headed for Dr. Azarian's house first."

"Is that . . . Diesel?" Lee said, and tried to raise his head up to look.

Diesel's enormous head appeared over him. His metal earring caught the light and reflected silver in the artificial light.

Lee stared at him. "What are you doing here?"

"I volunteered to help. Rhino came too, but there wasn't room for us both in the ambulance. He's over there helping the officers keep people away."

Lee looked across the street to the cadre of police lining the sidewalk and saw Rhino's powerful, compact form among them.

He looked up at Chuck. "How did—?"

"They said they knew you—that they were helping you on the case. At that point, I don't have to tell you, we were pretty desperate."

"Anyway," Diesel continued, "there was this old lady in the street."

"Blue hair and eye shadow to match?" Lee said.

"Yeah, right. We asked if she'd seen anyone matching your description, and she told us to go to St. Mary's."

"Sort of like an oracle," Lee said.

"Yes," said Diesel. "Instead of the Oracle of Delphi, she was the Oracle of Philly."

"Oh, something else I have to tell you," Chuck said. "You're off the case."

Lee looked up at his friend, who was smiling. "I don't get it."

"Internal Affairs requested that I take you off the case."

"Really? When?"

"Oh, about three days ago."

"*What*? Why didn't you say anything?"

Chuck shrugged. "Guess I forgot. I'm telling you now."

Lee laughed, and felt a stab of fire shoot through his ribs. He remembered the wound Nelson had slashed into his side.

"So—he's really dead?" he asked.

"Yeah," Chuck said, without looking at him.

"Dead at the scene, you said?"

"Pretty much, yeah."

Lee peered at him. "What do you mean, 'pretty much?'"

Chuck cleared his throat. "He was still alive when we arrived."

Lee looked back at Diesel, aware that they were both avoiding eye contact with him.

"Is there something you're not telling me?"

Chuck's jaw was clenched, and Lee could hear his teeth grinding. Diesel was looking down at his shoes.

"What? What is it?"

"I think you should get some rest," Chuck said, getting up and putting a hand on Lee's shoulder.

"For God's sake, what is it?"

"Look, we don't believe him," Chuck said. "We think he was lying."

"Lying about *what*?"

There was a pause, and Lee could hear the sound of car doors opening and closing. Scenes like this always drew far more patrol cars than necessary.

Chuck took a deep breath. "He claimed to know who killed your sister."

"We think he said it just to upset you," Diesel added quickly.

Lee's stomach took a quick dip, like a car lurching down a hilly road. "But if he was lying, why would he tell you?"

Chuck looked him straight in the eye. "Because he knew that sooner or later you'd find out what he said."

"Did he even know I was alive?"

"My guess is that he gambled on it. You were already being loaded onto a stretcher when he said it."

"And what did he have to lose, in any case?" added Diesel. "He probably knew he was dying."

"But people who are dying don't usually lie," Lee protested. "What if he was telling the truth?"

"Then he's taken the truth to his grave," Diesel replied.

"Come on, Lee, think about it!" Chuck said. "What does your experience and training tell you? What are the chances he'd know who—"

"You're right," Lee agreed, but a tiny doubt had lodged itself in his mind and was sprouting, a dark seedling stretching its roots downward, taking hold of his imagination.

"We called your mother and told her you were okay." Chuck rubbed his palms together, a gesture he made when he was uncomfortable or embarrassed. His nails were pink and manicured. Lee imagined Susan sending Chuck to a manicurist, when he would rather be playing golf or doing yard work. Susan liked everything just so—ironed shirts, starched collars, perfectly organized closets, manicured nails. He imagined Chuck submitting meekly to her prodding.

Thinking of Susan made him think of Kathy, and that made his stomach go hollow inside. He sank back into the stretcher and watched the rotating lights of the ambulance spin around and around, cutting through the darkness like a red blade.

Chapter Sixty-six

Two weeks later, Lee Campbell stood in his apartment looking out the window at the first buds of spring struggling to open in the March frost. The sidewalks were damp from a recent rain, and the late-afternoon sun bounced off the wet pavement, turning the concrete into a mirror, reflecting the street scene on East Seventh Street. The return of the sun had finally lost its terror for him, and he felt the swelling of the earth in his own breast, a gradual awakening as the warmer weather opened the pores of the maple trees, the sap flowing freely again. All the earth's transitions struck him as blessed. All four seasons had their unique charms, and they were all irreplaceable. Like people. No one would ever take his sister's place. He knew that, but now he felt closer to accepting the irretrievable loss.

He turned to the small, dark-haired woman beside him.

"How are you feeling?"

"Oh, I'm fine," Kathy said, leaning her body against his. "How about you?"

"Fine."

"You sound like your mother," she said, frowning.

"Not exactly, I hope."

"Pretty close."

"Wasn't it Oscar Wilde who said it is every woman's tragedy that they become their mothers—and every man's tragedy that they don't."

"That sounds like him. Wonder what kind of mother he had?"

"A hellion, no doubt."

"That's a word you don't hear everyday."

"What?"

"Hellion."

They stood looking out the window together for a while. Below them, the middle-aged couple from the back building strolled along Seventh Street, hand in hand, the woman resting her head on the man's shoulder. Her curly gray hair was abundant and shaggy. With the sun behind her, her head was framed in a silver halo.

Kathy and Lee were doing a delicate dance around the topic on both of their minds—her abduction and its aftermath, his betrayal by a man he loved like a father.

He turned to her. "Did you have nightmares last night? I don't remember you waking up in the middle of the night."

She continued to gaze out the window. "The sleeping pills help."

"Be careful—they can be addictive. I wish you'd reconsider seeing someone."

"Your therapist?"

"No, someone else. A specialist in post-traumatic stress."

"Maybe I will . . . soon."

She had been unable to talk about it for several days, and then, slowly, in the course of the past couple of weeks, the story had come out, of how Nelson had ambushed her on her way to her father's house—right in front of the church, just as darkness was falling—and dragged her inside. How she'd called out for Lee until she lost consciousness, and awakened to see him on the cross. The nightmares that came now were surreal, but no more so than the experience itself. The cuts on her chest were healing, but the scars—both internal and external—would remain. Fortunately, Nelson hadn't gotten very far—only a capital *T*, which was presumably the beginning of the phrase "Thine is the kingdom and glory forever and ever."

Amen, Lee thought, looking down at Kathy, her catching the early spring sunlight as it crept through the French lace curtains.

The hardest thing for her now was remembering—reliving, really—the feeling of being slowly strangled to death, and she would wake up in the night, trembling, unable to breathe. Lee would wrap his arms around her in the darkness and murmur soft, unconvincing words to her about how it would be all right, until she fell asleep again. This had become their nightly ritual, and he hated the feeling of helplessness it gave him.

He put a hand to her cheek. "I'm always going to be chasing people like the Slasher, you know—dangerous people."

"I know. But hopefully next time it won't be someone you work with."

They were both silent, as Lee thought once again how Nelson had managed to mislead them for so long—and how he had been caught almost by accident.

The sound of children's voices floated upward—a game of tag was going on in front of the Ukranian church. A stout boy with a red face was running, laughing, pursued by a girl in a lime green coat, as the other children cheered them on.

"Get him, Carey!"

"Come on, Jimmy—run! Move your fat ass!"

The boy collapsed in giggles on the steps of the church, as the girl's momentum took her careening into his arms. The other children closed in around them, laughing and cheering.

"Does it bother you?" he asked.

"Of course it bothers me. One of the things I like about my job is that I do my work after all the nasty stuff has happened. All I have to do is study nice, clean bones in the peace and quiet of my lab."

"So?"

"So I love you . . . so I'll deal with it."

"I still think you should talk to somebody."

"All *right*. Jeez, you're so damn persistent."

They looked out the window at the coming spring. The blossoms on the cherry trees looked as if they were ready to burst forth in bloom any day now. Lee thought he had never seen Seventh Street looking so magical, so . . . blessed.

"You know," Lee said, "I was blinded by my need for him."

"What do you mean?"

"I needed him to be the father I never had—so I misread clues that pointed to him."

"Oh, for God's sake, Lee, none of us suspected him! Why should we? He was one of *us*!"

"Exactly. He was one of us. And he misled us every step of the way. When I suggested there were two people at work, he steered us away from it time and time again. And then he called me over to his apartment just so he could fake that phone call. He played me."

"You can't blame yourself. No one else saw through him either."

"Yeah, but in retrospect it all makes such perfect sense. The unexplained absences, the drinking, his out-of-control behavior—we never put it all together."

She squeezed his arm. Her fingers were thin and strong. "A lot of things make sense in retrospect."

"He even used his expertise to create a 'signature' that would lead us to Samuel—although whether that was his idea or Samuel's, I guess we'll never know." He sighed. "Guess I don't have very good luck with father figures."

There was a pause, and then she said, "So your wound isn't bothering you?"

"Not too much."

She yawned, stretched, and walked over to sit on the sofa. "Come over here and let Nurse Kathy check you out."

"Well, if you put it that way . . ."

He was about to join her when the phone rang. He picked up the receiver, cursing himself for not turning off the ringer.

"Hello?"

It was Detective Butts.

"Yeah, hi. Look, I thought you'd like to know the results of some of our interviews with the neighbors and stuff. None of them could remember Samuel ever being involved with a woman of any kind—which is just what you had said about him."

"Thanks, I appreciate that," Lee said, but his heart wasn't in it. Right now he just wanted to forget about it for a while, to leave it all behind.

"Yeah," Butts went on. "We got that 'he was a quiet boy—kept to himself' thing, you know. Apparently he was very respectful, well behaved. 'Course, it's the quiet ones you have to watch out for—"

"Which wouldn't be you right now," Lee managed to interject.

"What?"

"Look, I'm sort of busy right now."

"Oh, okay. Sorry to interrupt. I just thought you might like to know."

Lee smiled. "Thanks, I appreciate that. I'll talk to you later. We'll get together next week, okay?"

"Right," Butts said. "Sounds good. Tell her I said hi."

"I will."

He hung up and turned off the ringer.

"Now," he said, "where were we?"

Kathy laughed and threw back her head. The lamplight reflected a perfect triangle on her exposed throat.

"I believe," she said, "we were at the beginning."

Don't Miss the next C. E. Lawrence thriller from Pinnacle
coming Fall 2010!